HANDY GUIDE TO MURDERVILLE

By Les Pobjie

Publisher: Inspiring Publishers,
P.O. Box 159, Calwell, ACT Australia 2905
Email: publishaspg@gmail.com
http://www.inspiringpublishers.com

A catalogue record for this book is available from the National Library of Australia

National Library of Australia The Prepublication Data Service

Author: Les Pobjie
Title: Handy Guide to Murderville
Genre: Fiction
ISBN: 978-1-922618-34-4

Dedication

This book is dedicated to all who, since the first marks were painted on cave walls, have persevered to write their stories: to inform, inspire, thrill, entertain. Without them our lives would be as empty as the libraries, our minds as closed as the bookshops.

HANDY GUIDE TO MANDERVILLE

Manderville, Jewel of the Plains

By Councillor Bruce Mercer, Mayor of Manderville

Manderville has a long and inspiring history going back to the beginning of the 20th century. Way back then, the early settlers established the pattern for what would become a country town to be envied. As it grew, it did so in an orderly fashion: the straight streets, fine buildings, spacious sports grounds and expansive, green parks for our citizens, all make Manderville such a joy to live in. As do, to a much greater extent, the fine people who make up our town population. You'll find them out and about, working and mingling and meeting with each other day and night in this town, Manderville, where anything is possible.

I, the humble proprietor of Mercer's Premium Meats, am proud to be, for now, mayor of this lovely town. I hope anyone visiting here, for whatever length of time, long or short stay, will see the advantages of living in such a peaceful, law-abiding, and, yes, loving community. Stop and chat with any Mandervillian you meet as you wander our streets. I guarantee that they will love to talk with you and tell you about their town, of which they are so proud.

1

JACK

WHEN the cops get here, I should tell 'em Dad's in the chook house. Should. Break my word. If I don't, Katie might. Can't hold us to a promise made to silence tears. Squatting among our few scrawny birds. Not many now. Enough to stink the place out. Worse after the morning rain on the uncovered half of the pen. Wet stink of straw and chook shit. And Dad's fear. Smelt that before. That time when the cops pulled him out of the wardrobe, dragging him past me and Katie in the hallway, Mum at the bedroom door, bent over, bawling. Smelt it. Saw it in his eyes, appealing for help from two kids that looked away. Heard him stuffed in the back seat with fists and boots.

Wire gate was the giveaway squeak, catch clinking shut, then indignant squawks, wings fluttering, tiny feet scrabbling. Drunken curses whispered. Now silence.

Hard to see, crouching in a corner, skinny back to the wall, away from the wire netting, crotch wet, shoes crunching on shell grit.

I can't hear him breathing. Just sniffing. Sure he can see me. Would have seen my long shadow first, stretching across the grass, from the kitchen doorway's golden rectangle of light. No doubt relieved mine was the only silhouette coming at him. Cops'll be here soon.

"Jack." A whispered croak. "Jack. Son. It's me…" A pause. "Dad."

So, not a talking chook. Pity. Would be more valuable.

"It's always you, Dad."

He stifles a sneeze.

"Mum asked me to see how you are."

"Aww, gee, did she? My love asked—"

"Beats me why. After what you did." Enough for me to call the cops. "Bloody hell, Dad. Mum's been crying her eyes out."

"But, Jack, Jack, she wanted to know how I am." Sniffle. And made us promise not to tell the cops where the bastard was hiding.

"This can't go on," I say. "I've had a gut-full. We all have."

"Shoosh," he says. "Quieter."

"You gotta leave, Dad."

"Not with bloody cops coming."

"Leave home. Get out of Mum's life. Ours."

"No. I love her. She loves… We've always—"

"Showed that tonight."

"Just the grog… I…" A long pause. Just. Bloody just. Too many justs. He shifts position, agitating a couple of chooks.

"What you gonna do?" As if it would be any other than sorrow-full, reality-empty promises. The wind stirs next door's over-burdened apple tree and a few plop to the ground. Their scrawny excuse for a dog barks once. Silence, as if trees and dogs couldn't be bothered offering any more than a token stirring and bark this drizzly night.

Softly, he says: "Just want a bit of peace and quiet, is all."

"What we want. What Mum wants. Can't have it while you're around."

"It's just…" Pause. "Who's laughing? At me?"

Jeez. "It's the Bradleys—"

"What's it got to do with me?"

"You're changing the subject. They're watching telly. Comedy. Canned laughter." Never heard them laugh. Reckon they let telly do it for them. "Dad—"

"Did Mary come?"

"She wanted to, but I told her to go back to bed."

"It's just—"

"Just shit. You could've said you didn't like the jumper. Enough." Would've saved all this.

"Son, all those colours… I couldn't wear that in the shearin' shed." Or the pub. "My mates would—"

"Mum's your best mate. Always has been. She worked bloody hard on it. Knitting on and on. Plenty of other things she could have done for herself. She was so proud of it. Held it up to us. Now, it's smouldering in a bucket."

"Well…"

"Shoving it in the fire. Bastard act. Raging around. Banging and chucking and…" What's the point? He doesn't say anything.

"I got the cops after Katie rang me."

"I didn't touch her."

"They'll talk to Mum. Katie. Me."

"Don't dob me in, Jack."

"What you deserve. Get you out of our lives for a while. Give Mum a bit of peace and quiet."

"Hide with me, Jack…"

"Cops aren't after me."

" Jack… Bit cool. Cold."

"Be alright."

Right. Jumper could've helped.

"Get my phone for me?"

"I'm not coming back out."

Might as well go inside. No happiness there either. The Bradleys' pretend happiness has stopped abruptly and the packaged laughing is followed by an equally false packaged deal spruiked by a fast-talking man. He is quickly silenced, too. Bedtime for the Bradleys. Lucky them. Yes.

I leave Dad trembling in the refuge he'd built one blistering summer day, before he needed a refuge. Tall then. Straight, strong, thumping the crowbar into the soil. Again and again. Deeper and deeper. With a wink at Katie and me sitting on the back step, he switched to the big shovel. Dirt flew high, scattering clods and brown crumbs, digging post holes.

Wiping sweaty dirt from his face, his brown hair splattered with darker flecks, he dropped rough-hewn posts into place. Dirt dumped back, tamped firmly down by his wild dance around the posts, like a Comanche brave around a totem pole. He grinned at us and thumped his chest. A quick drink from the second beer can then back hammering a plywood and wire netting coop together, partly topped with corrugated iron.

He stood back and smiled. We clapped and Katie spilt orange cordial on the step. He picked us up, one in each arm. Tall, straight. Strong as the sun. Sweat from dripping singlet and bare arms seeped into our clothes. I loved the wetness and the smell of work.

Tonight, a different man slumps in the dark corner of his creation. Not tall, straight, strong. Deflated like one of Katie's poorly tied birthday balloons on the front gate, substance vanished into the wind, flopping with no purpose among its plump fellows dancing merrily with the night breeze.

* * *

SUNDAY 9.38pm

At the back step, Jack turned and looked into the yard. He couldn't see his Dad. The rain had begun again, invisible drops falling through the darkness, burst into light on the path and pinged on the coop's iron roof. The wind had picked up and the leaves on the big tree in the corner of the yard were rustling, whispering as if disturbed by the sound of a car driving into the lane and stopping with a squeal of brakes.

Jack walked into the kitchen. His mother was on a chair, to the side of the black stove, crouched towards the dying heat, an untidy heap of firewood at her feet. She was now wearing a thin brown cardigan over the red and white dress she kept for special occasions. Embers pulled out along with the jumper had left burn marks near the hem. Her good shoes, the red ones with open toes, lay behind her feet, under the chair. Flames flickered through the half-closed firebox door. Inside, deformed plastic knitting needles ran wildly yellow over submissive wood chunks. The charred remains of the sleeveless Fair Isle jumper lay crumpled, sodden, in a tin bucket. Dead embers melded with the variegated wools.

Her sobs were quiet now, her cheeks blackly smeared.

Katie knelt, head and hands on her mother's lap. She looked up when Jack entered; Bev didn't.

"Cops are here," Jack said. "Pulled up in the lane."

The Durkins–except for Jack —didn't live in a street: their address was 14 Worral Lane, Manderville. Jack lived a few blocks away with his partner, Mary Bourke. The lane ran parallel with the Sydney to Melbourne railway line, a short walk from the station. Homes fronted the entire length, like in a normal street, but there was no footpath on either side.

Bev jumped up. "Don't say anything. Leave your Dad where he is." She looked at Jack.

"Mum, you can't—"

"Yes, I can. It's my fault. I should have told Dad first. Not surprise him." Did that.

The police banged on the front door. Katie jumped. Bev sighed and ran to the table. She hid spilt tomato sauce under a square of paper towel. Katie darted behind her father's chair and picked up a half-eaten lamb chop. Bev gave her a grateful look and dropped it in the bin, popping the lid open with a bare foot on the pedal. She grabbed the plates, all with congealed meal remnants on them. Jack told them not to bother. It was just cops.

The police banged again, louder and longer this time. Bev waved Jack towards the hall. He went and let them in. As he does.

There were two of them: uniformed. Jack knew them, summed up as good cop, didn't-give-a-damn cop. Smithson, tall, balding, awkward-limbed, moved jerkily—rumoured to be from an injury—reminding Jack of a wooden puppet. But his eyes were grey steel; Higgins, overweight, slow-moving, mouth wide, lips fat, as if they didn't get enough exercise, curly ginger hair.

They rasped out a few questions. Mostly Smithson, mostly to Bev, who kept eye contact while answering.

Higgins poked his head into every room. He leaned into the toilet and pressed the flush button. He ambled past Jack without a word and checked the backyard by opening the door and closing it before his eyes could have adjusted to the dark. Jack breathed again.

"Where is he then?" Higgins asked.

"We don't know," Bev said.

"He ran out," Jack said.

Higgins snorted. "Waste of time then."

Smithson looked exasperated but continued his leading-nowhere questions to Bev. They stood near the table. As Higgins wandered past the stove he looked down at the bucket. "Somebody been sick?" Nobody answered. Smithson shrugged and rolled his eyes to the ceiling. In the momentary silence, the only sounds came from outside: rain and chooks clucking and scrabbling.

Smithson said: "Better check out the back again, Constable. Something's stirring up the poultry." Higgins sighed and walked to the back door. Jack put his right foot up on a chair and retied a lace that didn't need retying. Bev poked the fire that didn't need poking. Katie went to the fridge without anything in her hand, looked inside and closed the door quietly. Smithson looked curiously at the three Durkins.

Higgins opened the back door, stepped outside. He stood in the rain for a minute or two before coming back inside and closing the door.

"It's just the rain beating on the iron out there, agitating the chooks. It'd irritate me, too."

Jack was tempted to say that rain didn't usually worry the chooks. After glancing at his mother, he said, instead: "Rain stirs them up. Don't like it."

Smithson looked at his colleague without saying anything. He turned back to Bev. "So it was just an argument, then?" Like, yeah, so just a crushing of hope. Just a breaking of a heart. Just. Just.

Bev sniffled. "Yes."

"You said he didn't assault you, just threw things around." Yeah, right. Just.

Higgins had returned to the kitchen after using the toilet, or maybe only flushing it again, He stood near the back door, looking at his watch every few minutes.

"He scared me." Bev said. "More than … ever."

"Scared me, too," Katie said, in a whisper.

"That's why we called Jack," Bev said.

"I called you guys," Jack said.

Smithson went to an upended chair, righting it near the table. He glanced at Higgins then back at Bev. "As I asked: Did he assault anyone?"

Bev looked at Jack before returning to the sergeant's sharp eyes. She shook her head. "No."

Katie stared at the brown-and-white Lino floor, as if the square pattern held a clue to solving their problems.

Jack turned away.

"I thought you got him blacklisted."

"I did."

Smithson touched the empty beer can on the table with his pen, "Didn't do much good then. For all your efforts, Mrs Durkin."

Jack went to his mother's side. "You saying we do nothing?"

"Not suggesting anything. Up to you, Mr Durkin. Blokes have mates—and family—who will always buy beer on their behalf." He flipped his notebook closed and walked towards his partner, who was studying his hands, held out, palms up, as if checking his own fingerprints.

"That will do for now." Smithson said. Higgins nodded. "Call us if Mr Durkin comes back tonight."

When they had gone, Bev picked up a cup from the table, took a sip and splattered. "Cold as..."

"I'll make you another," Katie said.

"Don't worry. I'll get one in a little bit."

Jack and Katie hugged her. Cold tea spilled onto Jack's back from the cup Bev still held. He jerked and Bev pulled away, splashing tea on the stove where the drops steamed and spat. She rubbed vigorously on his shirt, trying to dry it with a tea towel.

Katie laughed. Jack told Bev not to worry and he moved towards the door.

She began folding the tea towel neatly but abruptly crumpled it into an untidy lump. Katie took it and draped it over a chair.

"Dad's still out there," Jack said. "I'll go out the back when I leave. Make sure he's gone."

"He won't come back in tonight," Bev said. She bent and picked up her shoes, swinging them in one hand. "As my date has taken off, I guess we won't be going to the pictures." She paused. "Thanks for not telling them."

"Better if I had. Can't go on like this."

"I didn't want him hurt again." Bashed again.

"He deserves it," Katie said. "That beautiful jumper…"

"Just a bucket of vomit now, love." Bev gave a wry grin.

Jack hugged her shoulders. She stifled a sob. "You can go, Jack. We'll be all right."

Katie began clearing the table. Bev took saucers from her and rinsed them in the sink. Katie dropped cutlery beside them.

"The lamb was good, Mum," Katie said.

Tasty start to another meal that ended prematurely in tears.

Katie took a tub of butter to the fridge, pushed it in beside a plate with two slices of pink iced cake and a scattering of candles on it.

"You should kick him out," Jack said, knowing he was nagging at the wrong time. "Been too many years of this crap."

"He's never hit me, Jack."

"Some things might be worse than being hit." He paused. "I better go."

Bev touched his sleeve. "Yes. Mary will be worried. Dad will go to Meg and Doug's. All over for the night." She attempted a smile, but it didn't come out very well.

"Lock the door after me."

As he opened the door, he heard the chook house gate click shut. Stepping outside, he saw his father trip over one of the many wire-strung rabbit skins standing up like bizarre tombstones in a mini cemetery. He untangled his foot and scurried around the back corner of the house. Jack followed more slowly, but there was no sign of his father. He sighed, seemed the night's action was over.

The rain had stopped so he paused at the front gate to release the balloons he had tied there two days ago, despite Katie's protest that she was too old for 'that sort of stuff'. At sixteen she was too young for tonight's sort of stuff. The wind lifted the balloons into the black sky. Jack said: "Party's over."

On the way home, he tried to remember if he had locked the front door after seeing the cops out. He thought he probably had.

HANDY GUIDE TO MANDERVILLE

General Hospital

By Mrs Barbara Hoffman, Hospital Superintendent

We are a healthy lot in Manderville. Probably something to do with the country air here in the sunny climate. However, people do become ill from time to time. And at those times, the Manderville General Hospital provides the best medical services.

The hospital has a long history and during that time the original building has been added to, renovated and in parts rebuilt. I know the facilities we offer to our patients and to nurses and doctors are as good as any in the country. Our wards are roomy and airy, our equipment continually updated, our nurses are well trained and our resident doctors are expert in dealing with all manner of ills and injuries.

Accidents happen in the workplace, on sporting fields and at home - and the Manderville hospital team are ready and more than able to help the people seeking medical assistance. Our maternity section is first class and ably ensures our new citizens get a good start in life.

All of our dedicated staff live in Manderville and mix with the community at schools, sporting activities, in clubs, churches and even while shopping. As such, they have a special empathy with their patients and are able to offer advice beyond their health needs.

2

JACK

How the hell did it come to this? A family dinner at home. Now this. Standing here, looking down at Mum, my bashed, unconscious mother. Should have told the cops where the bastard was skulking. Should've let them drag him away. Should've. So should've Mum. Why did we think it was right to protect the mongrel? No answer here, in a hospital ward's white glare, nervy noises of hose-and-cord-attached, emotionally detached, machines.

No… if we… Guilt mixes with the shock of seeing Mum like this. Maybe my selfish guilt will dissolve in the face of reality: Mum's face. Shit. I never thought it would end here, near midnight, watching Mum not watching me. Not seeing me. Or anything. Not moving. Not Mum's face. Swollen, black, blue, wide orange smears across the soft, pale, skin as if someone used a highlighter pen to show where cuts were. To emphasise the cruelties inflicted on her pretty face. Other damage may be hidden by the mask she breathes through. Her left forearm is encased in plaster. And… I don't know. Her breathing is quieter than Dad's among the chooks. At least still breathing…

✳ ✳ ✳

MONDAY 12.15am

A nurse came in, acknowledging Jack only with a stern glance. She walked quickly, quietly, to the other side of the bed. He tilted his head slightly. There was something familiar about her, but he didn't know any overweight, middle-aged nurses, with an expression nobody would want to be caught with when the wind changed. He didn't know any sort of nurse, really.

Holding a ballpoint pen and pad, she briskly checked dials on a contraption attached to Bev, touched cords and tubes, lifted the mask a few centimetres and bent slightly to study the area around Bev's mouth and let it fall back over the bruised lips that had kissed his cheek a few hours ago, before he had abandoned her. After the cops had wiped their hands of 'just' another incident and gone away.

If only… He shouldn't have gone home. Mary would have understood. He had seen his father running off. He heard the front gate clunk shut. He thought it was safe to leave. His father ran off without his house keys.

His father wasn't a basher, inflicting other more long-lasting forms of hurt. Until tonight.

When Katie rang an hour or so ago, Jack had rushed back to a crying little sister. She turned her pale, wet face to Jack. No cheeky grin. No smart-arse quips.

And no Mum. No Dad. He wished the second was true. Feared the first could be literally true by morning. No Mum anywhere. He stood awkwardly, helpless. He wished the nurse would finish her tasks and leave the room. She was studying a chart at the end of the bed.

He knew Katie was safe, with Meg and Doug. But Mary was taking a while to come back. He hoped she was okay. Shocked. She said she shouldn't cry in the ward.

The nurse put the report folder back on the rails at the bed end. Jack was relieved when Mary came in. He put an arm around her waist. She put her hand with a damp hanky in it on the back of his and squeezed.

Jack told her nothing had changed. He looked down at the bed and said loudly: "Mum, we are –"

The nurse cleared her throat and wagged a finger at them. "Quiet, please. She can't hear you."

Mary broke away from Jack and said: "If Bev can't hear him, shouldn't he speak louder?"

The nurse ignored Mary's feigned innocence. "She isn't the only patient in the hospital."

"When you say 'she', do you mean my mother, Beverly Durkin?" Jack asked.

The nurse nodded and headed for the open door. Jack stepped towards her. "Excuse me". She turned and waited for him to speak. He was sure he had seen her somewhere. She tapped her fingers on the pad. Long ago. Tonsils. He was seven.

The nurse craned her neck around the doorway and looked along the corridor. She turned back with an impatient look. Jack saw she was about to walk away. She pushed her ballpoint pen into a top pocket. It drew a blue line on its way in, alongside other accidental scribbles. Jack didn't care to tell her the point wasn't retracted.

"Yes?" She half turned to go.

"How is … my Mum? Will she…"

"I'm very busy. A lot of legitimate patients to look after."

"What the hell do you call my Mum? Illegitimate?"

"Don't shout."

"Will. She. Live?"

"There are lots of sick people trying to sleep—"

"Mum's trying to live. Hanging on is what the doctor said. Isn't that legitimate enough for you?"

"I meant…" She sighed and looked around the doorway again. "People who get sick from natural causes, have accidents, unavoidable things. Not ones who choose to stay with–"

"Don't say it," Mary said. "You are a disgrace."

Jack was close to adding another illegitimate patient to the room. He clenched his fists and stepped towards her. Her expression hardened. She sucked in her cheeks, creating crevices on both sides of her mouth. She took a step back.

A memory from many years ago clicked into focus. Yes. He was seven. He remembered the nurse. She wasn't like the other cheerful nurses. He remembered thinking her smile must have slipped off.

Jack moved closer to her, his face angry. With surprising agility, she skipped backwards into the corridor.

"Look, Mr... Mr..."

"Durkin. You might remember me here in a bed. You shouted at me because I'd vomited on the blankets. I'd had my tonsils out."

"I can't recall every little thing." She studied him. "Must have been many years ago. Well..."

"I was seven. You were too slow with the bowl." His Mum had said that.

"Makes such a mess. Patients must hold it in until the bowl comes."

"Seven-year-olds don't know about that. I'd just come to from anaesthetic. Rolled over in a strange room, bed. Strange people."

"Little kids can't remember things that long ago."

Jack thought the statement was illogical, but he was through talking with the woman.

"We're very busy," the nurse said. "We're looking after her the best we can." She flapped her pad, looked at them, and repeated: "I am very busy."

Mary moved beside Jack and held his hand. She said: "You must have been too busy to attend the staff training session on compassion."

"We don't have -"

"Oh, perhaps they don't bother about such things," Mary said.

"We have security guards."

"So?" Mary said.

"And a police officer is coming tonight to guard this door. About time, too, I say."

Jack said: "Do they think Mum will escape?"

"To make sure Mrs Durkin isn't hurt again."

"We know that," Mary said.

Jack shook his head and returned to his mother's bedside. He bent and kissed her forehead, causing the nurse to shuffle back into the ward. Jack sat on the chair and Mary knelt beside him.

The nurse, like a dog with a bone, couldn't leave well enough alone. "Some injuries could be avoided by wiser choice of partner."

She turned and ran a few steps towards the door before slowing to a more professional pace. Jack jumped up and followed her as far as the door but couldn't think of anything worth shouting after her. He banged a fist into the door.

"Careful, there, Mr Durkin." Jack turned, recognising the hard voice of Constable Smithson. He had come down the corridor behind Jack. He waited for the officer to speak again.

"Constable Smithson." He flashed his ID card and pocketed it.

"I know," he said. "You're one of the cops who didn't protect my Mum from this." He flicked a thumb towards his mother.

Smithson said, calmly: "I hear you didn't hang around to protect her."

Jack ignored the comment. The cop was right. "Have you got him?"

"Who?"

Jack pointed at his mother again. "The mongrel who did that. My bloody father."

Smithson glanced at the battered, barely breathing woman. He turned back to Jack without changing his expression.

"Why do you say your father did it? Did she come to? Say something?"

"She? You mean my mother? Her name's Beverly Durkin." Pause. "Have you got him?"

"Him? You mean your father? Raymond Henry Durkin?"

Jack glared at him and asked again. "Have you got him? No? Why not?"

"Just hold on–"

"If you can't, I'll get him and he'll look a lot worse than my Mum there."

"Keep it down, sonny. This is not a pub."

Jack was close to exploding. Mary put a hand on his shoulder. She whispered that he would be no use to anyone if he was stuck in jail.

Smithson said: "We are dealing with it."

"He'll be gone by morning," Jack said.

"No. He won't."

"You don't know him like I do. He'll—"

"If you know him so well why did you leave -?" He paused. "-Mrs Durkin alone with just a young kid?"

"Katie's his daughter, for God's sake." He looked at Mary before limply finishing. "I know what I know."

Smithson didn't take his eyes off Jack. "Just means someone did it. We don't know who. Yet. We believe your father will stick around."

"Good. Cause I'm gonna get him."

"Jack," Mary said. He pulled away from her.

"Funny," Smithson said with no facial sign of amusement. "Your father said he's going to get you. Kill you."

Mary gasped and gripped Jack's shoulder.

Jack looked around the room, stared again at his mother.

"Why me? Is he out to get us all? Jeez, mate."

"Just you. He's after you for doing this." He waved casually at the bed. "He told us you bashed your mother."

"You believed the old drunk? Was he there?"

"Were you? We'll have to talk with you, Jack. Down at the station."

"No." Mary said, "Surely this can wait until tomorrow, Constable. Jack's not in a fit state to be questioned tonight. You must see that."

"It's essential, Miss Bourke," Smithson said. Jack wondered how he knew Mary's surname. "We'll call you when the interview is done so you can pick him up at the Station."

Mary turned away and Jack heard her soft "Bugger"

"Not an invitation." He paused. "It's for your own protection."

Jack spat out a brief, bitter, laugh. "You didn't protect my Mum very well."

"He rang his sister, Meg, and told her he's got a gun. Got his rifle from home. He intends to kill you."

3

SMITHSON

This young bloke looks set to explode. Fidgeting. Tapping on his knees, the side window, the dashboard. Must have a lot to say. Holding it in, seems. Mouth shut tight. Might have done it. Dunno. Says not. See how he copes at the station. Interviews catch a lot out. Been here, couple of years ago. Charged. Got off.

Not much traffic. Late. Never is at any time. Sooner we get to the station the sooner I can get this done. Get home.

Bugger, should be home. Great job. Cop. Kept out to all hours by bloody domestic dramas. Bloody drunks. Young thugs.

"Quit fidgeting, sonny. Distracting."

That stirred him. Shifting. Long as he keeps belt on…

"My Mum might die tonight. That's distracting. My Dad's out to kill me. That's distracting. By morning our family could be down to just one young kid. That's distracting, hey?"

Deserve that. This shit's keeping me from a warm bed. Get it over ASAP… if Higgins doesn't butt in with his irrelevant questions.

* * *

MONDAY 1.55am

Jack got out and slammed the door, bringing a rebuke from Constable Smithson. He knew this place. Cop Shop. Been here a couple of times. Once when he had been charged. And one night like this, many years ago, he had stood here with little Katie. The brown double front doors were closed that terrible night. Tonight, the doors were open wide–but still not welcoming. On the wall to their right, was the wooden shutter with 'ENQUIRIES' painted above it in red.

He knew that behind it there was a window with a half-circle cutaway at the bottom. It had reminded him of the ticket booth at the Saturday arvo movies. He and Katie had trembled before the cop shop shutter, shivered in their pyjamas and bare feet. Jack had to stretch on tip-toes to reach the shutter. He tapped and waited. They heard voices inside, but nobody came. Katie looked down at her brother's bent toes. After a minute or two, he banged. Three times. He dropped his hand and wrapped his arms around his body for warmth. Katie puffed and copied him. He feared the loud knocking would anger the police inside the probably warm interior. He saw Katie was about to cry again.

"It's all right, Katie. We'll go home if nobody comes soon."

The shutter flew out on its hinges and Jack stepped back so suddenly that he trod on Katie's toes. She yelped. Embarrassing.

"Yes?" A big-faced man was at the window. Light from the room reflected off the pink dome of his head and glittered on chipped spots on the glass cutaway. Jack, who had never seen a diamond, thought it sparkled like one.

The policeman's face was unclear, backlit, cheeks shiny red.

"Please, sir-" Jack began.

"Why are you kids crying out there? At this time." Jack didn't know the time.

"I'm not crying," Jack said. Katie sniffed, gulped, and stopped sobbing.

"What's the matter?"

Katie blurted it out, words and sobs tripping over each other.

When she finished, the officer nodded and turned to Jack. "Go again. Slower. You tell me, son."

Katie sniffled and looked at the ground.

"Mum wants you to come."

"You Durkins?" They nodded. Katie wiped her eyes. Jack lifted the bottom corner of his pyjama coat and wiped his nose on the inside.

"Dad's playin' up again. He's drunk."

"Would be. After closing time." He leaned into the glass and stared down at the two kids. "Haven't you got shoes?"

"Didn't have time, sir," Katie said. She stood on one leg and rubbed the back of it with the other.

The policeman pulled a scary face—he possibly thought it was a smile. He straightened and walked back into the room behind.

"He's a shearer," Katie said, to his back.

The officer called out something to somebody inside. "Let's go," he said, pulling the shutter closed.

It was dark in the back seat and it smelt of tobacco and beer and something like vomit. Jack and Katie screwed up their noses.

The town was dark, most people in bed by that hour. They drove into the lane and the kids saw their place was lit up like expecting visitors. Which, in a way, it was, Jack supposed.

They took Ray Durkin away. He went peacefully. They manhandled him into the car. They stood with their Mum close to the kitchen stove, listening to the bangs and thumps as they threw their Dad into the car. Heard the punches and kicks. His yelps. Groans. The car drove away. It was quiet in the lane and the house and the kitchen. Bev and her son and daughter soundlessly hugged each other. The silence was broken by Bev's anguished cry.

Smithson shouted at Jack to "wake up" and "get inside". They went into a small, windowless room. Smithson and Higgins faced Jack across a wide yellow wooden table. Jack clasped his hands in front of him, on the table. Smithson had placed his opened notebook on the table. He was clearly the one in charge. Higgins studied the water jug and two glasses. A tape recorder sat at the other end of the table.

"Don't worry about that, Mr Durkin," Smithson said. "You're not a suspect." Yet. Not being charged. This time. "This is just a little chat. Recorder's not on. Want a drink?"

Jack shook his head. Smithson tapped the notebook with his pen. "Detective Sergeant Brogan might talk to you a bit later."

Higgins asked: "Do you know DS Brogan?".

Smithson looked annoyed. "Let's get on."

Jack looked around the room. Not much to see, other than a child's tricycle against a side wall.

"Interesting that, hey?" Higgins said. Jack glanced, but the constable didn't elaborate.

Jack turned his focus to Smithson. "What about?"

The policemen exchanged puzzled looks.

"What about what?" Smithson asked. Higgins poured half a glass of water and touched it to his lips. He put it down, without sipping.

"The chat," Jack said. "With two of you."

"Right." Smithson turned over a few pages of the notebook, stopping at a blank one. "Where did you go after we spoke at the house?"

"Home."

Higgins said: "Do you mean your home, Mr Durkin?"

Jeez. Does he think I went to somebody else's home?

"Weren't you already there?" Higgins persisted.

"Mr Durkin doesn't live with his parents." Smithson said.

"Moved out last year," Jack said.

"Kicked out?" Smithson asked. "Have a row with your Dad–or Mum?"

"Nothing like that. Moved in with my girlfriend."

"I see. Name?"

"Yes."

Smithson sighed, dropped his pen on the table. "Didn't you hear me?"

"Yes. Yes, she has a name."

"Dammit, sonny. Enough of the time-wasting games. Everyone has a name." He glared at Jack. He picked up his pen and clicked the point out "What is it?"

"Mary."

"Is that your—" Higgins began.

"Mary who?" Smithson asked.

"Mary Bourke. Hampson Street. Fifteen." He looked at the jug and the one unused glass.

"I assume that's not her age."

"No. Our street number."

"Hampson's not far from your old place then?" Higgins said. "You didn't think your Dad would return and assault your Mum?"

Jack couldn't see the connection between the two questions.

"Never has," Jack said.

"Meaning never ever?"

Smithson sighed loudly. Jack ignored Higgins's question.

"Do you know anyone who would want to harm your mother?" Smithson said.

Higgins turned his left arm over to look at his watch.

Out of the side of his mouth, Smithson said: "Are we keeping you, Constable?"

Higgins picked up his glass, touched it to his lips, put it down after one noisy sip. Jack licked his lips. He wished he had accepted Smithson's earlier offer of water. The room was uncomfortably warm.

"Nobody else would've. Only my–"

"You," Smithson said. "Easily get back after the rest were asleep. You got a key?"

"That's bloody stupid."

Higgins leant forward as if to object, but Smithson put his hand on his colleague's shoulder. Higgins sat back. Jack was pleased to see his disgruntled face.

"Why're we wasting time in here?" Jack said. He reached over to the jug and filled the remaining glass. He drank half while staring at Smithson, not caring if the officer wanted a drink. Too slow.

"You got the wrong bloke in."

"Hang on," Higgins said.

"We haven't got anyone yet," Smithson said. "Just chatting."

Higgins put the glass to his lips again. Took another big swig.

Smithson watched Higgins, then turned back to Jack. "You have a record of assaulting people, Mr Durkin. You were the only one in that house last night with that."

Jack was not surprised by this sudden comment. "You know what happened, Constable. Know why. Know assaulting people is an exaggeration. Know—"

"I know you knocked a man down in the street. With a punch. I know that."

"One bloke isn't people. And I was saving a disabled bloke from a mugging. Got his wallet back and stopped him getting hurt more."

Smithson waved a hand. "OK. OK. But shows you're quick to resort to violence."

"So," Jack said, "a man running around with a rifle, set on killing his son isn't a suspect? But I am, for an incident I was found not guilty of? Oh, that's OK."

"Just hold it—" Smithson grabbed the jug and slammed it down, spurting water onto the notebook and bouncing the pen, which rolled towards the edge near Jack's elbow. He let it roll off.

"You're going the right way to get stuck in a cell tonight," Smithson said. Higgins nodded and muttered something like "Amen". Smithson mopped the notebook with his handkerchief. He looked at his watch. Higgins followed suit.

"I only care about my mother. She might die tonight. Get the one who did it. You must know it's Dad." He finished his water and carefully placed the glass in front of him.

"If Mrs Durkin dies, we'll be looking for a murderer," Smithson said. Jack thought he sounded like Higgins, stating the bloody obvious.

"I suppose the hunt will pick up then," Jack said. "Be more energetic… more…"

Smithson didn't bite. "Constable Higgins talked to your sister. She didn't see or hear anything. Seems whoever did this knocked your mother out straight away. Probably the first blow."

"He must've kept beating her while she was out," Jack said. "Jesus, man. What a bastard."

"Could have been more than one perpetrator," Higgins said.

"Perpetrator? You saw Mum. Take more than a bloody perpetrator to do that. Use English, for God's sake."

He sat back and put one arm over the back of the chair. He was weary. "I gotta go."

"Not yet. Do you know anyone who would do that to your mother?"

"Nobody. Not an enemy in the world."

"You reckon a friend did it?" Higgins said.

Smithson reached for Higgins's glass. Wiped the rim with his wet handkerchief. He emptied it into Jack's glass before filling it and almost draining it in one go.

Jack said: "Can we end this? Not getting anywhere."

Smithson dabbed the open pages of his notebook and closed it. He gave a wry smile at the jug. His fault. His temper.

What he had written was smeared. He shook the pen, wiped it, and put it back in his pocket. He roughly folded the hanky, ensuring the ink marks were out of sight. He stood.

"It's late. All we can do tonight." Bugger all, Jack thought. "You can go for now. Ask Jones on the front desk to ring the hospital for you."

Jack stood and turned towards the door.

Smithson said: "Do you want a lift home?"

"I'll ring Mary. She's waiting to hear from me." He paused. "Thanks."

Smithson turned to follow Higgins to the door. He waited for Jack to reach him. "Mr Durkin, do you have a gun of any sort?"

"No. Wouldn't know how to use it if I did. Why? Afraid I'll go father-hunting?"

"We don't want any deaths in this town."

"Don't look at me," Jack said.

"You said you wanted to kill him."

Jack looked away. "Was how I felt. Now we'll see."

The two men looked at each other for a minute, Jack was first to shift his gaze. Down the corridor Higgins walked into an office. Jack looked back at Smithson.

"Anyway," he said. "What happens depends on my father. I won't start anything. I'll find the bastard and see what he has to say for himself first. See how it turns out."

"Don't take the law into your own hands or you'll find the law taking you into its hands."

Smithson sighed. He patted Jack's shoulder. "Stay alert." He walked away and Jack went to the front desk. The officer there said he had phoned the hospital. Nothing had changed. Mrs Durkin was still in a serious but stable condition.

"Is Mum conscious yet?"

"No, sorry. She is still in a coma."

Jack rang Mary. She would soon be there. He went outside, walked past the shuttered window and down the steps to the footpath. A small car with frosted side windows drove past. He put his hands in his pockets and exhaled steam. He walked on the spot, stamping his feet, waiting for Mary.

He heard footsteps coming from the footpath across the road. A man in a brown bomber jacket walked, collar up, hunched over, hands in pockets. Jack watched him until he turned the next corner. Jack suddenly felt exposed. Hurry up, Mary. He walked away from the police station to the relative shelter of the Court House next door.

HANDY GUIDE TO MANDERVILLE

Courthouse

By Margaret Houston, President of Manderville Law Society

We owe it to our early settlers and their foresight that the town has such a wonderful example of architecture. Built from imported stone from various places including Italy this proud building denotes the very basics of justice for all.

Wide stone stairs leading up to the imposing columns across the frontage in the building assures our citizens that justice will not only be done but that it will be seen to be done. No one who crosses the line into criminal activity can escape being seen and heard in this building. A sentence is pronounced always after a fair trial of course

Built in the late 1890s the Manderville courthouse exhibits all the best of that period's architecture and has a strong presence from its height overlooking the street across from the Post Office. Most weekdays citizens walking in this area or driving past are likely to see some symbols of justice being done by wigged judges, suited barristers and lawyers' secretaries coming and going as the law goes about its business. It's all public as it should be and easy as it is throughout our fair land. For a town of this size Manderville is fortunate indeed to have such a strong showing of the meaning of justice for all.

4

JACK

Smithson'll be in bed before me. Warmer, dryer. Safe from a drunken hitman. Wasted all our time. Talking. Going through the motions. No better driving around, pretending to be proper investigators while the crimin—perpetrator, perp—runs free. Free to shoot me. Thanks, cops.

Mary's taking her time. Handy dry spot this. Bit out of sight among these big columns. Massive brown stone, dragged in its natural state from some faraway quarry, shaped to corrugated roundness, stuck here without any say in the matter by pretentious strangers, to posture incongruously before a bush town Court House.

Jeez, place's got me thinking like Mary. Only matters that it keeps most of the rain off.

She must be close. Need her, plain need her. Surely Dad's not out there, in the rain, the cold, watching from across the street. Would've seen me walk from the cop shop. Come on Mary. Cold wind. God, what a night.

* * *

MONDAY 3.22am

He and his mother had stood outside the Court House several years ago. A cold day. They shivered on the footpath, backs to the wind. Twitchy leaves played kiss-and-run with their legs. Grey clouds padded the sky like a dirty quilt, threatening rain. They could have stood inside, but neither wanted to spend any more time than necessary inside the Court House. Inside, a stranger would decide Jack's future.

"Bloody cold day," Jack said.

"Looks like rain," Bev said.

"Has for some time," he said.

"Do farmers some good, if it did. Rain."

Both spoke without looking up from the ground. Nothing talk. Jack shook a leaf off his arm. Who gives a shit about the weather? Or the farmers? He knew his mother didn't. She rubbed her hands together; breathed steam into them. She stamped her feet on the cement. But Jack knew it could pelt with rain, hail, snow even and she would hardly notice. He knew all too well the pain his mother was suffering; the heartache he had caused her.

"Weather is keeping people off the streets," Bev said. "Good."

"Yeah," he said. No sticky beaks about, she means. There were a few cars angle parked, tail into the kerb. More would come about ten to park close to the doctors' practice, around the corner from the Post Office, which was across the road. Jack hoped they would be called before then.

"Not many about yet," Bev said. Relief in her voice.

"You don't have to wait, Mum."

"I'll stick around," she said.

They turned at the sound of voices. Bev groaned when Mrs Hooper and Miss Carlisle came around the corner. They walked along the street towards them. They were smiling as they always did when they sensed gossip was coming.

"Look, here's Bev and Jack," Mrs Hooper said.

"How nice to see you both," Miss Carlisle said. "What are you doing out on this chilly morning?" Her tiny smile told Jack she knew why.

"Like you, just out," Bev said.

"Not going to the doctor's now, are we?" Mrs Hooper said. "Nobody sick, I hope?"

Jack turned away.

"We're all fine," Bev said. "Got some things to do in town."

"Good, good," Miss Carlisle said. "Was that your car we passed down near the boot-maker's?"

"Hard to know what cars you saw," Bev said, with a sweet smile.

"We wondered why you parked so far away from the town centre."

"I'm sure you did," Bev said.

"We said that to each other when we came around the corner and saw you standing here," Miss Carlisle said. "Didn't we, Lily?"

"Just standing, not, you know … actually going…" Miss Carlisle said.

"Like you're doing," Jack said. "Standing. Not going."

Bev said: "We were deciding what to do first."

"Didn't think standing in the street was anyone's business," Jack said.

"Oh," Miss Carlisle said.

Mrs Hooper said: "We just—"

"Durkin! John Douglas Durkin! Calling John Douglas Durkin."

The court official stood on the top step, looking around the street as if there were lots of Durkins, only one of which would be a John Douglas.

"Oh," said Miss Carlisle again. "Is that you, Mr Durkin?"

Jack didn't answer. He walked up the steps and spoke to the official, who pointed him inside. Bev started to follow, turned and smiled at the two women, who smiled at each other.

"Ahh, there we are," Bev said. "Mystery solved."

"That was a surprise, wasn't it, dear?" said Mrs Hooper.

"Lucky your son happened to be standing here when that man came out and called his name," Miss Carlisle said.

"It was lucky," Bev said. "While we're in there I'll renew our Standing-in-the-Street Licence." She ran up the steps into the Court with Jack.

He had got off that day: charge dismissed. But he still remembered the humiliation his Mum had felt that day. One more…. No secrets in a small town.

* * *

The blaring of a car horn jerked Jack back to reality. Mary had arrived. He jumped in with a mixture of relief and annoyance.

Mary leant across and kissed him on the lips before he had fastened the seatbelt. As the belt clicked in, he pulled away and waved his hands towards the road. She took the hint and accelerated away from the kerb. The windscreen wipers swished metal and rubber, intermittently across their view.

"Sorry you got wet," Mary said.

"Where the hell were you?"

"I had to stop for petrol and… I was asleep when you called. I'm sorry I kept you–"

"Just go."

"What's …"

"Go. Please. I'll tell you about it on the way."

She gave him a quick glance. "I rang the hospital," she said, "Bev's stable but– "

"I know. Still unconscious."

Neither spoke for a few minutes, then Jack said: "Cop at the Station rang the hospital. Not good."

She touched his arm. "Jack, I'm… We can go there now…"

"In the morning." After another silence he said: "Dad's out there. Waiting to kill me."

She pulled her hand away and wiped it dry on her skirt before gripping the wheel with both hands again. "No. You don't believe that, do you? Ray wouldn't."

"I believe Aunty Meg. She told the cops he rang. Said he'd got his rifle from home. Vowed to kill me."

They stared ahead at the dark, wet street, no cars or pedestrians. The only sounds were the engine and the wipers sliding on the glass.

Jack turned to Mary. "Better check Katie's all right."

"I checked. Aunty Meg said not to worry. She and Doug will look after Katie for as long as needed."

"I'll talk to Katie tomorrow," Jack said. "May be problem if Dad calls in there, wanting to be hidden."

"Meg won't do that."

"Not for her brother, you reckon?" Jack said. "Might be better to have Katie with us."

Mary said: "Will you be safe at home? Where can we go?"

"Just home. Lock up. I'll stay up." She turned into their street and slowed as they approached the driveway. He touched her elbow. "Maybe you should go to your parents for a while."

"I'm sticking with you," she said. Then she screamed.

Jack swore and flung the car door open.

Mary yelled: "Stay in the car." She grabbed his right arm. "I'm driving in." He pulled the car door closed with a bang that he regretted.

"Quiet," Mary said, so low he barely heard it. He didn't need to. They must be quiet. Get in the garage and turn the engine off. Mary had stopped the windscreen wipers.

She clicked the remote control. The garage door's screech sounded louder in the darkness, grating on their nerves. Jack slapped his thigh. He was sure the door was much slower than usual. They held hands and watched the black painted words 'I know the truth You will pay for our new grief' disappear into the roll above the door. Mary drove in and clicked the control again. The squealing door descended, and they sat in the dark.

HANDY GUIDE TO MANDERVILLE

Putting Our Arts Into It

By Ms Yvonne Greebstreet, OBE, Manderville Art Society Chair

It is a fact, little-known even by many of our own citizens, that Manderville has a flourishing, inspiring and invigorating artistic community. While sport stars are recognised widely for their achievements —and rightly so, some may say— our poets, novelists, artists, singers and musicians are attaining great heights in their chosen fields. I am sure these wonderfully talented people would receive more plaudits if they ran or swam fast, tackled, punched or wrestled on grass or in squares they ignorantly call rings, kicked balls over and between sticks, used sticks to hit balls into small holes in the ground, jumped over sticks or used very long sticks to jump over ever higher sticks.

Be that as it may, Manderville is blessed to have such a vibrant arts community.

How proud we all were when Winnifred Potter's artistically offbeat self-portrait, 'Winnie and Fred' was hung among the entrants in the Archibald Prize at the New South Wales Art Gallery. This is now proudly displayed in the Society's office, on the second level of the Mackie building.

Also worthy of note are Percy Mumton's vertical landscapes and Marigold Bright's skilfully rendered paintings of insects. Especially eye-catching is 'Stick Insect on a Twig'.

We must not neglect to mention our brilliant performing artists who have entertained us on stage for years with music and singing and dramatic shows and comedies. What a world of talent we have here. The Madder Musical Society, in particular, has staged three shows a year for decades. I don't know how they do it. Such wonderful actors and singers in the musicals. Who could ever forget the hilarious stage appearances of Beverly Durkin, who added her own cheeky interpretations to shows such as *Calamity Jane* and *South Pacific*. But, perhaps, most of all, we remember Beverly's moving one-woman show *Verses from the Heart*, several of which she penned herself.

In another great stage presentation, Joel Perkins enthralled us with his magnificent acting in *Death of a Salesman*.

At many local events we all have been stirred by the martial strains of the Manderville town band. Well done, lads and lasses. And of course, I must mention...

5

RAY

You do your best bringing 'em up and they turn on you. Jack and I used to be great mates. And sweet little Katie, so sweet. Yet she could've killed me that night last year, with the fork. Poor Bev gave that boy everything. Would have given her life for both kids. But not this way. Given, not taken. She might die the cop said. Wouldn't let me see her. My Bev. All right when I took off. Crying, sure, heard her from the chook house, but still… all right.

Never thought Jack would raise a hand against his Mum. Sometimes close against me. Cop said I was a suspect. Dumb bastards. Reckon I was too drunk to know what I was doin'. Me? Never that full. I should know, sure.

Who else would've? Jack, for sure. In a hurry to get away from me outside the chook house. Obvious. Came back after the cops had gone and Katie asleep. Back to have a crack at Bev. To blame me. Said he wants me outta the place. Should've gone back in after cops left. Not skulked off.

Shouldn't have run away from the cop. Should've gone to the station. Well. Ha. Well. Too fast. Still got it. I'll front up to the cops. Take what's due to me after I've done right by my Bev. Oh, Bev, forgive me, please, if I did it. I never... Not hit, not really. I was full. Did I… tonight? Steamed up. Angry. Got close to it but… fuzzy…

Oh shit… Shouldn't have burnt the bloody jumper. Fairy aisle or something she called it. Can't expect me to wear all those fancy colours. Could've asked me first. Asking would've saved all that… Before doing all that work. I didn't ask her to knit for weeks. Surprise is no excuse. Jeez, was that. Bloody Smarties explosion. Don't think I hit her. Said I hated it. Mongrel act. I saw your eyes water, and I hated that, so much more. When you cried Bev, love, when your face crumpled, I … You shouldn't have tried to take it

35

back, I … I just… you can't blame me for throwing it in the fire. That was enough. Wouldn't bash her as well. Unless…. Scared her. I'm scared now. Jack won't …

* * *

MONDAY 4.45am

Ray felt secure, in a safe place, among familiar bushes, well hidden. From his hiding hole, even at this late hour, he could see some distance across the playing fields, past the brick toilets and facilities block. As long as he was careful, he wouldn't be seen. And nobody could creep up on him from any direction. Not if he was awake. The high metal fence and bushes along it protected his back and kept him safely out of sight from the street. Not likely to be anyone about at this time, anyway. Shrubs and a few trees surrounded his spot. Once was his and Bev's spot—one with happy memories that tonight made him cry silently.

The rain had stopped a while ago, but the grass was damp. His rifle lay a couple of metres away, relatively dry under a bush.

He needed a smoke. And a beer. Bloody water bubbler outside the team dressing rooms was enough to drive a man to drink—if he hadn't reached that destination many years ago.

Wind shook the leaves. The only sound now. Whatever had rustled the bushes some minutes ago – if anything had— was gone. Maybe a rat or a cat or the wind.

Nobody about. Unlike match days. Oh boy.

Great days. Running out as fullback for the Manderville Mugs. The name began as a joke, but none laughed after they won the Harper Cup. The next season—just as successful—Ray won an ever more valued prize—not that he dared call Bev that, not after the first 'trophy' joke.

He didn't drink in those days. Only started to fit in with shearer mates after a shed cut out and, eventually, with teammates after a game.

Every game Bev was there when he came off at half-time. Slim, in slacks and casual top, her fair hair peeking out from her brown-and-gold Mugs cap.

"Hey, love, how you reckon we going?" He always knew how they were going. Asked it to hear her invariable answer. "Good as gold." In those days, things were always 'good as gold' to Bev. Not any more. She often added things like: "Should win from here" or "Need another Ray Durkin try or two".

He'd grin and hug her, usually spotting her top with mud. She never cleaned it off until he was back on the field.

Most weeks, Bev said she loved his try he scored at the start, or at the end or just before half-time. Most weeks he scored at least once. And kicked several goals.

Bev exuded joy at his play. "… so fast, zipping around that fat forward bulldozing right over their halfback. Jeez, we laughed…"

Ray slumped down on a large stump and wiped a tear away with the back of his hand. So long ago. Now he's hiding here and…

That lovely face was now battered, bruised, eyes shut, mask covering lips that may never smile again. He had run away when the cop told him he was suspected of causing all that damage. That he wasn't permitted to see his wife in hospital.

Tears ran down his cheeks. He didn't wipe them away. No one to see here; only him to grieve in this black hole. Tears were the least he owed Bev.

After home matches, he and Bev had often crept here, after all the coach's and team manager's spiels and man-of-the-match awards. They lay there for a private after-match celebration. Sometimes they heard others with similar intentions murmuring nearby. Sometimes they just lay in each other's arms, listening to the passion around them. He would rudely joke. Bev would giggle, smile and gently kiss his lips, while sliding a hand into his shorts she would feign astonishment, brown eyes wide open.

"No wonder you won man-of-the-match."

"Sounds like some around here are trying to win it," he said one day.

He smiled at the memory, now flickering in his mind like fading sepia photographs.

She gave a cheeky grin and said: "We can't have that, can we?"

He lay again near the stump, not caring, at that moment, if the cops found him. Tonight, there were none of Bev's perfume and perspiration scents; only the smells of shrubs and damp earth and grass.

Sometimes, like that day, he knew her grin was a prelude to embarrassment. Often, he tried to silence her with a hand over her mouth, only to have her push his hand away.

Tonight, he lay, face down in the grass, watching faded images stutter across the blackness of his closed lids. He heard a rustle nearby but couldn't bear to open his eyes, focused on the past when small amounts of alcohol brought only fun to each of them.

That afternoon, sometime, when, not now. Anymore.

Hearing her words, seeing that grin, he knew he shouldn't encourage her. But he made the mistake of saying: "Sounds like she's enjoying herself… him."

Bev rolled her eyes and winked at him, her face alight with mischief. She gasped and groaned loudly and thrashed about and cried out as if calling for her creator to ease her pain—or ecstasy. A plea of such passion that God may have wished he had a Red Sea to part or a safe bush to burn.

All the while, Ray lay on his side, head supported on a bent arm, a smile on his red face. Anyone within earshot could have wondered why a Pentecostal meeting was being held in the bushes. Ray reckoned his teammates concentrating on their own attempts to provide sexual satisfaction would have listened in envy.

She enjoyed play acting, whether on stage or lying here in the bushes. When her performance was done, Ray clapped before he rolled over onto her. They took their time, quieter now, in no hurry to part and go home. Bev was all whispers and one-syllable exclamations, ending in a rush of soft murmurs. And Ray's equally quiet "You're welcome. My pleasure."

Ray blinked at the night surrounding him. He sat on the stump he used to put his footy kit on and where Bev put her cap and purse. Tears blurred his vision. He wiped them with the back of his thumb, the tears stinging cuts around his knuckles. "Must have punched the side of the house or the gate post," he muttered. "Or…" A noise broke into his thoughts. Footsteps? Not close. A door banged. The public toilets alongside the clubrooms. Only one outside light worked now but Ray saw a man come out and walk up the slightly sloping driveway and go out the gate. In a few minutes a car engine started. Ray relaxed and lay down on the ground to rest. He fell asleep.

When he awoke he cursed his carelessness. He didn't know how long he had been asleep. He couldn't see his watch face. He guessed it might be about four in the morning. It could be later, close to dawn. Better get going, find a daytime hideout. He leaned over to get his rifle from under the bush. His hand scrabbled in the grass. Nothing. Gone. He stood and shuffled around, peering into the dark, willing his feet to make contact.

"Bugger," he said. Someone had his rifle. He stopped moving, listening for sounds of someone else in the bushes. Someone with a rifle aimed at him. Nothing, except the whisper of leaves. He sat on the stump. Sitting target. He stood. Face it. The rifle was gone. Probably the thief, too. Ray crept out of his hideout. He hoped he could cross the open fields without being seen by the man with his gun.

"Any luck, Bert?" Ray froze at the sound of a man's voice.

Whoever Bert was, he hadn't had any luck at whatever he was trying to do.

"He's got away, then. You got sharp eyes, spotting him standing in the trees."

Ray relaxed slightly. The men were outside the grounds in the street. Bert said: "Gave him a start, by the way he jumped when he saw me looking at him. Gave me one too, I don't mind saying. He took off, heading the other way, thankfully. Didn't know he had a gun at that stage. Shit."

"That'll teach you not to take a piss in the bushes next time, with the toilets right over there."

Both men laughed. Ray wished they would go away, even if they might have unwittingly saved his life.

"Bert, we better tell the cops. Hiding in the park with a rifle, could be the bloke they're after."

"Radio also said not to approach him."

"That's why I didn't run too hard."

"Me either."

As the men's laughter faded down the street, Ray breathed more easily.

But he had to get going. He stood for a moment, studying his surroundings, and was satisfied there was nobody there now. He saw bushes and trees silhouetted against the lighter sky. Dawn soon. He was alone. And somebody had his rifle.

6

BEV

Strange. Why strange? I... who... bright light... but blu . Strange. Where are people? Who are people? Girl... yes little... strange... Big boy.... I... who? Not place mine... who? Where? Kitchen gone. Bright blur... Humming... What is... Big man. Not boy called who? Love him and her and... who are... Name... name? sleepy... humming... no people. Who... then black. Floor rising... up and up. Fast. Hard. Blood. Yelling... who? Where? Pain... not now... Sleep... need sleep ... no. Wakeup... nightmare go... where's love... Man crying.... man I... I... I... Who... love... screams. A woman... frightened... so sleepy... Ray… Jack… Katie…Good... good to sl...
   "Rob…"

* * *

MONDAY 12.45pm

Mary ran to the door of Bev's ward. "Quick. Someone. Come here." The constable jumped off his chair and reached out as if this mad woman was about to run amuck.

"Whoa, there, madam. How did you get in there?"

"Saw you go to the toilet. Just went in. I didn't disturb Bev. Kissed her forehead. Hey! Her eyes opened for a second. She muttered something—"

"I could arrest you. That room's off limits."

"For Pete's sake. There's no signs. Look. Look." She waved her arms wildly and the constable put his hands up to fend her off. "Nobody around. What sort of security is that?"

A tall nurse ran towards them with rapid short steps, looking almost as if running on the spot. "What's going on?"

"Ahh, now there's action around this high security room." She grabbed the nurse's arm and the policeman grabbed Mary's shoulder. Swivelling, Mary somehow manipulated the trio around to the ward doorway.

"What's wrong?" The nurse rushed to the instruments beside the bed. She bent and studied the dials and looked back at Mary.

Mary slipped away from the policeman's grip. He looked at the nurse, as if seeking further instructions from someone a head taller than him.

"She - Bev, opened her eyes. Blinked. Said something—"

The nurse straightened and walked back to Mary, standing anxiously at the door with the constable's arm across her path.

"Well?" Mary asked.

"I'll tell Doctor Robbins when he comes through on his rounds."

"When he just wanders through whenever that might be. Get him now. Bev might be waking up."

"She may be coming out of her coma but—"

"Yes. Yes. Get your strolling doctor. Now."

The nurse rolled her eyes at the policeman. "He will explain it to you. All the signs there - " She gestured at the block of data recorders attached to Bev. "- are showing her condition has not changed."

"Bugger your instruments. Dead boxes of wires and and... stuff. I saw a living person open her eyes after days unconscious. I'll wait until your Doctor Bobbin gets here."

"Robbins."

"Whatever. I'll wait until Doctor Robbins comes bobbing along."

The constable gently turned Mary around and guided her to a short row of green plastic chairs against the corridor wall. She saw his smile transforming into a straight line as she turned to sit on the chair closest to the ward. It wobbled on the uneven flooring.

"I could get you a drink," the constable said, pointing to the cold-water dispenser further down the corridor.

"You can't trust me. Or leave me alone."

"It's just there." He paused. "Maybe you better get it yourself."

She got up and went to the dispenser. After filling a plastic cup, she called out: "Want one, too?" He nodded as if not wanting anyone to hear him enlisting a civilian to get him a drink. She smiled and took the first cup to him before getting another for herself.

"What's your name?"

"Constable Watkins." He took a long drink.

"Me and Jack are really not violent characters. I promise. Jack is breaking up inside because he wants so much to see his Mum, to hold her hand, kiss her face."

Constable Watkins looked uncomfortable and didn't reply until he had drained the cup.

"I believe all that, but I have to follow orders. What if my judgement is wrong? It happens." Mary believed that. "And if your boyfriend assaulted Mrs Durkin again…" Mary stood and started to protest. "I know, he might not have done it in the first place."

He went to the ward and stood looking in. He turned back to Mary. "I just have to keep all except hospital staff out."

"I went in a while ago. Important that I did." Mary said.

"I could get reprimanded for that. Had to go to the toilet."

"Couldn't you get one of the staff to go for you? Or bring you a bottle?"

He looked at her as if considering the absurdity of that. Her smile changed his face from set serious to wrinkled amused. She looked both ways along the corridor, sipped some water. "Where's that doctor? Must have stopped off for lunch." She glanced at her watch. Clicked her tongue. "My lunch break is nearly over. Lost too much time walking here."

"Don't you drive?" Watkins asked.

She stood and walked to the middle of the corridor. "We only have one car. Jack didn't pick me up. If he doesn't come to drive me back, I'll cop it… sorry, I'll get into trouble."

"Here's your doctor," Watkins said.

Not my doctor, she thought, turning to see a small, neat man in a white jacket come around the corner. His hair matched his jacket.

"Mary." She turned at the shout. Jack hurrying towards her from the other direction.

"Speak of the devil," she said, hoping it would be Jack's more angelic side today. He looked flustered. Not a good sign.

He reached her before the doctor who was walking at a leisurely—infuriatingly slow, to Mary—pace alongside a nurse.

"I heard your Mum speak."

He grabbed her shoulders so hard she winced. "Mum's awake?"

He started for the ward door, but Watkins held a big hand up in his face.

"She's not awake," Mary said. Jack turned abruptly from the constable's grim barrier.

"What're you doing to me? Is Mum awake or not? Is... Who's this?" Doctor Robbins had joined them. The nurse stood a discreet distance away against the wall. Constable Watkins stepped back to stand at the ward entrance.

Mary said: "Jack, this is Doctor Robbins, who can tell us how your Mum is. What speaking and opening her eyes means." She squeezed Jack's hand. He put the other hand on her waist.

Dr Robbins looked into Mary's face then Jack's before speaking. "Sister Johannsen told me you had seen and heard signs that have raised your hopes, Miss -"

"Bourke. And good afternoon doctor."

"Miss Bourke." He turned his eyes back to Jack. "And you, I presume, are the patient's son."

"Tell me what's going on. Mary heard my Mum say something. And saw her eyes open."

"Hrrumph. We only have Miss umm Bourke's word for that."

"If anyone was actually in there caring for Mrs Durkin," Mary said, her words loud in the quiet corridor, "you know, looking after a woman who has been brutally bashed within an inch of her life. If anyone around here cared, someone else would have seen and heard what I did."

"Don't dare question Mary's word. She's the most honest person I've ever known. How about doing something to help my mother get better, to come to."

The nurse pushed forward. "We are doing all we can—"

"Doesn't seem you can do much then," Jack said.

Dr Robbins raised his left hand, palm facing the angry young couple, reminding Mary of a traffic cop past due for retirement.

"You must calm down. Quieten. You are assuming Mrs…" He consulted the notes in his right hand. "Durkin is the only patient in here."

"We know that, doctor, but she is the only one we care about and we want someone in here to care also." Mary had quietened her voice.

Seeming to ignore this the doctor continued. "Comas caused by this sort of thing usually don't last longer than four weeks. Some much shorter. But two to four weeks is common if they are going to recover."

"So Mum could be unconscious for weeks yet? Or never wake up. Jeez, man."

Mary held his hand around her waist pressing closer. "Doctor, I saw evidence that Bev was —"

"Now then. Coma patients often recover gradually, becoming more and more aware over time."

"What sort of time?" Jack asked.

Doctor Robbins stuck to his explanatory script, not acknowledging Jack had spoken. "They may appear to be awake and even alert at times. On the first day it may be only for a few minutes."

"Like today," Mary said, excitedly. "This could be the first day of regaining consciousness."

"Patients may wake for longer and longer times. Gradually over time." Bloody time again. In time. Over time. At times. Must be driving Jack mad. Wonder he's kept his cool.

"So, we just have to wait?" Jack asked.

"Yes. Wait and see."

"Any idea for how long, doctor?" Mary asked.

She could have guessed the answer. "Time will tell."

Constable Watkins joined them. "If Mrs Durkin regains consciousness do you expect that she will be able to tell us about the attack? Identify the culprit?"

The doctor seemed to be considering the question, scratching his nose.

"Well, doctor?" Mary asked.

"I'll get the bastard if she does."

Mary squeezed his hand again.

Doctor Robbins said: "She may well be able to do that. But maybe not immediately after she completely emerges from the coma. She may never do so."

Jack shook his head and turned towards Mary. "What did Mum say?"

'It wasn't much. Just one word. It sounded like Rob.

Jack looked as if he was about to cry. "Oh," he said.

Watkins said: "That's something. Could be trying to say robber."

"Or Robbins, as in Doctor," Mary said. Jack said nothing.

Watkins said: "I had better notify the boss. This could be a clue. We may have to increase our surveillance here."

Jack pulled away from Mary. She felt his agitation.

"None of you know anything. Come on, Mary. Gotta get back to work."

7

JACK

Where is she? Said she would be here by seven. I'm worried sick about Mum. Need Mary with me. If only that cop up there would go away. Go for coffee. Go for a piss. Just long enough for me to get into the room. Where is she? Won't order coffee yet. She might be another half hour. Bloody hell. I love Mary. But sometimes… sometimes she can be infuriating. She just … loved her when were only kids in primary school. Probably thought we did. But now, after what, two years or so, can't imagine being without her. Or without my mum. Or Katie. Last week I would've said that about my Dad. Now… I can't live with him. I can't stand all this turmoil. Out of nowhere. From nothing. Brightly coloured jumper. To this. Hanging around the hospital. Waiting for my mother to die or live. Waiting for the cops to grab Dad. Waiting for him to shoot me. But all I'm waiting for now is to see Mary back here. Where is she? At last…

* * *

MONDAY 7.05pm

The hospital cafeteria was quiet, with few customers. Jack and Mary sat at a table near the door, two tables from an elderly woman. At the far end, two women in nurses' uniforms talked softly, leaning towards each other, elbows on table, cups in hand.

Jack tapped rhythmically on the table with all fingers of his right hand. Mary touched his forearm.

"They're going to close soon," she said.

He nodded. Kept tapping.

The peaceful atmosphere was interrupted by china and trays rattled by counter staff. He looked into his half-finished coffee.

Mary watched him, her hands around her mug. A man wandered in and studied the display of pastries to the side of the serving area. Mary thought he was a doctor.

"Good that your Mum may be waking from the coma." He nodded. "Lucky I came when I did. Nurses might have missed that."

"Yes," he said. "Thanks." He drank a few more sips. "So, your boss was all right with you being late back this afternoon?"

She wrinkled her nose. "Not so pleased, but grudgingly accepted I had a good reason. I was only a little bit late anyway."

"Generous man."

"Accountants not known for generosity."

"Did he know what happened to Mum? Probably town gossip by now."

"Yep. He tried to sound sympathetic. But when I said I was leaving work to come back here tonight, he asked me to work back a short while to make up for my 'long' lunch."

Mary watched the possible-doctor move to a table near the two nurses, plate in one hand Coke can in the other. She turned back to Jack. "Do you know what Bev was trying to say?"

"She said Rob. That was the name of the baby that was never born. Robert would have been between me and Katie. Miscarriage."

Mary put her arms around him. "I am so sorry. Poor Bev. I didn't know that."

"Kept it quiet. They had a few hard years before Katie arrived."

"And now, you all have so much... bad stuff to deal with. I wish I could ease your pain some."

"Nobody can. I need my Mum home and well. And I need to get my Dad, the one who did it."

Mary didn't want to ask what "get" meant. She placed both her hands on his.

"He wouldn't be running away, hiding, if he didn't do it."

"Maybe he's just frightened of being blamed for it."

"He tried to frame me. Told cops I did it. Bastard."

The elderly woman sitting alone stared at Jack for a few seconds. She frowned and looked towards the serving counter, apparently wishing someone would bring her order. She had nothing in front of her. Oblivious of anyone around them and Mary's quiet pleading, Jack went on: "He said he would kill me." He looked at her without speaking for a minute.

A slender man in operating theatre garb turned to look as he glided past. The woman saw the waitress approaching with her tea and cake and stood. She gestured with her hand to a table further away. Mary saw her eyes were red and thought she might have been crying before she and Jack came in.

Jack said: "We used to be good mates." His voice was quieter now. "He taught me how to kick a football. Punt it. Drop kick, pass and catch. He helped me become a pretty good junior player."

"I used to watch you."

"I know. I used to look for you on the sideline. That made me drop the ball once or twice." They both laughed.

"You were pretty good."

"Not as good as him. He was Manderville's best. Captain, too. Mum used to watch him. Like you did, me. Before they were married." He slid his mug around and studied the swirling of the coffee. Mary could see he was a bit embarrassed. "For a while afterwards, too."

"Then he just gave it up? Retired in his prime?" Mary accompanied her words with a smile, but she knew better. Knew why champion football hero Ray Durkin stopped playing.

Jack shook his head. "Nah, the grog. Started drinking after games—mates talked him into it. In a year or two he was gone. Ruined him. His shearing tallies dropped, too. Bloody grog."

She reached for his hands and squeezed them together. She looked around at the almost deserted cafeteria. "What a sad place. Hospitals are so depressing. I hate them."

Jack didn't look around. "Who could like them?" Mary thought maybe doctors did when they saved lives, maybe nurses.

"Dad has every reason to steer clear of them."

"Like you, cops keep him away from his loved one."

"Way before this." He paused, and Mary thought he was delving into a long-ago memory. "When he was about five his dad, my grandfather Isaac Durkin, was pretty sick in this hospital. My grandmother, Edna, tried to protect young Ray. They didn't take him to see his father. But one day she dressed him up and told him they were going to see his Daddy."

"That was only right. Lovely—"

Jack held both hands up. "No. She and her sister took him to the dentist, who took out a tooth."

Mary sat back, "That was a dreadful thing to do to a little boy."

"A few days later Granddad worsened, and it was obvious he was close to death. He asked to see his little boy."

Mary felt the story wouldn't end well but sat staring intently into Jack's face.

"So, they told him his Daddy wanted to see him. They dressed him in his Sunday best, slicked his hair, shined his shoes, and the little boy set off hand-in-hand with the two women walking down the street."

"Jack, did he—"

"He suddenly pulled away from their hands and ran away. I don't know where to. Maybe up alleys or into bushes in the park. They found him, crying, later that day and—"

"Poor little bugger," Mary said in a whisper. "And I suppose he was all messed up by then. Not a good state to see his dad for the last—" She saw the look on Jack's face, the tears inching out of his tightened eyes. "His Daddy died without seeing him."

"Bloody thoughtless," Jack said.

A stout man came from the kitchen and stood behind the counter. A young waitress screwed up her face and said something that Mary couldn't hear, and the man nodded. He called something into the kitchen and walked to the end of the counter.

"Time we left," Mary said, dumping the sodden serviettes in the nearby bin. The elderly woman walked hesitantly towards Mary. She stopped about a metre away. She waited until Mary looked up before speaking. "Your young man isn't very considerate of other people, is he? Such language."

"I'm sorry he disturbed you.," Mary said. "I can see you are grieving, too."

"I am and ..." Her face softened, and she interrupted her thought. "Oh, are you… do you also have someone close who is very ill in here?"

Mary gently touched the woman's arm. "Jack's Mum. She might die. She's in a coma."

The woman dropped her head and spoke without looking up. "Is that the poor woman who was beaten up?"

"Yes."

"I'm so sorry. She is only young, isn't she? So much of her life in front of her still. My sister is older than me." She looked up at Mary. "Sadness every way you look." She sniffed and turned away, sobbing.

Always is. Always has been in one way or another, Mary thought. Jack had been watching them and seeing she was alone again, he went up and added his scrunched up wet paper to the bin.

"Who was that?"

"A sad lady. Her sister is dying. We should offer her a lift home."

"We've got enough on our plate. Do you know she needs one?"

"No. I'll ask her."

He turned away. "She'll be fine. Let's go."

Ignoring Mary's protests, he headed for the entrance without saying anything. Mary walked quickly to catch up. Seeing his grim face, she didn't press him about helping an old lady.

"We've got some steak in the fridge. I can cook that up with some chips tonight," she said.

Jack kept walking as if he hadn't heard Mary.

"What do you think?"

"I'm not hungry now. Maybe later."

Like when I'm in bed, Mary thought but didn't say. "How about steak sandwich then? We've got some lettuce and tomato and onion…" Sounds good to me. Make one for myself then.

Neither spoke again until they were in the car. Jack was driving.

"I'll drop you off then go out again."

"What on earth for? You're tired, Jack, go to bed if you're not wanting to eat anything."

"I have to find Dad. Get him to give himself up." He turned the car into their driveway. The threatening graffiti had been removed—at some considerable cost to their finances and to Jack's fragile mental state. "I can't just tuck myself into bed as if all is fine in the garden," he said.

He activated the garage door and drove into the space lit only by the headlights. He turned the lights off and triggered the remote to close the door again. They sat in the dark in silence, looking straight ahead. Mary reached over and turned Jack's face towards her. Leaning across, she kissed him. First a peck, then more passionately.

"Jack," she said, drawing back for breath. "This will all pass and we'll—"

A loud bang, like a door slamming, startled them. Jack shouted, "Front door," and sprang from the car. The garage light switch was nearest Mary and she was there before Jack had rounded the rear of the car. Mary opened the internal door and Jack pushed past her into the darkened house.

"Someone's running away," Mary said. But Jack was already opening the front door. Mary ran to stand beside him on the veranda. They looked both directions, but nobody was in sight. Jack ran down the drive. Mary peered into the bushes on the left side of the front yard.

"Did you see him?" Mary asked.

"Nahh. He's gone," Jack said. "Bloody fast bastard," he said, walking back to the veranda. He reached for Mary as she stepped up to join him and pulled her close.

"Better call the cops again," she said.

"Check if he took anything first, I guess."

They went into the house and Jack turned the living room light on. Mary gasped.

"The ... mongrel..." Jack cursed and punched the wall beside the window. "Not what he took. It's what he left."

Jack slumped against the wall, beside the door jamb. Mary slipped slowly to the despoiled carpet. Her eyes were wide. Frightened. She began to cry.

8

MARY

Hard to comprehend the hatred behind this sudden violence. Even when spelt out in dripping black letters. Been one thing after another. Now it's like a bomb went off in here, spattering words of terror. Vile threats, on our walls.

He needs comforting. So do I. I want to cuddle him. Be cuddled back. I know, I know. His grief is so much greater than mine. But I feel their pain. I love them all. Bev: kind, compassionate, non-judgmental. Katie's a wonderful, clever girl, sorry Katie, young woman.

He's lying with his back to me now. He doesn't seem to know when I snuggle up against him. He doesn't notice my nakedness, my nipples against his back, my thighs against the back of his. I just want him to turn around, to be beside me, to be around me, over me, inside me, out of me, rolling away, rolling back and kissing and kissing until our tears mingle with each other's. Last night he didn't go to bed at all. Listening for any sounds of the spray can man returning. He told me he slept a bit last night. I heard him pacing, talking to himself. Is it wrong for me to feel the way I do? Is it bad to desire this? Just touching his chest over his stomach and then into the bush finally breaking through into a dead end. Like this when we lose the cricket… God, sorry Jack, sorry. What is wrong with me? Sorry Jack, so sorry trivialising this terrible trauma. My mind so often goes down tracks my mouth would never wander. Or hardly ever.

This is a million times worse than a game we watch on TV or listen to on radio. A dark presence living among us, walking our streets, watching us, listening to us, breathing our very air, then striking and vanishing like a trapdoor spider. He doesn't move. Not a sign from him. If we don't love tonight, if we don't embrace tonight, enjoy the bodily comfort that we can give each other, we'll lie here in the dark alone, each with our own grief. We'll be alone, alone in our concern and care and love for each other. I hope he's aware of my feelings for him, my concern, I'm so sad and lonely. What can I do? What can I…

TUESDAY 7.15am

When the alarm woke Mary she stood and stretched and went to the wardrobe to gather the day's clothing which she placed on her end of the bed. The sounds, low as they were, woke Jack, who checked the time and sat up.

"What you doing at this hour, babe?"

She turned on her way to the bathroom. He looked at her nakedness the way she wished he had last night. "Got work to do."

He stretched out his arms and gestured to her.

"Come back to bed. Too early to be doing any work. I feel like—"

"Too late. Had your chance."

"When? Not this morning. Come on. I'm ready." He pulled the sheet back and she saw he was. Temptation made her take a step towards the bed, but she stopped.

"Sorry, Jack. Tempting as it is, another time." Last night would've been a good time. She continued towards the bathroom, fully aware of how he would be affected by the sight of her backside.

"I have to be at work by eight-thirty," she said, closing the door on his protests. The shower noise blocked anything else. When the water stopped there was no sound from the bedroom.

He wasn't in the room when she came out in her bathrobe. As she dressed, she heard spitting sounds from the kitchen and smelt the aroma of bacon frying. Yum. He was making a more substantial breakfast than usual. It smelt delicious and she wished she had time to eat some. Hope he understands. Oh yeah, you reject me then you reject my breakfast. Two marks against me this morning. Better not mention last night's rejection.

She put on a cheery smile and walked into the kitchen. "Smells delicious, honey. Feel inspired?"

Jack was tipping two fried eggs and a lot of bacon onto a plate he held in one hand. He put the empty frying pan back on the stove.

"Just for me. Didn't think you'd want to hang around this morning." Without looking at Mary, he slid a heavily buttered slice of toast under the eggs which burst yellow over it. He hadn't put a tablecloth down and there were crumbs and specks of rind on the red Formica top.

She kissed his cheek then filled the electric kettle and popped bread into the toaster. "I want to hang around. But I have work"

"Can't even be a bit late when there's a crisis."

She bent and hugged his shoulders. "I wish I could. But I've got a bastard as a boss. I've got to kow-tow to Hardwicke or he could sack me. Drop of a hat."

"It's only accountancy stuff. What could be so important?"

She laughed. "Our clients. That's what." She made a pot of tea and spread apricot jam on two pieces of toast. She sat opposite Jack. "And don't knock accountancy. It's what I do."

"I was counting on you to visit Mum today."

"I am. In my lunch break. Come with me. About one?"

"I'll join you there." He took his plate and knife and fork to the sink and dropped them in from an unwise height.

"Did the plate break?" Mary asked.

"Nup. More important things to worry about." He returned to the table. "Any tea for me?"

"Of course. Haven't got mine yet, either. Waiting for it to draw." She poured two cups of tea—both with milk. She put one on the table at Jack's place. He sat again. Nodded thanks. "What's..." She bit into her toast. Better I eat than ask what's eating him. Just bring out the bitch in me again.

"We can meet after work and visit your Mum again then, too."

"What about finding my Dad? Doesn't he matter to you?" He drank his tea.

"I know. Of course, I know." She patted his forearm. "But he might be out to hurt you."

Jack plonked his mug on the table. "I can deal with that."

Mary took her plate and half-full mug to the sink, emptying the mug and turned the tap on to rinse them. The plate slipped from her grasp and crashed into the sink.

Without turning, Jack said: "Did the plate break?"

Mary ignored the question. She dried her hands on the little towel hanging on the oven handle. She went to the bathroom without looking back. Jack called after her: "You're in a hurry."

No answer. Mary returned in a few minutes. He was standing at the sink, turning the tap on and off. She went up and put her arms around his waist. She kissed his neck and he turned and kissed her lips.

"Sorry if I'm a bitch."

"Sorry to be a bastard."

They kissed and Mary slowly pulled away. "Have to go. I'll walk." She looked at her watch. "Fast. Car keys are on the dresser." She went quickly to the door. Stopped suddenly.

"Oh God," she said. She turned around, her face pale.

"Jack. He's been in here again."

Jack rushed across the room. She held a note out to him but he let it fall without touching it.

"Fingerprints," he said. "I'll call the cops."

"He must've come in while we were in bed," Mary said.

"Not necessarily. He might have put it there last night and we didn't notice it when we ran out the door."

"It was another threat," she said. "We would pay."

"You go to work, love. I'll make the call and tell you about it later. Don't worry. We'll be right."

She was shaking, not convinced. He hugged her. They kissed. Jack let go and took a step back. "I missed you this morning. Why didn't you come back to bed?"

She glanced back with a toss of brown hair and grinned. "Blame the netballers. Kiwis beat us." Her grin widened and then she was gone. The door closed gently over Jack's question. "What's that supposed to…" Click. "oh…"

She began slowly, legs still wobbly, but then almost ran up the driveway and turned right onto the footpath. If Jack didn't turn up at lunch time, she would have to walk to the hospital, there and back perhaps. Be cutting it fine. Old Hardwicke would be watching the time as closely as she watched the same big white-faced office clock as knock-off time approached. Some days Mary was sure the long, black hands crept slowly past the Roman numerals as if they were dying for a last look at the past.

She broke into a jog, causing a brown terrier-cross to leap at the fence, barking with a pretend ferocity as she went past. Her fingers waved it a rude sign. Another block of jogging put her in sight of the shopping centre and she slowed. She might be on time after all.

"I can't afford to lose this job," she said to a tabby cat posing on a fence post. "We can't afford to." The cat gave no indication of caring less.

9

COLIN MARTIN

They all told us, Edie and me, that time heals the grief. That the pain fades with the passage of years. They were wrong. Its black stare follows me like eyes in a portrait. Through the kitchen window a grey shadow moves over the backyard, as if my eyes were dragging a small cloud in front of the sun as they passed over the weather-faded swing and its rusty chains, over the little bike leaning against the tree, the ladder up to the treehouse and the toy gun lying on the platform.

I switch on the light in Peter's room— we still call it that — the black maw follows my unblinking eye over toys and books and cards and model aeroplane on shelves and desk, uncolouring them all, and down onto the sneakers poking out from under the bed.

All those years we have suffered the pain of Peter's death.

Oh, they were so good at work. To both of us. Mr Hardwicke, uncharacteristically for such a stern boss, was kind and sympathetic. We needed the time off he granted us. Sadly, our loss must have brought it all back to him: his own loss. Heartbreaking to come home from work to find your wife and two little kids gone, leaving a note. She had gone off with one of his best mates. All the office staff, so wonderful, especially my assistant Mary, trying to be comforting, trying to find the right words when no words can ease our pain–not even after a decade.

And now they tell me our pain should have been greater, our grief deeper – and Edie urges me to do more… To avenge this horror.

* * *

TUESDAY 7.30am

On the second morning after Bev Durkin had been attacked, Katie left Uncle Doug asleep on the lounge to sit in the front garden. She leant back in the wrought-iron chair and put her Coke can on the table, set in the neat, well-kept front garden. She breathed deeply, relaxed by the crisp, early morning freshness and the scents of flowerbeds and new-mown grass. So peaceful, away from Uncle Doug's tedious TV watching in the smoke-filled living room. She wasn't used to smoky rooms; her parents didn't smoke. Unusual for a shearer. Maybe he considered one addiction was enough. When she saw her uncle nodding off in front of two women and a man discussing a whiz-bang vacuum cleaner, Katie had crept away. Out here the air was clear; the only sounds birds and the occasional passing car. But, there in that smoke-free, prattle-free environment, her mind was even more filled with thoughts of her mother lying in the hospital bed and her father hiding somewhere, probably frightened. She couldn't understand why anyone would hurt her mother. Everyone loves her. Dad more than anyone. Dad couldn't have done it, despite his frequent drunken outbursts. Often he had thrown things about, but never had he hit anyone. She shivered… Unlike Jack– and her.

She heard a car brake. She looked up and was surprised to see a car pull up in front of the gate. A bit early for visitors. Could be the police or news from the hospital. The driver turned the engine off and she got out. Katie stood. She was shaking. She hoped the woman now walking towards the front gate wouldn't notice. If she did, she didn't say anything.

"Hello, are you Katie Durkin?"

The woman was vaguely familiar to Katie.

"What's wrong?" Katie said. "Who are you? Is it my Mum?"

The visitor bent and unlatched the gate. She looked up, walked in, shut the gate, all the while keeping her eyes on Katie.

"You might remember me," the woman said. "There has been a development."

Katie put a hand to her mouth. "What? Is Mum–"

"Settle down, dear. I'm here for you."

"What? How come you?" Katie didn't know her. Not really.

"I'll drive you to the hospital." She smiled. "I'm Edie Martin. We met at the Hardwicke Accountancy's Christmas party. Do you remember?"

"Sort of." She had gone with Jack and Mary. It was a brief conversation. The woman looked somehow different from the brunette she met at the party. For a start, this woman was a blonde. Dye? Wig? At the party Edie was charming and smiled a lot, putting on a brave face after the tragic loss of their son: drowned in the creek. Today's smile was different.

"I met your husband, also. He was very nice."

"He is a very nice man. We went through a lot of grief over the years." She raised clasped hands to her chin and gazed at the ground. She looked up and said: "But you know all that."

Katie looked around. Nobody in sight. Not in the car. Not on the footpath. Few cars speeding past. And Uncle Doug asleep in the living room. Edie patted Katie's arm but pulled her hand away when Katie stepped back.

"Now listen, dear, Jack and Mary want to see you at the hospital. They were called into the Police Station. Jack said you didn't answer your phone."

Katie gasped. Her phone was dead. Charging now in the kitchen. "But, but…" She struggled to understand what she was hearing from the virtual stranger who had walked unannounced into the garden.

"Jack asked me to come and get you. Colin said Mary could take the day off." Yes, Mary works for Edie's husband. Should be all right for me to… "I'll drive you to the hospital where Jack and Mary will meet you later."

Katie asked: "Are you sure Mum's not worse?"

Edie stood and said: "There is no change in poor Bev's condition. We should go now."

"I better tell Uncle Doug."

"Is Meg out?"

"She's rostered on with Meals on Wheels this morning. There's only Uncle Doug here." Edie didn't appear surprised at this. "I'd better tell him."

Edie moved closer and held Katie's hand. "I don't know how to say this, but Jack said it's important to take you away from your uncle."

Katie laughed. "That's ridiculous. He's a harmless old fellow." She turned towards the house. Edie held her hand more firmly. "Katie, you must listen to what your brother said. He was adamant it's important for your safety. Let's go."

She walked towards the gate, looking back at Katie. "Come on, dear."

Katie followed her, tentative at first, with backward glances at the house. Then, making up her mind, she sped up.

Edie opened the front passenger door and Katie got in. Edie got in the other side and drove away.

After a while, Katie said: "Mrs Martin, why are we going this way?"

"Call me Edie. I have to pick up flowers for your Mum at home. And a vase, to put beside her bed. Won't be long."

"How far away do you live?

She didn't answer immediately. Katie waited a few minutes before asking again. "How far, Mrs Martin?"

"Not far out of our way. Don't fret. Visiting hours haven't started. You'll be there in plenty of time to meet Jack and Mary and spend as long as you like alongside your poor Mum. Dreadful, isn't it? So dreadful this happened to you and your family."

She sounded sincere, but Katie wasn't sure if she could trust this woman who called herself Edie Martin. It had all seemed more credible then, than it did now. Katie's bewildered protests were hushed with vague insinuations that Uncle Doug was a threat. She found this hard to believe. But someone unexpected had attacked her Mum. The person she trusted completely was in a coma. Unreachable in any way. She felt tears run down her cheeks.

She jiggled the door handle.

"Don't fiddle with the door," the woman said. "It's got a childproof lock on it. Tighten your belt."

"I'm not a child. I don't need a childproof anything."

"It's for your own good. I told you that." She sighed. Katie knew Edie hadn't said any such thing, but she understood the threat in the words. She moved her hand from the door. She put her right hand over it to stop the shaking.

"I need to concentrate on driving. Just trust me."

"Like you trust me? Locking me in."

The car turned into a driveway of a house Katie had never seen. "Here we are. Behave now. No screaming."

Katie trembled. What was going to make her want to scream? This woman had told her that she was in danger. The man who beat up her mother was still out there. Katie considered jumping out on the driveway as soon as the lock was released and running to Jack's place. Her heart sank when the garage door automatically swung up and the car went in. The door clanked down. They sat in semi-darkness until the woman got out and the interior car light went on. Then the garage light.

"Come on, Katie. We're home."

"Not my home. Please get your flowers quickly, Mrs Martin."

Edie smiled in a non-smiling sort of way. Without replying, she opened Katie's door and pulled her out. Katie cried out. She struggled to pull out of Edie's grip on her arm but it was bigger and stronger. The more she jerked, the more it hurt.

"Enough of that, you silly girl."

Oh, oh, where is Jack? I want him: bursting in, temper flashing, fists ready to rescue me from this jailer. No hope of cavalry. Jack will think she had run away from Meg and Doug's.

Edie pushed Katie through the internal door, into a lounge room. "Settle down. Stop crying; or do it quietly. Yelling and screaming could be dangerous. Even fatal."

Edie nodded towards a doorway behind Katie. "You can wait in there for now."

Katie didn't look behind her. "I'll help you get the flowers ready." She knew there weren't any flowers for her mother.

Edie said: "Don't worry about the flowers. For now, you can rest on the bed in the room behind you."

Katie looked around the sparsely furnished room and through a doorless entry into a kitchen with red bench tops.

"I don't need a rest. I won't go into another room, I'll just wait on the sofa."

She took a step towards the sofa, but Edie blocked her path. Katie felt a chill of fear.

Suddenly, a hand came from behind and covered her mouth. Another hand grabbed her elbow and she was dragged back through the doorway. She kicked backwards. "Bugger you," a man said.

She tried to bite the hand and it moved away. Her scream was silenced by a cloth across her mouth and tightened at the back of her head. Both hands were free now and she punched wildly. But it was a momentary respite: both Katie's hands were grabbed by her unseen assailant and tied behind her back. Despite her struggle, she was carried into the room and pushed face down onto a single bed. When she turned her head, the man was gone and Edie was standing at the door. "Now don't be silly, dear." Stop calling me dear. "All for your own good. Very dangerous for you if anybody hears frightening noises and comes knocking. Be a good little girl. I'll be back soon with some sandwiches and a drink."

Garbled sounds came through the gag. She thrashed around on the bed, stopping only when she was about to fall off. "Now just relax and have a sleep."

Katie heard the door lock and lay still, sobbing, wanting her Mum and Dad. Just sixteen and I'm a prisoner in a cell, being roughly treated by a friend of Mary's. She thought of Aunty Meg returning home and finding her gone and silence deepened her despair.

10

JACK

Damn. Hoped they wouldn't have put the guard on Mum, yet. Just as well, I guess. Dad's roaming around. Me, too, cops might say. Me, the only one with a record. But that's old stuff. Dad and his gun could open a new Durkin record before day's over. Good shot. Used to be. Dunno now. Maybe when sober. Doesn't scare me. Mary should be safe in the reception area. He loves her. Thought he loved Mum. Never said he loved me. ... Not lately.

Cop's watching me. Good sign. On his toes. Don't know this bloke. Talking to that nurse. About me? Looking at me, not each other. Keep walking, act… What's the word? Nonchalantly. Surely they'll let me see Mum.. After Jacobs gave me the morning off. Give it a go.

* * *

TUESDAY 9.30am

"Excuse me sir," the policeman said as Jack walked towards his mother's ward. "We can't let anyone go in there."

He moved to the centre of the open doorway. A bulky man, he blocked much of the room from Jack's view. Jack stretched to look past the wide body of the law. Bev was lying on her back, unmoving – as he had expected but hoped against.

"My Mum's in there," Jack said. "You can't keep her son out."

The nurse patted the constable's arm, looked, unsmiling, at Jack, and went back into Bev's ward.

"I've been instructed to only let medical staff in. Identified medical staff. You aren't a doctor or a nurse, are you Mr Durkin?"

He knows me, Jack thought.

"It is Durkin isn't it? John Durkin?"

64

"Yes. I want to see her. Touch her. Kiss her."

"Somebody 'touched' her too violently already. Until we know who that person is, we are restricting who enters here."

"You're wrong if you're implying it was me. No way." He paused, calming his building anger. "Hard to admire the local force's efficiency. My father's out there with a gun after bashing my mother. And you won't let me see her." He paused. He gazed at the stolid constable blocking his way. "Is anyone investigating the death threat painted on my garage door, on my walls?"

The officer stared impassively at Jack while he spoke, then he said: "We're on it."

So, word has been passed on about that, at least. And this cop guarding a hospital room may also be involved in finding the maniac who graffitied their garage and broke into their house.

"Shows it's my Dad you want. Not me."

"Did you recognise your father's handwriting on the door?"

Jack gave the officer a disbelieving look. Was he kidding?

"Don't think big, dripping, spray painted print resemble handwriting with a pen."

"We're looking into all possibilities." He paused. "I'm sorry, Mr Durkin, I understand you are upset…" Upset! "but I can't let you in there."

"I want to know how she's going. Is there a doctor around?"

"It is a hospital."

Jack turned and looked back along the wide corridor. Nobody. No one the other way either.

"Try the nurses' station." He flicked his thumb in that direction.

Jack shook his head. The suggestion didn't deserve any comment. The nurses' station was deserted. He turned away and saw a doctor and two nurses come around the far corner. One of the nurses was talking animatedly, arms and mouth constantly moving. The doctor, eyes on the carpet, nodded occasionally. The other nurse looked straight ahead as they walked in Jack's direction. He recognised her as the outspoken woman he had clashed with the first night. She seemed to recognise Jack, alas. She said something to the doctor. They stopped, looking at Jack, as if a hole had unexpectedly appeared in the road. The animated nurse stood, arms dangling, mouth closed. The doctor had looked up from the carpet, studying Jack instead. He said something and they resumed their stroll.

Jack strode towards them, intending to get some answers.

* * *

TUESDAY 10.20am

Mary closed the magazine she had been idly flipping through and asked: "How is Bev?"

Jack plopped down beside her on the reception area bench. He rubbed a hand across his forehead, ruffled his hair. "Buggers wouldn't let me see her. Got a glimpse from the door, past the fat cop. That's all."

Mary dropped the magazine beside her and put a hand on his knee.

He gave her a crooked smile. "Grabbed a doctor. Man called Robin somebody."

"Robbins," Mary said.

"What?"

"His last name. Robbins." She kissed his cheek. "Sorry, darling. Shouldn't interrupt. Go on."

"He said no change. He expects Mum might improve in a few days. Might not for weeks. Mary, she's so…" He stopped. Mary brushed his cheek and leant across to kiss him on the lips. Her movement caused the magazine to slide to the floor.

The front desk receptionist, a middle-aged woman in the hospital's standard pink blouse — a white cardboard tag poking out from the hem indicated it was probably new—opened the door in the counter and hurried towards them.

Mary picked up the magazine. Jack determined that if the woman with a serious, over-made-up face bearing down on them reprimanded Mary for dropping a magazine, he would scatter the lot over the floor.

He stood, body tense, ready to grab magazines from the small coffee table in the corner. Mary looked nervously at him. She stood and held his hand.

"It's back on the heap now," Mary said.

The receptionist walked up, ignoring Mary. She said to Jack: "Are you Jack Durkin?".

"Yes, Why? Is it my Mum, Mrs—"

Mary squeezed his arm tightly.

"There is a phone call for you. It is your Aunt Meg. She says it is urgent. Sounds upset." She turned back towards the counter. "You can talk to her over here."

Mary whispered: "Phone off again? Even at a time like this?" They followed her to the counter. She went behind it and handed the phone to Jack.

"Don't be too long. Many people call for assistance or information on that line."

Jack didn't know how long 'too long' was. He said "Hello". As he listened, colour left his face. He mumbled something into the phone. Then, more clearly, he said: "We'll be right there." He dropped the handset on the counter and ran for the door. Mary ran after him.

11

RAY

This place scares some people. Watch too many horror movies. Never scared me until tonight. Now I'm in a horror reality. Scared a bit. Not the place, but it doesn't help. Weeping willows in corner. Weeping willows, for god's sake. As if there wasn't enough weeping goes on here without getting trees to do it, too.

Bloody big Mander mausoleum stuck in the middle to lord it over everyone else. Too late, mates. They're all dead. Gives me a bit of cover in that direction, so thanks for that, Josh.

Don't expect any company tonight. No one wanders around a cemetery at this hour. Seldom did years earlier when me and Bev came for a bit of loving. Sex in the cemetery. Good name for a movie. Our trysts among the tombstones. She'd laugh, back then, at the romance of it.

Here's the spot, behind old Fred Turner's oversized and chipped headstone. Silas whatsisname's next door not much smaller. More chipped. What do they do in here? Maybe the cowboy on his rider mower.

Chipped or not, they made good cover for a couple of horny young lovers. So many nights.

Bev's shenanigans spoilt it for a while. Her sense of fun gets out of hand sometimes. Used to.

Scared the hell out of me when she started that night. Funny though.

Not so funny for old Jake Smith and Ron Woakes. Bet they never took that shortcut home from the pub again. Their carousing along the path was cut short by Bev's exaggerated shrieks and howls from behind the gravestones… would've scared a ghost, let alone a couple of until-then-happy drunks.

"Is that you Malachi?" Jake asked in a shaky voice. Bev giggled and I wondered who the hell Malachi was.

She called out in what she thought was a spooky voice, but what I thought was cute: "Whooo wants to know-wo-wo?"

I popped my head up to see the two men clinging to each other. A broken beer bottle lay between them, beer and maybe some other liquid spilled at their feet.

My grinning, tree-shadowed face unfroze their feet and they shuffled backwards. When Bev's bare legs shot out each side of the headstone and waved in time with her cackles, that did it. They screamed and ran for their lives—or so they probably thought.

She pulled me down beside her and kissed the laughter from my lips and tongue.

"Was that scary enough?" She had that mischievous look I love. It was too late to ask Jake and Ron, the sound of their running feet fading in the distance, screams falling among tombstones.

"No," I said. "I could tell you were faking."

She pushed me down and fell on me. I put my arms around her naked back, brushing away dried leaves. Soon the leaves didn't matter. Soon nothing mattered. Soon I knew she wasn't faking anymore.

Hurts to remember, here, now. Have to suck it up, because I can't forget. She always had this little, smile, afterwards, like a secret message to me that said, "Good as gold."

So much fun in her, so much mischief, so much love. A cemetery, of all places.

And I had to look for more in a bottle. Will I ever beg her forgiveness again? For real this time? They must let me in.

Lonely here. Now a sad place. Never again be a loving place for me and Bev behind the tombstones.

Reckon I could hole up here through the day, too. Neglected area, no flowers–dead or alive. Is that how I'm wanted? No new graves in this bit. One of us Durkins might be next. If it's Bev, Jack'll soon follow.

* * *

TUESDAY 11.15am

The living room at his old home was dimmer than Jack remembered when he crept in. Such is memory when you're the ripe old age of 22. He turned the light on and it hardly brightened the room. All in the mind. The future was blacker than he could have imagined before dinner Sunday night. Before the family was shattered and had to wonder if they'd see dawn, let alone breakfast.

Now Katie has vanished. He could not be sure any one of them was safe.

How could that be? Any of it?

Mary had dropped him off and gone to pick up Aunty Meg, who had rushed home as soon as she got Doug's call. There, she had demanded an explanation from her anxious, shame-faced husband. He had no idea. Jack imagined Aunty Meg's reaction. Almost wished he had been there.

Meg would leave the car with Doug in case Katie rang or returned.

Jack poked around the house, hoping –but not expecting– to find a clue to his sister's disappearance.

He was careful not to make any noise as he moved around his former home. Something he had never bothered about before. Katie wasn't in the house or outside. Not in wardrobes, not under beds. Not down the back yard. Not in the chook house. "Must feed them before I go," he said quietly.

His father wasn't there either. Not behind a door, rifle ready.

The living room added to Jack's depression. The thick green curtains blocked most sunlight. He left them closed. Dark furniture—dining table, six chairs, brown, three-seater lounge. Grey-and-green carpet, scuffed patches around the chairs and the radio's walnut cabinet standing in the corner, a clear glass vase with dying gladioli, struggling to stand tall.

They used to sit in here, listening to cricket in summer, Rugby League in winter, Jack at the table, Ray perched on a chair near the radio, Katie on the floor, alongside her father's legs. That all changed when television arrived, belatedly, in their home. Same sports plus loads of other programs that competed for attention in their household.

Unusually for a shearer, Jack presumed, his father preferred reading books to watching the new box in the corner. His collection was stacked on the four-shelf unit in another corner, beside the lounge.

His 'library' was shoved every which way, vertically and flat. Among the untidy stacks were *Les Miserables*, *War and Peace*, several by Jules Verne and Charles Dickens.

Jack checked his watch. Where was Mary?

Dog-eared westerns, most by Zane Grey, jostled for space between the classic novels.

To hell with the books. He wanted to see Aunt Meg. Where the -

Familiar voices from the hall startled him. He hadn't heard the front door open. He heard it close.

"Jack. Are you in here, darling?"

"In the dining room."

"It's very dark," Aunt Meg said. "I can't find the hall switch."

"Sorry about the light," he said. "I didn't know if Dad was here, too." He didn't add "…waiting to shoot me dead".

He went out and turned the hall light on. The two women stood in the hall, faces sombre. Mary raised her hand to shoulder height and wiggled it. "Hi," she said, no smile on her pale face. Aunty Meg hugged him. She stood back holding his shoulders at arm's length. Mary walked around Meg to kiss Jack's cheek. She carried a paper bag.

Meg said: "So, Katie's not here, then?" Jack shook his head. Meg gazed around the room, which obviously only contained the three of them. "I mean, she's nowhere … anywhere in the house?" Jack shook his head. "Oh Jack, where can she be?" Jack knew: "Or him?" was the unspoken extension of that question. And has he got Katie? Whether or not, she might be in danger. God.

Mary handed the bag to Jack.

"You didn't have breakfast this morning, love. I bought you this." He held it away from his body, dangling from his left hand as though it contained spiders. For a second he was about to throw it on the floor.

Mary patted the bag. "It's a burger and chips."

He nodded and lifted the hamburger to his mouth. He grinned at Mary after swallowing the first bite. Mary moved closer and kissed his lips.

"Hmmm, tasty sauce." She dipped into the bag and ate a few chips. "Good chips," she said. "Have some, Aunty."

Jack offered the open bag to Meg.

"No thanks. He didn't say he was coming here."

Jack and Mary exchanged a glance.

Meg sat on the lounge. She adjusted her dress over her knees, as if arranging the yellow and orange flowers. She frowned at the result and fiddled with the white buttons on her brown cardigan. She lifted her eyes, face startled, as if suddenly realising what she had said. Jack and Mary were staring down at her.

Mary said: "You've spoken with Ray? You didn't tell us."

"Have you seen him?" Jack said, anger in his voice.

Meg appeared flustered. She looked at Jack, but if she hoped for her nephew's understanding she didn't get it.

"What did the mongrel say?" Meg jerked back as though struck. "That he was sorry for bashing Mum? For abducting his daughter?"

Mary put an arm around him. "Darling, we don't know that–" He pushed her arm away and strode closer to Meg, who shrank back on the sofa at the violent, rapid-fire outburst.

"He… Jack, dear… he's my brother. We're all family…"

"Did you hear what I said about my mother, my sister, about my life under threat? Our family's buggered."

He clenched his fists, glaring down at Meg. Mary tried again, standing firm this time, holding his right arm. Meg stuttered something about her brother but Jack cut her off.

"Your brother put grog first… Don't talk to me about family." Meg stood, shaking her head. Wisps of grey hair fell over her forehead. She brushed them up with a quick flick of a hand, but they fell down again.

"Ray thinks you attacked Bev."

Jack cursed and turned his back to study the bookshelf. Mary sighed and looked helplessly at Meg.

Outwardly unperturbed by his rudeness, Meg continued: "He was adamant he wasn't so drunk he didn't know what he was doing."

Mary spoke, changing the focus back to Katie. "Where do you think Katie is, Aunty? Who could have a reason for taking her from your home?"

Meg licked her lips. "Katie's just gone. Left our place, alone or with someone, while Doug was… I hate to say this… while the lazy bugger was asleep. That's all we know. What we told the police."

Jack had turned from the bookshelf, his arms hung at his side, his hands open. He faced Meg. "I hoped she'd come home. To her own bed, own room. That's why I came." He paused. "But when I saw the kitchen… I knew she wouldn't stay here."

The women stood without speaking or sitting.

Jack grabbed Meg's arms. Shook them. "No way Katie's here. So, where the hell is she? Did Dad take her? Did he?"

Meg struggled to release her arms. She winced and asked him to let her go.

Mary said: "Jack, Meg doesn't know anything. Please let her go."

He loosened his grip. Meg pulled away. She said: "Don't do that John. Katie was asleep when Ray rang from a phone box. I didn't tell him she was in the house."

"What did he want then? Just a friendly chat?"

"He was hungry. Wanted food—and beer. Then he hung up."

"We better get you home, Aunty," Mary said.

Meg nodded and walked to the front door.

"Coming, love?" Mary asked him.

"Can you come back and get me? I'll have another look around. Make sure everything's locked and turned off."

She kissed him. "I won't be long."

Waiting for Mary, Jack looked over his father's collection of western novels. He noticed several of his old comic books. He leafed through them before stuffing them back among the books.

He wandered into his parent's bedroom. His cot had long gone, of course. He had slept in it, in his parents' room, longer than little kids usually did. Until they could afford a bed.

A round clothes hamper was in the space where his cot had once stood, against the wall furthest from the window. The site of his earliest memory–well, his parents' earliest memory anyway–occurred at the cot. He had heard it over and over for years from his cackling parents. He woke one morning to see his Daddy standing over the cot, a colourful, flapping, thing in his hand. Waving it, he said: "Look what Daddy's got for you."

Toddler Johnny could not have known what it was. But he laughed at his Daddy, who was so excited by the flimsy object. The toddler wobbled up to stand at the foot of the cot. His tiny hands gripped the top rail as he waited to see what Daddy would do with his odd paper surprise. He didn't wait long.

"It's a Hopalong Cassidy comic," he said as if it was one of the greatest gifts a father could bestow on his little son. "A collector's edition," he added, handing it to Johnny. In later years, Jack pointed out that a two-year-old would not have understood a single word his father said.

He may have thought it was food. As soon as it was in his hands he put it in his mouth, losing his grip on the rail in the process and falling back onto the quilt.

Dad was horrified; Mum amused. Their toddler trying to eat Hopalong– Bev called it Chewalong–Cassidy. In between chewing and sucking, Johnny found great fun in tearing the pages. Stupid memory from his baby years. But better than memories building up now. Or yet to come.

Jack was stirred back to the present by the sound of his car pulling up in the lane. He went into the hall. He heard Mary's footsteps running along the path, clattering up the wooden steps, pattering over veranda floor boards. Before he could open the door, Mary burst in. Her face was flushed.

She shouted: "Jack, I've seen your Dad."

"What?" He was already out the door, following Mary. "Where?"

They jumped in the car and Jack started the engine before Mary had her seatbelt fastened.

"He was hiding among the trees on the dividing strip in Meg's street."

"Did Meg see him?" He was speeding now.

"Don't think so. Slow down love… It was after I dropped her off."

"Right. We'll get the bastard now."

"Not so…"

12

MARY

He should've let me drive. Thinks he's better. I'm safer. Would be now. Calmer. Asked twice. Bit my head off. No way, he says. Right. No way we'll survive at this hellbent rate. Ignoring my alarm will only save a couple of minutes. He's so uptight. Not thinking of us here and now. Not concentrating on the road. Or—hell—the footpath.

"Jack!"

Ignores me. Me. The woman he's likely to die with. Today.

"Argh!" Any minute. Not got to marriage ceremony yet. Not promised to stick with him until death do us part. Ooh, woo. Nearly shot that old fellow into heaven or…

"Hell! Jack!"… That dog, hope heaven doesn't have pets. No, that'd be hell.

"Oh, shit! Jack! For God's sake."

Gone deaf. Why am I here? I love him… but? He's copped a load of pain. Out of nowhere. Maybe. Ray's always … He…we… don't know if Katie's alive or if Bev'll recover.

"My God…Jack…"

Not himself. Manderville's not itself. Concentrate on the mansions flashing past as we career around narrow streets of the bloody highfaluting Patterson Heights Housing Estate. All the hoo-ha when it launched years ago. Pompous speeches, band, balloons and long queues. Our small town had never seen anything like it. Sales reps didn't mention it was built on an old rubbish dump. Asbestos Heights might've been better name.

Bloody hell! That woman's dropped her grocery bag. Jumping out of the way. Lucky she wasn't holding a baby, he says.

Meg and Doug were sucked in. Sold their cottage in South Manderville to move here. Could only afford single-storey place.

Too fast. Calm. Calm. Clasp hands. Kiss Jack when—if—we get there. Will Ray be there? Might. Soon, please. Slowing now. He's relaxing, sitting back, holding wheel with stretched arms. No longer crouching over it like a dingo with a rabbit. He parks and looks at me.

"Hey, Mary, why you been swearing. Not like you." And praying. Not like me either.

* * *

TUESDAY 12.25pm

Jack propelled himself out of the lounge chair again, pushing so firmly with his legs that he was halfway to the hall door before taking a second step. Standing in the doorway, he turned his head each way, index finger lightly rubbing has upper lip, as he peered at the hall's four closed doors. Sunlight, filtered by a pale green panel in the front door, subtly deepened the primrose walls and, spilled into the living room, added its cheeky intrusion to the window's over-lording illumination. Except for quick sideways glances at each other, Meg and Doug kept their eyes on Jack. Sitting side-by-side on the lounge, neither looked at Mary, sitting to their right in a single-seater lounge chair. Mary thought they were like a couple in Poirot summing-up, fearing he would swing around and point his finger at them.

Meg twisted a pink handkerchief around and around her fingers. Doug seemed poised to leap up, his right foot tapping rhythmically on the off-white shag carpet, his left leg bent back to touch the lounge.

At last, with no significant movement other than her eyes, Meg asked: "What's wrong, Jack?" Silly question. Mary closed her eyes for a moment. What's right would have been harder to answer. Jack didn't reply. Meg said: "You remember where the toilet is?"

More silent minutes, during which Mary sat smiling, unnoticed by them, at Jack's unsmiling aunt and tap-dancing uncle. Jack didn't answer Meg's toilet question. He stepped fully into the hall. Mary feared he might go down the hall, opening every door, showing he distrusted Meg and Doug. Maybe best if he did. He turned and looked at them. Mary had never seen him so haggard. Weary, hurting, sad. He needs cuddles.

Jack returned to the room. "You sure she's not here?" Mary could tell he wanted to search the house. To satisfy himself that not only was Katie not here, but also that Ray wasn't, either.

"Jack," Doug said. "We've told you he isn't here. Do you think we'd lie about that?" Maybe, Mary thought. Depends on where 'here' is.

"All the doors're shut out there." He waved his left hand towards the hall.

"Tidy habit, dear," Meg said. She smiled at Mary as though seeking confirmation of an obvious housekeeping tip.

Doug said: "Meg is as upset as you."

Can't they see him? Mary bit her tongue. Jack looked at her, slowly shook his head.

"It's a small town," Doug said, "we'll find Katie soon enough."

"Soon enough has passed," Mary said. "By my watch it's already half past 'worried sick.'" Jack's strained smile showed he agreed.

As if Mary hadn't spoken, Doug said: "Can't be far. As for your Mum, it was Meg's brother that did it. Blood is thicker–"

Meg slapped his shoulder. He shut his mouth. "The police aren't saying that."

Mary couldn't think of anything thicker than Uncle Doug. She stood and went to Jack, who was standing in the middle of the room. She held his hand. "We believe you haven't seen Katie." She didn't add "or Ray." When she didn't, Meg turned to whisper something in Doug's ear. He nodded. Mary was sure they knew more than they were letting on.

Mary sat in her chair again. Jack plopped into the single-seater next to Mary.

"Good," Meg said. About believing them or for sitting back down? Nobody spoke. Doug picked up a TV guide and opened it. Meg took it out of his hands and threw it on the coffee table. It nearly missed and hung over the edge. All eyes focused on the dangling magazine until, sure it wasn't going to fall, they went back to looking at each other in silence.

Mary was uncomfortably hot.

The curtains were wide open, allowing the sun full rein to heat the room. The air conditioner wasn't on. No wonder she was sweating. Maybe they couldn't afford high electricity bills on top of a high mortgage.

Mary said: "Do you think I scared Ray off when I saw him this morning, Aunty Meg?"

Meg looked at Doug before answering. "He may have recognised you if he was where you say."

Doug stopped tapping, his slippered toes paused on the upbeat.

"Maybe he wanted to see me," Meg said.

"That's probably it, dear," Doug said.

"About what?" Jack snapped.

"Calling in for a cuppa and a chat?" Mary asked with a smile that neither Doug nor Meg returned.

"Have you reported this… 'sighting' to the police?" Doug asked.

"That's our next stop," Jack said.

"We rushed here first," Mary said. "In case—"

Doug interrupted: "Police won't find anything, anyone, here. No point in reporting anything."

"No, dear," Meg said, looking at Jack, "think of the neighbours. Doug and I don't want police turning up, sirens wailing."

"I don't think they'll put sirens on for a house call," Mary said. "Not like the house is going to run away."

She had an image of this little house on the run, Doug, in slippers, shooting from a pistol and Meg, hair in curlers throwing fruit and vegetables through the back door at the pursuing police car, with its siren screaming.

She tried to stop an entirely inappropriate giggle and triggered a coughing splutter.

Meg leapt up. "I'll get you a glass of water."

Jack stood. Mary, red-faced, followed suit.

"Don't worry, Aunty," Mary said. "Just a…"

"She's stressed about all this," Jack said, steering Mary towards the hall.

Mary flapped a hand in front of her mouth, as if cooling it. "Yes. Just a stress bubble."

Meg saw them to the front door. A click from the lounge room as Doug turned on the TV. Meg gave an exasperated sigh and rolled her eyes.

"Now, mind you tell us as soon as you find Katie," Meg said. "And we'll keep in contact with the hospital about Bev. No need to call the police here, is there? Both of you go carefully."

Back at the car, Mary offered to drive, but Jack said he'd be right.

After a few minutes of silent driving, Jack said: "Notice they didn't apologise for not properly looking after Katie?"

"Was odd. Meg, particularly, fusses over us but doesn't say 'sorry we let your sister get abducted'."

"Bloody weird. Probably in it with Dad."

"Surely not. That would be… Very stressful time for everyone. They would be feeling guilty."

Jack said: "Brother and sister."

"No. Meg wouldn't protect anyone who attacked your Mum."

Jack slowed as he turned the car into York Street, two blocks from the Police Station. It was late afternoon and there were a lot of people on the streets, heading home from shopping or work. Traffic slowed their progress. A car in front stopped and slowly reversed into a diagonal spot, drove out again and retried it. Jack cursed. Mary playfully rubbed his hair. Not good to get stirred up before they see Constable Smithson.

The car reversed out again, turned, and accelerated away down the street.

"There you go," Mary said. "He's given up. Good spot, close to the station."

"Yeah, lucky sometimes."

He drove directly into the space.

* * *

Fifteen minutes after Jack and Mary left, Meg was peeling potatoes over the sink when she heard a cough behind her.

Without turning, she said: "Have a good sleep?".

"Didn't mean to sleep so long."

"You needed it, after roughing it in the bushes here and there."

"I'll go soon. Have a bite and beer."

"No beer for you. Done enough damage. A cuppa for you."

She poured tea into a cup, added two spoons of sugar, and slid a cup and saucer in front of Ray. "Here's a sandwich, too."

He nodded thanks. "Yeah," Ray said, begrudgingly. "Rough. Bit hard on a bloke."

"Hard on Bev," she said, while rinsing the peeled potatoes under the tap. She glanced at him, then turned back to cut them into pieces.

"I didn't touch her, Meg. Never have. Never would. For god's sake, you must know that."

She turned to face him, wiping her hands on a green-checked tea towel. He was chewing a mouthful of corned beef sandwich.

"Who did, then?"

"Must be Jack."

She threw the tea towel on the bench. "Not Jack. Less likely than you."

He leant his hands on the back of a chair. "Shit, Meg, you know how much I love my Bev. Worship the ground she walks on."

"What about the ground she was knocked to?"

"Let me be. I wouldn't, couldn't..."

"Not the same man when you're on the grog." She swung back to the sink and dropped the potatoes into an aluminium saucepan. A piece bounced off the rim onto the floor. Meg swore. Ray bent and retrieved it. She took it from his hand and threw it in the open-top bin. She put the saucepan under the tap and turned it on. The saucepan wasn't accurately placed under the tap and most of the water gushed into the sink. She clicked her tongue in annoyance. She moved the tap arm across, holding it until water covered the potatoes. She put the saucepan onto a hotplate. She didn't turn it on. After adding a shake of salt, she carelessly dropped the plastic container on the table. It rolled towards the far edge. Ray stopped it and set it upright.

"I'd better go," he said.

"May be best. Jack might be telling the police you're around here."

"Why'd they think that?"

"Mary saw you hiding in the bushes on the median strip. Not a really smart hiding place, Ray."

Ray stood silently, leaning on the table, watching Meg add another shaking of salt and put the lid on the saucepan. She shook her head, said to herself: "Did I do that already?" She put the salt container near the sink.

Ray watched her start peeling carrots.

"I'd love some watermelon," Ray said.

"Sorry, got none." She didn't turn from the sink.

He looked down at his hands. "Oh." He looked up. "Remember when we were kids on bloody hot days, sitting in the hall, backs against the wall, gobbling chunks of watermelon?"

She laughed, turning to face her brother, peeled carrot in hand.

She said: "Legs straight out, towels and bowls on top. Front and back doors open for the breeze."

"Stinking hot some summers, Manderville," he said. "I could do with some watermelon now."

"Out of season," Meg said.

"Like me," he said. "Where's Doug? Watching TV?"

"More likely TV's watching him."

He nodded. "Uh ha. Asleep."

Meg was almost finished her work on the carrots, wielding a yellow-handled peeler, long strokes curling strips into an orange topping over potato skins. She stood looking at the peel for a minute, before grabbing an onion, which she proceeded to peel and slice into rings.

Ray moved to stand next to his sister. Without looking up she said: "I love you so much, Ray, and would defend you with my life. But sometimes the forces against us are too powerful to fight—"

"We can beat the bastards."

"You must go, now. Take this Thermos of tea, sandwiches and other goodies."

She handed the food and drink to him and kissed his cheek.

He pulled a chair out and sat at the table.

"Oh, Ray." She checked her watch. "The police could…" She touched his shoulder.

He put his head in his hands, elbows upright, red and white tablecloth scrunched up around them.

"I've got nothin' left. Bev's likely to die. Jack hates me. Katie's missing, probably hates me, too."

Meg rubbed his back. "Don't give up. Remember, Ray Durkin always had another try in him."

"Not this time, Meg. Game's over. Cops after me. In the wink of an eye; all buggered up."

"You gotta go. For me, and Bev and your kids." She gently helped him to his feet and handed him the food and drink.

"I was somebody once."

"Still somebody," Meg said, pushing him towards the door. Maybe a dangerous somebody, she thought. She dismissed the thought. No, not Ray.

He said: "Back to skulking around, hiding in bushes, among tombstones, filching scraps…"

They hugged at the front door. Meg cried. She dabbed at her eyes.

"The onions."

His eyes were watery, too.

"You and Doug were breaking the law. Having a wanted man in your home. A basher, the cops reckon."

Best if he hadn't run away, Meg thought, but didn't say.

"We'll cope with whatever happens."

"Gotta go. Get Jack."

"No. Keep away from Jack. He's as torn up as you are. Jack believes you attacked Bev."

"Bloody liar… Sorry, Meg."

"And he's distraught about Katie."

Ray pulled away from Meg. "I'll be lookin' every-bloody-where for Katie. Whatever's happened, Meg, I tell you this: Somebody's gonna pay."

"Hurry. Go. Hide in better place than the middle of the road." He went. Fast as a will-of-a-wisp like the Ray Durkin of years long past.

Meg stood in the hall for a few minutes after the front door closed with a click. Doug came out of the living room.

"What's going on now? Who slammed the door? Woke me."

"You poor, suffering bugger. Ray's just gone. To a rougher night's sleep than you'll be enjoying. And the door wasn't slammed."

She opened the front door and flung it shut again. "That's a slam."

He gazed at her for a second, then said: "Pretty cut up about Katie, I suppose. Does he blame me?"

"No good blaming anyone now." She went and turned on the hotplate under the saucepan. "We'll have bit more veggies than usual for dinner."

She paused. Looked at Doug with sad eyes.

"He's my brother, but Doug, I can't help being uneasy while he's around. Not the same as he was."

"He's had a bad time lately," Doug said.

"He's run off to…. I don't know." She turned the heat down under the saucepan and went to the fridge. She took out a plate with steak on it and put it on the table. She reached towards the knife block on the bench. Her hand froze in mid-air. "Doug, he's got our big knife."

13

SMITHSON

What's young Durkin expect. Staring at me as if I'm Hercules Poirot or Columbo or … Expecting me to know all the answers. Not sure I know all the questions. Bloody mess. Woman attacked in her home. In a coma. Husband accuses son. Son accuses dad, who's run off, with a rifle. Threatening to kill son. Son vows to kill him first. Threats spray-painted on son's garage. His sister abducted from under uncle's sleeping nose. So he claims. Or did she run away? Boss must think I'm up to it. But expect he'll call Brogan in sooner or later. Durkin's waiting for answers. Let him wait, might think my leafing through these reports means something.

Girlfriend discreet, looking around, not staring at me. Wouldn't mind those big brown eyes staring at me. Expect she'll be more reasonable.

Check hospital later. Please don't let this become a murder case.

And this bloke—a suspect —has the cheek to sit here waiting for me to solve it all. Elbows on the table. Staring.

* * *

TUESDAY 2.35pm

"Well?" Jack said when Smithson looked up from his handful of papers. Mary put a calming hand on Jack's arm. He was disconcerted by the police officer's lack of urgency. They should be combing the town for his father and Katie. Not sitting here drinking water and reading files.

After all, they had waited seventeen minutes – he had checked his watch – before Smithson had appeared in the interview room.

They had rushed in to report Mary's sighting to the front desk. Mary had asked to see Constable Smithson. A constable took them to the small room they were now in and put a tall green jug of water and three clear glasses on the table. And then they had waited, mostly in silence.

"He mustn't think we're dangerous," Mary said, pointing at the glassware.

"He should be here by now," Jack said. "Wasting time when he should be out looking for Katie and Dad."

Raising his voice, he added: "Three crimes and he's sitting on his arse waiting for something to happen."

She said: "Shh, surely there'll be plenty of uniforms combing the town." Hearing the door click, she nudged Jack. He flashed her a look that said he'd heard it, and didn't need a dig in the ribs. The door creaked.

"For your information, Mr Durkin," Smithson said, "I have been out, as you require, since 6.30 this morning. I returned only fifteen minutes ago. I am hours past my normal lunch break. Break, you understand, not lunch hour that workers such as yourself enjoy."

Workers like me, too, Mary thought. The door slammed, and Smithson walked over and sat opposite them.

Now, after several painful minutes, he seemed ready to hear what they had come to say. He opened a notebook. He took a ballpoint pen from his shirt pocket and held it over the notebook.

Mary thought he looked bigger than he had in the hospital corridor, and balder. Jack had said he was surly afterwards at the interview. She thought he had an agreeable face. She could imagine him laughing occasionally. Good. Surly and short fuse didn't make for a happy meeting.

"Thank you for sparing the time for us, Constable Smithson," Mary said. "Sorry we have interrupted your fleeting chance for lunch." She smiled. Jack looked as if she had lost her mind. Smithson smiled, revealing a strip of lettuce in his teeth. Had time for a bite of salad then.

Smithson said: "I hear you might have seen Raymond Durkin in the street."

"Mary saw him skulking among trees on a dividing strip near my Aunty Meg's place."

"She is his sister, right?"

They nodded. She said: "We've just been there."

"He's not there," Jack said.

Smithson looked from one to the other. "Really?"

"No, we—" Mary stopped, as the officer's sarcasm sank in.

"We might have found him if you had informed us immediately, instead of racing out there like Keystone Cops."

"Didn't have much faith in you guys," Jack said.

"Wouldn't call you two, either. Seeing as you came back empty-handed." Touché. Mary gave a little smile.

"Are you sure you saw Mr Raymond Durkin, Miss Bourke? Or perhaps 'think' you did is correct term?"

"Think?" she said. "I'm not blind, Constable. I saw him all right. Among the trees and low shrubs. Trying to hide, but not much cover in middle of the street."

Smithson wrote in his notebook.

"It was him," Jack said, louder than the other two had spoken.

Smithson ignored Jack and said to Mary: "Any sign of a young female person with Mr Durkin?"

"You mean like a ... teenage girl? Like, say, a Katie?" Mary said. "With Ray?"

Smithson looked at her without answering. Waited.

"No," Mary said.

"Does that mean anything?" Jack asked, leaning forward again. "Do you reckon my father could be involved? Think he's hiding Katie?"

"We don't consider that likely, Mr Durkin." He paused. "We've found evidence your father camped at the cemetery for a short while. No sign of any girl being there."

No young female person then.

"Are you sure he wasn't in the house?"

"They said he wasn't." Mary realised how weak it sounded. "We trust Doug and Meg."

"I'm sure you do, but nevertheless—"

"We couldn't search the place after they gave their word," Jack said.

"We could. In fact, a couple of officers are there now doing just that."

Mary didn't show any emotion: She was pleased they would soon know if Ray or Katie – or both – were in the house, but knew – could see – Jack felt he had betrayed his aunt and uncle.

She said: "They also told us Katie wasn't there."

Smithson took a drink. He put the empty glass down near the table edge. He looked at it and pushed it further. "Why would she be? Mr Durkin reported to us that his sister, Katie…" He checked his folder. "…Anne Durkin, was missing from your aunt and uncle's home. Do you suspect she was being held in there against her wishes?"

"We don't know where Katie is," Jack said, heatedly.

"We need more information about Katie."

Mary said: "Katie's vanished. We don't know where. Or who's got her."

"Maybe nobody's got her," Smithson said. "Might have wandered off by herself."

"She'd be too nervous to do that," Jack said. "Not with all this stuff going on. She's only sixteen."

"She may have wanted to see her mother. We are keeping a watch on that."

Jack sat back. "That's no–"

"Oh good," Mary said, "but I agree with Jack. Katie wouldn't have wandered off without telling anybody. She even left her phone behind."

Smithson asked if Jack or Mary could give him the names of Katie's friends, who might know where she was. The list was short and somewhat vague. Smithson said that they would check it out. He paused, looking at his open notebook. He looked up at Jack.

"We have found two black paint spray cans in the bushes at McGovern Sports Fields."

"That's where he hid, then?" Jack leaned forward. "He used to play footy there." As if that matters a damn now. Time ravaged. Beer sozzled. No longer strong, fast or heroic.

"No sign of anyone. Just the cans."

Jack banged the table. "Jeez, mate. Constable, too slow again. Never there when it's happening. What's the - ?"

" - point of you blustering Mr Durkin. If you hadn't kept vital information to yourselves for so long a prime suspect might not have got away."

The constable's face was red. He glared at Jack.

"We thought if we drove there immediately, we might see Ray," Mary said calmly. "Sorry, Constable Smithson, for our misjudgement."

"We'll soon know if he's there. Thanks for the information. Pity it wasn't sooner." This brought a flick of a glare from Jack.

"Fingerprints. Must be fingerprints." Mary said.

"We always check those things."

Jack sat back. "So – "

"So," Smithson interrupted, " if you can't give us any more timely information that might help, we'll continue following normal procedures."

Jack stood so violently that his chair fell to the floor behind him. Smithson jumped to his feet as if he thought Jack was about to attack him. His chair also fell over and he shoved it away with a sideways kick.

"You had better leave, son. Keep on like this and you'll spend the night in a cell. Come on. Out." He jerked his thumb towards the door.

"Why won't you cops try to save me and my sister? Do I have to do it alone?"

"We haven't got manpower to put a guard on each of you, so keep alert for yourself while we hunt for your father and sister."

Jack and Mary walked in front of Smithson. He quickly strode around them to open the door into the hall.

Jack and Mary went into the hall and stood there. Smithson closed the interview room door, clearly expecting them to keep walking, but they didn't move.

Mary pointed to the folder under Smithson's arm. "May I ask, is there anything hopeful for us in that file?"

"I think not, as such." As such. No wonder Jack blows his top with this fellow.

"But we have a few leads to follow up."

"What are they?" Jack asked.

She said: "Can you tell us, Constable Smithson?"

"Not in detail." He paused and considered the two young people. "However, I can warn you to be careful..."

"About what? Being careful when someone went into our home and bashed my Mum?"

With lowered hands, Smithson indicated they should keep walking. They did, slowly. Then Mary stopped and looked at Smithson.

"Are we in danger?" Mary said, her brown eyes wide and unblinking as they looked into the officer's dark eyes.

"We have been alerted to a link with a couple of ..." Pause. "... suspicious..." Mary waited for him to say deaths. "... events."

He resumed walking towards the reception area door. Jack and Mary followed.

"Oh," Mary said. "I'm surprised that a more senior officer hasn't been appointed to this case. No offence intended." But unavoidable.

They were almost at the door. Smithson turned and looked at Mary. "My superiors have complete faith in my abilities. They know I am up to the job." His voice was grey iron hard. "They are kept informed of progress. If it develops into anything more serious than a domestic assault and a teenager running away from home, that may change. At the moment, this is not a major case, Miss Bourke, no offence intended." He smile was as metallic as his eyes.

Jack said: "Katie didn't run away. She was bloody-well kidnapped. Isn't that major enough for you blokes? Or are you waiting for our mother to die so it becomes a murder case?" His eyes blazed at the constable and Mary feared he might lose it. His fists were clenched. She moved in front of Jack. He pushed at her back but said nothing.

Keeping a tight rein on her voice, Mary said: "That was extremely insensitive Constable Smithson. It is no surprise to me that you are still a constable."

"Yeah," Jack said.

Mary reached behind and squeezed his right fist. It relaxed. He dropped both hands to his side.

"You can't leave us up in the air like this," Jack said.

Without a word, Smithson held the door open for them.

As they walked past him Mary said: "Thank you Constable. You've been very..." She smiled. Smithson shook his head. He walked quickly back along the corridor to a door, which he opened and disappeared without another look or word. They went out into the sunshine. Both breathed deeply, relieved to be out of the station. Jack kissed Mary. They embraced, ignoring the stares of passers-by.

"And you criticise me for stirring Smithson," he said, kissing her again. "Let's go get a strong drink."

14

MARY

I'm sure he's a frustrated racing driver… now racing to get me into the next world when all I want is a coffee. Racing off to get a drink… did he say a strong drink? Oh my god. This is Ray's example. Surely not. I misheard. He wouldn't say 'strong'. He's never been a big drinker. He's seeing what addiction does. No I misheard. Sheez, so fast. Where is a cop when you need one?

Slower please.

Never spoken about wanting strong drink before. It's all this family trauma. This shit. Looking at me. Asking why I'm jumpy.

Phew. At last. The MegaMall car park. Good spot not far from the main entrance. Better still, parked wrong end of mall for the bar.

* * *

TUESDAY 3.50pm

Jack strode quickly across the car park towards the entrance. Mary had to walk quickly to keep up. When they were inside, Mary reminded him that the bar was at the other end of the mall. He looked surprised.

"Does that matter to you?" he said.

"I thought you wanted a strong drink."

"Where did that come from? I want a strong coffee."

Mary hugged him and kissed his cheek. "That's exactly what I want, too."

She pointed to a coffee shop across the way, its multiple doors folded back. She said: "This is a nice place. Good coffee."

They chose a table for two in the sparsely occupied café.

Jack leaned across the table to kiss her. She grabbed the small vase of artificial flowers that his sleeve threatened to tip over.

His lips met thin air when she pulled back. She slid the vase away from the centre of the table.

He straightened and looked around, silencing the snickers of two girls at a nearby table. He turned back to Mary. "The table's too small," he said.

"Hmmm, Depends what you intend," she said. "Too small and crowded for lovers."

For a moment he looked confused. "I - I didn't mean that sort of thing," he whispered.

"What sort of thing," she said, with mock innocence. "Wherever did you get such an idea?" Jack began to bluster in protest, saw Mary's smile, and closed his mouth, reshaping it into a big grin. She laughed, and in the midst of all his despair, it was like the moon breaking through dark clouds, briefly lighting the sky before disappearing behind rolling clouds again.

He relaxed onto a chair. "You're right. Only here for a coffee."

Still standing, Mary asked: "What can I get for you?" He gave his usual answer of "the usual" followed by "I'll share whatever you get". Yeah, sure you will.

Mary returned from the counter and sat facing Jack. "I've ordered the coffees and a blueberry muffin for us to share."

"That's not what I –" Her face showed she wasn't serious.

"No, love, I got your usual – ham, cheese and tomato toastie. No need to share."

He sat back in his chair. Its legs squeaked on the tiled floor. "We've got the cops offside." He ran a hand through his hair.

Mary nodded. "I think we may have upset the local constabulary," she said. "But we're more than a bit upset ourselves."

"Interview was going nowhere. I got impatient."

"Not like you," she said.

"Do you reckon anybody's looking for Katie? I mean seriously searching?"

"Surely they are," she said. "A missing person.

She reached across and held his hand. They looked up when their coffee and food arrived. Mary smiled and whispered a 'thank you' to the teenage waitress.

"I said things I shouldn't have I suppose." He took a bite of the toastie. He washed it down with coffee. "Should have learnt by now to keep my mouth shut."

Mary didn't disagree, concentrating on eating her muffin.

Jack said: "Something to do with getting older."

Mary laughed. "Yep. Ripe old age of 22."

"Extra responsibility. You know…"

"I've heard your responsible mouth a few times, but I still love you. Maybe Smithson does too." Her grin disappeared behind the uplifted coffee cup.

Jack wiped crumbs from his mouth. Mary continued: "You and I go back a few years. Back to our first date."

Jack looked into his cup, saw it was empty and put it down. "At the movies?"

"Well before then. You were all of 11 years old. Your birthday party."

"Come on, Mary." A smile flickered on his face. "Hardly a party. You were the only one who turned up." Jack rubbed his chin. "Is this a first memory of your love or my temper?"

"See what you think." She smiled. "We were at the big table in the living room. I remember it being quite … dim."

He squeezed his eyes shut, and sat silently, facing down, as if viewing the scene again. After a minute or so, he looked up at Mary. "Dark you mean. It was the thick curtains. Mum closed them whenever we had visitors."

Mary knew visitors were rare at the Durkin home – then and now.

"Why?"

"She was ashamed of our carpets and furniture. 'Past their best', she'd say. Well past now. Turning the room light on didn't help much."

"But you shone out as the birthday boy." Mary couldn't recall if he had or not. He was just a friend from school; one she liked more than most.

She remembered it was a subdued party— too grand a word for the trio at the table that afternoon.

"Happy Birthday!" Bev carried the cake waist high, eight candles burning, three smoking, blown out by her rush from the kitchen. One was leaning at an angle, dripping wax onto the red icing.

Katie said: "Are you eight today?" Bev said "Shoosh, don't be silly".

Mary said: "Some candles are out, Mrs Durkin."

Bev looked as if she wanted to shoosh Mary. She put the cake in the centre of the table, pushing the fairy bread plate aside. "No worries. I'll light them again." She pulled a box of Redhead matches from an apron pocket and did so.

"There. As good as gold."

As she stood back from the cake, one of the newly lit candles went out. Mary saw her swear under her breath.

"Don't worry, Mum," Jack said. "I'm going to blow them out anyway."

Bev wiped sweat from her forehead with a corner of her apron. She puffed wisps of hair from her face. She re-lit the candle.

"We have to do things right for your birthday. Pity you don't have many guests to celebrate it." Pity his Dad was at the pub, too. "You're a good friend to Jack, Mary. We're glad your Mum let you come."

Mary didn't let on it took a tantrum before her mother allowed her go to a place in 'that lane'.

Bev said: "We're disappointed that Rod and Jerry both accepted Jack's invitation, but didn't come."

Mary spoke quickly. "They were coming, Mrs Durkin, but - "

"We had an argument," Jack said. "We were playing in the lane with our cap guns and I said Rod was 'dead' and he reckoned I missed. We shouted a bit…"

Mary said, "Rod said he didn't like Jack."

Katie followed the discussion wide eyed, while tucking into fairy bread.

"I said, he'd change his tune tomorrow. Would come crawling to my party. Gobble up all the cake and lollies and drinks."

Bev sighed. "Your mouth, Jack. Not the best thing to say."

She moved the fairy bread plate out of Katie's reach. The three-year-old squealed. Bev gave her a muffin.

"He said he wouldn't come and was keeping the present for himself. Said it was a beaut present."

Bev said she would buy something to make it up.

Jack stood and walked around the table to get a bowl of potato crisps, which he took back to his place.

"Another one's out, Mrs Durkin," Mary said. Bev glanced at the cake and nodded.

"Jerry took Rod's side," Jack said. "I told him—"

Bev held up her hand. "I can imagine what you said. I don't think we need to hear any more. Come along. Blow the candles out. They're burning low. And out."

Jack had no trouble blowing the candles out—there were only five alight by then. Happy Birthday was sung, mostly as a solo by Bev, followed by a desultory three cheers.

Party games don't work well with only two players and they quickly lost interest in the three games Bev enthused over.

Mary didn't mind her mother coming early, and skipped down the path dangling her lolly bag in one hand. She paused halfway along, turned and, very politely, thanked Bev for the party. Her mother didn't get out of her Volvo.

Jack held the last of his toastie, a triangular corner piece, melted cheese on the crust edge, between his thumb and forefinger. Looked into his empty cup, then at Mary.

"Long time ago." He shook his head. "Wasn't much of a first date."

"I loved the cake," she said. "And the candle dramas."

"Poor Mum. My temper wrecked that birthday party before it began."

"Not only you. It was a stupid boys' fight. I mean a boys' stupid fight."

"So, my temper goes back a long way; how about the love you spoke of?"

She put a forefinger to her lower lip. "Now, let me–"

"Hey, Jack, mate."

Jack turned, surprised to hear the once familiar voice. He smiled at the tall, solidly-built young man with ginger hair and freckled face, who was striding towards them. Jack shook his hand vigorously.

"So good to see you, mate, after what? Must be a year or so."

"Must be."

They hugged briefly. The newcomer smiled at Mary.

"You're as beautiful as ever, Mary."

"Thanks, Tucker. You're looking pretty good yourself."

Despite the friendly greeting, handshaking and hugging, Tucker's smile was tight and soon disappeared.

"Are you all right?" Mary asked. "Jan and Luke well?"

He hesitated. Before he replied, Jack said: "We've been out of touch, mate. How–"

Tucker stepped back without speaking. Mary thought he was about to cry. He adjusted his mouth a couple of times, as though unsure how to get the words out.

"It's Luke."

Mary and Jack looked at each other. She moved beside Tucker and put a hand on his shoulder.

"Is he ill?"

Tucker's mouth wobbled again. "He was badly hurt. Hit and run. You didn't hear? Read?"

Mary put her arms around his shoulders and gently led him to a chair and sat him at the table. She and Jack sat at the table and waited for Tucker to continue. After a while he looked up.

"I thought you would have heard. Jan and me, we… we… Well, we sort of collapsed. Didn't think of who to tell after … you know…"

"Oh God, Tucker," Mary said, "that's not important. What happened?" She leaned forward, hands on the table.

"He was hit by a speeding car. Thrown to the side of the road."

Jack reached across and held Tucker's hand.

"Hit-and-run, eh?" Jack said.

Tucker nodded. "Cops reckon probably a drunk. Bastard. Still investigating."

"How is he now?" Mary said,

"Busted ribs and a broken leg. He was unconscious for a while in Wagga Wagga Base Hospital."

"Where did it happen?" Jack asked.

"Near home. Been at a mate's place just down the road. Close. He stayed later than he should have, but still a bit light. Just a few metres from our front gate." He choked back a sob.

"Someone must have seen it," Mary said.

"No one has come forward. You know our little chicken farm, Jack. Bit isolated. A few homes around."

Mary went to the counter and returned with a glass of cold water. She handed it to Tucker, who smiled and nodded 'thanks'. He took a sip.

"When did it happen?" Mary asked.

"Couple of nights ago."

Mary gasped. Jack glanced at her.

"It was in the paper, not that we saw it."

"We missed it because–"

Jack interrupted her: "Mum was bashed a couple of nights ago. In her home. I heard it was in the paper, too."

"Not a drunk driver then," Tucker said.

"Just a drunk."

"We don't know that, love – not the 'drunk' bit," Mary said quietly.

Tucker said, "I'm so sorry, mate." The two young men stood and embraced.

Mary said: "Nobody has been arrested and nobody has seen anything. In either case, it seems."

"And Katie – You remember Katie? – has disappeared."

"Abducted," Mary added.

Tucker pulled away from Jack.

"Bloody hell, what's going on?" He paused. "Does your father drive?"

Jack flushed. "Not usually. But drinks always."

"Odd, this. Cops want to talk to me tomorrow morning. Don't know why. They did say they haven't located the hit-and-run driver."

Mary asked how Jan was coping.

"OK, I guess. Twitchy, nervous. Anxious about safety. Bloody graffiti on our shed didn't help."

"Oh, shit," Mary said. She grabbed Jack's arm.

"You too? Someone sprayed threats on our garage."

They looked at each other. Nobody spoke. Then Tucker turned to go. Mary spoke quickly, to delay him, learn more. "Is Luke doing all right now?"

Tucker turned to face them again. The waitress walked to the other side of the table and began clearing it, concentrating on the task without looking up. They watched her for a few seconds.

"As well as could be expected, I guess." He paused. "You know, funny thing is, Luke's more interested in someone else's accident. We took him to the pictures one night as a treat. Afterwards, a young fellow, about 18 or 19, slipped over on the footpath. Hit his head, lying on his back, bleeding a bit."

Mary said: "How horrible for poor Luke."

"No, that's the thing. It's become a memorable event for Luke."

Mary stopped herself from asking "How come?" They didn't interrupt.

"Others crowded around and a few bent over the poor fellow. In between his crying he called out 'Mummy, Mummy'. Over and over, 'Mummy, Mummy'. His mother wasn't there. Not anyone he knew. The ambulance came as we left."

Mary couldn't contain herself any longer. "But how did this affect Luke?"

The waitress had stripped the table clear and was putting a new cloth on it. She asked if they wanted more coffee. No one did.

"Luke can't get over a big man crying for his mummy. Keeps wondering how that can be. A grownup calling for his mummy."

Jack put a hand on Tucker's shoulder. "You know, Tucker, no matter how old we get, we always need our mothers."

After Tucker left, Jack and Mary went to the car and discussed going to the hospital.

"Bastards won't let me see her." He banged a fist on the steering wheel. She put her right hand on his fist, felt the tension in it.

"They might let me in. I'll whisper in Bev's ear that you love her. That we all love her."

"Except her brutal husband."

"I won't say that. I know your Dad loves her, too."

"While you're in there — if they let you — I'm going to have a look around the place, inside and out. See if Katie's there. Hiding in bushes maybe."

Mary thought it was worth a shot, but didn't think it very likely. She kissed his cheek.

"Be careful. The cops will be watching you."

15

KATIE

How can this be for my safety? Shoved onto a bed, hands tied, mouth gagged. Said my life's in danger. Implied Jack and Mary's, too. Lies. Tricked me. Dumb. Scared me in the car. Not like the Edie I met at the party. How can Mary like her?

Drove like crazy. Her face was scary. Staring ahead, teeth gritted. Swearing...

Wish I was wiser. Hard to tell who to trust. I need Mummy. I need Jack. I need…

Don't know where I am. I want to see Mummy. See her smile at me. Hug me. Wipe my tears.

* * *

TUESDAY 2.20pm

Katie was relieved when, after what had seemed hours, she heard the door being unlocked. Edie came in carrying a plate of sandwiches and a can of Coke. She placed them on the bedside cabinet.

"I made these for you. Before I untie you and take the gag off, you must do what I say." Katie heard only don'ts, no do's in Edie's list of instructions. "Don't make a fuss. Don't cry out. Don't scream. Don't bang on walls. Don't make any noise to attract attention from outside. Do you understand?" At last, a do. She nodded, telling herself that understanding wasn't the same as agreeing. Edie untied her hands and removed the gag.

Katie flexed her fingers and wobbled her mouth. "I want to go to the toilet."

"I can help you with that."

Katie shuddered at the thought of being taken to the toilet at her age. Edie smiled down at her. She knew there was an evil woman behind the smile and the sandwiches.

"Why did you kidnap me?"

"Not kidnap, dear. Eat your sandwiches now."

"It can't be for my own good. This is terrible. This is bloody terrible. What have I done to you?"

"Not what you have done. Be patient. Only be as long as necessary."

Katie wondered what 'necessary' meant. She was afraid to ask.

The woman backed to the door. "Rap quietly on the door if you need the loo."

Surely she didn't mean a portable loo. How long could she hold on?

Katie cried when the door clicked shut. She picked up a sandwich. Ham, cheese and bit of lettuce. White bread tasted at least a day old. She preferred wholemeal, but this isn't a restaurant serving food as ordered. Do you want freedom with that? Eat what you are given or go hungry. Or… How long did it take to starve to death? She would Google it, if she had her phone. She would call for help if she hadn't left it behind.

She popped the can open and drank, thankful it had come sealed. She read too many crime novels, like Mary did. Never wanted to be in one.

She put the empty can on the cabinet top and fell back on the bed. She lay, staring at the white ceiling, wondering how she could escape.

It wasn't long before she regretted drinking all the Coke. She needed a pee. Damn. Hold on. Sleep impossible. Different positions didn't ease the pressure. Nor did sitting up. Walking. No alternative: she couldn't avoid going to the toilet any longer.

She knocked on the door and waited, hoping someone was home. After a leg-crossing wait, Edie unlocked the door.

She wagged a finger at Katie. "Remember, not a sound."

"I'll try to pee quietly. Is that OK?"

Without a glimmer of a smile, Edie said: "Don't endanger your brother and his girlfriend." Not to mention myself, Katie thought. "Big responsibility, hey, Katie?

"I know things have changed suddenly for you, but you must know that this is not a game. This is reality."

"I need the toilet. That's my reality, right now."

Holding Katie's arm in a firm grip, Edie led her across the room and swung the toilet door open.

"You must do what is required. Must."

Katie nodded, muttered under her breath and went into the toilet. In response to Edie's "Good girl," Katie slammed the door.

"Oh, sorry," Katie said.

Back in her 'cell' Katie sat on the bed. Edie turned to leave the room. Katie took a big breath, and spurted out a cry for help. Edie stopped and turned to the teenager.

"I'm so scared. And sad. Won't you help me?"

Edie took another step, put a hand on the door handle. "I'm the wrong one to ask for help."

'I don't know how Mummy is or where Daddy is." Her voice trembled and tears trickled down her face. "I just want to go home."

"Now you know what it's like to ask for help that never comes. You'll know what it feels like when no one will help you. When your cries for help are ignored."

Edie went out and locked the door.

Katie watched the door close and heard the key turn in the lock. Right, I'll help myself then. She gazed around the room: Orange metal frame single bed, white wooden bedside cabinet with a small lamp atop, chipped blue metal chair, a single-doored, built-in wardrobe. There were no pictures on the walls, but three hooks showed where some once hung.

She picked up the remaining sandwich and studied it. Ham and salad. She took a big bite. As she ate, she thought of the noisy dinners at home. Tonight, she longed for those chaotic, often argumentative mealtimes because they were with her family.

She knew that eating plastic sandwiches alone in a locked room distorted her view of past occasions. Meals that became unpleasant, nasty, even abusive.

As her father's drinking increased, so had his scary behaviour. Happy family times broke up with shouting, swearing, throwing, breaking, door-slamming, wall-kicking. Crying.

Sometimes he picked on Jack, sometimes on her. But mostly their Mum copped the brunt of his toxic, alcohol-induced rages.

He was often jealous, like he was that night… She shuddered.

Katie looked at the remnant of a sandwich in her hand, screwed up her face and plopped it on the plate. She sobbed quietly and wished she hadn't recalled the night of the fork – as Jack called it.

She had seen it coming. It had begun small, as these things often did, and blew out of proportion. Ray criticised the steak. Bev said she got it from the most popular butcher in town. Must have been popular; he is now Mayor.

Katie looked at the drained Coke can and wished she had more.

That night, Ray wouldn't let it go. "We all know why he's so popular– with women anyway. They get more than fine cuts of meat from that man."

"Don't be so silly," Bev said. "He's just a pompous man with an inflated image of himself but he sells good quality meat."

"And gives away –"

Jack said: "Just shut up and eat up."

"Sticking up for that … that bastard."

Katie pleaded with him to let them eat in peace "for once".

"Ray, take Katie's advice please," Bev said. "It's perfectly good meat."

He half stood, then sat again. "You get the best meat because you spread your legs, like the other sluts."

He looked at his plate, picked up the steak and threw it towards the stove. Bev screamed, Jack swore.

Katie threw her fork at her father. Three mouths snapped agape; three pairs of eyes stared at the fork projecting from his forehead like a unicorn's horn. Ray looked at them through stunned eyes, seemingly too shocked to say a word. Katie was crying. Bev sat beside her and put her arm around her shoulders, all the while staring at the fork stuck in her husband's head. A thin trickle of blood ran between his eyes, over his nose. Three little spots fell on the white plate.

After a few minutes, Ray reached up and pulled it from his forehead. Bev pulled tissues from a box near the sink. She bent and dabbed his head. He reached up and took them from her hand while standing. Without looking back and without a word, he left the room. A few minutes later they heard the bedroom door shut quietly.

Bev assured Katie he would be all right. It wasn't a deep wound. She treated it later with antiseptic.

Katie was still hungry. She ate the last bit of the sandwich. Her silent meal finished, she lay back on the bed and hoped sleep would soon shut out all her realities—present and past.

Next morning, she was awakened by the door unlocking, and Edie saying, "Here's your breakfast, dear."

The hours dragged through the day with lunch and toilet breaks being the only interruptions. Late in the afternoon she was dozing when the door opened. She kept her eyes closed. "Dinner time," Edie said.

Katie heard a plate clunk on the cabinet top. She opened her eyes to see an unappetising meal and a plastic cup of red liquid.

"I'm not hungry. I have a headache."

"Bit of gratitude would be a fine thing," Edie said. "Up to you, but best you eat while you can. You complained about a headache before. I put a couple of soluble aspirins in your cordial."

Katie closed her eyes and waited until she heard the lock click. She sat up and looked at what Edie had brought her. The meal, of congealed gravy slurped over two fat sausages, mashed potato and a sprawl of exhausted grey beans, did nothing to revive her appetite. She knew she hadn't mentioned a headache to Edie; it had only started half an hour ago. She suspected the cordial would taste 'funny'.

At first, Katie had no intention of eating. Then she remembered her Mum stressing how important regular meals were to "keep your strength up", because "you never know what might happen". Right. Katie knew what was going to happen: she was going to escape. Somehow.

She chewed her way through the no-longer-hot meal, using the plastic cutlery. She ate as much as she could stomach and picked up the cordial. Cordial? I'm not a child. She put the flimsy cup to her lips and sipped. Was that odd taste aspirin or… She went to the wardrobe and emptied the cordial in the back corner, ignoring the pink stain on the carpet. Closing the door, she returned the empty cup to the cabinet.

She lay back on the bed and closed her eyes. She heard voices raised in argument. Edie and a man. Katie concentrated and picked up occasional words, then partial sentences. The man's voice was dominant.

"Only … way… … that little … caught… then …the"

"But… be reasonable … wait…"

"No… must do… about eleven rid…"

"How…"

"Get rid of her…"

"Shhh…"

"Tonight. Right."

Then silence. A short time later a door slammed and a car roared away. The key turned in the lock and Katie lay still with her eyes closed.

"Are you alright there, Katie? Finished your dinner?"

Katie didn't answer, feigning sleep. She heard the plate being lifted and Edie saying: "Good girl, you drank all of your nice cordial."

As the door clicked shut, Edie said: "It's for the best, dear. Asleep when–"

The door closed. The lock clicked. Silence.

Katie lifted her wrist. Nearly nine o'clock. What did eleven mean? Who was 'her'? The 'little'. Was someone going to be killed? Her?

She walked to the door, placing her ear against it. No sound. She went to the chair and sat, looking hopelessly around the room. How to get out? Before eleven? The door? Out of the question. Window? Not likely. She investigated. Locked, of course. Smash through? Could be seriously injured by shards of glass. And the noise would bring Edie running. At worst, she could be lying on the floor bleeding to death.

Despite the obvious objections, the window was the only option. She lay on the bed and cried into the pillow. After about ten minutes, she sat up. Still no apparent escape route. She sat on the chair and checked the time again. She wished she had a drink. At least she wasn't drugged.

She went to the door and turned the light off. She returned to the chair and half lifted, half dragged it across the carpet to the window. With great effort she lifted it to shoulder height and threw it. The chair banged into the wall next to the window. Shit. The noise. The… She stood, shaking, silent, barely breathing. Something scraped in another room. Desperately, Katie grasped the chair and with fear-driven strength lifted it high and threw it at the window.

The chair smashed through, taking timber and glass with it.

"What are you doing?" The key turned, the door opened, the light clicked on, the woman screamed.

"Gone. You silly little bitch. You don't know what you're doing. He'll kill me for this."

Her voice was tinged with panic. She ran out the door, yelling: "You won't get away."

HANDY GUIDE TO MANDERVILLE

An Enviable Sporting reputation

By David Michelwhite, Chairman of the Manderville Sporting Association

For a town of its size Manderville punches well above its weight. Lots of people from this little town have gone on to star on state and national stages. Boys and girls, men and women, young and old, enjoy the wonderful facilities of this town to practise and improve their skills and then move on to state teams in the sports of their choice. Athletes from our little town have gone on to become acclaimed players in cricket, baseball, basketball, netball and rugby league. We've even had a few who played AFL.

One such star is Mervyn Faulks who made a name for himself on the country's tennis courts, heading to number nine in the country a few years ago. His sister Trish starred as a netballer leading the Manderville Sprites to win the district competition four years out of six. Well done girls! And Teddy Mawson exceeded averages of all sorts in this area of New South Wales in the number of wickets he's taken. A lot of batsmen around this period breathed easier when Teddy Mawson decided to retire.

Of course nothing can be said about Manderville sporting traditions without mentioning Ray Durkin, fullback extraordinaire. He came into our team and led it to victory four years out of five. He played for the Manderville Magpies when they were known mockingly as the Manderville Mugs. The season after he began playing Mugs became Magpies once again and won the Harper Cup. This was just the beginning of the legend that grew up around Ray Durkin.

Crowds increased not only on our grounds but for away games as well. Legendary for his speed and nimbleness, Durkin was hard to catch and could tackle hard. Week after week his name figured among the scorers of tries, often not just one but several. It was a sad day for our rugby league team when he decided that he would retire. His name continues today on the Ray Durkin Trophy which is awarded each year to the team's best and fairest player. His name will forever feature in the history of sport in Manderville. There were hopes that he would return as a coach after his retirement but circumstances prevented that.

Blessed by plentiful sunshine, people most weekends head for the cricket or the tennis or swimming in our beautiful Hardy Ralston Memorial Pool. It is wonderful to move around this town on Saturday afternoon or Sunday and see so many people taking a healthy option of getting out there and playing a game.

16

RAY

Gamblin' on cops given up watchin' here. They had no idea I was watching them. Pushing sticks into bushes, sniffing around like dogs that have lost the scent. Lookin' for my rifle as well, I reckon. Hope they catch the bloody thief. Wastin' taxpayers' money, searchin' for me, an innocent man. Uniformed ring-ins from god-knows-where don't know Manderville like I do. My town. Once was. Hero cheered on the field. Now a drunk mocked in the lane.

They loved me down there. On that big green rectangle. Tackled like a… ran like a… scored… What's it matter now?

And always there was Bev, smiling so brightly, eyes shining… hair tossing as she clapped and cheered and waved and… But now… Oh, Bev. What did I get you into? Better if you had never loved me. Better if … All gone wrong?

What's that? Someone? Not here—

* * *

WEDNESDAY 11.15pm

"Hello, Raymond. Or would you prefer I call you Ray?"

The intruder, who had come so quietly, so suddenly, into Ray's bushy hideout, pushed branches aside. He stood smiling at Ray, as if waiting for an answer.

Ray squinted, trying to see who it was. Friend or stranger? Foe? He was tall, broad-shouldered, in a buttoned-up suit. In the shadows his hair appeared dark, grey-flecked. Getting no answer, the man, still smiling, parted the waist-high shrubs and, not waiting for permission, entered Ray's private domain. "You are doing it tough, I hear, Raymond." His thin smile didn't convey any depth of sympathy.

"Bloody hell, scared the life out of me."

"So far so good, I suppose. Considering…" the intruder said.

"You a plain-clothes man? Detective?"

"No. I am not. I am–"

Ray interrupted. "Why you poking around here late at night?" His voice trembled. He was annoyed at that. Mustn't let this bloke shake him up. "Go home to your family," Ray said, not knowing if the man was even married.

The man licked his lips, his tongue wiping the smile away. "There is no family now, Raymond. Did you know that?"

"I apologise," Ray said, his voice more controlled now. "I don't know what you've got. You must have a home. This isn't it."

"I will go soon, Raymond," the man said. His humourless smile had returned.

The man reached behind him, causing a bush to shake. Ray edged sideways, his eyes on the knife lying nearby.

"Bloody good job," Ray said. He turned, looking for a quick way out of the little hideout. Too much bush. Branches.

"You are not very hospitable, Raymond. Or sympathetic. You never get over losing a loved one. Odd. Seeing as you have got one hanging by a thread in—"

"You bastard."

Ray punched him in the chest. He copped a thump on the forearm from his rifle, which the man had pulled from a shrub at his side.

Staggering back, Ray shouted: "You. You bashed Bev."

"Not what the police are saying, Raymond. They are out in force after you."

"Give me my rifle." Ray grabbed at it, but was knocked off-balance by a blow from the swinging barrel.

"As I was saying, one in hospital; another missing—"

"You've got Katie, too? What's going on? Two of—"

The big man laughed, like an unhappy kookaburra. "Three, Ray –may I call you Ray?— you are the third."

Ray sat heavily on a log. This was beyond him. The man's mad. "You — you—"

"Bastard? Is that what you were struggling for, Raymond? People in my business get a lot of insults. Often from people who are more articulate than shearers. I am sure you understand, Raymond. Businessmen of any ilk have to balance the books."

"Like bloody bookmakers do. They look after themselves all right."

Ray stood, drawing himself taller and straighter than he had for several days. He stood face-to-face with the man, who stepped back, moving the rifle from side to side, as if covering a group of attackers.

"People, Raymond. Lives. I am not just talking Durkin lives. A few families are in debt in my books."

Ray slid a foot in the knife's direction. The rifle stopped moving, aimed directly at Ray's chest.

"Stop. You can't reach that, Raymond. I've calculated the distance so don't think you can beat my bullet."

Ray stopped moving. "They're my bullets, mate. My rifle. You're crazy. This is my place: where I was the hero of the town."

"Down there was your stage, Raymond, but the fans have long departed and the lights have gone out. We are now off stage, in the wings. Others will judge my standing in the town's history. In the meantime, Raymond, I will keep going until my books are balanced."

Desperately, Ray looked around. At the bushes and the trees and the man with the gun. "Go away. Leave me." Ray didn't think his demands would get rid of the frightening intruder. "Can't see you balancing anything, seeing as you're unbalanced," Ray said. "Nothin' you've said adds up." He smiled at his little joke. He gazed at the grim-faced man with the wavering rifle and rock-steady eyes, hoping for a glimmer of amusement. None. Distract the bugger with small talk.

"So," he said, "what sort of bloody businessman are you?"

The rifle stopped wavering, aimed steadily at Ray.

"This sort, Raymond."

17

Wait. Wait. Don't breathe. Not deeply; suck up dust. Mustn't sneeze. Or choke. Too busy bashing and abducting to vacuum under beds.

Can't hear her now. Sure she ran out the front door. Hope. Hope. Didn't slam it. Maybe still open, Standing near it. On the path.

Like the night Jack 'ran away' to escape punishment. Cruel on Mum. Panicked, running up and down the lane, calling him. Jack was under my bed. I giggled into the pillow. After a while, he crept out the back, ran around to the front door and walked in, to be hugged by Mum like he'd returned from the grave. I won't hang around for any hugging. Likely to end in a grave.

Can't hear her now. Better risk it. Might come back. Or him. Where'd he go? Why? Get out while the going's good. Is it? Scared or not, I gotta go.

* * *

WEDNESDAY 11.20pm

Katie strained her ears. No sound from inside the house. No sound outside of running feet or yelling. Time to scamper. She took a deep breath of oxygen and dust and crawled headfirst from under the bed. She lay still for a few seconds face into the carpet. She strained, listening for any sound. It was so quiet she heard the fridge humming in the kitchen. She sat up and stretched. Leaning on the bed, she pulled herself up, at every heartbeat, fearful of hearing the woman's voice and the front door slam.

She ran out of the bedroom, her head swinging wildly around the living room as she sped through it. Nobody there; no Edie sitting on the lounge sipping tea. Fortunately, her sneakers made little sound on the soft carpet, or even on the kitchen tiles. She moved quickly to the back door, opened it and went into the yard.

She stood for a moment, adjusting her eyes to the dark. From the front of the house, came the sound of running steps on the footpath. Katie froze on the spot, wondering what to do. No safe hiding place. There were two beds of assorted vegetables, a bare rotary clothesline and a big tree at the back fence. Katie was dismayed to see the fence of green aluminium slats was too high for her to scale. There were no footholds.

The woman's voice screamed from inside the house. "Where the hell are you?"

Katie wasn't about to answer that. She scurried to the back fence. She tried to get a grip on it, but her feet scrabbled against the shiny metal, slid down each time she tried to climb. The banging of room and cupboard doors opening and closing and the woman's frenzied shouting terrified Katie. Turning to the tree, she jumped to grab a flimsy, low-hanging branch. She pulled herself up on it, but it bent under her weight. Her feet touched the ground.

The kitchen suddenly lit up and a square of light from the window settled over the vegetable garden.

Desperately, she grabbed the trunk and somehow got a grip with her feet and arms and scrambled up like an arthritic monkey. She crawled onto a thick branch, burrowing into a leafy area.

The back door opened and more light spilt across the yard. Katie quietly pulled herself higher into the thicker foliage.

She peeked towards the brightly lit doorway. Hardly breathing, she inched along a branch that hung over the back neighbour's yard.

Risking a look behind her, through the leaves, she gasped. The man had returned.

"How did you let this happen? For god's sake, woman."

"She... she–"

"She outsmarted you. That is it, plain and simple."

Edie came out and stood on the lawn, facing the back fence. Katie froze, stretched along the branch. The man appeared in the doorway, his face lost in the silhouette shadows.

"She smaa… smashed it," Edie said, "frrr..ame and all… ww… ith with the ch… chair... I thought—"

"The trouble with you, woman, is that you do not think." The man stepped into the yard.

Realising speed was more important than secrecy now, Katie scurried along on all fours, until she was hanging on a gently bouncing branch, over the neighbour's backyard.

"I see you, you little bitch," the man said, in an angry whisper. "You will not get away. There is a fierce rottweiler in there. Better come back here." He banged on the fence, as though trying to arouse the dog.

Squinting into the dark, Katie couldn't see a dog of any size, nor even a kennel— or a big cage for that matter. Shaking in trepidation, she rolled around the branch and dropped to the ground. There were no lights on in the house. And no growls in the yard. Lying bugger.

Her late night intrusion into the yard had stirred neither man nor beast. There was a short fence and gate blocking her escape route. It ran between the house and the side fence. She ran to it, hoping the gate wasn't locked. The fence and gate were too high to easily climb over. It wasn't locked. She lifted the simple latch and pulled the gate open. A cement path led to the street. There were two wheelie bins against the fence, for household and recycled waste.

What to do? What to do? Her abductors had banged and kicked against the back fence a few times, but quickly gave up and ran through the house. Katie heard door slamming, then feet running in the street. They were running around the block.

She took off for the street. She knew her pursuers could come around the nearest corner at any moment. Soon be at the front of this house.

No time to panic.

She ran to the bins and upended them. Garbage rolled and rattled out on the path. Leaving the gate ajar, she ran into the backyard to the fence near the tree.

Panting, she leapt at the branch. She got a grip on it, pulled herself up. She scrambled back along it and dropped into the yard of her former prison. She sat against the fence catching her breath.

She heard the man arrive at the neighbour's side path and curse.

"The little bitch thinks this will slow us down." He laughed. "Dumb bitch expected us to come over the fence. She thinks this mess will trip us up. Ha!"

"Hey. Why're you going through our bins?" Another man's voice shouted.

"We… we saw them tipped over," Edie said meekly. "We saw the mess from the street. We came in to put them upright."

Katie heard a window squeak open.

"Who is it, Fred?"

"Couple of drunks, knocking our bins about," the angry man said. "Call the cops."

Katie, smiling, stood, ready to run for it. In the neighbours' driveway, her abductors were protesting.

"No need for that," Edie said. "We didn't do this."

"Let's get out of here."

"What's happening, Fred?"

"Go back to bed, Beryl."

Taking the male abductor's advice, Katie ran across the yard and into the house. Running through the kitchen, she suddenly stopped and ran to the drawers under the bench. Muttering "just in case", she pulled a large knife from the third drawer down then escaped through the front door, closing it quietly. A battered blue car skulked on the driveway, its left headlight broken, the bonnet dented.

She was almost past it when an idea struck her. Swiftly, she bent and stabbed the two nearest tyres. She jumped back as the car sank towards her. Certain she could never stab a person as she had the tyres, she turned to throw the knife into the flower garden alongside the path, but changed her mind and ran into the street with it in her hand.

She knew she didn't have much time to get out of this street. She expected the man and Edie – in that order – to come around the nearest corner any second.

Blinking away tears and fighting panic, Katie ran fast, as fast as she had ever run, faster than when she won the school cross country race, faster than when she almost missed the bus to the Cootamundra Music Festival, but possibly not fast enough to outrun the big man with soft hands and vice-like grip.

She fled along the street, stirring up a couple of dogs as she sped past a high, wire-netting fence. At the first intersection she slowed, beset by two more problems. It had begun to rain, and she didn't recognise the street names on the post. This part of town was new to her. It was a major housing estate that had grown haphazardly on the northern fringes of Manderville, like blisters on a gravedigger's thumb. It was considered a posh area, with large, predominantly two-storey, houses that almost filled the small allotments. The residents had too many cars to fit in their garages, parking the overflow of vehicles and boats on driveways and in streets.

Aware she was wasting precious seconds, Katie made a pure guess. She turned left into a street lined with big autumn-tinted plane trees. She soon found she had to run around yellow-and-brown circles of fallen leaves, made more slippery by the rain. Bad choice. Slowed by the slimy patches, she considered running on the street. But the leaves were there as well. Although there was little chance of being hit by a car at this hour, if one did come along she would be too scared to hail it in case they were now after her in Edie's car.

She veered off the path and ran beside the fence to get around a small white boat with a green half-cabin parked across the driveway. She thought she heard people running not far away, but when she looked back saw nobody. With renewed fear, she spurted on.

Further along the street, an even bigger boat— cabin cruiser she thought— blocked her progress. She abruptly changed course to the road edge. Turning back towards the footpath, she slipped on a patch of wet leaves and fell hard on her left knee, scraping it across the edge of the kerb.

She cried out in pain; instantly regretting it. She gritted her teeth and rubbed her knee through the torn fabric, feeling a thicker wetness. Shit.

Despite the bloody stinging, she had to keep going. She pushed herself up leaning on the boat's trailer and hobbled towards the fence, determined to continue. It was painfully obvious that she was too slow.

From down the street came a shout. His. Bugger. Katie turned around. Bugger again. From the other corner, Edie's voice shouted back. Trapped. Not a second more could be lost to fatigue, pain, rain, blood– or, especially, panic.

The nearby fence was too high, so she limped back to the boat. Somehow, she dragged herself up onto the trailer and over the side of the boat. She rolled backwards and slid into a corner under cover near the wheel. She ignored the tears streaming into the rain on her face. She didn't try to wipe her face dry. She slumped against the bulkhead; scared and miserable and cold and bleeding and she wanted her Mummy and Daddy.

She heard footsteps approaching from two directions. She stiffened, trying to control her shaking.

Then her heart almost stopped. They had caught up. They had rushed together at the driveway and were now standing at the back of the boat.

"This is stupid," Edie said, panting between words. "Running madly when we don't know which way she went. She could be with the police now."

"Nothing I do is stupid," the man hissed. "You make me sick. I thought you were made of sterner stuff." He took several deep breaths.

"I just–"

"You have more to lose. She knows you."

Katie wanted to straighten her injured knee, but didn't dare. She hardly dared to breathe.

"I've run as hard as I can," Edie said, panting less now.

Katie heard the man walk away from the boat.

"We cannot stand here all night," he said. "Peter is depending on us."

"You go. My side still hurts. I'll go in a minute."

"Right," he snapped. He started running.

Edie called out: "You're so cold and calculating. Everything done by your bloody book, as if that's the most important thing in the world."

"It is the only thing," he shouted. Then his footsteps faded away.

"I just need a minute," Edie said to herself. "Treats me like…"

Startled at first – thinking the woman was speaking to her – Katie was relieved when Edie's resentful muttering trailed off.

She was immediately startled again when a grey cat leapt on the side of the boat. It took two steps and stopped, mid-step, looking down at Katie who was alarmed by this new visitor. She was allergic to cats. Mustn't sneeze or sniff or cough. The boat moved slightly when Edie leaned against it. Katie had never been as frightened as she was now. She looked at her watch but couldn't see the time in the dark. Time froze as she slumped, uncomfortably, a few metres from Edie's back, and the allergy-loaded cat stared at her. Katie back at the cat.

Suddenly the boat moved. Katie looked up to see Edie running across the street. She breathed normally again and waved her hands at the cat. It leapt away into the night.

She bent her injured leg a few times and gingerly stood. Looking in all directions and listening for any sound of footsteps, Katie slowly lifted herself over the side and on to the footpath. Her knee hurt. She limped, walked slowly, faster, then ran in a different direction to those taken by Edie and her partner in crime.

At the next corner she took a punt and turned right.

She knew she was running blind, but hoped to soon come upon a familiar landmark or street name. Her feet were hurting, and she was out of breath. At every step she feared hearing the kidnappers again.

She almost cried with joy when she turned another corner and there was the Salvation Army Hall. She stifled a 'Hallelujah'. Now she knew the way to Jack's house.

She slowed to a fast walk when she reached Jack's street. There was a police car parked outside the house.

"Great," she said to herself. She was safe. Now she'd tell the cops about it.

But when she got to the neighbour's fence she shrunk back. Jack's front door opened and in the rectangle of light, Jack appeared, a police officer on either side. They moved onto the veranda and walked towards the steps. Mary followed. She had her hands over her mouth. Even from the street, Katie could see the tears glistening on her cheeks.

The policeman escorted Jack down the path to the car. Mary watched from the veranda.

"Jack," Katie shouted.

The policemen and their suspect froze, Jack half in the car, held down by one officer, the other poised to slam the door, like a tableau in a crime museum, mouths agape, eyes white and wildly staring at the slim, bedraggled, muddy, bloodied, teenager, rain running down her lank, clinging blonde hair, carrying a brown leaf from her shoulder onto her chest as if to comfort a wildly beating heart, flowing further to dilute the red around the left knee into pink rivulets.

And they stared at the big knife in her right hand.

"She's got a knife," Constable Higgins said, his bleedingly obvious statement breaking the spell and the figures softened into movement again.

"Katie," Jack said. "Are you all right?"

"Miss Durkin," Constable Smithson said. "Where have you been?"

"Oh, Katie," Mary called out. Katie didn't catch the rest of her sentence.

"Just keep away little girl," Constable Higgins said. She thought that was a silly command because he was closing the distance between them. And she wasn't a 'little' girl. "Drop the knife."

Smithson pushed Jack down into the car. Jack twisted his head back towards Katie.

"Do what they say, Katie," he said.

Katie looked at her hand for a moment.

"Don't do anything stupid," Higgins said. "Your brother's in enough trouble as it is."

She dropped the knife, and everyone looked at it as it clattered on the cement. Higgins moved, crouched towards the knife. He kept his eyes on Katie until he was in reach of the knife, then grabbed it so quickly it was a wonder he didn't cut his hand. He wrapped it in a cloth from a coat pocket.

"Where are they taking you?"

Smithson had paused and stood above Jack as he wriggled into the back seat.

"They say I killed Dad."

"But he'll show up soon,' Katie said. 'They'll see he's alive."

Jack pulled back against Smithson, trying to stand again. Smithson held him firmly.

"Katie, Katie," he said, in a calm, controlled voice, "Our Dad is dead."

Katie screamed and ran towards her brother. Higgins grabbed her. She thrashed with her arms and kicked the constable's shins. He yelped, holding her with one hand, while trying to keep the wrapped knife out of the way.

"Stop that. You'll cut yourself."

Mary ran down the steps and onto the lawn. She stopped several metres from the red-faced constable and the flailing, hysterical teenager.

"Just drop the bloody thing," she shouted.

He dropped the knife; Mary ran across the yard. Her voice still raised, she told Higgins to "Step away". Katie dropped her arms and stood limply. Higgins didn't obey Mary's second command until she put her arms around Katie and hugged her tightly.

Higgins moved towards the car. He shook his head at Smithson, who had put a hand over his mouth.

"Time we got out of here, Constable," Smithson said. Higgins nodded.

Mary kissed Katie's forehead. "Come inside with me, Katie. Get you dry. Clean clothes and a hot drink."

"No, I need Jack, I need Mummy, I need Daddy." Tears ran down her face, already wet from rain. Mary wiped her eyes with a tissue she pulled from a pocket in the dressing gown that Katie hadn't been aware of until then.

With her arms still around Katie, Mary caught Smithson's attention as he was opening the opposite back door.

"I've told you, Jack was here with me all night. He wouldn't leave me alone after a deranged vandal did all that stuff inside our home."

"A murder's more important at the moment," Smithson said.

"What happened to our Daddy?" Katie said, her words distorted by her sobs.

Jack, who had opened the car door, leant out and said: "Cops say he was shot dead."

Katie slithered out of Mary's grasp and crumpled to the ground. Higgins slammed the door on Jack.

Mary bent and helped Katie to her feet. She put her arms around the crying girl's shoulders and turned her towards the house.

Smithson got into the back seat alongside Jack. Higgins started the engine. The car roared away as Mary helped Katie up the few steps to the veranda. They paused and saw the taillights of the police car disappear around the next corner. Mary looked across the street at a small group of people watching. Too weary to wave them away, she turned and led Katie into the house and closed the door.

18

SMITHSON

Don't need to look sideways to know the young bloke's struggling to hold his emotions in check. Hard at any age when thing like this happens. I couldn't when I … Lot older then. Won't want me looking at him. Not even in the dark. Not me. The cop who dragged him out of his home at midnight with a double whammy. Good evening, son, your father's been shot dead, oh, and by the way, we're taking you in. You're the prime suspect. Bugger of a job, this. Not made easier by bloody Higgins' tuneless humming. Can't drive anywhere without demonstrating his utter lack of musical ability.

Wiping his eyes. Lot more tears to come — if he'll let 'em show. If I know him, he'll tough it out. Pity. Brogan won't give him an easy time. Good luck to them. I'll be in bed.

He's sniffing.

"You crying, kid?" Higgins showing his sensitivity again. "Get a grip."

"It's me, Constable. Touch of hay-fever." Hope my sniffing's convincing. Oh, Durkin, cheeky bugger's punched my arm. Gently. Just as well.

Here, thank God. Now to get the kid in to meet Brogan. And me out of ear range of Higgins' bloody humming.

* * *

THURSDAY 1.05am

Detective Sergeant Brogan strolled into the Manderville Police Station interview room, past the uniformed officer standing against the wall. He dropped a green folder on the table where Jack had been waiting for more than half an hour.

"Mr Jack Durkin?" Jack nodded. "Detective Sergeant Brogan. I am sorry to keep you waiting."

"Only been half an—" He checked his watch, "–forty-seven minutes."

"I was in bed," Brogan said. Jack looked him over. He hadn't seen the plain-clothes man before. He was dressed like an executive ready for a nine-to-five city job, in a navy pinstriped suit, crisp white shirt with maroon tie. Not at all like a detective called to work in the early hours of the morning, Jack thought.

Jack had draped his wet, black bomber jacket over the back of his chair. A thin pool had spread under it.

"Like you," Jack said, "I found it's hard to be woken unexpectedly in the middle of the night." He looked at the clock on the wall to his right. "But they let you sleep a bit longer than they allowed me."

Brogan ignored the sarcasm. He unbuttoned his coat and settled on the white plastic chair facing Jack across the table. There was a jug of water and two glasses near Brogan's left elbow. He reached across with his right hand and lifted the jug to pour himself a full glass. Jack watched the detective drink half in one go and wipe his mouth with a blue and yellow checked handkerchief.

"We finished?" Jack said.

Brogan folded his handkerchief and returned it to the pocket in his coat before looking at Jack for a few seconds. Jack tried to return the gaze, but his eyes were drawn to Brogan's eyebrows; thick, black, neatly rectangular. Somehow familiar. Brogan blinked and looked down at his folder. He opened it flat and shuffled the few sheets it contained.

He looked up at Jack and finally answered his cheeky question. "We have not even begun, Mr Durkin.

"Now, I have got to find who killed your father, Mr Raymond Charles Durkin. That's my job, not to be all sympathetic, huggy, teary.

"It is for you and your loved ones, to support each other during this grief event."

He paused and took a sip of water. Jack kept his eyes on him without speaking. "I have to make sure, in the first case, that a loved one is not also the cause of the grief event."

Jack had never heard any level of police officer talk like this. "If you're going to catch the killer of my Dad, you'd better stop spouting mouthfuls of shit and get into detecting. That's a fact event."

Brogan stared steadily, silently, at Jack, who stared back, unblinking. Neither man changing expression nor, their focus on the other's eyes. The only sounds were the whirring of a fan in the corner, Brogan's papers fluttering in the fan's breeze, and the normally unobtrusive clock ticking high on the wall.

Although he would never admit it, Jack regretted his outburst. He needed this man to get his father's killer.

And he wanted to get himself a glass of water but wasn't about to flick his eyes at the jug. He licked his lips. Without shifting his focus on Jack's eyes, Brogan reached for the jug with his left hand.

"Water, Mr Durkin?"

Tick. Tick. Tick.

"Thank you." Jack felt he had won something.

"You can thank me after I give it to you."

Jack's eyes slipped away from Brogan's steady gaze to settle on the water jug, to which Brogan's eyes now moved, before flicking his gaze back on Jack's face. Bugger. A draw? This cop might be too good for Dad's killer.

Brogan pushed a half-full glass of water across the table.

"Thank you," Jack muttered. He drained the glass while Brogan leafed through his scant papers, not looking up until the glass clinked on the table. Jack glanced at the constable standing near the door, who was licking his lips, no doubt wishing his boss would offer him at least a sip or two. The room was warm.

"You can be assured, Mr Durkin, that I will find the killer of Raymond Durkin. This may give you hope or may arouse fear. My hope is that you are encouraged; my fear is that your quickness to anger may have caused a deeper grief than your family is yet aware of." He turned over a page.

"Listen, Mr Brogan–"

"I am Detective Sergeant Brogan. Please address me as such. Or Sir."

Jack chose neither. "I did not kill my father. I was at home with Mary till your blokes dragged me here."

Brogan blinked up at Jack, and quickly down at the paper fluttering in his hand. He moved it out of the stream from the fan. "Your short temper, Mr Durkin, has got you into trouble before this."

Jack sat up and leaned forward across the table.

"Before this? What this? There's no *this* involving me or my alleged temper. Your cops are ignoring the record. Again."

"Firstly, Mr Durkin, they are police, not cops. And they are your police, not mine. We belong to the community.

"Secondly, I noted your quick response to what I first said here in this room. And I also know you have been in court because you attacked a man in the street."

"I was acquitted. Why do you guys ignore the record and treat me as a criminal? I'm not. If you really were my police, I wouldn't have been charged at all. I helped a disabled man, a bloke in a wheelchair. I actually stopped a crime. He was being mugged. A well-known thug was robbing him."

Brogan raised both hands, but Jack continued regardless.

"I know you would've read the file and you know the truth."

Brogan reached for Jack's glass and half-filled it. Jack murmured, "Thanks."

Brogan looked down at the paper flapping in his hand, like a freshly caught fish. He put it down under his palm, sliding it out of the breeze. Jack realised what his subconscious had probably known for some time: the fan was fixed on the detective, not the suspect. No wonder Brogan looked cool while he was hot, as was the sweating statue near the door. Jack suddenly wanted to cry. He took a long, slow drink and wiped his mouth with the back of his hand.

As if he had been waiting for Jack to settle himself, Brogan looked up and said: "The truth of the matter is that I am investigating the murder of a man."

Jack half rose, about to interrupt but changed his mind and sat down again. He wanted to turn the fan to get a fair share of its breeze but sat tight. His Dad was dead, for god's sake. What's a little bit of bloody sweat?

Brogan said: "I am interested in the man you assaulted."

Jack spluttered a few "buts", murmured "shit" and subsided into his chair, leaning back, hands dangling.

"Do you recall the name of that man?"

"Course I do. Mullins. So what?" Jack didn't change his slumped posture, belying his mixture of anger and curiosity.

"He reported you for assault. You ended up in court."

"I was acquitted," Jack said. "We've just been over this. Ancient history. Irrelevant."

He lifted his glass, as if it contained more water than the wetness on the bottom and sides, and slowly sipped the last drops.

Brogan waited until Jack put his glass down.

"Not necessarily. Sometimes history reaches into the present."

Jack looked up in surprise.

"Did you bear any ill will against Mr Mullins, even though you were acquitted?"

"I hated him. Still do."

"Interesting," Brogan said, writing in his notebook.

"Maybe interesting to you," Jack said. "Only three things interest me: who killed my Dad, who bashed my Mum and who kidnapped my sister. Probably the same person. But I bet it's not Mullins. He's not even in Manderville anymore."

Broken gave a wry smile. "No, he isn't. Have you seen him in the past…" He paused. "Three weeks?"

"Not the past three years. Longer."

Brogan wrote again.

"So forget that red herring event. You're looking for one bloke, but it isn't Mullins. Don't waste my time on bloody history lessons."

Brogan's odd eyebrows pushed wrinkles up his forehead. "Please moderate your language in here."

Jack saw a glimmer of a smile come and go on the damp uniformed statue.

"All… interests are being pursued. Are you sure you haven't seen each other anywhere recently?"

Jack sighed theatrically. "I can't know if he's seen me. I told you I haven't seen him. Never want to again."

"Mmmm," Brogan said, studying his open notebook. Jack checked his watch and fumed. After Brogan took the time he apparently needed, he turned his attention once more to Jack. "Now, Mr Durkin, I have in front of me the only person known to have said he wanted to kill Raymond Durkin. You are my prime suspect.

"Do you understand my dilemma? It is all on my head."

Jack slid his glass noisily across the table and then back towards his chest. "All on your head? You poor bugger. Drive around in late model cars, secure job, well paid, well fed, respected and feared, power of the law." He waved his hand around the room. "Get to sit in a cool office. Even in this bare room you ensure the bl… the fan's all on you, overloaded head and all."

The statue's mouth cracked into a grin, a tongue flicked out, licked sweat off the top lip, quickly resealed again. Brogan raised a hand and was about to speak, but Jack didn't pause.

"Finding Dad's killer's all on your head, officer? Katie and me have a lot on our hearts. So overloaded they've broken. Our Dad is dead. We didn't get to say goodbye. Might not get to say goodbye to our Mum, either."

Brogan looked around the room. He got up and set the fan head to oscillate. Sitting again, he said: "Beats me why this room is always so hot, even when it's miserable outside."

Jack thought it was miserable inside, too, but was grateful for the cooler air intermittently blowing on him.

Brogan cleared his throat before speaking.

"I am aware of the overwhelming grief you and your sister are going through. I hope I can make a small dent in that sadness by catching the person responsible.

"No question I ask is irrelevant to my investigation. Therefore, I have to ask you what you were doing last night between seven pm and midnight."

Good cop-bad cop in the one cop, Jack thought. "I've told you that. You should write these things down, so you don't forget so quickly."

"Sonny, you can either help me find your father's killer or you can stuff around like this, being a smart arse. Of course, if you confess, we can go home – except you, Mr Durkin. In that case, we'll pop you in a cell for some time."

"I didn't kill Dad," Jack said. "I want him to be alive, not dead. I want…" He struggled to continue. Paused. "I was with Mary at the time he was killed — at the time they told me he was killed."

"We need corroboration. Someone to back up your claim."

"Mary was there. All the time. She'll give you your corroboration."

"She's sure to back you up. After all, she is your girlfriend."

"Mary wouldn't lie, not even for me. Nobody else was home with us. Just me and Mary, all night. Same as every night. Until I was removed. Mary wouldn't protect me if she thought I was a killer."

"Were you both asleep during those five hours?"

"I went to sleep on the lounge around nine and Mary went to bed a bit earlier."

Brogan said: "So you sleep in different rooms?"

Jack flushed. "Only last night, not normally, until your guys banged on the door and woke both of us at midnight."

"Convenient."

Jack let it ride, apart from an angry glare.

"So, you could have gone out without Miss Bourke knowing?" Brogan smiled, as if chatting with a friend about a family outing.

Jack stood, pushing the chair back with his right leg. His jacket fell to the floor.

The statue came to, taking a step towards the table. Brogan stood. He told Jack to sit. He did, glaring at Brogan, who turned and gestured for the constable to return to his post.

Jack picked his jacket up and draped it over the back of his chair again. Droplets slid down it to rejoin the pool on the floor. He sat and put both hands on the table. Brogan took his place again.

"I had no reason to go out in the rain. I slept until I was woken by banging and shouting. And Mary was also asleep until then. Your… our guys scared her." He paused. "Probably the neighbours, too. And a couple of dogs."

A thought struck Jack and he said: "If I had been out during the night, the floor and my clothes would've been wet when the cops - " Brogan winced " - burst in."

"Not necessarily so, Mr Durkin."

"Smith — Constable Smithson saw how wet Katie was. Knew how wet he and his offsider were."

"I will accept that, for now. For the moment, I think we're looking for someone else."

Jack slapped his hands flat on the table. "So finally you can see there is someone else out there bashing and killing. You think Manderville has a killer who isn't me or my Dad."

Brogan nodded and blinked and his eyebrows jumped on the spot. "Settle down, Mr Durkin. The investigation is still in progress."

The detective rifled through his papers, and pulled out a small sheet. "Mr Durkin, I can tell you that your mother may — the doctor stressed 'may' – come out of the coma before long."

"Mum," Jack said, leaning forward, knocking both glasses over. They were virtually empty but drops splattered towards Brogan's papers. The detective pulled the handkerchief from his pocket and wiped the spots between the overturned glasses and the folder of papers. Jack ignored what he had inadvertently done.

"Is she awake? Talking? She can tell us who bashed her."

"Not quite yet," Brogan said. "She can't tell us anything yet. She may soon, but you're right, she may point the finger at the person who is doing this. Who may have killed your father.

"However, Mr Durkin, I may have raised your hopes prematurely. Doctors are hopeful but warn it is too early to be sure."

Jack slumped back in his chair.

"We may have more questions for you. You will have to spend the rest of the night in a cell."

Jack swore. Brogan ignored the 'language' and continued speaking.

"I will interview Miss Bourke and your sister tomorrow morning. In a few hours, in fact."

He closed his notebook, flicking water off it. He nodded to the constable, who had moved towards them. Jack stood and put his jacket loosely over his shoulders and was led away.

<h1 style="text-align:center">19</h1>

MARY

What's happened to our world? Our tiny bit of the universe? No longer Mundane Manderville. The quiet town of my life so far has slunk away, without so much as a by-your-leave, without warning that the backwater would be flooded with violence. Nothing stable beneath us, nothing solid to lean on.

It's like riding the Manderville Show Ferris Wheel, enjoying its gentle, predictable path through lows and highs, present, past and future clearly seen, but suddenly tossed every which way, pitched out, scattered by out-of-control machinery, leaving us staring at the wrecked circle of fun, our innocent expectations lying in the dirt beside us.

Ohh, me again. Jack says I catastrophise and fantasise at the same time. Fantastrophise? But... oh ... What a...

Jack a murder suspect. And Bev... poor dear... And Katie, wrapped in my arms, our tears re-wetting already damp faces, hair and clothes... How can she deal with such tragedy? Any of us?

And at the centre is the black hole left by tormented, loving Ray sucking hope from us.

I can't calm my mind, stop my catas...

Horrible reminders mock us from the walls as we cry.

Painted words smear the futures we've planned. Who hates Jack's family so much? Jerking them around as if by a psychopathic puppeteer.

Sprayed threats drip colour and ooze evil.

We sit on the lounge and we cry.

She wipes my tears with a wet hanky. Says, stammers, "Kidnappers." Edie. Why? Looks down at her hanky, scrunches it, wipes it against her jeans.

Trying to tell her about Jack. About Ray. Ask about her… looking at me with glistening red eyes, asking on and on… Questions, answers tumbling over one another, gasps and stutters and cries… How did her Dad die? I tell her what I know. Too little. Oh, Katie, Katie, talking to me but I can't focus. Tears soak our words tumbling from lips, in unintelligible sentences, as unhelpful as our wet wadded tissues.

* * *

THURSDAY 1.11am

After a while, when crying eased into sobs, eventually subsiding into sniffs, Katie bent and wiped her eyes on the hem of Mary's dress. As she dabbed, Mary gently patted the back of her head, ruffling the damp hair. She touched her own head.

"We should dry ourselves," Mary said. "Get into dry clothes." Into pyjamas at this hour.

Katie nodded.

"But first," Mary said, touching Katie's injured knee, "We must clean this wound." She stood and turned towards the main bathroom. "Take your jeans off. I'll get stuff from the medicine cabinet for your poor suffering knee." She smiled down at Katie, who managed a small smile. Both smiles looked misplaced, as if carelessly stuck on the wrong faces. For the umpteenth time that night, Mary wished Jack was home, wished she could ring the police station and ask, nicely, if they would let him go. She knew he hadn't killed his father. But, of course, they wouldn't take her word.

Katie sat quietly while Mary cleaned and bandaged her lacerated knee, wincing only once, when antiseptic was applied.

"There," Mary said. "Good job, if I say so myself. That somewhat inelegant waterproof covering will protect it in the shower or if you go jogging in the rain, again." She smiled up at the serious faced girl looking down at her.

"Thank you, Mary. For being here for me. You're the only…" Her voice broke, murmuring syllables that never quiet became words. Mary put a finger on Katie's lips and kissed her cheek. After a few seconds of silence she said: "I know who killed Dad."

"How can you know that? You've been locked up somewhere." Mary looked into the teenager's wide, grief-ravaged eyes.

"Edie," Mary began. "Is Edie involved? You said her name earlier." She regretted the note of disbelief in her voice.

"Not her. The – "

"Phew," Mary broke in, "I didn't think – "

"Edie kidnapped me. The man killed Dad. And attacked Mum. I'm sure of it."

Mary slumped back, slapping both hands flat on her head. "It can't… Edie's a lovely… Are you …" She stopped, knowing Katie was sure. Oh my God.

"It must have been my kidnapper. The man."

"Colin? Not Colin? Col's my line manager. My friend."

"Don't know who he is. They were close, but I thought she was a bit scared of him. I never saw the man in the house, or when they were chasing me."

She looked apologetically at Mary, who nodded for her to continue.

"He and Edie are in it together. He was going out to get someone, finish him. Not very clear through the locked door but I had no doubt he meant to hurt somebody."

Mary put her arms around Katie. "So horrible to be in the hands of that monster."

"He said he was going to do something at 11 o'clock. Frightened me. I - I thought he intended to kill me." Katie's voice trembled. "Now I know that was when he killed Dad. I was going to be next."

She dropped her face onto Mary's chest and cried. Mary cried, too.

After a while, Mary said: "Edie and Col. I never would've thought." She paused. "Then, nothing these few days could've been imagined."

Mary held Katie's hands in her lap. "We'll tell the police about it tomorrow. You've had too much tonight, let alone the past few days."

Katie shook her head so fiercely, hair flicked across her face, strands sticking over her mouth. She pulled them away, revealing the determined set of her lips.

"First thing tomorrow. I'm gonna make sure the cops get them."

Mary said she was grateful and amazed that she had got away from the killer. Katie calmed a little and told how she had taken the chance to escape while the man was out because she reckoned Edie would be easier to trick than both of them.

Mary sat transfixed, alternately shaking her head and smiling broadly, as Katie told how she had pretended to be drugged, smashed the window to feign escaping while she hid under the bed. "I got out the back and up a tree in the nick of time," she said. "He came back before I'd got over the fence into the neighbour's yard."

Mary clapped. "You are so brave. And so clever. You outsmarted those bastards. Oh, excuse the—"

A smile flickered across Katie's face. "It's what they are. Then I ran like hell. A cat nearly undid me. When I hid in a boat."

Shaking her head and giggling, Mary said: "Neither man nor beast could stop you. Ray would be proud of you."

"I can't … anymore… talk to him. Tell him…"

Mary pulled her closer. "Somehow, I think he'll know already."

Katie beamed. "I hope Mum will know."

"If she doesn't, we'll tell her tomorrow."

Katie said: "I want those two," she paused, "*bastards* caught. That's what propelled me through the streets."

"Wait a minute," Mary said. She got up and left the room. Soon she was back and sitting beside Katie again.

"I called the police. A Detective Sergeant Brogan is coming to see us tomorrow morning."

"Here?" Katie said. "I don't have any clean clothes."

"Mine should be a make-do fit."

"What about Jack?" Katie asked.

"First thing I asked. The detective has just interviewed Jack. We won't see him until tomorrow midday at the earliest. Sad to say." Katie groaned. Mary added that Jack had not been charged. "There seemed to be an implied 'yet' at the end of his sentence," Mary said. "But I'm probably being paranoid."

She went to the kitchen and returned with hot chocolate and cookies. After several minutes of drinking and munching, Mary said: "Katie, I know it's hard for you to consider this tonight, but do you think you could find that house?"

Katie finished a cookie, brushed crumbs from her blouse and took another slow sip, before answering. "Don't know, maybe. Dark and I was running for my life in strange streets." She screwed up her eyes. "I think it was in one of the rich new estates. I don't know the name."

"Right," Mary said. "Not where Col and Edie live then."

"If that means anything," Katie said.

The two young women finished their drinks in silence. Then, putting her mug on the coffee table, Mary spoke with a touch of excitement. "How about we give it a go tomorrow?"

"Without the cops?" Katie said.

"To help them. We can try to locate the place. Not go in. Probably taken off by now, but we won't take any chances."

Excitement building in her voice, too, Katie said: "Yes, yes, we'd be giving the cops a head start. Sooner they get on the trail the sooner they'll get them."

"Right," Mary said. "We've got a plan. Soon as the detective leaves tomorrow we'll set off. But, first part is to get some sleep."

She took the mugs and plates to the kitchen. Returning, she sat beside Katie. "Guess we'd better get into the shower and our pyjamas and sleep in the few hours left."

Katie nodded and snuggled into Mary.

"The bed in the spare room is made up."

Katie nodded, more slowly this time.

"I'll get you a towel and… and a …" She couldn't think of how the sentence was meant to finish.

Katie's head swayed, but didn't quite become a nod.

They didn't get to the shower. In five minutes they were asleep on the lounge.

20

MARY

Smart suit and tie, nothing unbuttoned, loosened or rolled up, silver–in-colour pen, notebook and unusual eyebrows, he sits gazing at us, ready for business. May be all show and he'll end with nothing to show for it. Be no closer to catching the killer, to ending our fear.

Seems a serious sort. Right sort for a murder case. Who knows? He may catch the bastard.

Appearances can be deceptive. On both sides of the law. I might have spoken with the murderer without realising it. Scary thought. They don't wear labels.

This bloke's making sure he'll recognise us next time. Staring at me, then Katie, then back again. Katie gazes at him as she picks up her glass. She takes a long drink without taking her eyes off him. Miss Cool–on the outside. Trying to show more calmness than I feel.

About time. He's got the pen in his hand, pops the point out, looks down at the notebook and opens it to a new page.

His black eyebrows, oddly familiar. Neatly shaped, matching, blocky rectangular things. Who cares? Trivial. Get started.

Ahh, crazy. I see it now. Like miniature Groucho Marx moustaches. Solid black, not salted like his greying hair.

He raises his eyebrows and I strangle a giggle into a cough with a hand around my throat. I avoid his and Katie's eyes, scrunch a hanky to my mouth. Here we go…

* * *

THURSDAY 8am

Brogan sat in a light brown lounge chair facing Mary and Katie, who sat close together on a matching three-seater, their backs to the closed front door about four metres away. A low coffee table with a dark red laminated top was between them.

The young women sat demurely, their neat appearance belying the frantic rush in the half hour following Brogan's seven o'clock phone call. Mary's lemon blouse was a bit big on Katie, but the blue jeans were about right. Mary sat back, hands in her lap, in a below-the-knee forest-green skirt and dark green blouse.

Sunlight slanted in from two front windows, brushing over the room like an artist's touch-up, adding dabs and dashes of brightness, filtering through Mary's dark hair, glowing golden, halo-like, around Katie's head, glistening on tall, dripping, glasses of orange juice, highlighting a mug's rim with a whiter circle, glinting silver on the detective's pen, finally splashing brighter yellow on daffodils fading beneath the scrawling spill of black letters across the pale mauve wall and tropical island picture. There, behind Brogan's back, the malicious graffiti sapped sun from the light.

In the early morning flurry, Mary had pulled the curtains open, then closed them to dim the vandalism. She had considered for a minute before defiantly pulling the curtains as wide as possible. Let the investigator see it in all its inglorious crudity. I won't be shut off from the sun by a killer, Mary vowed.

She was relieved when Brogan had arrived alone. Maybe an informal interview. She had offered him tea or coffee. He opted for orange juice, as had Katie. Mary made herself a mug of instant coffee.

Brogan took a sip and put the glass on the table.

"Detective Sergeant Brogan," Mary said, "would you prefer a jug of water?"

He stared at her for a moment, perhaps weighing up if it was a serious question.

"No, thank you, Miss Bourke. Orange juice is fine."

Mary smiled. Sure it is. More choice than at Police Station interviews. She shifted her gaze away from his comical eyebrows, which surely had no place in a murder investigation. It was her fault. She determined to keep her imagination in check. Try, at least.

She looked at Katie, who flashed her a nervous smile. Brogan dropped his eyes to the notebook, then up again.

"Thank you, ladies, for giving your time to help us solve this case," he said.

Not that we had any choice, Mary thought.

Katie said: "Maybe just a case to you, Sir, a job. But, it's personal to us. We want you to get my Dad's murderer, a lot more than you do."

Mary said: "The sooner you catch these mongrels, the sooner you take your eyes off Jack and let us go back to our normal lives– if that's ever possible.

"But thanks for addressing us as ladies." While her tone was pleasant, her face friendly, the corners of her mouth were set in a distinctly sad curve.

Brogan's lips moved as though about to form a smile but he appeared to think better of it. "Ladies, we all agree with that, but it will be easier to achieve if everyone co-operates with us." He leaned forward and had to grab his notebook to stop it slipping off his knee.

"We will, of course," Katie said.

"Fine. Now, Miss Bourke, you said 'these criminals'. You think there are more than one?"

Mary and Katie exchanged glances.

"Katie was abducted by Edie Martin and a man, who might be her husband, Colin." She paused. Katie was leaning forward. "Why don't you ask Katie herself? She was there. She was their prisoner."

Brogan wrote briefly in his notebook, which was still precariously balanced on his knee. He nodded at Mary, then looked directly at Katie. "Are you saying that Mrs Edie Martin and her husband Colin are behind all this?"

"I didn't see the man's face, but I am sure that man killed my father, I don't think Edie was involved – not directly – in any killing or assault, but she was his accomplice. She kidnapped me and locked me up."

Brogan nodded without comment. He didn't write anything.

Mary suspected he knew more than he was letting on.

As if reading Mary's mind, Brogan said: "Of course, Miss Bourke, we value your succinct summary of Miss Durkin's experience that you gave when you rang the station. However, as is often the case, in this…" He hesitated, as if trying to avoid using the same word twice. "… investigation, we are following several other lines of enquiry. Other–"

Mary interrupted. "Other murders, attempted murders, and threats sprayed inside and outside houses?"

She waved an arm towards the graffitied wall. "Like this."

Brogan didn't need to turn around. "Disgusting," he said. "Off the record: yes."

Katie cried out and grasped Mary's arm. Mary said: "Are they Aunty and Uncle, Meg and Doug…"

Brogan blinked twice, his eyebrows twitched in sync and Mary lost the thread, couldn't remember the surname. She looked away, down to her lap, biting her lower lip.

"They are safe at this moment." Brogan said.

Katie exhaled loudly, but Mary wasn't about to let him off too easily.

"At this very moment?" she said. "How can you possibly say that? A few days ago we all thought Bev was safe. And Ray and Katie. I mean, with respect, get real."

"We deal with realities, all the time, Miss Bourke, so we must get down to business." He paused, tapping the notebook with his pen. "I find you and Mr Jack Durkin exasperating at times."

"Sorry, Detective Sergeant Brogan, I guess we should have read Being a Suspect For Dummies."

Brogan ignored both her comment and the smile that followed it.

Katie grinned and shook her head at Mary.

He said: "Where were you, Miss Bourke, last night between seven pm and midnight?"

Katie gasped. It was obvious what he was getting at. Mary clasped the teenager's hands. "I have been here all night."

"At home all night?"

"Yes, you could put it that way, also."

"Can anyone verify that?"

"I can," Katie said, so quickly that Mary half expected to see her hand waving in the air, but she was sitting quite still.

"I was here from about midnight until…" She turned to Mary, who was tugging her sleeve. Their eyes met, but Katie continued. "… until now and – Oh." She put a hand to her mouth. "I'm sorry, Sir, that doesn't count, does it? After the time you … When…" She began to cry. Mary put her right arm around her shoulder. Brogan watched in silence.

"I …I was mixed up…"

"It's all right, Katie. We'll be OK."

Brogan wrote briefly, then looked at Mary. "If I may continue–"

"I'm sure Jack has already confirmed he was here with me from early evening until a couple of police officers woke us with their banging and dragged him away from me.

"Right after telling him his Dad had been shot dead. Poor bloody Jack."

Katie, who had just dried her eyes, sobbed anew. Mary whispered "Sorry" in Katie's ear before continuing. "You will have recorded the exact times Katie arrived and when Jack was taken away." Brogan opened his mouth to speak, but Mary ignored that. "I was with Jack right up to our midnight dramas and from then until now I've been here with Katie. Rephrase it as you like."

Katie sniffled in her seat and added: "There was a crowd across the street watching, too."

"There you are, Detective Sergeant Brogan," Mary said. "A stack of people who can give you the verification you seek." Despite her cheeky confidence, she knew there was no legally acceptable corroboration for the fatal hours before midnight.

Katie said: "Can you please now concentrate on getting my father's killer, who is probably also my mother's attacker?" Her voice trembled. Mary squeezed her hand.

"Time you got off this false trail," Mary said.

"I see," Brogan said. Mary wondered what he saw. "Were either you or Mr Jack Durkin asleep while the other was awake?"

"How could anyone know what was happening while he or she was asleep?" Mary said, knowing the implications of Brogan's question. "But I think Jack and I were asleep at about the same time."

"How could you know that, when you and Mr Durkin slept in different rooms?"

Katie put a hand to her mouth. Brogan's eyebrows smiled triumphantly.

Before Mary could answer the detective pressed on. "If you were asleep in the bedroom, how can you state Mr Durkin didn't leave the house?"

"No, no," Mary said. "You can't assume I wouldn't have heard Jack go out. Apart from other noises he might have made, the front door squeaks a lot. Needs oiling."

He made a note. Mary hoped it wasn't 'What about back door?'.

"You must've heard that yourself when you came in."

Brogan's eyebrows twitched above a blink. "I didn't notice that. I will pay more attention on the way out."

"Of course," Mary said, hiding crossed fingers under her right hand. "Sometimes it doesn't. Squeak I mean."

Katie gave her an anxious look.

Brogan said: "Now, Miss Bourke, why was your partner sleeping in this room and not in the bedroom? An argument?"

"Nothing like that." There was amusement in her voice. "We have a very loving relationship. Do you want to hear about that, too? Is it pertinent, Detective Sergeant Brogan?" She gazed at him, wide-eyed, innocence.

Brogan wrote quickly in his notebook.

"Why did Mr Durkin decide to sleep in the lounge room last night?"

"He wasn't planning on sleeping anywhere." Groucho eyebrows tilted up, then remained still, as if poised for the punchline.

Mary said: "Jack stayed up to protect me, us."

Katie sniffled and rubbed her nose with a tissue.

"He was guarding the house against whoever attacked his family and did this."

"But he went to sleep," Brogan said.

"He fell asleep," Mary said. "He didn't intend to."

"You cannot know what Mr Durkin was doing while you were asleep."

Katie jumped up. "Hang on, how—" she began, looking down on the seated man. Brogan's eyes narrowed, and the eyebrows obediently clumped down, but Katie didn't step towards him. "Of course, he bloody fell asleep. Do you really understand what torment my brother and me have been going through over the past few days?

"Detective do you really understand anything about people? You are buggerising around after an innocent young guy whose mother's been almost killed and now his father's been shot dead and all you can do is go on about sleeping arrangements and creaking doors and other crap."

Her voice cracked as she raised it to an unaccustomed loudness. She sat heavily back on the lounge. Mary restrained herself from clapping.

"I have told you who's doing these terrible things, who the murderer's accomplice is. Yet you have done nothing."

Brogan shifted in his seat, uncrossed his legs, crossed them again, but didn't say anything. Once he glanced at Mary, but otherwise he remained focused on Katie.

"Will you, Detective Sergeant Brogan, try to find the killer of our father, who also tried to kill our mother— and me?"

"Wow," Mary thought. She said: "Are you looking for Edie and Colin Martin, Sir? That must be a more fruitful line of enquiry."

Brogan opened his notebook, poised his pen over it, but didn't write anything.

"Miss Bourke, Miss Durkin, it is an error of perception to assume we are doing nothing, just because you can't see it.

"As in every police investigation, we must check everything, everybody—"

"That may be—"

Brogan gestured Mary's interruption into silence.

"We don't normally, as a matter of practice, go around to witnesses and possible suspects in a murder inquiry to keep then updated on what we're doing out of your sight. It doesn't mean we are sitting on our hands."

Mary couldn't argue with that. She nodded at Katie, who looked abashed.

"Sorry, Detective Sergeant Brogan," Mary said. "I believe you and your officers are doing your job with full diligence."

Her mouth and eyes smiled at Brogan but if he was mollified he didn't show it.

Katie said: "Have you spoken with the Martins? What—"

Brogan waved his notebook to interrupt. "We have not. Both Martins have disappeared. We are searching with..." He paused. "Due diligence. We will find them before—"

"Before he kills another one of us?" Katie said, the directness of her clear, young voice making it more a statement than a question.

Brogan frowned and the Groucho moustaches slowly tensed below his creased forehead. He rearranged his features and spoke calmly. "Do either of you know of anyone who might have wanted to harm Mr Raymond Durkin?"

"No," Katie shouted. "Everyone loves … loved my Dad."

"Obviously, not everyone," he said. Katie glared at him. "What do you say, Miss Bourke?"

"No one disliked Ray enough to kill him. Not Ray Durkin. This is Manderville after all."

She felt Katie's eyes on her and wished she had been more positive. Nobody disliked him enough to kill? For goodness sake.

"Manderville is the town where Mr Durkin was shot dead."

Katie shook her head and looked helplessly at Mary.

Brogan said: "Miss Bourke, how did you get along with Mr Durkin?"

Mary hesitated. She poured herself a glass of orange juice and took a sip. Nobody had been drinking much. She considered offering coffee, but decided against it. This had gone on too long already.

"We were okay. Fine. Got along all right —"

"All right?" The detective raised his eyebrows. Mary quickly refocused on his mouth. "Did you and Mr Durkin–Raymond Durkin–ever argue?"

Mary put her half-empty glass on the coffee table. She put her hands back on her lap. "Nothing serious." She realised Katie was looking at her. "It was just a little family squabble. This is ridiculous."

Undeterred, Brogan said: "He didn't like you living with Jack did he? He wanted to break you up?"

Katie rested a hand on Mary's hands.

"No, that's not how things were," Mary said. "Who's been telling you this?" Meg? Doug? Her mother?

When Brogan didn't answer, Mary said: "He was drunk. He got angry because I stuck up for Bev." She glanced at Katie, then back at Brogan.

"He said vile things about her. He didn't like me interfering."

Brogan studied Mary for a moment. "Did he threaten you?"

She shook her head. "Just told me to keep out of it —"

"Or he'd do what?"

"Nothing, really. Said he wanted me out of the house, out of the family."

"Are you in the family? I didn't think you were married to Jack."

"No. But everyone treats me as if I am part of the family. As I said, he was drunk. Shouting, pushing chairs around. Knocked one over. Said stupid stuff to others, too."

"How did Jack react to this?"

He was writing while talking now.

Katie said: "Jack wasn't there. And Dad cried later, after Mary left. He was very upset at what he said."

Brogan nodded at Katie, then turned back but spoke to Mary. "Did you threaten him? Physically or verbally?"

Mary laughed loudly. A scoffing laugh. "You must be joking. Me threaten Ray Durkin with violence? No, I have never threatened him physically, verbally or fantasyly." She didn't think there was such a word. Katie giggled. Brogan exercised his eyebrows and wrote in his notebook.

"Did you express any disagreement?"

"I disagreed, of course, and I said I wouldn't let him break us up. Jack and me."

He wrote again. "Did Mr Durkin—Raymond—threaten his wife during this fracas?"

"No, way," Katie said. "Nobody threatened to do anything to anyone."

"Except perhaps implied threat by Miss Bourke in defence of her relationship with your brother."

Mary said: "Excuse me, Mr Brogan." His eyebrows skipped up and down. "I would never threaten anyone. No matter how you may interpret my words."

Brogan scratched the side of his nose. Said nothing.

"What are you doing about my kidnapping?" Katie said. "Isn't that important to the cops?"

Mary silently cheered Katie's directness. She said: "I'm sure our local police force is right on the case. Following up all the clues you've given them."

She paused, then: "They have interviewed you about your evidence, haven't they?"

She knew they hadn't, other than this side-tracking interrogation.

"Not in my presence," Katie said. She smiled at Brogan who glared back.

"Pity," Mary said. "Solid first-person information."

"We are checking certain things, Miss Durkin. It would help if you tell us where this house is and where you were, allegedly—"

"Actually," Katie said. "Not allegedly."

"—held prisoner. Your brother gave us some sketchy data about the day you disappeared from your Aunt and Uncle's home."

"I don't know the address but—"

"But we'll find it for you," Mary said. "Won't we, Katie?"

"Umm… I suppose we… Yes, we will. I'll get that info for you."

Mary smiled sweetly at Brogan.

"There you are Detective Sergeant Brogan, that may give the investigation a shove along."

"How about you leave all that to us." Brogan wrote some more words. "Now, Miss Bourke, I understand you work for Hardwicke Central Accountancy?"

"Yes, I'm a senior clerk there, studying accountancy. Mr Hardwicke's my boss."

"Simon Hardwicke?"

She nodded. "What's this about?"

"Mr Hardwicke told us he hasn't seen his deputy, Mr Colin Martin, who you have mentioned already, for a couple of days."

Although it wasn't a question, Brogan looked at Mary as if expecting confirmation. She kept him waiting for a second or two.

"Colin's my line manager. He's also an accountant. A good one. He does a lot of work away from the office. Not unusual for him to be 'missing' for a day here and there."

Mary waited while Brogan wrote again. She said: "Their only child, Peter, drowned several years ago."

"Actually," Brogan said, " it was eleven years ago."

Mary nodded in agreement with this clarification. Was this heading somewhere? Apparently nowhere. Brogan closed his notebook and dropped the pen on it. However, Mary wasn't finished.

"Another thing, Detective Sergeant Brogan, have any of your lines of inquiry led to the person who has painted these vile threats on our home? If I may return to the question of people making threats. Have you any data on that matter?"

"Miss Bourke, all these threads seem to be connected to the same perpetrator or perpetrators."

Mary gave an exaggerated sigh. "A policeman's work is never done. Sorry to keep pestering you on these things, but as one person has been murdered and another may well not survive, these are rather serious matters to us."

Brogan picked up his pen and opened the notebook. He scribbled something, closed it and dropped the pen, from a greater height this time. It rolled across the table to fall over the edge. He left it on the floor.

"Thank you for your time, ladies. You will be contacted, Miss Durkin, for more da… information about your… abduction." Mary picked up his pen and handed it to him.

"Thanks. Anything further you can supply us with in the meantime will be followed up." He snapped the notebook closed, and held it and the pen in his left hand.

Mary ushered him to the front door and held it open. He released the catch on the screen door and pushed it open. There was no squeak. He went out and gently closed the screen door. No squeak. He looked at Mary who shrugged. She reached forward and pushed it open. It squeaked. She smiled, suppressing a wink. Brogan looked at her as if she was a magician who had performed a trick he couldn't figure out.

She closed both doors; the first squeaked, the second gently clicked.

"Phew, that was close."

Mary murmured, "Yes" and turned to see Katie struggling to hold a sad smile in place.

They stood, several metres apart, weakly, almost shyly, smiling, as if knowing smiles were inappropriate.

Neither moved or broke the silence of the room. Outside, children shouted and laughed, two women talked interruptedly, their words unheard in the lounge room, a vehicle whooshed past, brakes screeched, tyres squealed, women shrieked, children howled, a dog barked. Male and female voices added an abusive chorus to the climax of a demonic opera.

The two women in the house stood unmoving, undistracted, seemingly oblivious to all this, but, as the street noises diminished, the fragile smiles faded and the faces crumpled.

Mary knew she was about to cry, but Katie started first.

Mary ran and hugged her tightly and began crying, too.

HANDY GUIDE TO MANDERVILLE

Focus on Education

By Thaddeus Morgan, Chairman, Manderville Education Committee

Manderville children are truly blessed with the range of educational opportunities available to them. They – and their parents – have many choices (subject to residential eligibility): Central Primary, Manderville East Primary, Manderville High, plus Catholic primary and high schools.

The diligence of our students and their natural abilities, along with the dedication of all our talented teachers is shown in the results they produce each year in examinations, particularly in the high schools' HSC examination. Most years at least one of our high school students features in the state's top 100 in one subject or another. One recent stellar year twelve Manderville student starred, reaching the first hundredth in various subjects.

That year, Mary Bourke and Reginald Jobson attained the top 30 in English and History respectively. Ms Bourke also represented Manderville High in that year's regional debating competition and out-argued all-comers to win. Great achievement.

The sporting side is not neglected in any of our town's schools, either. Manderville students excel in many sports and have maintained a strong tradition that goes back to the school days of Raymond Durkin. John Durkin was selected to play in the district schoolboys' Rugby League team, which came third in the shield.

In her last year at high school, Sharon Grey, the daughter of another sports star, gymnast Charlotte Grey, reached the final four of several tennis tournaments.

21

COLIN

Weeks ago sitting in our lounge room, drinking our tea, eating our cake, the detective, matter-of-factly, broke our hearts again, telling me and Edie, that our facts were, in fact, not facts, after all. After all. All the fears and tears and years of grief, he sat, telling us that the boy watching from the walls and the buffet shelves had been murdered.

Eleven years not knowing the truth. Not an accident. Not now. Not ever. We grieved too little. For the wrong reason. Not knowing how much worse Peter's death had been. Poor Peter.

We reached, eventually, a form of acceptance. It was a tragic accident. Nobody's fault. But now. Murder, the detective said in between tea and cake. Crumbs on his chin. Our only child taken by murderers — unknown, unblamed, unpunished, unhated.

Edie cries a lot now. Grief has deepened, and I can hardly … I cry, too. I want revenge somehow. Edie says other people must grieve as we do. She's stronger. Have to deal with this—the best we can.

We have to do the right thing by our poor boy.

* * *

THURSDAY 9.53am

Mary opened the desk's bottom drawer and pulled out a map. She unfolded it and spread crumpled, creased Manderville out below them.

"See if you recognise any of these street names," Mary said.

"I'm not very good at reading maps," Katie said, bending lower. She flattened a couple of raised creases with the heel of her hand and peered at the irregular grid of streets.

Mary poked a finger at a spot towards the left. "This is our street," She ran her finger along another street.

"How about Jolly Street?" Mary said. "It runs down to join our street."

"Hmm… maybe," Katie said. "It wasn't jolly for me".

Nevertheless, she bent over to look carefully at where Mary was pointing.

"Not sure. What's that long one there?"

"That's the other end of Jolly Street."

Mary pulled the drawer open again and folded the map. But changing her mind, she held it towards Katie.

"Are you sure you're up to this, Katie?"

Katie took the proffered map.

"I'm all right. We must do this as soon as we can." She spoke firmly. "I owe it to Mum and Dad to help the cops find those two… I'm the only person who can find that house."

Mary nodded. "It doesn't seem like Brogan's team will be around to see you for a few hours. And Jack won't be home before midday. God knows why they don't just let him go."

"Let's give it a go," Katie said.

"Right," Mary said, tapping the map in Katie's hand. "We can do it without this. Follow our noses."

Katie took the map back to the desk. She paused, looking down on the open drawer. She lifted a paperback book out. She dropped the map in and held the book up to Mary.

"What's this? Handy Guide to Manderville. Who needs it?" She turned pages over. Mary laughed.

"I know. Who needs a guide to this place?"

"Road map out would be more popular," Katie said, still leafing through the book.

"The council thought it was a good idea a few years ago."

"Hey, you're in it," Katie said. She raised it, fingers holding a page open. "Woo hoo. Champion debater."

"My ten seconds of undeserved fame."

"Too modest. Talking of undeserved… That sleazy butcher's got himself a plug."

"Yep," Mary said, "But I got in it without being mayor, as he was at the time. One term, thankfully."

Katie flicked over more pages.

"Here, this bit by Sharon Mortensom, admin secretary of the art society. Is she the Sharon who beat up– "

"Jack. The same. That's her married name."

"Poor Jack," Katie said.

She closed the book and dropped it in the drawer. Mary put her hand out to keep the drawer open.

"There's some good stuff in there about Ray Durkin, the town's football hero."

Katie's eyes lit up and she reached for the Handy Guide again. Mary smiled and lifted her hand from the drawer, but Katie pushed it shut with a bang. She gave a faint smile. "That's lovely," she said. "I'll leave that till later, when we get back."

Mary brushed Katie's cheek with the back of her hand.

"Wait a bit if you want to read it now," Mary said.

Katie shook her head.

"I'll read and cry more later. Thanks."

Mary looked doubtful. "Really? Are you ready for a bit of a drive around Manderville streets this morning?" Perhaps a drive into danger, she thought.

"Absolutely," Katie said.

"Right. Let's get ready and hit the road. See how we go."

22

KATIE

Feel silly. This big floppy, black hat and sunglasses. Stand out more. Like a movie star on the Riviera. Mary wants me to slump down in the seat. But between the hat and the slumping and the sunglasses I might never recognise the street let alone house.

This area doesn't look right. Older houses. My place… Ha, my prison higher quality than these ones. Mary doesn't know this part of town either. Bit further out, I reckon. Odd, me giving directions, when I don't have much idea. Nevertheless, I suggest; she nods and turns. And turns.

A new estate. Might be getting warmer, but I don't remember running along the streets in the dark. I was so scared I probably wouldn't even know them if it had been daylight.

Mary is taking it all in her stride. As she does. But she must be exasperated by my inability to know where I am, know where to go. Should've brought the map… No, that'd be no use to me either. You'd think where I'd been locked up would stick in my memory. Hope I'll know it when I see it. That old car could be stuck on the driveway, thanks to my creative knife work.

So impressed by Mary's strength. Calmly driving along, like she was going on a picnic, not visiting a killer's home. Turning left and left again, then right, on and on, around and around.

I'm thirsty. Hey. This corner is a turn for the better. Newer houses, bigger. Close, now. I know it.

* * *

THURSDAY 10.22am

Katie straightened in her seat watching houses go past. Mary sensed Katie's sudden movement.

"Do you see it?" Mary asked.

"I'm sure this is the area. I think I ran past a boat along here."

"You mean a car?"

"No, boat parked in a driveway. I remember that alright. Dog dashed out barking at me."

Mary slowed; Katie peered left and right.

"There," Katie shouted. "I knew I was right."

"Ship ahoy," Mary said.

"That bloody dog … See, barking mad mutt."

"Want me to run him over?" Mary veered towards the dog as if she meant it, then straightened and sped up, leaving the dog with nobody to bare its teeth at. The two women look at each other and laughed. Their mirth was tinged with fearful excitement. But as the car slowly moved along the street a grim mood filled the interior.

"Is it near here?" Mary asked. "You'd better keep down a bit more now."

"No, it's around to the left. Twice. The house backs onto the ones in this street."

Mary accelerated, turned the next corner and the one after it before slowing again. Katie suddenly banged on the dashboard. Mary jumped, but kept her hands steady on the wheel and her eyes on the road.

"What the hell, Katie."

Katie stretched forward and pointed, prodding the windscreen. "There…That's the place. See?"

"Keep your belt on. Might take off suddenly. Lot of houses. Look much the same to me. Which—"

"That one," Katie said. "blue car in the driveway. I wrecked the tyres."

"They could still be there," Mary said.

She slowly turned the car into the kerb and turned the engine off. Katie looked surprised. "Don't stop here. Go closer."

Mary shook her head. She, too, was surprised. She thought Katie would want to keep her distance from the house that could have become her murder scene.

"Better not park in front," Mary said. "They could still be there."

She was about to suggest they drive away and tell the police, but Katie was already opening the car door.

"Maybe. Let's go and have a squiz."

Mary got out and joined Katie on the footpath.

"All right. We'll have a quick peak to make certain it's the right place. Then tell the police."

"Yep," Katie said, stepping around a puddle. "Think I trod in that one last night."

Mary took hold of Katie's elbow, slowing her in her tracks. Katie turned impatiently back to Mary.

"We might catch them. Can't let them get away."

Mary wondered how much of the teenage girl's bravado was an act to control her fears. Because she had escaped once didn't mean she could do it twice. She shivered as the wind picked up, lifting dead leaves across their path, dropping one-foot-in-the-grave yellow ones around them.

"Catch them?" Mary said. "How can we catch two people who may be armed with your Dad's rifle? They might have other weapons too."

"We'll be very careful. We'll be all right in daylight. In a public street."

"Might be a public street," Mary said, "but there's nobody around. Hardly seen a car going past."

They looked at each other for a few seconds. Mary grabbed Katie's hand and they walked towards the driveway with the crippled car. There was no sign of life around the simple, brick house that –solely because it had been Katie's prison – loomed ominously before them. When they reached the driveway they bent double, hiding behind the car.

"This is silly," Mary said, standing straight. "Like kids playing hide-and-seek.

"If anyone in there is looking out, they'll see us whether we're bent down or standing."

Katie stood beside her. "Yeah, Looks suspicious, ducking around."

"Hey." As if hearing her words, a man shouted at them. "What are you up to?"

Mary sensed movement in the corner of her eye. For the first time since setting out that morning, she was frightened. Katie grabbed her arm, pinching the skin.

They turned, breath held in, and looked over the car. What now? They stared in the direction of the voice and relaxed, breath exhaling, bodies slumping limply, like the punctured tyres at their feet. The women exchanged glances. Katie suppressed a giggle.

This was no kidnapper of young women or killer of unarmed men.

An elderly man was standing in the next door driveway, hands on hips, obviously waiting for an answer. He wore a loose-fitting brown shirt, baggy green shorts and sandals. Long white socks stretched over skinny, clamped together, tanned legs up to knobbly knees that looked, to Mary, like two cheeky pups peeking over a picket fence.

The young trespassers, self-consciously guilty and, at the same time, fearful of who might be watching from the house, were in no mood to laugh at the ludicrously officious neighbour.

Mary answered: "We were hoping to catch our friends at home." Oops, Mary thought. unconscious use of 'catch'.

"That couple, they were your friends?"

Katie bit her tongue. She wanted to say "No, they held me prisoner and were going to kill me". She let Mary speak.

"Not close friends. Did you see much of them?" She trembled, squeezing Katie's arm, while she spoke.

The neighbour dropped his arms and put his hands in his pockets. "Kept to themselves, those two," he said. "Surprised to have them living next door." Mary wished he wouldn't talk so loudly.

"Didn't know the Tylers had rented it out."

Katie said softly to Mary: "Rented."

Mary asked: "So, the Mart… our friends didn't own this place? We weren't aware of that."

"No," Katie said.

He studied them for a moment, as if suspicious of people who didn't know everything about their friends. He looked around the street and saw a soft drink can near the kerb.

"Filthy pigs."

At first, Mary was taken aback by this apparent insult, but when he picked the can up, she realised he was referring not to her and Katie, nor to the Tylers or their tenants, but to a long-gone stranger.

He crushed it in his hands before shoving in a pocket of his roomy shorts.

Katie whispered: "Wish he'd go away. We've gotta hurry."

"Yes. Just hope none of our 'friends' has got an eye on us."

Returning to his former position the man said: "The Tylers are in Europe for a month or so. Never seen those two before." He sounded as if he hoped to never see them again.

He paused to feel his shorts. A wet stain was spreading around his pocket. He swore and said something about filthy pigs not even emptying cans before dumping them.

Mary and Katie watched with growing impatience while he rubbed a wet hand on the side of his shirt. They each repeatedly turned to see if the curtains were still closed, unmoving.

"Come to think of it," he said loudly. "I haven't seen or heard anything of them since late last night, when Vonnie and me were going to bed. There was a racket in there." Pause. Mary hoped he had finished telling the neighbourhood all about it. She and Katie glanced at the house again.

"Come to think of it," he began again. For goodness sake, stop thinking. "Must have been later than that. Ruckus woke Vonnie and she nudged me. Heard nothing from there since."

Mary wanted to ask him why he was talking so loudly, but she fumed in silence. In the corner of her eye, she caught a flash of movement at the front window. She turned to see a sparrow sweeping past the house. The curtains were not moving.

She turned back to the man, who had taken the can from his pocket to empty the last drops on the grass under a tree.

He held the can up, with a disgusted shake of his head. Mary wasn't going to wait for another thought to come to him.

"Well," she said, "they might have left without letting us know. We'll knock and see if we can raise anybody." By now she was sure they had fled. "Thank you for your help Mr…"

The man turned back towards his house, not offering his name. Fine, Mary thought, you go and explain to Vonnie why you wet your pants in public.

She said to Katie: "I reckon the house is empty. That fellow's loud talk didn't bring anyone to the door or window."

Katie took the cue and strode up the path to the porch. She looked over her shoulder at Mary, who quickly caught up with her. Centimetres from the closed door, their bravado petered out and they stood together, looking at the doorbell, then each other, as if suddenly realising their next step was not only foolish, it could cost their lives.

Mary took a deep breath and raised her finger to the button. She hesitated. Katie put her hand over Mary's and pushed it.

They jumped at the loud ring that seemed to echo in the house for several fear-filled seconds. But nobody opened the door.

"They've gone," Katie said, her whisper betrayed her uncertainty.

Mary pushed the bell button again. Still no sound from inside the house.

"We'll go around the back," Mary said, heading off to the side of the house, past the car.

Katie ran a few steps to catch up. Debris from Katie's escape was strewn across the side path: a broken chair and scattered glass and pieces of broken window frame.

"All my work," Katie said.

"You didn't muck around, did you. I'm in awe of your vandalism."

"That's the room they locked me in."

Mary smiled. "I gathered that. Not strong enough to hold you."

Mary moved closer. Carefully avoiding shards of glass projecting from cracked woodwork, she pushed the curtains aside and peeked in.

"Oh God," she said, backing away from the window so quickly she cut her hand.

"What is it?" Katie said. "Oh, you've cut your hand. I've got a clean hanky."

Mary gently pushed her away.

"No. No, that's nothing… There's …" She pushed Katie further away. "Not my cut. There's … It's.. . We must get away …"

She started crying.

Katie paled, frightened by Mary's distress. "They still there? Did they see you? Quick…"

She turned to run. Mary put out her right arm to hold Katie back.

"They are gone. I'm sure. I'd better borrow your hanky first. Dripping blood everywhere."

Katie wrapped her handkerchief around Mary's left hand. The white cloth was soon red. She put her arm around Mary's shoulder and hugged her.

Mary turned tearful eyes on the younger woman.

She wiped her face with her sleeve and whispered: "There's a body in there."

Katie pulled away, almost falling backwards over the broken chair, face pale, her mouth open.

"Someone is dead in that room."

"Did you see who?"

"He, or maybe she, is lying on the floor. The end of the bed covers the … head. A blanket's over it… him…

"There's a lot of blood."

Katie tried to move around Mary. "Let me see."

Mary firmly held her back. "Don't go there."

Katie didn't try to force past Mary's outstretched arm. "Man or woman?"

"Could be either… Trousers or slacks… feet under the bed, I think. Job for the police.

"Are you up to going to the police now?"

Katie nodded. "Whatever. Wherever. We gotta get out of here quick," Katie said.

They ran past the sabotaged car and down to her car. Sitting in their seats, Katie took a bunch of tissues from a box and wrapped them around Mary's hand. It was a chunky bunch, but Mary was able to start the car and drive off.

Mary said: "Katie, this has been a big shock on top of your already… I can take you to Aunty Meg or a doctor or–"

"Nah," Katie said, "We told Brogan we'd find the house. We've done more than that." After a pause, she asked: "But, is your hand okay to drive?"

Mary nodded and, as if to prove it, accelerated down the street.

Mary shouted: "Detective Sergeant Brogan, here we come. It's your lucky day, talking to us ladies twice in the one day."

HANDY GUIDE TO MANDERVILLE

Joshua Mander 1856 – 1957

By Anna Cornwell, Manderville Historical Society

When young Joshua Madder rode into the little village of Sparrow Grove in May 1878, it is unlikely that he had an inkling, nor any expectation, that not only would he become its leading citizen and contribute mightily to its blossoming population, but that he would alter his name to one that would, in time, become part of the name by which the rapidly developing town is known today—Manderville.

Joshua set up Sparrow Grove's first butcher's shop, having gained experience in a butchery in Wagga Wagga. Then known as Madder Meats, is now called Mercer's Meats, and is owned by our current Mayor, Councillor Bruce Mercer.

Within six months of arriving in the town, Joshua had met, wooed and married Martha Hogan, eldest daughter of the district's wealthiest pastoralist, Wilbur Hogan and his wife Winifred.

It was not long before the young couple welcomed their first child to their union, Harold, who was to be followed over the next several years by Maud, Arabella, Silas and Bramwell.

Mr Hogan generously bestowed a large parcel of land on his new son-in-law. Joshua and Winifred moved to their new property and he installed a manager in his shop, Mr Bertrand Mercer, great-grandfather of today's master butcher.

Joshua set zealously to work establishing a large sheep empire by buying up many surrounding properties.

He became quite eccentric as he aged and folk began saying "There's nobody madder than Joshua". This mockery spread to the schoolyard and the Madder children were teased by other pupils. This caused tears in some Madder children and regular fighting by others, predominantly, but not only, by Silas.

Eventually, Joshua decided to change his surname, rather than forgo his eccentricity. The family name became Mander. On his death bed, at the wise old ago of 101, Joshua Madder is reported to have said to the three generations gathered around him: "I have done my duty to God and fellow man. I leave this earth knowing I have created a better, safer town where residents can live without fear of lawlessness, able to pursue their lives in peace."

23

BROGAN

Keeps getting worse, this. Common domestic abuse call-out, perpetrator gone, we leave, woman battered, in hospital near death, daughter abducted, father shot dead, a hit-and-run, and now, it appears, another murder. Lot of blood the women said. Too right, according to Smithson. Two murders could become three. Plus those two blokes. God give me strength.

So much for the quiet time in a little country town I was expecting. Be a lot more time for me and the kids, Margie said.

Even read the guide book. Shows you can't believe everything you read.

It's my job, so get on with it. Only few hours since I interviewed these two. Seem more subdued, in shock. Don't blame them. Tough on a couple of country town girls, caught up in murder and violence. Shocks me, too, even after all my years.

* * *

THURSDAY 11.50am

"Well, ladies, here we are, back again."

"We are back again, but for you, Detective Sergeant Brogan, it may be 'still here'," Mary said, looking Brogan directly in the eye. Brogan kept his gaze steady. Oh dear, he sighed to himself, shocked but still feisty. At least she addressed me by my rank right away.

"Yeah," Katie said, "we've actually been out looking for evidence to help the cops."

Brogan winced but let 'cops' go.

"Thank you for reporting your discovery immediately, but you should not have interfered in a police investigation and possibly put your lives in danger. We have enough crimes to investigate at the moment, thank you." He saw both women were about to speak but he kept going.

"Despite your…" He paused. "self-satisfaction, I don't see any evidence of evidence, Miss Durkin." He smiled, pleased with his play on words. "Rather than evidence, you two have found a body. A body for which we require evidence to help us solve yet another violent crime."

Katie said: "I'm sure you'll find more evidence inside the house where I was kept prisoner."

"Our men," Brogan said, "are going over the place right now."

Mary shifted in her chair, leant both forearms on the table. "They'll find my blood," she said. "Around the broken window. Outside."

She waggled her hanky-and-tissue wrapped hand, strips of red-and-white tissue flapping like streamers from a footy fan's car.

Brogan nodded. "Constable Brady will apply a proper dressing before you leave," he said. "Is it okay for now?" Mary nodded. "We'll take a sample at the same time, to check against other blood there."

Mary said: "It's only on–"

Brogan put a hand up. "We can't take your word. It is a crime scene, despite the best efforts of you two to contaminate it."

Mary looked away from the detective's face and bit her lower lip. Brogan thought it showed she felt chastened.

Katie offered her addition to the crime scene. "They might find my fingerprints."

"No doubt, Miss Durkin. In fact, I believe the only fingerprints we're likely to get there, will be yours, and a few of Miss Bourke's."

Katie and Mary exchanged guilty looks.

"I was too focused on getting away to wipe my prints from everywhere I'd been."

"You've both left enough evidence around to be added to our list of suspects, I'm afraid," Brogan said, without looking afraid at all.

"That's just plain silly," Mary said. "The major part of the evidence which you say put us on your alleged suspects list was Katie's fingerprints. Surely evidence that she had, indeed, been there—of the victim, not the culprits."

"It confused the scene," Brogan said.

Katie said: "Edie always wore thin rubber gloves when she brought my meals. I think the man had gloves when he grabbed me from behind. Not rubber, maybe leather."

Mary stood. Katie looked surprised, Brogan annoyed. He gestured for Mary to sit down.

"Not done yet, Miss Bourke."

Mary opened her mouth to speak, but Brogan waved a hand at her to sit, so she sat, silenced.

"This is no kids' club adventure," he said. "There's somebody extremely dangerous out there." He silenced them with both hands patting the air. "I know, you are fully aware of that. It's personal for you. But we don't want any more victims of this killer. Ladies, please don't take that lightly."

"How could we ever forget it?" Katie said. Tears welled in her eyes.

Mary said: "We know danger's all around us. A killer targeting certain people. Knowing that, however, if not for us, you wouldn't know about this new murder."

Brogan rubbed the side of his head. "Right, another to add to the growing list…" He stopped, looking down at the table and over to the skirting board, avoiding their eyes, like a child who had said too much to a suspicious mother.

"List?" Mary said. "Of more–"

"We don't want any more bodies," Brogan said.

Katie began crying. Mary reached across to hold her hand.

Brogan pulled a handkerchief from his pocket, looked at it, put it away. He changed the subject.

"You seem to have a lot of time off," he said, gazing at Mary.

"Necessary at the moment. Does it bother you, Detective Sergeant Brogan, that I may have more time off than you do?"

"I'm used to it. Most people work shorter hours than I do." And have more lenient bosses. He sighed. "So, Mr Hardwicke is quite generous in allowing you time off?"

"We only came to report our discovery. We should go."

Brogan looked at his notebook and wrote something in it. He looked up briefly at Katie, then at Mary.

"Have you seen Colin Martin today?"

Mary put a hand to her mouth. "I haven't been in today. Why do you ask?"

Instead of answering, Brogan changed the subject. "The boy who drowned some years ago. Peter Martin. That unfortunate lad was Colin and Edie Martin's son, wasn't he?"

Mary blinked. Looked at Katie whose face mirrored Mary's bewilderment.

"I'm sure you know that; why do you ask?" Mary said. When Brogan didn't answer, she said: "He… That really hit them hard… Of course.

"Long time ago. It was an accident."

The detective's eyebrows bobbed. "You think? We know that was the accepted verdict on the tragic event."

"Event?" she said. "It was an accident. Tragic. His parents will never get over it."

Once again, Brogan abruptly changed the subject. Mary sat back, took her hands off the table and placed them in her lap. She gave Katie a quick look, but she was watching Brogan.

"Do you know where your friend Jack is?"

"I'm expecting him to be outside, waiting for us. He rang me after he was released here, this morning.

"We didn't expect to be here this long."

Brogan closed his notebook and stood. Mary and Katie followed suit and headed for the door after him. He paused with his hand on the doorknob and turned back to them.

"Oh, Miss Durkin, you can visit your mother any time. Tell your brother that, too. With an officer in the room."

They walked quickly into the reception area. Jack got up from a chair against the wall. Katie and Mary raced to embrace him.

Mary was the first to disentangle herself. She waited for Katie to let go and pulled him towards the street.

Katie stopped Mary at the door.

"What about your hand? That constable was going to bandage it properly."

Jack lifted her arm and asked her what had happened.

She shrugged. "It's all Katie's fault." She smiled at Katie. "I don't see her." She hesitated. "Let's go. I'll fix it at home."

"But what about the blood sample?" Katie said. Jack looked puzzled.

"They know where to find me."

24

BEV

I'm scared... Unknown voices from unseen faces. Where are mine... Ray and Jack and Katie? Voices that fill my life? Hiding? Giggling together in a wardrobe? No... silly... So silly. Crazy, my mind. That... scares me. So much. Only strangers' voices around me, kind, impatient some, not one a friend, not one loves me. Frightens me ... my can't think clear... Murky. Sometimes clear... Not sure where... Or why? Man from nowhere... Pain from everywhere... Can't grasp it, slides out of my grip. Not my home, my kitchen, my bedroom, my anyplace. My wonderful Ray, oh Ray, Jack, Katie. Not here and no tears come. Why can't I cry? I must... so scared. Trying to sleep again... am I asleep? My eyes won't open, too heavy, so... My life withering, fading... No control... Feel ... what is ... Scared... So ...

* * *

THURSDAY 2.15pm

Jack, Mary and Katie came out of the lift on the second floor and headed confidently towards Bev's ward. The policeman on duty watched their every step. Katie said: "Mum's door's shut."

"Will be sometimes for ... Umm ... hospital sort of reasons," Jack said.

The door opened and a nurse poked her head out. She looked both ways and said something to the constable. He nodded. She withdrew and closed the door.

"She should be looking after Mum, not chatting to cops," Jack said.

Mary chuckled. "Give her a break. I'm sure she's giving Bev proper attention."

"Might be making a date for after work," Katie said. "He's a good sort. Young."

Mary took her arm. "Hang on, girl. Haven't you got your hands full already with—"

"Excuse us."

A doctor and nurse rushed past them, heading for Bev's ward.

"That's Doctor Robbins," Mary said.

"They're going into Mum's room," Katie said.

"Still shutting us out," Jack said.

"Come on," Mary said, "we'll find out what's going on–if anything is."

"Why did they close the door?" Katie said.

"Maybe some medical procedure," Jack said.

"Might be shut from time to time. When we've not been here," Mary said.

Jack and Katie nodded, eyes fixed on the door. Mary saw she hadn't persuaded them that this was an everyday occurrence any more than she had persuaded herself.

Another nurse came out and spoke with the constable. He nodded several times while keeping his eyes on the three would-be visitors standing near the closed door. The nurse quickly turned and re-entered the ward.

When Jack stepped towards the door, the policeman moved faster, planting his considerable self in the centre of the corridor, blocking any further approach to the ward entry. He held up his hands.

"Hold it there, please, folks. I can't let you in this ward at this time."

"I only want to see my mother," Jack said, taking another step. "To find out what's happening."

The constable stood firm, both hands up, palms facing them.

"We need to know if Mum's alright," Katie said.

"I am sorry, I am not permitted to allow any visitors in here," he said, emphasising this by pushing the door with one hand to ensure it was properly shut.

"But —" Jack began.

"That's not fair," Katie said, moving alongside her brother.

"Now, Ms Katie Durkin, you are not one to say it's not fair that we stop you from entering the room of a woman who has already been attacked by a person, or persons, unknown. I believe you were running around the streets with a carving knife the other night."

Mary said: "She didn't harm anybody with it. She'd escaped from abductors, probably killers, that you guys didn't even know about. Having a weapon was a good idea, under the circumstances. Don't you agree?"

The officer didn't say whether he agreed or not, but his unmoving posture indicated they had to offer a bit more to shift him. He looked about Jack's age; too early in his career to depart from strict instructions.

Mary turned away, but before the constable could respond in any way, she swung back, smiled with a sort of non-smile.

She said: "Katie got tired of waiting for the local constabulary to rescue her."

Jack said: "Detective Sergeant Brogan told us we can visit Mum."

"Yes," Katie said.

"I am aware of that, Sir. However, this is not a police requirement. There is a medical matter requiring attention."

Katie cried out and clutched Jack.

"Don't you think Mrs Durkin's son and daughter should be told what's happening?" Mary said.

A tall, sun-tanned, nurse in her 30s, rushed briskly along the corridor, patting the air in front of her with both hands, .as if clearing a way through underbrush.

"Hush, hush, don't you know there's a lot of sick patients around here? Especially right in there."

"That's my Mum," Katie said. "What's wrong?" Jack said. "Tell us, for god's sake."

"You will have to ask the doctor."

"Will you see if Doctor Robbins will come out?" Mary said.

The nurse looked at the constable, who shrugged.

"I don't think doctor could leave his patient right now," she said.

"We understand. Perhaps you could check with the doctor." She smiled at the nurse and then at the constable, figuring she might get extra mileage from one sweet smile.

"Maybe Doctor Robbins will be ready for a break, soon," she suggested.

Without a word, the nurse went into the ward, quickly closing the door before anyone could see inside.

Mary hugged them together and they stayed in a tight group waiting for news to come through the door. It came in a few minutes with the return of the nurse.

They separated into individuals and looked at her unsmiling face.

"Well?" Jack asked.

"Doctor Robins is very much occupied in treating Mrs Durkin. He regrets that he can't talk to you at the moment."

"Is Mum going to die?" Katie's voice wavered.

"He must tell us what's happening," Jack said.

The nurse said: "You will have to go outside if you can't behave quietly."

For reasons best known to himself, the constable apologised to the nurse, adding: "They will be leaving soon, sister." He turned back to the noisy three, who were not showing any sign of leaving.

The constable said: "I can't do anything about this. You must all leave now."

As if to ease their concerns, he said: "I am sure it will be as the nurse said. The doctor will inform you as soon as there is anything new to report on Mrs Durkin's condition."

He moved to stand beside the nurse, facing the other three, waiting for them to leave.

Jack swore under his breath. Mary squeezed his hand and whispered that they weren't going to get anywhere and might as well go.

She took a few paces towards the two guardians of the ward. The constable stiffened as if uncertain of Mary's intentions. He spoke quietly to the nurse, who also seemed ill at ease.

"Excuse me, Sister," Mary said, "We would appreciate it if you could tell us what you know about Mrs Durkin's condition."

"You have to ask the doctor that." Of course, we would.

"Bloody hell," Jack said. Mary grabbed his swinging right arm, stopping it an instant before his fist would have banged on the wall.

"Stop that," the nurse said, alarm raising her voice to a level above what visitors were permitted. She glanced at the officer, who shifted from one foot to the other, but didn't speak.

The nurse turned away from Jack and spoke to Mary. "Look, miss, I can tell you that Mrs Durkin is still unconscious —"

"Oh Mummy," Katie said, grabbing Jack's arm. He hugged her.

He said: "Detective Brogan told me Mum might be coming out of the coma."

"Unfortunately, sir, detectives are not usually medically trained."

The constable coughed away a smile.

"There has been a setback today. That is obvious to you." She looked at each of them in turn. "However, there have been signs that Mrs Durkin may come out of the coma. Slight signs. Don't get your hopes up just yet."

She started back along the corridor. As she passed them, she said out of the corner of her mouth: "You didn't hear that from me." She hurried off.

Mary turned to the constable. "That was kind of her," she said. "Quietly bending the rules without the world ending."

She flashed him a bright smile. "Constable, we are arranging the funeral for Mr Raymond Durkin. We need to know when his body will be released." She hoped she was using the correct terminology.

The answer didn't surprise her. They would have to talk to Detective Sergeant Brogan about that, or maybe the Coroner. He wasn't sure.

They left, Jack angry, Katie crying, Mary frustrated because she couldn't take away the causes of the anger or the pain. Helpless to stop crying and swearing, she herself struggling to keep from doing both–out loud, anyway.

As they walked across the carpark, Katie said she wondered if her mother would have heard their voices through the closed door, even while in a coma. None knew. Each hoped so. Each, more deeply, feared what news the next 24 hours would bring.

25

SMITHSON

Young Durkin calls it police harassment. Can't blame him any. Young bloke's got a lot to cope with. How it is. No way we can solve crimes without questioning folks. Getting in their faces. So Jack, here I come, going where Brogan wants me.

Won't appreciate me popping in here. Might keep lid on his smart-arse stuff. Being under eye of his boss. Customers, too. Acts–that's probably it, acts– composed for a young bloke whose family's reeling in midst of murder and mayhem. Strong? Hard man? Able to hold emotions together in public. More than I did … Then … Or is he the one who… Doesn't add up.

Ahh, sees me, the intruding nemesis. Frowns as if a blowfly has buzzed across his face. Shakes his head.

His middle-aged customer turns. Sees me. Says something to Jack. They laugh. Just have to wait.

Then, we'll hear what Jack has to say about our latest revelations.

* * *

FRIDAY 11am

When Constable Smithson walked into the small hardware shop, Jack looked over the customer's shoulder, his face a mixture of surprise and annoyance. The manager, Clive Jacobs, at the far end of the counter, poring over paperwork, pen in hand, reading glasses tight on nose, also looked displeased when he raised his head. However, he returned to his papers after glancing at Jack.

Smithson was sure Jack would assume he hadn't come to buy a lawnmower or even a chisel.

It wasn't his choice to speak with Jack at work. Plenty of other hours in the day, he had argued. But Brogan had insisted, which

175

was as good as 'ordered' when a detective sergeant was doing the insisting.

Still, Smithson had begrudgingly told himself the new information inserted intriguing possibilities into the investigation.

Smithson stood just inside the door, waiting for Jack to finish serving a man, who wanted to buy an electric drill. Jack was describing the features of three drills in boxes on the counter. The man asked to hold each drill, "to get the feel of it, you know".

So, Jack unpacked the drills. The customer wielded each in turn, bouncing it, moving his hand from side to side, lowering it below his belt, then quickly raising it and aiming it around the shop, sometimes closing one eye.

Thinks he's an Old West gunfighter, Smithson thought, wishing the fellow would holster the weapon and buy the bloody thing.

This new information was going to shake Jack up. Whether it was relevant to this case was another matter.

He resisted looking at his watch. Too obvious. He studied the display stand near him. Its plastic shelves were untidily stacked with books, magazines, leaflets, all implying that anyone, all-thumbs beginners, could build decks and retaining walls and treehouses and trellises and benches and sheds and fountains and …

Smithson turned from the pack of lies aimed at would-be home handymen—and, no doubt, handy-women, he thought, his do-it-without–you wife in mind. He sighed.

Jack flicked occasional glances at the policeman, standing like a guard near the door. Smithson turned to study the shop's products. It wasn't his sort of store, but a few items attracted his interest, all power tools. He would return for a closer look when things settled down. His eyes roamed over the arrays of power and hand tools, bigger implements for the garden, from lawnmowers parked near the window to brush cutters, chainsaws and line trimmers on the side wall. There were wall and floor tiles, small containers of nails and screws and …

His eyes stopped their lackadaisical wandering to focus on the paint corner, where more than a dozen spray paint cans were lined up, chest high. There were gaps in the ranks. Smithson noted a wider gap between the last black can and two red ones. Higgins had not reported anything useful from his roundup of hardware and similar stores. Not surprising. It was Higgins.

He went to Jacobs, who was still bent over two piles of papers.

"Excuse me, Mr Jacobs," Smithson said. When Jacobs looked up, he introduced himself and asked if the store had a record of spray can purchasers.

"Of course. Normal business practice."

"Who bought the missing black spray cans?" He pointed at the display. Jack was watching them. Jacobs turned around and sat at a small desk squeezed into a corner behind the counter. After a minute or so pressing keys and peering at the screen, the manager turned back to Smithson.

"Mr Colin Martin. An accountant, I believe. I checked it after your colleague asked the same question a couple of days ago."

"You told him that?" He spoke through gritted teeth.

"He hasn't been back. I asked him to give me twenty-four hours. I was busy with a customer at the time and he couldn't wait."

Bloody Higgins. "Thank you, Mr Jacobs. Constable Higgins has been tied up." Should be.

Smithson headed back to his post by the door, fuming inside. He was relieved to see Jack's customer had made his choice. It was a solid-looking, shiny red machine and Smithson surprised himself by wishing it was his. That would cause a few disbelieving laughs at home. If he ever mentioned it.

He wondered if Jack might give a discount if he treated him right, within the law, of course. Nahh. Specially not if he was arrested for murder.

Before the man walked out, face shining, hugging his new toy, Smithson was striding towards Jack, intent on beating any new customer who might walk in. He hardly needed to bother. Jacobs was free and the junior assistant, Edwin, had returned to the shop after his lunch break. This was just as well, because a young man in blue overalls sauntered in. Seeing the policeman heading for

Jack, the customer changed direction towards Jacobs, who was standing behind the counter on the right.

Jacobs was watching Smithson approach Jack and jumped when the man in overalls said: "I want advice, if you're not too…"

Jack slowly raised his head from the remaining boxes when Smithson stood at the counter. He didn't speak.

"Excuse me, Mr Durkin, can you spare a few minutes, please?"

Jack looked around before answering, as if checking, hopefully, for a line of customers waiting, but even the man in overalls was about to leave, thanking Jacobs for the bulky plastic bag he was handed. Edwin shuffled sideways to join his boss.

Smithson waited another moment for Jack to reply. Then he said: "I have new information that may help our enquiries–"

"You've got something on the killer?" Jack said. "Have you got him?"

Smithson held up a hand. "I need to ask you about matters that have come to our attention."

If Jack was worried by Smithson's words, it didn't show on his face, but he glanced along the counter, avoiding the constable's eyes for several seconds. Smithson followed his gaze to see Jacobs and Edwin imitating an illiterate couple trying to understand instructions on the side of a paint can; a task made more difficult because they held it upside down.

Jack and Smithson exchanged a split second of smiles.

Back to business.

"Can't it wait until tonight? I'm going to the hospital with Mary in a little while."

"Sorry, Mr Durkin. I understand that any time is bad for you in the present circumstances. I heard your Mum suffered a setback yesterday. How is–"

"Doctor said she's stable. Suppose that means no worse, no better. Mum's tough. Hanging on."

He checked his watch. Smithson ignored the hint.

"Good. I'm sure the doctors will do everything they can." He paused. "It's best we talk now. Surely Mr Jacobs will give you a bit of slack. Not too busy." Smithson thought he should've asked the manager first.

"It comes and goes. He's been pretty good. I'm only in today to help with re-ordering stock." Including black paint spray cans? "Okay," Jack said. "Let's get it over with. What is it now, Constable?"

He got straight to the point.

"Did you go to school with Gregory Mullins or Harry Jones?"

Smithson saw Jack was taken aback by what must have seemed an irrelevant question. He gave him time to take it in. Then: "Ring any bells?" It obviously did, but what tune was playing?

When Jack spoke, he was composed, expression neutral. "Both. We weren't mates."

Smithson noted Jack hadn't asked why the police were interested in fellow school students. Perhaps too weary, laden with family distress, to care. Get it over, he had said.

"They left Manderville a while ago," Smithson said. "Separately, not the same time."

"I heard that. But I lost track of them after school. We all — most of us — went our own ways."

"It happens," Smithson said. "Were they popular, well liked?

"At school?" Jack pulled back from the counter so abruptly he trod on an empty box. His scoffing laugh was loud in the small shop and Jacobs gave him a disapproving look. Edwin giggled.

"Hated. They were well hated. Bullies." He stopped suddenly and bent to pick up the box, which he placed on the counter, carefully, as if it still contained a fragile item as the label cautioned.

Smithson gazed steadily at Jack while he opened the box flaps. He put his hand inside. Closed the flaps again. The officer waited.

Two men walked in and stopped. They spoke quietly to each other. One said: "Yeah, yeah. Let's..." The rest of the sentence was lost as they turned and walked into the street.

Jack tapped fingers on the box. When he spoke, it came in a rush: "Why are you asking about Jones and Mullins all of a sudden? Brogan asked about Mullins, too. Why the sudden interest? In the middle of an investigation into my Dad's murder? Did they do it? The two of them?"

Smithson checked to see if anyone was within earshot. "Our enquiry has widened."

"Who now? Is — " He looked alarmed.

"Nobody close to you has been harmed."

Jack leant forward, hands on the counter. His relieved outrush of breath rustled a label remnant on the box.

"You said you didn't know where Jones and Mullins live now." He paused. "I'm afraid they don't live anywhere. They are both dead." He spoke softly but clearly.

Jack stopped fiddling with the box and pushed it to the floor.

"Both deaths are considered – are known to be – suspicious," Smithson said.

Jack stepped back, his feet tangled with the box. He grabbed at the wall for balance. Swearing, he stamped the box flat. He straightened and turned to Smithson, who was keeping his lips zipped, ensuring no smile escaped.

"Murdered?" Jack said. "Two more murders?"

"We have reason to believe that neither death was accidental."

"Murdered? Both? Together?"

"Not so loud." Smithson held up his right hand and looked across the shop. Jacobs and his assistant were moving a lawnmower to another spot nearer the window, trying to do so as quietly as possible, whispering as they manoeuvred it into place. Smithson wondered if they were concerned about disturbing the interview or to hear it better.

He continued: "Not the same time. Not the same day. Jones died in Sydney. Stabbed to death late at night in a hotel car park. Mullins was found dead in a farm dam, not far from Wagga Wagga. He had drowned."

Jack listened without interrupting, occasionally glancing at Jacobs.

"Do you know anything about their deaths, Jack?" Enough of Mr Durkin.

Jack shook his head. "First I've heard of them."

Smithson didn't reveal the details of their tortured ends which would give him nightmares for years.

Jack asked when they had been killed.

"About two weeks before your mother was assaulted," Smithson said.

Jack wrinkled his nose. "But I don't get what do these things, in other towns, cities, have to do with–"

"There is a link with Manderville. We now know of a past murder here in town and two former Manderville citizens probably killed as a consequence of that earlier murder."

"Earlier? Not Dad?"

Smithson shook his head. Out the corner of his eye he saw the other two men were quietly doing nothing. "Not directly."

"Either did or didn't," Jack said.

"About ten years ago, a young boy drowned in the creek here. Peter Martin. Do you remember it?"

Jack hesitated, clearly unsettled.

"It was big news. Tragic accident."

"Tragic, certainly. Maybe not accidental."

"Shit, man, you saying the poor bugger…" He left the sentence unfinished and ran a hand over his head, ruffling his hair, leaving black tufts sticking up and a spiky ridge over his forehead. Smithson resisted pulling his comb out to tidy it.

Jack muttered, as if to himself: "After all these years …" He looked up. "Why?"

Despite the implications of the new information, Smithson couldn't help feeling sorry for the young man. Lot of traumatic stuff for anyone, let alone one not many years past his teens. He had been a dozen years older when his inattentive driving had killed Pam. Didn't help that he had been punished with a permanent limp or that the other driver was convicted. Remarrying hadn't shaken off the guilt, an ever-watchful tail lurking in the shadows.

Now, he was going to add guilt to Jack's already heavy load of black emotions. Must be better jobs. Here, for example, even with old Jacobs as boss.

Two men came in and went to the paint section. They talked loudly about a big paint job. Smithson turned his head to look at them. Abruptly, their conversation dropped to whispers. One laughed, the other said something that brought a nod from his mate. They headed for the door so fast they gave the gesticulating, fast-talking Jacobs no chance. By the time he reached the door, the potential customers were lost, several metres away, crossing the road. Jacobs came in mumbling under his breath. He gave a wry unsmile at Smithson.

Jack said: "Better move into the kitchen, Constable. Be a bit out of sight."

His hand indicated an alcove behind a short length of wall. Kitchen was too grand a name for the small space. But they would be hidden from much of the shop. Squeezed into the alcove were three unpacked cartons and a bar fridge, which jutted out from under a green bench. A tap dripped into a sink, which was surrounded by an untidy jumble of tea-and-coffee-making items: mugs, partly crumpled carton of long-life milk, a yellow plastic bowl containing coffee-speckled sugar, teaspoons, large jar of coffee, open box of teabags, chipped white saucer of swollen used teabags. A jug and toaster stood at the back, plugged into a double adaptor.

It was an uncomfortable fit for the two men – made more so when a red-faced Edwin squeezed past to go to the toilet, which was behind a green door at the end of the alcove. Smithson took a deep breath, sighed. Jack looked at him and shrugged, as if saying "when you gotta go, you gotta go". Smithson wished he could go out of the shop and back to the station. He finally checked his watch and sighed again.

They waited in silence for Edwin to come out. Smithson was relieved - as was, no doubt, Edwin – when the toilet flushed and flush-faced Edwin wriggled past, apologising to the constable.

When the young shop assistant was back behind the counter, Jack said: "You won't scare customers away in here, Constable."

"At least there's that," Smithson said.

"I have to go. Mary will be waiting for me."

"One more thing.'

"Always is," Jack said, with a theatrical sigh.

"Maybe so. Jack, we found a confession on the front seat of Mullins' car, which was parked close to the dam, in which his body was discovered. By the farmer's wife, by the way."

"Confession to what? You said Mullins was dead when someone bashed Mum. To killing the boy?"

"Our enquiries point to Peter Martin being deliberately killed."

"By Mullins and Jones?" Jack asked.

"This was long before this week's crimes in our town."

"But what did the confession say?"

Jack's impatience was plain to see, but Smithson knew he had to be careful in what he said. He also wished he had called a spade a spade. Crimes? Murder and attempted murder and…

Smithson asked Jack if Mullins and Jones had bullied him at, or after, school. No. Although they were older, Jack was bigger. He reckoned they were afraid of him.

"Typical bullies," Jack said. "They only picked on smaller kids."

"Such as Peter Martin?"

Jack nodded. "What did Mullins confess to?"

"It was hard to read," Smithson said. "Scribbled under duress." Torture. "It said–"

"Please excuse me, officer." It was Jacobs.

"Toilet?" Smithson asked. Damn.

"No, no, no," Jacobs said. "Just wondering if you will be much longer. I could do with some coffee." He smiled.

"All right, Mr Jacobs, I don't expect to be much longer. I am grateful for your patience." If Brogan had listened, this would have taken half as long at the station. He waited until Jacobs left them.

"Jack, were you there, on the creek bank, on the afternoon that Peter Martin drowned?"

Jack took a second gazing past Smithson into the shop before answering. "I was there before that happened. I didn't know until later that night." He paused. "Not on the bank. On the bridge. Above that part of the bank."

"You and Thomas —"

He nodded. "Me and Tucker."

Smithson moved to be half out of the alcove. He was pleased to see both manager and assistant serving customers.

"Better wrap this up. Your boss has waited long enough for his coffee."

Jack grinned. "Don't worry about him. Jacobs doesn't drink coffee or tea." His smile disappeared. "I always thought Peter was alone when he fell in the water or somebody would have tried to save him."

"According to Mullins' purported confession," Smithson said, studying Jack's face, "there were two other people there that afternoon, besides him and Jones. He named you as one of the two who refused to help the little boy."

26

MARY

Something's wrong with him. Something more. More than bad news about Bev. We discussed that. Shore each other up. Something else in his silence. What more? How can anything be worse? Plain to see, impossible to hear. Brushes my concern away. Who now? Not Katie. She's safe with Meg and Doug.

His eyes are tired, red, but more than that. Not focusing. Looking at me, but don't think he's seeing me. Speaks, barely parting his lips. Kisses like he speaks.

He snaps at me. I shut up. He rejects my hug. I stand, limp, try to understand. Oh, great. Now tears. I turn away, wipe them. Be strong.

Emotions pull at his face, like a baby's exploratory fingers. Sadness. Despair. Hopelessness.

Something new. Fear? How can I tell? Never seen that. He's never been frightened of anything. Might see it, newly minted, on my face. I'm scared as hell... For Jack. For me. For us. For Bev. For Katie.

We all must wear ravaged faces. See here, folks, the new-season Durkin look...

Don't cry. He reaches for me but drops his arms before they touch. I hug him again. He stands, almost slumps, unresisting, unresponsive.

I dread asking again what's wrong... But I must. We're together in this.

* * *

FRIDAY 6pm

Mary looked down at Jack, slumped in a lounge chair, staring at the floor, hands together, arms dangling between his legs.

"Please, darling, tell me what's wrong," Mary said. She waited several minutes but Jack didn't look up, let alone reply. She tried again, moving to him and touching his hair.

"I love you. I want to share this… this thing that's causing you so much … new pain." Or fear?

He looked up now and for a heartbeat Mary thought he was going to cry, but he got up and went to her, and hugged her so tightly that she wondered if she could live without breathing. Then his mouth closed over hers and she no longer cared about such mundane matters as breathing.

After too few minutes, they parted and Mary said: "Tell me, Jack."

He paused, took a deep breath and told her. "Three, Mary," he said. "Killed."

She pulled away to arm's length, her heart thumping, mouth dry, face pale.

A simple question. An horrific answer. Some questions are better not asked. But how would that change anything? It is what it is. Too much for Jack to bear alone.

She was afraid to speak. Afraid to ask who.

"Not again. More –" She paused. Don't beat around the bush. "Who now?"

The answer surprised her.

"Mullins and Jones."

Mary dropped on the three-seater and fell back in relief. She felt guilty about that relief, knowing it was an inappropriate response to news of deaths.

Jack sat alongside Mary and put his arms around her. He kissed her cheek. He clung to her and his breath tickled her throat and she felt the wet of tears on her face. She was suddenly afraid again. There was more to come. Jack had named only two of the three people he said had been killed. She trembled and he asked if she was cold. She shook her head and waited, with foreboding, for more explanation.

She knew Jack had never been close to the two bullies. Quite the opposite. And she was sure they had been at the forefront of those who had mocked Jack in his humiliation at the park that terrible day. So, why was he in such a state? Was everything catching up with him? No surprise. She hugged him tighter.

"Mullins and Jones? From school?" she said, stating the obvious, so unsettled by Jack's distress at this 'unrelated' news that she was unable to come up with anything else.

"The …" She stopped herself saying "bullies". This was not the time to label them as such. After all, they were murder victims.

Jack had no such compunction.

"Yes, the school bullies have been murdered." He put both hands on his knees.

Mary anxiously waited to learn who the third victim was. However, Jack sat without speaking, apparently lost in thought. She decided to ask. Instead, offered to make coffee. "Later," Jack said. She was craving a cup but it was important to stay with Jack until the whole story was out. He was still edgy.

"Yep," she said, "Let's wait a while." She covered his hands with her right hand.

He repeated himself, softly, almost as if thinking aloud. "Killed. Murdered."

"Both?" she asked, knowing the answer, trying to encourage him to name the third person.

And, hopefully, relax when the words flowed, taking her into his confidence. She squeezed his hands.

"That's two," she said. "What about the third person? Or did you mean two—?"

He pulled his hands away and stood, glaring down at her.

"Don't treat me like an idiot. You pleaded for me to share what I had to say, but then you tell me I don't know what I'm saying."

Shocked by this outburst, Mary stood and went to him but he pushed her away. She sat back on the lounge and waited for him to continue. She hoped he would.

When Jack didn't speak or move for several minutes, Mary got up without a word and walked towards the kitchen. He spoke then.

"That's right walk away. Where the hell are you going?"

"I need coffee. Can I —"

"I said I didn't want any bloody coffee."

She shuddered but left the room without a word. When she returned, coffee mug in one hand and a biscuit in the other, Jack was sitting on the lounge. She sat, took a long drink and put the mug on the small table. She drank and nibbled as she waited for him to say something. No shouting. Anything, please. Except shouting.

"Mary," he began, as she brushed biscuit crumbs off her blouse, not caring about them falling on the rug. Not tonight..

"Smithson came to the shop today," he said eventually. "Told me about Jones and Mullins and…" Paused. "Other things."

Mary nodded sagely, as if this was, all normal so far, but dozens of questions were clamouring for answers. She decided to leave the number of victims for now. She would let Jack tell it his way.

Mary asked: "Why did Constable Smithson tell you?"

"Mullins supposedly left a confession to another murder."

Mary couldn't see how this answered her question. It only added others to the hand-waving queue in her mind. She would need more coffee before the night was over.

"Did they kill your Dad? Did they come back to Manderville?"

Jack said the two had been killed before his Dad was shot, and his mother assaulted.

"So, what was the confession about? Stealing pocket money from little kids? Did he tell you?"

"He did." He was tight-lipped, grim. Like a grey day without hope of the sun peeking through, Jack's clouded face offered no prospect of a smile ever appearing.

"Those bastards killed Peter Martin —"

"No." Mary grabbed Jack's shoulder so hard he winced but any peep of pain was lost in her shriek. "No, Jack, no."

She released her grip on his shoulder and turned to him, eyes wide, blinking, searching, as if for a sign she had misheard. Tears glistening on her cheeks showed she knew she hadn't. Every word was clear, it was the fact that was inconceivable.

She took a couple of tissues from the box on the coffee table and wiped her eyes.

"But why? why would they do such a terrible thing to an innocent little boy?"

"I don't think anybody knows. Smithson couldn't give me a reason."

Jack jumped up and went to the kitchen. He returned with a glass of water and sat next to Mary. He drank some water and put the glass on the table. Smithson said: Mullins confessed that he and Jones did it. Mary struggled to believe anybody, let alone, former students at her school, could commit such an horrendous crime.

And why would he write a confession after all this time?

Jack picked up his glass again. Put it down without drinking.

"He didn't write it of his own free will."

Over Mary's gasps he continued. "He was tortured. Badly beaten and … other things. It was all spelt out on a page lying on the car seat."

Horrified, Mary feared there might be worse to come, but needed to know more. So, like a horror movie heroine tentatively climbing to the black at the top of the stairs, she pressed on.

"But… but. What…" A pause. She began again. "Who killed Mullins and Jones?"

"The man – cops believe it's a man – who killed my Dad."

"Oh my God, Jack." She pulled him closer, but he moved away again. He looked at her, his face a montage of emotions.

She said: "Everyone thought Peter fell in the creek. It was running full after a lot of rain. Poor kid didn't have a chance."

"He didn't have a chance," Jack said, his voice expressionless. "Held under until he died.

Mary was shaking, hand over her mouth. She had been caught in a nightmare for more than a week and now it was like she had sleepwalked into another terrifying room. Where was the way out? No exit sign from where she sat.

At last, she gained a modicum of control over her voice. "I taught Peter in Sunday school. A lovely, quiet boy; always attentive, respectful."

Mary stood, feeling the tears coming again. "I'm tired." She went to the kitchen and made herself another mug of coffee. She went back to the loungeroom and asked Jack if he would like one now. She was tempted to say "bloody coffee" but the night was fraught enough. She feared it would get more so. Jack was still on edge. She was sure the crunch was yet to come.

Jack shook his head. She sat and drank while Jack began speaking again.

Hearing his first words, Mary stopped drinking, the mug poised just below her chin.

"Smithson asked me why I hadn't told the police that I could have intervened."

"Shit, Jack, what are you saying?" Her hand was shaking, and she hastily put the mug on the table, leaving a trail of drips along the way. "Were you there? With those bastard murderers?"

"No," he shouted. "I wasn't there then. Before. Didn't know what happened after I walked away."

"Walked away? Leaving Peter with those… those… You could have saved his life, Jack." She tried to quieten the anger that sprayed her words out. Listen calmly until the full story is told. Will it get worse or better? Can't be as bad as… Not Jack.

She took a deep breath. So did Jack. He looked at his clasped hands and tried twice to continue but stopped each time. He looked at Mary as if needing her to explain it all. She kissed his cheek.

He was obviously struggling to find the right words. She thought none existed to justify what he said had happened.

He gave up and said weakly: "Nobody would've expected school kids to drown another kid. Would you have?"

"No," she said, a calmness in her voice that belied the screaming in her mind, "but I would not have expected Jack Durkin to walk away from anyone in need of help either. The Jack Durkin I know took action, stepped in to save a man from being robbed by one of those same bullies."

She put a hand on Jack's forearm. They looked at each other in silence for several minutes. In her mind, Mary re-arranged her words, adding and rejecting others, seeking a kinder way to express the way she felt; the way she wished she didn't feel. She wasn't a judgemental person; she got enough of that at home. Yet, here she was… like mother like daughter? No. Never. There was no gentler, honest, sequence of words. So she let it stand.

Jack broke the silence. "I'm sorry, Mary. I should have helped Peter. I never… We didn't think enough about the situation… It was an ordinary walk home from school. We didn't know it would become a murder scene. Not then. Not until Smithson told me."

"No," Mary said. She went to the round-backed cane chair at the desk and plopped down, head bowed, hands clasped. Jack murmured something she didn't catch, except for a mumbled "sorry". Too late for sorries. Too late for Peter. Too late for Edie and Col.

She needed coffee. Jack, too, probably. She stood, but before she could offer to get it for both of them, Jack spoke.

"This stuff happening now… It all started with me —"

"Darling, you can't be responsible for what's going on today." She stopped herself from adding "That's silly". She relaxed back in the chair. Not coffee time yet.

"Please, Jack, let's clear this up now. Tell me what happened back then. May help clear your mind."

Without looking at Mary, he began. "That day, however many years ago," Mary knew but didn't interrupt, "me and Tucker were dawdling along, talking about what sort of jobs we'd do when we left school in a year or two."

"As you do," Mary said.

"We'd had a careers symposium or expo at school that day. I suppose we were full of it, excited by jobs beyond Manderville. Flight engineer sounded good. Odd to think of it now. Don't think they even have them anymore."

Mary thought he was putting off the nitty-gritty of that terrible afternoon.

"Or even if there was such a job then. Brochure a bit tatty."

She wished he would get on with it, but listened intently, eyes fixed on his face. She also wished she had got coffee before Jack began talking about flight engineers.

"Tucker, ignoring that we both knew he would end up on his parent's chicken farm, was going on about being a surveyor. We were on the bridge by then and we heard a shout. A young boy shouting 'Tucker'. We stopped and heard other, quieter voices. We couldn't make out their words. Even if we had, I wouldn't remember them after all these years. Then the boy shouted my name.

"It was coming from below us, from the creek bank. We leaned over the railing. Peter Martin from third class was standing on the bank with Mullins and Jones who were facing him. His school bag was a few metres away in the grass."

"Little Peter," Mary said. "He must have been so frightened; bailed up by those hulking guys."

Jack didn't comment on that.

"I asked what was going on. Three faces looked up at us. The bullies smiled, Peter had a worried look."

"Who wouldn't in his situation?" Mary said.

"Tucker thought he might start crying. He yelled out that they were taking his pocket money and they were going to hit him if he told his parents.

"Then bloody fat Jones called out 'He's all right. Just chatting'. He gave Peter a playful shove."

"Peter wouldn't have been in a playful mood," Mary said.

"Sorry, my wrong word." Pause. "Mullins smiled even wider than before and agreed with his bully mate. He said, we should ignore kid's 'baby whinges'."

"So, you did," Mary said, jumping up, walking towards the kitchen and back again. She sat heavily at the end of the lounge away from Jack. "Go on," she said.

"Peter wanted us to go down and help him. He said we were 'as big as them'."

"Why didn't you?"

"We… we sort of …"

His voice faltered and Mary saw the glint of tears in his eyes. She patted his knee. "Take a break. I'll get us coffee. Won't be long."

"No, I'll get it."

He went to the kitchen and returned a few minutes later. "Jug's on."

Mary nodded and they waited looking at each other without speaking. A noise from the kitchen startled Jack. "What the bloody hell?" he said.

Mary was up. "No water in the jug." She ran to the kitchen and turned the jug off. She filled it at the tap. Jack stood in the doorway.

"Did I burn it out? Is it busted?"

'It's fine." she said, smiling. She clicked it on. "Be ready in a minute."

"I can't even boil water," he said.

"Sure you can. Just didn't have any water in there to boil."

"You better make it."

He turned and went back to the lounge. The jug automatically switched off. She sighed and made the coffee. She joined Jack on the lounge after placing two mugs on the squat table. Jack waited until Mary had taken a long drink. He didn't pick up his mug.

"They kept smiling at us, as if it was a big fuss about nothing.

"Peter said he wanted to go home. He said: 'Mum will wonder where I am.'"

Mary put her mug down. "Was Peter crying?"

"I don't think so. Whimpering a bit."

"Oh, Jack, the poor…" Mary put a hand to her mouth, muffling her words.

Jack kept talking and her sentence muttered to a stop "Me and Tucker told them to let Peter go."

Wow, Mary thought, that was taking strong action.

Jack continued: "Mullins walked across to get the schoolbag. He shoved it at Peter with a 'here you are, matey.'"

Mary remembered the schoolbag was found in the creek, with lolly wrappers, cap gun and sodden homework sheets. Edie had told her that months later at work. Mary sobbed into her hanky. Jack glanced at her, and paused a moment before continuing.

"They mumbled something to each other. Then smiled up as if to see what we were going to do."

"What did you do, Jack?"

Her eyes, now tear-free, stared fiercely into his. He tried to speak but under Mary's unwavering gaze his words tangled. He broke the optic link and looked everywhere except at Mary. After several uncomfortable seconds, he spoke in a whisper. Mary said she couldn't hear him. He looked up at her and said loudly what Mary already knew but was hoping not to hear…

"We walked away." As simple as that. "Tucker turned away. Then me. We kept walking across the bridge. We didn't hear any crying or anything from the bank. There weren't any other kids or adults around. Just cars going past."

"Maybe one was driven by Edie, searching for her little boy," Mary said.

Jack didn't seem to have heard Mary, still back on the bridge.

"We walked on, comparing the merits of surveying and flight engineering —".

He stopped suddenly when Mary screamed: "Enough of the bloody surveyors and flight engineers."

He half rose then sat again, his face pale. She hated herself for adding to the horrors already filling his mind. "Sorry Jack," she said, voice tinged with hysteria. Calmer, girl, calmer. "Darling we're here now, not in the past. What's done is done." She reached over and picked up his untouched coffee. Cold now. She drank most of the remaining coffee in one long swallow.

"Not over for me, Mary. More punishment coming."

Crazy stuff. She finished the worst coffee she had ever drunk. Pulled a face.

"Punishments?" she said. "Nobody's talking of punishments."

"Why do you think Mum was bashed, Katie kidnapped? And why do you think Dad was shot dead?"

She could only stare at him, in disbelief. This was all beyond her understanding. He was talking nonsense.

"You see, Mary, he wants me to suffer the mental agony he has gone through. Kill my loved ones not me."

"Shit, Jack, this is crazy. He must be crazy."

"Or them," Jack said... "Or her. It could be Edie, I suppose, with the unidentified man."

Mary struggled to see the logic of what Jack was saying. An avenger from a decade ago. Vengeance from beyond the grave of a little boy? Murders in peaceful Manderville, even reaching kilometres away into another small town and further on to the big smoke — Sydney.

"But... but not just you," Mary said. "Tucker was there, too." She instantly regretted her words. Wished she could bite off her tongue.

"I knew you would blame me." Suddenly, angrily, stunning Mary. "You said it."

Mary's entreaties were buried beneath the ferocity of Jack's outburst. She went back to the cane chair. She turned towards Jack again.

"You do think I am the cause of Dad's death. You think Mum's in hospital because I left Peter to die ten years ago."

He stopped and glared at her.

Mary spoke quickly in the pause. "You're not to blame for what this maniac is doing. "You were schoolboys, what, fourteen? For goodness sake, Jack. No way you —"

"You think we could have saved Peter. I know you believe it."

Mary turned her face away from Jack's glare.

He ran to the desk, kicking one of the legs. Mary leapt out of the chair. She stood behind it, hands on the back.

"Jack. Jack, don't... don't do this. I do not think you caused any of the violence against your family."

She wondered if a stranger looking in just then might think otherwise. "How could you be blamed? You were just boys."

Jack sat in the chair vacated so quickly by Mary without a word. Mary put a hand on his shoulder. He shrugged it away. She stepped quickly back from the chair.

"Please, calm down. I'll get us something to eat. And decent, hot coffee. You didn't touch yours."

She turned towards the kitchen. Jack banged his fist on the desk. "I don't want any food or bloody coffee. Didn't you hear me before? I thought you loved me. Now you're saying I'm a killer's accomplice."

She stood aghast, stunned by a Jack she had never known. "You know I don't think such a ridiculous thing."

"So you're saying I'm stupid. That what you think?" He paused, glaring at her as if daring her to disagree. She blinked a tear away.

"No. Jack, darling, I love you. You must know that." Could love live in a whirlpool of murder, assaults, kidnapping, hatred, suspicion, fears, guilt, revenge and overwhelming grief? At this moment Mary doubted it. She had no strategies to deal with any of it. I'm just a bloody accountant.

She realised Jack was speaking again. She focused on his face, which was no longer its usual striking tan. It had coloured from its earlier sudden pale to a flushed red.

"I need somebody to love me, no matter what," he said. "To support me through all this shit. Unquestionably." She teared up, saddened that her support wasn't apparent. "I needed you, Mary."

She wanted to hug and kiss him but was sure he would push her away. Wait until he was talked out.

"But… Hey, what do I get? Hey? I find out your true feelings. You know I caused Dad's murder and… Mum… all that. Me. You blame me. So do I. I can't bear all this."

Mary's protests went unheeded. Jack strode out of the room without another word or a backward glance. Mary winced as the bedroom door slammed shut.

She stood, shaking. Too many tears to blink away. She wiped her eyes and cheeks, with tissues. After a while, she lifted the chair and pushed it under the desk. She pulled it back out and sat on it. She slumped forward, dropping her face onto her crossed arms.

Soon, though, she stood, her mind made up. She pushed the chair back. It caught on the carpet and she almost overbalanced.

She grabbed a handful of tissues to mop her face and forearms.

It was still dark outside when Jack came out early the next morning. The lounge room light was on. It was immediately clear that Mary was not in the room. He called her name several times and went into other rooms. She wasn't asleep in the spare bedroom. In the kitchen, he saw a note taped to the fridge door. He went closer, one single hesitant step after another, as if approaching a sleeping snake. Another step and he recognised Mary's neat printing. One more step, head bent, and the snake awoke, as he knew it would. And, as he expected, it struck, and he cried out in pain.

He ripped the pink notepaper off the fridge and re-read it. He crushed it into a ragged ball and threw it on the table. He filled the jug and switched it on. He took a mug from the shelf. He reached for the instant coffee jar. It had a new label – on pink paper – 'Bloody Coffee'. A grin escaped but he knew tears were not far behind.

He lifted a teaspoon of coffee towards the mug, but dropped it on the bench, spilling brown grains across the red top.

He left it and sat at the table, where he picked up the balled-up note and rolled it in his palm before unfolding it.

He read it again: 'My Darling, Please believe that though my love for you may appear buried beneath all this trauma it remains as strong as ever. But I can't stay with you, upsetting you the way I have. I am going to stay with Mum and Dad, for now. Better not to come to see me there, Jack. It will only cause you more stress. And I don't want that. We will be together again soon. Be on guard always. Love forever, Mary.'

Dropping it on the table, he stood and leaned his face against the fridge and cried out: "Mary, I need you, I am so sorry."

He switched the jug on again, and went to sit on the lounge, hands on knees, looking at the floor. The jug boiled, clicked off. Jack didn't look up.

HANDY GUIDE TO MANDERVILLE

Churches

By Reverend Ralph Pickins, Manderville Ministers Fraternal

Every Sunday hundreds of Manderville people, good Christian folk, gather to worship the Lord in the churches of Manderville. The main denominations are all represented in town. Christian folk here, support each other's faiths.

There is a thriving Minister's fraternal here in Manderville. We do a lot of good, helping those in need of food and spiritual support.

Our worship services are joyful occasions. We are all equal in the love of God. Despite what some unbelievers think, we Christians don't point the finger at anyone. All people, believers or not, are welcome to join with us at any time.

Whether a resident of the town or visitor, all are welcome to join any of the many functions the churches of Manderville hold every week. Details of activities are on the noticeboard outside each church. Please join the fellowship of the Lord Jesus Christ.

27

MARY

I better go. Before Mum does. Only been two days, nights. Better go… Oh, too loud. Must think we're deaf. Not good if Mum goes. My problem. Sorry Jack, not a problem. You have the problems: sadness, grief, shattered family, fear—and me. Now me. Bugger. She's coming. Phew. Here, not the front door.

* * *

SUNDAY 2.10pm

"You just sit right back down there, Mary," Mrs Bourke said, rushing into the living room, her long floral dress swirling around her thick legs as she tugged at a green apron tied around her ample waist. She clicked her tongue twice, gave up pulling and reached behind to fiddle with the apron strings. Undone, the apron dropped. She grabbed it centimetres from the carpet. She roughly folded it and held the bundle in her left hand. Mary remained standing near the wide window, looking into the garden, hoping for a glimpse of Jack. But the front porch was not visible from there. She turned and looked at her mother.

"Having trouble with the apron strings, Mum?"

"I won't have you going outside to see that man."

"If by 'that man', you mean Jack, he needs to see me. His father has been murdered. His mother may yet die." She paused. "You know that."

She strode towards the door to the hall, inadvertently knocking her mother's arm as she brushed past. The impetus of Mary's passage unbalanced her mother, who dropped the apron.

"Mary, don't be silly. You can't help him now. What you just said reinforces what I am saying — it is dangerous to be around that family."

Mary stopped at the door to the hall and turned back, her face angry.

"That family? That family is my family, too. No matter what you say. I love Jack Durkin and I am part of that family as well as this one."

Mrs Burke sat in a black leather lounge chair, arranging both hands together in her lap, on top of the apron. She looked at Mary.

"You know what I think of that family. I never liked you mixing with them. They are well-known to the police." As I am now, Mary thought.

"Mum, you are such a snob. You don't know how to value people."

Mrs Bourke looked flustered for a moment, then rearranged her face back into its smug, I-hold-all-the cards look.

She said: "I was the only parent to allow her child to attend that birthday party."

"Mum, we were just little kids."

"Nevertheless, I drove you there, into that lane. No other parent allowed their children to go. So, I guess you're right. I don't know how to evaluate people." She sat back with a thin smile. "In those days, anyway."

Mary said: "That wasn't the reason I was the only..." She stopped. It wasn't worth it.

"He might be a nice lad but look at his father. He's a drunk. And I hear he attacked his wife." She patted the bundled apron.

Mary went to the window and pulled a curtain aside and looked out again hoping to catch sight of Jack. If he was still at the door, he had given up knocking. Oh God, he'll walk away, rejected again. She felt trapped in an endless cycle of arguments; coming from both sides. No wonder she felt so tired.

With a sigh, she turned back to her mother.

"He's not anything now, Mum. He is dead. Shot. By the person who tried to kill Bev Durkin. "You know that, so why do you speak so disgracefully? I'm sorry, Mum, but that's what you're doing."

She paused. Mrs Bourke avoided eye contact.

Mary continued. "Jack needs me to help arrange his father's funeral. Bev can't help. She might die any time herself."

Mary waited at the window for her mother's response. She wouldn't wait long. She wanted to catch Jack, who had knocked once more.

Mrs Bourke frowned at the sound but didn't comment on it. She said: "It doesn't mean he didn't beat her up."

Mary strode to the centre of the room. A loud knock, repeated three times, stopped her two angry steps from her mother's chair. She half-turned about to return to the hall. But anger swung her around to face the focus of her fury.

"Bloody hell, Mum, you have no heart. I don't know you. Not like this." She was standing, hands on hips, staring down at her mother, who had shifted in her seat and was gazing out to the garden through the partly open curtain.

Mary went to the window, blocking her mother's view. She saw Jack walking up the path to the front gate. No. Don't go. Don't… Mary whirled and headed for the hall.

"Mary, I saw Mrs Durkin with that young teacher."

With one step in the hall, Mary turned around once more.

"Hell, Mum, that was years ago. Mr Hanrahan was helping Jack with his English."

Mrs Bourke laughed. "Sure, that was the story they gave. We knew better—"

"Who is this bloody 'we' that supposedly knows the real truth, but which is really only nasty, hateful gossip?"

Mrs Bourke stood and fiddled with a vase of flowers on the coffee table, pulling them out, shuffling them, putting them back, moving the vase a few centimetres across the table. Mary watched, waited patiently. Finally, Mrs Bourke looked up.

"We don't use that B-word in our house, Mary," she said. "My group of other mothers; we know what's going on around town."

Is 'bitches' an acceptable B-word, Mary wondered. "The filthier the better," she spat out. "I know better than all that rotten gossip. Jack talked to me about how he was struggling with English, with the book he was studying. Mr Hanrahan saw his potential. Knew the difficulties he faced at home and volunteered to help him over that hump." She had to end these delaying tactics and get out to Jack. There had been no knocking for a while now.

"Ha, you are so naive, Mary. You know I saw him and Mrs Durkin at church. I told you the Reverend Holcroft asked Mr Hanrahan to sit on the other side of the church, away from Mrs Durkin, when they arrived together. I was behind them—"

"I know, Mum. You gloated about it often enough. Your big ears listening for any hint of scandal."

"They had no right walking in together. Side-by-side. Our minister was quite correct separating them as they walked in."

Mary was disgusted by the triumphant look on her mother's face. She turned once again for the door and stepped into the hall. She called back over her shoulder: "So much spouting about Christian ethics, but no place for good Samaritans today, hey?"

"We have a very active charity auxiliary. We hold a meeting every month," Mrs Bourke said to her daughter's back from the hall doorway. Mary pulled her hand back from the front doorknob and turned to face her mother, who stood, face grim, arms folded. Mary knew the pose. Her mother was sure of her position and was waiting for Mary to acknowledge it and apologise. Not this time. Not this girl.

"Does anyone ever go outside that church hall? To see actual human beings? Real hurt? Real need? Real suffering? Or would that interrupt your cake and tea?"

Under this volley of questions, Mrs Bourke's arms unfolded and jerked around, as if unsure how to regain control with emphatic gestures. With a meaningless shake of both hands she retreated to the lounge room.

Mary followed her. "Trouble was, hardly anybody was helping poor Bev and her kids. Things were hard for them. And all you and your nasty-minded mates could do was spread malicious untruth about them. You disgust me."

"Mary," Mrs Bourke said in a calmer tone, "there's no future in this for you." She sounded close to tears. "Can't you see what this blot on our little town means? This is Manderville, not some dirty Sydney suburb." She flung her left hand towards the window, index finger aimed at one or the other place. Mary wasn't sure, though most likely it was wonderful Manderville. Mrs Bourke turned away from Mary and looked out the window.

"Still out there. Can't take a hint." She turned back to Mary. "Still hasn't replaced that old car," she said, clapping both hands together in a downward swipe, as if clearing them of dirt. With a case-proven glance at Mary, she said: "As I told you, many times, no future."

"It's my future. A future with loving, non-judgemental people. And you don't have to search far to find blots on the community. Turn your spotlight on your fellow members of the gossipers' auxiliary, who go to church every Sunday to worship a swear word."

Mrs Bourke gasped and lifted a hand to her mouth. Mary went into the hall and out the front door, slamming it. She stood for a minute on the doorstep. She felt guilty and regretted her angry — to her mother, certainly blasphemous —outburst.

Her mother shouted "Mary." Mary heard it as an appeal, not a command. She would try to apologise later.

She was probably on the phone to Dad right now. Something else to deal with later. Thank goodness she doesn't know Jack may have caused all… But for now…

Mary ran into the garden. Jack wasn't in sight. Her spirits lifted when she saw his car was still there and instantly sank at the sound of the engine starting.

She was happily surprised at the burning need she had to hold him again. First, catch him before he drove away. The car was slowly moving. Risking injury, she ran in front of it to the driver's side. The car jerked to a halt and Mary slid along the fender and down onto the bonnet, her shoes slipping on the road. Suddenly she was face-to-startled-face with the love of her life, through the windscreen.

Regaining her balance and poise, she tapped on the side window and blew him a kiss. He grinned widely and pushed the door open so quickly that Mary yelped and skipped back. She rubbed her right knee.

With her skirt hitched halfway up her thigh, and still vigorously rubbing the knee, she said: "Could have just asked me nicely to leave."

His face showed concern, his words something else. "Can I kiss it better?"

She stopped rubbing and her skirt dropped to a more proper place.

"Better not. Mum's probably watching. Already seen your violence, don't shock her further with your lust."

"Put me in her bad books?"

"Been there for a long time. Me too, now. I expect I'll be sent to my room without dinner tonight." She kissed away his sudden dismayed look with a peck on the cheek, which slid quickly to his mouth; and then he was embracing her and kissing her with the passion that she thought had drained from him. She was teary and when she pulled away from him his cheeks and shirt collar were damp.

A passing driver tooted. She smiled sadly and wiped her eyes.

"Mary, it's so terrible without you. I… I… Can't we…"

She pulled him gently towards the front gate, which was swinging open. Another mark against her, she clicked it shut and they walked hand-in-hand into the garden. They sat on a small, green, wooden bench. They looked into each other's eyes, like lovers who had been apart for months.

"Jack, I love you and I need you, but I also hurt you when you're suffering so much."

"I was confused, upset," Jack said. "I was wrong." He let her hand go to brush a fly from his forehead.

Mary kissed him again but pulled away before he could respond with the same wild abandon as in the street.

"It hurts me to be away from you, Jack. I want to help you. I will help you, the funeral, Bev, Katie."

He opened his mouth to speak, but Mary added "I'm so afraid that we'll break up forever."

"No, we won't, Mary. Not you and me." He stood and bent to kiss her forehead. "We know how to handle it now. Please." She took his hand. They looked around the garden, peaceful, serene, greens and browns and reds, yellows and whites. Quiet. A calmness. Calm after the storm? Or, Mary feared, calm before a bigger storm?

"We'll be all right," Jack said. "You'll see."

"I'm sorry, Jack." His face dropped and for a few seconds Mary wavered, and almost changed her mind. She bit her lip and squeezed his hand. "Just give it a bit more time. Maybe just a few days. I need to collect myself. I must be stronger for you."

"You've always been stronger than me."

"It's an act," Mary said. "For the audience. You're stronger than you realise. Believe in yourself."

"Never. Now, see how my weakness has destroyed our family. So…"

She heard the self-loathing in his voice and almost cried. What was she doing? How dare she make decisions like this, pretending to be wise, when all the time she was floundering, trying to make even one iota of sense from the tragedies spinning in her mind like dark clothes among a load of white in a washing machine.

She looked away following the flight of a white butterfly between two blue-speckled plumbago bushes. For a moment, she envied its carefree fluttering. She blinked back to reality at the sight of a spiderweb fanning out from the side fence onto a tall bush.

Jack said: "You're right, of course. What we have is too precious to risk losing through rows and misunderstandings."

He reached for Mary's hand. "I'd better go now. Your curtains are flapping unnaturally."

Mary laughed. "Might mean curtains for me when I go inside. Where will you go now?"

He looked at his watch. "Got an appointment, of sorts, with Tucker in twenty minutes. At the Memorial Gardens."

"Are you right with going there?" Mary asked. He nodded.

"Outside. Won't go in." He turned away for a few seconds, then back at Mary. "Tucker's clearing out for a while. Getting family to safety, he says."

"Hell. Jack. Maybe you ought to do the same."

"Can't. Not with Mum in hospital and Dad's funeral. Anyway, I won't leave you and Katie."

"Jack," Mary began.

"Don't, Mary. It's okay. For now."

He put his arms around her waist and kissed her cheek.

She saw his eyes conveyed a different message than his words. It was too much for her. She quickly kissed him on the lips, turned and ran into the house.

Jack walked back to his car and drove quietly away.

HANDY GUIDE TO MANDERVILLE

Our memorable parks and gardens

By Councillor Charles Brewster, Chairman of Manderville Parklands

Manderville is sometimes referred to as the 'Green Patchwork Town' because of its many large and small patches of green, dotted from one end to the other, from edge to edge. It is a beautiful sight from the air.

Of course, there are many colours as well as the varying greens of lawns and shrubs and trees. The Council's talented and highly experienced gardening staff, headed by Jim Brewster, ensures that there are many other colours of flowers and shrubs and also the foliage and blossoms of the trees. Liquid amber, maple, jacaranda and plane trees, along with many beds of annuals and perennials put on an ever-pleasing display of Mother Nature. These lovely oases are enjoyed daily by residents and visitors, young and old alike.

Peaceful places for rest and recreation are just minutes away from any home and even close by the main shopping precinct, where the pocket handkerchief Danton Park sits opposite the carpark.

Our town's greatest natural glory is the magnificent Manderville Memorial Gardens. Our largest parkland, these gardens are a showpiece of our gardening staff's skill and knowledge. As well as the well-chosen profusion of flora, there are tables, benches, barbecues, sheltered areas and a playground for children, who often spend hours happily playing together. A pond with ducks is another attraction in these beautiful grounds.

At the very centre is the outstanding monument to Manderville young men who gave their lives at Gallipoli and elsewhere. It is both sad and inspiring to stand and read the names of those brave citizens.

A memorable monument in memorable public gardens.

28

JACK

Funny how people say it's a nice day just because the sky's blue and the sun's shining. Like today. But it's a bugger of a day for me. Parked near the main entrance—forever the exit from my humiliation. No wonder Mary was surprised I was meeting Tucker here. Won't go in. Nice day then, too—for everyone else. Whole bloody town. Not me. Worst day of my life. Now it's way down the list.

Never leave my memory. Ever. Stuck in memories of everyone I've grown up with. Memorial Gardens, right. For me, not to the noble Anzacs' defeat, but to my ignoble thrashing.

Mary's right. Not a good place for me.

Where's Tucker? Should be here soon.

* * *

SUNDAY 3pm

Jack was impatient. The dashboard clock showed Tucker was late. Bugger. Tucker had picked this place on the road out of town because he was in a mad rush to get away.

A small bunch of school-kids ambled past, talking and laughing loudly. A couple of boys pushed each other back and forwards. Late alright. School's out.

Just kids having fun. Like they had been that Saturday arvo. Kids playing around in the sun. Yes, hot like today. He remembered sweaty.

Trouble is, like sometimes at his old home, fun at the start isn't always fun at the finish…

Arnold and dopey Bruce started it. Idiots then; still today, for that matter. Doing their imagined version of wrestling. Pushing and shoving each other. Half a dozen girls stood gossiping, pretending they weren't watching.

Jack smiled at the memory. Such young innocence in the sun. How did it go so wrong?

He stood well away from the two boys showing off. They tumbled, over and under each other, rolling near the girls' feet. They jumped back and giggled. Except for Sharon. Rather than skip away, she kicked out, connecting with Arnold's back. He yelped. Somebody laughed.

Sharon mocked their so-called wrestling. Boasted she could beat both of them "with one hand tied behind my back".

Where the hell is Tucker? Must think I've got nothing else to do.

Everyone laughed. Jack, too.

Bruce, who was under Arnold, poked his tongue out at Sharon. Unfortunately for him it coincided with Arnold's elbow unintentionally clamping Bruce's mouth shut.

"You silly, stupid bastard," he lisped. "See, You just made me bite my tongue."

His lisping speech only caused laughter, so he gave up and sat up, feeling his extended tongue.

"Oh, poor little boy, Sharon said. "Have you hurt your tonguie, wongie?"

Janice butted in: "You weakies wouldn't have a chance against Sharon."

"Who cares who can beat who?" Jack said.

"Yeah, who cares about sissy little girls?" Bruce shouted, pushing Janice in the back.

"Sharon could beat you, Bruce, and you, too, Johnny," Janice said.

Sharon started to walk away. Jack said he didn't give a stuff and turned away.

There was a bit of yelling and jokey insults and someone egged Bruce on to fight Sharon. He held his right elbow and reckoned his arm was "probably broken". Jeers and sneers, but no sympathy greeted his excuse. "Don't you mean your tongue," said Mary who had been quiet until then.

Suddenly, Jack was pushed into Sharon, who was looking the other way, smirking at Bruce. She had both hands in the pockets of her baggy khaki shorts and almost lost her balance, before whipping her arms free to flail about.

Arnold said: "Go on, Johnny. You're the best fighter here."

Jack didn't know where he got that idea. Mary said he wasn't. "This is silly," she said. "Leave him alone."

"You show her," Bruce said, shoving Jack at Sharon again, his arm apparently no longer broken.

Jeez, where's Tucker? Late. I need to get going. See Mum.

Sharon swore and turned on Jack, her face twisted in fury. She looked him over. Jack averted his eyes; he had seen enough of her watching her in past scuffles, so had no need to look her over.

She wore a loose-fitting brown shirt hanging out over her shorts. She was stocky, bit shorter than Jack.

He said he didn't want to fight anyone. Especially not a girl. That didn't sit well with the kids, excited now by the prospect of a battle of the sexes.

Other kids had come in now, including younger ones, who had run across from the playground, as if expecting something more thrilling than the see-saw and slippery slide.

Jack glanced around the faces sooling him and Sharon into a fight.

Katie and Peter Martin were among the littlies from the playground. Jack hardly knew him then, or ever. Mary, so little then, had edged her way to the front. Shook her head at Jack, who wasn't sure if she was urging him to fight or not. Most likely, she hoped he would walk away.

"I gotta go home," Jack said. Soppy, even for an eleven-year-old.

Jeers of 'scaredy cat', 'sissy', 'wimp' and 'coward' shook him, wiping away any possibility of him backing out. He saw Tucker to the left gesturing that he'd take Jack's place. No way, that was worse than the jeering.

Two bigger kids walked up. Mullins and Jones. They grabbed a kid's skateboard and flung it away towards the path. Peter said something and Mullins threw his red cap deep into the bushes. Peter scurried after it. The bullies joined the spectators.

Katie stuck up for her brother, but her tiny voice was lost in the louder hubbub. Jack saw her squeeze through the yelling kids to the side. What's she up to? She burst from the jostling pack and ran towards the street.

He was supposed to be looking after his little sister, and here she was turning onto the footpath and running as fast as her little legs could carry her, yellow sundress swelling around her as if by wind gusts.

Jack knew he had to fetch her back. She was too young to run around the streets by herself. The noisy excitement of the crowded kids filled his ears. He would never live it down if he ran after Katie.

He turned back to face Sharon, who stood grinning, hands on hips, waiting for Jack to make the first move. He felt wretched. He was letting a little kid run off alone when he was supposed to be looking after her. He would chase her, bring her back and make her sit while he fought Sharon. That wouldn't take long.

Was she running to get Mum? Oh no, what could be worse than being dragged away in the middle of a fight by your Mum?

Minute-long seconds passed while Jack hesitated. Kids were chiacking, impatient for the promise of a fight to be kept.

"Are you two going to dance or fight?" A voice from behind him. Laughter all around them.

He didn't know how a bloke started a fight with a girl. Ladies first?

Arnold started it, shoving Jack at Sharon and his left hand banged into her face. She yelled and went at Jack. Too late to back out; to find Katie.

Sharon punched him in the chest. Before he could retaliate, she was all over him, pinning his arms and dragging him to the ground. She was like an enraged beast, arms and legs lashing out at him, seeming to come from all directions, mouth cursing, eyes glaring with malice.

He tried to break free, rolling across her, but she jerked his left arm hard behind his back. He stifled a scream, blinked water from his eyes.

Too quick, too strong. He couldn't get a firm hold, hands fumbling, held back by a modest mind. They scrabbled around on the grass, flailing at each other, no more like professional wrestlers than Bruce and Arnold had been.

Jack's fist hit the side of Sharon's head. She yelped. Good.

Desperate, he grabbed at her shoulders. His fingers closed on her shirt. She twisted, pulling away. Buttons ripped off and her shirt gaped open. He heard someone gasp.

She swore again, spluttering spittle on Jack's shirt. She attacked with renewed vigour and jerked his right arm up his back, swinging him around.

Blindly, he grabbed with his free hand and squeezed hard. Now he gasped. Bare flesh.

"You perverted bastard," Sharon screamed, possibly as much in anger at the crowd's laughter as in pain.

"You've got her tit, Johnny," someone advised unnecessary.

Raucous laughter. Jack's face reddened. He quickly let go. "Sorry," he yelled. Sharon snarled and punched wildly, apology not accepted.

Jack flailed about, wishing he could go home, lie on his bed, and cry.

Sharon rolled him over, face down. He tried to kick himself over, but she pushed a knee into his back. She paused astride the struggling boy, looked around the almost silent crowd and took a few deep breaths.

Spotting something in the grass, she shifted her leg off his back and slid him a short distance to squelch his face into a mound of dog shit. It smeared over his face and into his mouth.

Someone had cried out "No. No." There were gasps and laughter. He was crying from the pain and the smell and the taste, but mostly from the humiliation.

Sharon let go and slumped away, one hand holding her shirt front together. Jack rolled over and sat up, tears glistening with the brown mess on his face. His shorts were pulled up, as if from a wedgie, and one of his balls was hanging out.

He looked up at the row of laughing faces, turning to each, side to side like the clown head in sideshow alley.

The laughter died down as the kids wandered away. He poked himself back in his shorts.

Now and then he heard brief bursts of laughter in the distance but in a while even those faint reminders of his disgrace faded from his hearing and he knew he was alone. He dropped his head.

A girl had beaten him up in front of his mates and he was crying and had dog shit in his mouth and in his nose and in his hair and his sister was gone. He lay down, face into the grass, and tried to stop sobbing.

He heard voices and sat up. A couple of men were walking on on the path. They glanced at Jack without comment. Apparently not concerned about a kid with a bloody nose and a dog-shit mouth. The sky was darker and he knew he had to get up. Go home. Find Katie. Do… what first?

Someone touched his shoulder. He turned over. Mary stood there, holding a pink-and-white hanky in one hand and a toilet roll in the other.

"I got this from the toilet."

She bent and wiped around his mouth, rubbing to an "argh" and "erks" accompaniment. The brown filth gradually disappeared, revealing the redness of embarrassment.

Jack had protested and squirmed at first but soon settled, reflecting his relief. He wouldn't have to walk home with a shitty face. Mary didn't say much as she worked, tongue out, on her self-imposed task. The hanky was soon ruined. She dropped it to the grass and tore pieces off the toilet roll.

"Sorry, Johnny, that's the best I can do. Not much good at this."

"Probably not many are," Jack muttered, tentatively scratching his nose.

Mary wrapped her hanky in toilet paper and tossed it, accurately, into the nearby bin.

Jack sniffled and wiped his sleeve across his nose.

Once again, he looked down, triple-checking no private part was poking out of his shorts. Not in front of Mary. Already all those kids saw my nuts. he thought. Might have to leave school.

Mary said: "Look, Johnny, more help's on the way." Katie was running towards them. Bev was close behind, carrying a bucket and towel and, no doubt, disinfectant wipes.

Jack was about to call Tucker when a car horn honked behind him and his friend's familiar dark-green station wagon loomed up in the rear-vision mirror.

"About bloody time," he murmured. Despite his impatient grumbling, Jack was pleased Tucker had not taken off without a farewell chat. He was part of this stuff, too. He got out and waved a greeting to his mate, who was standing beside his car's open door. Tucker waved and bent into the car to say something. Jack waved to Jan, who was in the front, and Luke behind her, amidst piled-up luggage. Hope none of that falls on his broken arm, Jack thought… Neither waved back; they were focused on what Tucker was saying.

Tucker bobbed up straight and strode towards Jack, rather more quickly than he usually did.

"Hey there, mate," Tucker said. They shook hands. "Sorry, Jack, took bit longer than l thought it would. Packing all the stuff in the wagon."

"No worries," Jack said, realising instantly how far from the truth that mindless phrase was. Would it ever be true again?

"I was a bit worried. You know, something might have happened. These times." He shrugged.

Tucker patted his arm. "What could happen, hey?" He paused, as if he, like Jack, knew the reality disguised by his careless bravado.

"You know… we're watchful now and —"

"—and you're clearing out with your wife and son, in case something happens."

Tucker's seldom-absent grin left his face. "It's not me, Jack. It's my family. Cops told me—you, too, I'm sure—that this bastard's not after you and me. He wants us to suffer the loss of people we love."

Jack said: "I just want to get my hands… Have you copped any more shit?"

Tucker shook his head. "Nobody hurt but the bastard sprayed our shed with red threats saying we'll pay and learn what it's like to lose a loved one who no one helps and… well, you know."

"You got a longer message than us."

Tucker gave a wry grin. "We got a big shed. We cleaned it off, after the cops had a look."

"What's it supposed to mean, anyway?" Jack said. "We've got people we can count on…" He paused. "A few." He rubbed the side of his nose.

Tucker looked back at Jan in the front seat. She waved him back. "Maybe," he said, "not too sure."

"Cops're convinced it all started with us," Jack said. He saw Tucker was distracted.

"So cops say. But we couldn't foresee Mullins and Jones killing another kid. Schoolboys don't think they're mixing with murderers in the schoolyard."

Jack saw Jan waving again. He didn't tell Tucker.

It didn't matter. As if sensing his wife's impatience, Tucker half turned and waved to Jan. "Look, mate, I must go. Jan's in a terrible state. Scared."

"Can't blame her," Jack said, patting Tucker on the back.

"No. You look after your lot. Mary, Katie and your Mum when she gets out of hospital. And yourself, too, mate."

Jack was alarmed. "Why Mary? She's not related. Not married."

Tucker began walking to his vehicle. "Cops said loved ones could be in danger, not just relatives. Goodbye, Jack. For now."

Jack called after him. "Where you going? Far?"

"Promised Jan I wouldn't tell anyone. She's very scared. Imagines we're being watched, followed. Gotta get away." Pause. "Out of New South Wales."

"Be warmer there, then."

Tucker looked back. "Yeah." He grinned.

Enough said. Jack knew Jan's parents lived in Bundaberg, Queensland.

He got into his car. The green station wagon accelerated past with three honks of the horn, Jack raised an arm in weary salute. His mate hadn't asked about his Mum or how Katie was. He turned the key in the ignition. He felt very alone.

He did a U-turn and drove slowly away leaving the garden of bad memories for a room of sad reality, where Mary and Katie sat alongside his unconscious mother.

29

THE BOOK KEEPER

This is no time for doubt. I have no use for doubt. It was Mullins. Mullins and Jones. They would have gotten away with it if not for my sharp eye. It was that little book, the so-called *Guide to Manderville*. A tiny item in a small book, but I spotted it, just as I spot clues to misdemeanours in clients books. Just a hint. That is all I needed.

The possibility of two boys near where Peter drowned.

The pocketknife in the grass clinched it for me. It must've been the same…

Those bloody —excuse my language, I am speaking frankly. I am angry, as you, no doubt, have noticed. Anyway, those bullies showed their ugly characters long ago. Sent my little Peter home crying. On Christmas day. I know, you know.

I never thought I could love as much as I did that day. Me. I deal with numbers, dollars and cents, adding and subtracting, balancing, staring at the hard data, until my eyes burn and it softens into a blur and I have to rub my eyes into focus.

But that Christmas Day, in my car, that sunny afternoon, half a block away, I rubbed my eyes to dry them.

I know you have experienced such emotions in the past. Yes. Even now. Let me.

The young fellow was so happy, so proud, running around with a few mates in the community park, a dashing cowboy. At first, I could not see him from my unobtrusive vantage point, but when the kids ran close to the front edges, I could easily spot him in his brand-new cowboy suit.

Do you mind my going over this again? Yes? Maybe that is a 'no'.

He thinks… thought it came from Santa. Seeing his happiness there, I was jealous of Santa getting credit for my gift. Silly. Ah well, I thought then, there would be plenty more gifts coming from me over many Christmases, birthdays and other occasions.

He went home crying that day.

Please indulge me in reciting these painful memories. Some I did not know until much later. Not fair, was it?

Of course, Peter had no idea I had followed him – that was not wrong, was it? Just so I could enjoy his pleasure. Reminds me of other Christmases.

He did not know about bullies at his age. I did not know schoolboys could be so evil.

Did you? I thought not. Yes, you did once say that.

He was the envy of all his mates. Great cowboy outfit, if I say so myself. I did not spare any expense. It showed. Best leather. Brown-and white vest, red-and-brown chaps, even a gun belt with plastic bullets and a holster for his silver cap gun.

He certainly looked the part and the other kids played with him and laughed with him and tried to draw their guns faster than each other.

For a magical hour or so, the little park was his Wild West world. Then the bad guys came into town. But I was not there. I had driven away. I did not see the two big boys go into the park.

I did not know the raucously happy boys would soon need a sheriff. But none came.

Peter told us. I know you know. They claimed they just wanted to join in, but they ruined the game. They pushed the smaller children over and grabbed toys and other new gifts from them.

Peter did not know their names, but I found out – Mullins and Jones, bullies even then. As I told you, when Hopkins mentioned he had heard that they might have been the last to see Peter alive – sorry, I feel your pain, also, but I can't sweep it from my mind – I remembered that Christmas Day and what they did then. Mullins was showing off his big new folding knife, flicking the blade out, swishing it through the air, sending pretend cowboys screaming away, closing it one-handed, flashing it out again.

Well may you stare at me. A kid getting a knife for Christmas.

Jones wanted to wear Peter's cowboy clothes. Peter shook his head. They were too small for a big kid, anyway, he said. Jones kept pestering Peter, who tried to walk away. But Mullins joined Jones and those big brutes stripped his beautiful dressing-up clothes off him and dropped him on the ground like an empty hamburger bag. I know, I know. Breaks my heart, still. Yours, too.

Jones tore the vest while stretching it over his fat body. It tore again when Mullins pulled it off him and tried to wear it.

Peter cried his eyes out. He did not tell me this, but I learnt it later.

Your tears can't help now.

My brave little fellow fought to get his cowboy suit back, but he had no chance. They pushed him over, mocking his tears. They scattered all the plastic bullets in the grass and threw his holster and gun into the trees at the far side of the park. Peter ran to search for them. A couple of mates helped, the others ran home.

Peter retrieved the holster and gun. He went back to where his ruined gift was lying in dozens of pieces. Mullins had cut up the belt, vest and chaps with his Christmas present. Jones had stomped on the white Stetson-like hat. It lay flattened into a green-stained, torn disc.

Peter learnt the details from one of his mates who had returned to the park with a large paper bag. The subdued, much reduced band of cowboys gathered the pieces and dropped them into the bag. Most of the bullets were recovered and dribbled onto the ruined remains of his briefly loved, too soon mourned present from a fake Santa.

Peter didn't know who they were. But I found out you wanted to call the police. Remember? Yes? Too late for that. I am my own debt collector. They ended up destroying more than a kid's beloved cowboy suit.

I never forgot that Christmas Day and made a note of the debt I was owed. Of course, I had no reason to inform you of this, but I kept it simmering. Did you notice? No?

Others had suffered at their hands, but those do not belong in my books.

I hate bad debts. You must, too. Sorry about the inconvenience. It will not be long. Things always end—one way or another.

30

BEV

Ray … And … And … Where are you? I've been … Looking … Listening … Shadows flickering. Like through sheer curtains blowing in the wind. Faint voices … in and out. So far away. Jack, Katie … No Ray and Rob … Gone … Where are my tears? Come home Ray … I need you always … …Are you caring for our kids? Keeping us all safe … As you … Quiet …

* * *

Sunday 5.45pm

Mary and Katie were almost jogging to keep up with Jack as he strode along the corridor towards Bev's ward. He barely slowed as he approached the police officer standing outside the door. She apparently knew who they were and nodded them into the ward. At last, after so many days and a scary setback, Jack was alongside his mother's bed.

Mary moved back for Katie to join her brother. They stood, side by side, at the bed edge. Jack put an arm around Katie's shoulders and gently pulled her closer. They looked down at their Mum's now-thinner form under a light, grey blanket, unmoving except for the rhythmic, almost silent rise and fall of precious breaths, face relaxed, still, except for occasional quivers of pale lips, eyes closed.

The policewoman watched them from the doorway. A tall nurse brushed past her and moved quietly to the other side of the room. She stood against the wall, hands clasped, fingers entwined, fiddling, eyes on the visitors.

"Be careful not to touch any cords or equipment," the nurse said.

Nobody responded, although Mary was tempted to point out that they would need orangutan arms, because most of the equipment was on the other side of the bed, but they kept away from anything that was attached to Bev or might affect her treatment.

"You're so beautiful, Mum," Katie exclaimed.

"You always have been, Bev," Mary said.

"Yes," Jack said, "but look what that bastard did."

Bev's face still showed signs of the violent attack. They quietened.

Mary looked helplessly at the constable, who dropped her eyes to the floor. Katie was trying not to cry. Jack felt the tremble in her shoulders.

He released his grip and bent over to touch the blanket. The nurse tut-tutted and waggled a finger at him, as if he was a five-year-old caught with his hand in the lolly jar. He gazed at her for a moment without lifting his hand. Katie's sobbing dropped to whisper level.

"Mummy," Katie said, reaching down, touching the blanket near Jack's hand.

The nurse took a half step forward.

"Mummy. I miss you so much."

The nurse stepped back to the wall. The constable nodded at her.

Mary moved to stand close behind Jack. She put a hand on his shoulder. She gave the nurse a reassuring smile as if to say: Don't worry, your patient is in no danger from these emotional visitors.

Katie looked at Mary and said: "Do you think Mum can hear us? She hasn't opened her eyes."

The nurse said: "She may well hear you, darling."

Jack looked up for the first time since he had been reprimanded. He looked from Mary to Katie without a word, then bent low. "Mum, I love you more than you could have ever known. I'm sorry for my silence. I should have said it during those tough years, when you were suffering alone. I should have said it when

I knew you could hear me. Mum, one day you can tell us if you heard us now. Just in case: I love you. We all love you. We're so worried about you."

Mary hugged him tightly. He turned to her. Mary kissed his cheek. She wiped her eyes.

Katie looked up at the nurse and said: "Hope you're right. Made me cry."

Mary gently squeezed between Jack and Katie and bent down closer to Bev.

"Bev, it's me, Mary. You'll be very proud of Jack and Katie. You have amazing kids. You and Ray."

Katie turned away and burst into loud crying.

The nurse went to the end of the bed and quietly said: "That will have to be enough, folks. We mustn't tire her out. It's still early days."

They straightened up and turned surprised faces to the nurse. Katie sucked in her sobs. Hiccupped. Jack checked his watch.

"We've hardly been here any time at all," he said louder than Mary thought was wise.

The constable put her hands up and asked them to lower their voices.

Jack took a deep breath and continued at a lower volume. "Detective Sergeant Brogan said I could visit my Mum."

"As you have done and now it is time to leave," the officer said, speaking softly and patiently. "We must take notice of the medical staff."

"I have waited days till you cops finally relented, finally trusted me not to attack my Mum." His voice broke and he swallowed, attempting to control it. "Your boss didn't say how many minutes I could visit her for. He just said I could come and spend time with her." He looked from face to face: the constable turned to the nurse, who nodded agreement.

Katie and Mary put their arms around Jack.

"The constable is correct. As I said, for Mrs Durkin's welfare, it is time to let her rest."

"Rest?" Jack said. "That's all she's been doing day after day. Surely our short time here can't have worn her out."

"I am sorry, sir," the nurse said, moving closer to the top of the bed. "Your mother may be fully conscious soon. You will all have lots of time together."

Mary whispered in Jack's ear. He nodded and took hold of Katie's arm. She pulled away but Mary touched her arm and she turned from the bed. She was sobbing and Mary's eyes glistened above damp cheeks.

"Okay," Jack said, "we'll go for now." He briefly turned back to the bed. "Bye, Mum, there is so much love for you here and—" The thought ended in a crackle. He paused and tried again. "We'll bring it back to you very soon."

"Be back soon, Mum, with even lots more love," Katie said.

Mary said: "And, Bev, we want you to see us the next time we see you." She wrapped her arms around Jack as they headed for the door.

Katie wriggled in and held his right hand. Mary kissed her cheek.

"I… My Ray…"

They spun around at the sound of the soft voice from the bed. As one, they hurried to the bedside.

Bev's slight figure lay under the blanket, as still as before. The nurse was quickly by the bed, leaning over Bev.

"Don't touch her. Just be calm." She bent low. "Mrs Durkin. Can you hear me, Mrs Durkin?"

No response. Concerned eyes flicked helplessly from face to face. The constable had moved closer.

Jack said: "Mum, we're all here." They knew it was a lie, but this wasn't the time for the truth.

The nurse pressed a button on the wall. Within a minute another nurse rushed in.

"What is it, Carol?" She gently pushed Katie aside and leant down over Bev.

"She spoke. Just then. Said a word."

"Three words," Mary said. "I, my, Ray."

"Is Mum coming to?" Jack asked, looking at the newly arrived nurse, who had taken control.

"Not necessarily. But it is a good sign." She studied the dials and tiny screens.

"What will you do now?" Mary asked. The senior nurse didn't reply.

The first nurse said. "We'll ring Dr Robbins. He'll want to know about this change."

"In the meantime, we'll keep a close watch on Mrs Durkin."

"As we always are," the other nurse cut in quickly.

Mary asked if it was all right for them to stay a little bit longer in case Bev spoke again. The nurses looked at each other. The senior nurse nodded and said they could, as long as they stood away from the bed.

"There are things we have to record. We need access to our patient." She paused to write on the clipboard at the end of the bed. "Also, Dr Robbins may require you to leave."

Jack, Mary and Katie shuffled backwards to stand against the wall. They stood holding hands, their eyes on Bev. She didn't speak again and in about an hour they quietly walked from the room and left the hospital.

They got into the car, and Jack started the engine. He reached across to hesitantly touch Mary's hand. He smiled and she squeezed his hand. She smiled sadly, knowing what was coming and knowing the sadness her answer would cause for the man she loved with all her heart. She released his hand and brushed her fingers across his face. She was conscious of Katie watching from the back seat. The engine was idling.

"We off home now then?" he said.

"Jack, darling, soon." His smile faded and she told herself enough was enough. "But, maybe—"

"Come on, Jack," Katie said. "Take Mary to her parents' place and get us home. Don't rush things."

Jack put the car into gear and drove off. "Okay."

Once out of the carpark and on the road, he said: "Will you be all right, Mary?"

"Yes," Mary murmured. "Soon."

He said: "We'll hope soon is sooner than a normal soon."

Mary wasn't sure what that meant but she laughed and gave a more positive "Yes".

Nobody said much more on the drive through the dark, almost deserted streets. When they arrived at Mary's new, but, she hoped, temporary home, she kissed Jack and Katie and said she would see them at their father's funeral Tuesday.

As she walked up the path to the front door, Mary tried to fight off the fear that Ray Durkin's funeral might not be the last his family would have to endure this year, this month.

31

MARY

So many people. Nearly full already. Jack baulks at the first row of pews, says something. I don't catch it. He takes a deep breath, straightens and walks tall towards our seats at the front.

He stares ahead, Katie and I discreetly gaze around, our heads hardly turning. She says "Oh" and moves her hand in a barely perceptible wave to three school friends near the back. I nod at our GP, she nods back with a wan smile. What a wide cross-section of Manderville society. Wasn't expecting this. Don't know everyone. Not closely. Not by name.

Jack's gaze drifts side-to-side, pauses on a row of men to our left. He whispers to us, "Players in Dad's cup-winning team". His voice is shaky. A worry.

Supporters of the Manderville Mugs, filling the next two rows, many of them resplendent in the famous brown-and-gold jerseys, scarves and caps. Bev still wears the scarf in winter… wore… wears. Almost as many women as men; a young boy, a football on his lap, sits next to an overweight man in a tight-fitting jumper. Mostly mature, but steadfastly loyal, they look expectantly to the front, much as they did all those years ago, when Ray Durkin magic lit up the field and their lives.

Dad smiles at me, waves. A pang of memory jolts me. Often happy then, singing the team song, after Sunday arvo victories. I loved his boyish excitement as he related incidents in the match. Mum wasn't interested. I was closer to my Dad on those winter evenings than at any other time in my life.

Now, the thousands of fans have dwindled to a dozen or so, gathered today not to cheer, but to sorrow.

Group from work, to our right. So nice of them. I acknowledge them with one of Katie's small waves.

Half a dozen of Ray's drinking mates— "blacklist busters", Jack whispers—are crunched together, like books squeezed onto a shelf, keeping each other upright. Unfair of me. They're talking softly, nodding, looking around, perhaps estimating, for personal reasons, the sort of crowd a drunkard can draw to his funeral.

Katie's giving her shy wave again. It's Meg and Doug; she sombre-faced, he looking as if wishing he was home with the telly—sorry, unfair again.

"Shearers," Jack says; three men about Ray's age and one about mine. All neatly dressed, smart shirts and ties.

We reach the front pews and shuffle sideways to our places.

Before I sit, I look over the congregation. Some look me over. So many here. Disappointingly, but not surprising, town gossips are scattered around, like lint bobbles on an otherwise fine jumper. Eyes swivel like radar antenna, locking onto mourners, guiding heads to the targets, turning, dipping, bobbing tongues wagging, whispering inside hand-concealed mouths. Women here not to show their respect but to collect intelligence for those who couldn't make it today.

I sit. Jack is between us. No one mentions the space at the end, beside Katie, the order of service lying on it.

Jack's grasping Katie's hands. Her face is wet, a pile of tissues on her lap. Mine, too. Jack is silent, unbuttoning, rebuttoning his suit coat, pulling his tie. I feel the tension in his body, in his grip on my forearm, I'm sure Katie feels it. She looks at Jack and then at me. This is all new to us. Don't know how a young brother and sister can cope with the funeral of their murdered Dad. And while their Mum lies in a coma.

Jack is steeling himself for what he must do—insisted on doing. Speaking before a crowd is scary for most people, but here, now? Oh boy.

He can't take his eyes off the coffin lying stolidly in front of us. Tall gladioli stand guard in a row of five vases.

Ray's jersey, with its big orange number '1' on the back, is draped over it, reminding us of our days in the sun, and the rain and the wind, watching our tall, dark, hero—the only one Manderville has had really—whizzing in and out, speeding away from would-be tacklers, palming off body-graspers, leaving all floundering, staggering and flopping on his way to the try line.

Even as a young girl standing for the first time near the sideline with Dad, I was thrilled by the excitement of the moment, even while bewildered by what was happening. Dad's stop-start explanations left me more confused. I was little.

Now, he lies in that shiny wooden box with golden handles. Now quiet, still. So missed.

The Reverend Graham Mathers is saying a few words of welcome, then speaks of a man he knows little about. Hasn't been here long. At least, he seems to understand the loss Manderville has suffered. Might not know the loss happened many years ago. Not days ago when he was shot. No, way back, when he took off his superhero costume to appear in the guise of just another town drunk.

Former Mugs' coach Fergus Spackman is up the front. Still got his loud rasping voice, lost his hair, gained a bigger stomach. What? Concentrate. He's talking about someone before our time. For goodness sake. A Greek god. Not Ray. Must be leading up to Ray. Now it's a Roman centurion. Sheesh. The only possible link I can see between Ray and Caesar's Legions is the Romans' deadly short sword, the gladius, and Ray's massed display of gladioli filling the Durkin front yard every summer.

The insignificant lane attracts many people, who wonder at the glorious colours of the flowers with sword-shaped leaves. That can't be the link.

Jack looks puzzled. Katie and I stifle giggles at the coach's well-intentioned but absurd tribute. Jack pats my hand, misinterpreting my burble of inappropriate emotion. He looks at me with a sad, twisted smile. Concentrate. Distracted by my need to hug Jack and Katie.

The rotund coach bravely presses on. Reminding us of other towns paying loads of money for 'marquee' players from Sydney clubs. The imports, near the ends of their careers, were no help, he says. Our team won four premierships in five years…

A couple of cheers from the back. Jack wriggles on his seat and whispers in my ear. His Dad didn't belong on a pedestal. I squeeze his hand. He turns to whisper to Katie. I bite my lip and worry about Jack's eulogy.

Mr Mathers thanks Fergus. A few forget where they are and clap. Someone cheers, seemingly from 'drunks' row'. We sing, or mouth the words of, a hymn with too many verses. Meg's choice? Jack stands looking at his feet, mouth closed in a tight line, not even pretending he's singing. He's nervous. Nearly time for his turn up front. He checks the order of service. He shuffles his feet, as if practising to walk in front of everybody without tripping or…

The discordant congregational 'choir' fades out, some reaching the end later than others. We all sit again—except for Jack. I pull his coat. He looks around and abruptly sits. Titters are silenced when I turn and glare at the patchwork blanket of faces.

He's hardly settled before Mr Mathers calls on him for the eulogy.

Jack rises. I reach out to give him an encouraging pat on the back, but he moves too quickly, and my hand pats his bum. He gives me a quizzical look, then strides to the front. He's shaking. Wobbles on the three steps to the lectern. He places both hands on it to steady himself.

He licks his lips, lowers his head and looks at me and Katie. We smile.

His eyes sweep across the church interior, taking in all the congregation. He coughs and I wish I had a glass of water for him. He begins speaking, his voice cracks and he struggles to control the tremor that's distorting his words.

Katie slides across to me and we hold hands.

"Oh, Mary—" she whispers, but suddenly Jack is speaking louder. Firmer.

Thanking Fergus for his "kind words" he pauses for several seconds.

Then: "I was a bit puzzled by stories about some legendary person. Not my Dad. He wasn't a Greek god, although our Mum said he looked like one." Quiet laughter from behind us. Quiet sobs from beside me. "He wasn't a Roman legionnaire, either, although rival players may have felt much like Rome's enemies did when the legions rolled over them."

Someone in the fans' mini-stand cheers.

"Or, just to be clear, our Dad wasn't a World War Two fighter pilot or jungle explorer."

Another pause. To my right, on the other side of the aisle, Cathy Morgan is writing in a reporter's notebook. Done well since she left school, a year before me.

"No," Jack says. "Ray Durkin, our Dad, Katie's and mine, was a drunk."

Katie's gasp is just one of dozens in the church that morning. She moves on the seat and for a moment I think she is going to stand. To do what? Shout at her brother? Walk out? Do both? I touch her arm. She settles back. She's shaking. I put my arm around her shoulders. I can feel dozens of eyes on our backs. Many more are on Jack.

I wonder how Jack can keep going. I want to be up there, hugging him. But he's looking confident, standing straight, strong. Tall, dark and oh-so-handsome in his new navy suit, white shirt and red tie.

He gazes around the church, keeping us waiting, aware, I'm sure, that this gathering of Manderville citizens has been hanging on his every word, sitting so silent you could hear a pin drop–they're expecting a bomb. I'm not.

Jack's eyes settle on Katie and me. He continues.

"Why do many of you look shocked at that? Isn't that how you referred to Ray Durkin when you saw him staggering home, helped him remain a drunk by supplying him with grog, against the spirit of the law, if not downright illegal?"

The silence is broken by mutters, coughs, sniggers and shoe shuffles. Only seconds are passing on my watch, minutes in my mind. There's a palpable air of discomfort.

I turn at a commotion. One of Ray's drinking mates is pushing his way along the row, treading on toes and poking his hands onto a convenient face here and there for balance.

Jack rolls his eyes and waits until the apparently insulted man has walked, somewhat unsteadily, out of the church. He takes up where he left off.

"You were right. A drunk he was. But our Dad was more than that. That word doesn't describe the whole man. So, more than a drunk; less than a Greek god.

"He achieved a lot in his forty-eight years. His chequered career as a drunk didn't fill all his years. You know, we hoped it would end soon. He was working on it. We'll never know what the next stage of his life would have been." Katie sniffles and grabs another tissue. "Dad was, without question, the greatest footballer Manderville has ever known, probably the best the district has seen."

All eyes are on him as he pays a glowing, but not overstated, tribute to Ray Durkin, the rugby league player. He tells of the nail-biting finish to his first grand final, won in the last minute by a Ray Durkin try. That began five magnificent years for the team that had been derided for a decade as Manderville Mugs. The Magpies threw the mocking name back in their rivals' faces by officially embracing that name and winning four premierships.

Jack's tales of his Dad's exploits on the footy field grips the crowded church, with barely a sound, unlike the cheering, whistling, clapping and screaming that reverberated around football grounds when Ray's exquisite (my word) talent was igniting sports grounds. Packed with adoring fans and despairing rivals.

Muted affirmations –"Too right", "You beauty", "Yeah, yeah"– punctuate his sentences.

Jack pauses, looks around his crowd again. He says, almost conversationally now: "But, you know, Ray was also a gun shearer–"

"Bloody oath!" Must be a shearer, loud and proud. Jack smiles and nods at the interrupter.

He has us with him now. I hear it wavering through the silence, a murmuration, so low it can only be heard when listening to the quietness, like gradual awareness of sounds in a silent room: rustle of curtains in a breeze, hum of fridge, drip-drip of leaking tap. I'm so proud of him, bravely steady and articulate, despite his inner turmoil. Katie sniffles and closes her hand over mine.

"Dad may not have been in the Jackie Howe class, but his daily tally was pretty good. He was not only fast, he was clean and careful. Seldom called the tar boy for cuts and nicks.

"When the shearing and crutching seasons were done each year, he turned to yet another role, a rabbitoh– trapping them, not a player with the Sydney footy club.

"All in all," Jack continued, "our Dad was a hard worker and we were seldom short of money."

Supportive mutterings from shearers' direction.

Jack pulls out striped hanky, brushes it over his eyes and then, as if it was his original intention, quickly blows his nose. Transparent attempt to hide his sudden tears.

Katie is sobbing. I hear someone else nearby. It's me.

"But, let me tell you, beyond all those things, our Dad was a dad. A fun-loving, storytelling, rolling-around-the-floor-with-his-kids dad. Dad. Not always, not much in recent years. But, at heart, our Dad was a simple man who greatly loved Katie and me, and above all, our Mum, the love of his life, who doesn't know the love of her life is being buried today.

"We loved him and the light shining on our family has dimmed."

He says his love for his Dad didn't waver even when unjust anger almost consumed it. He doesn't speak of blame, doesn't speak of distress. He says his father was a good man—his bright blue eyes sweep over the congregation, as if daring anyone to disagree.

"He was brought low by an addiction he couldn't control."

My darling looks spent. I want to kiss him better. Katie and I, we hug each other. He pauses. Deep breath. Continues.

"And finally, a bullet fired by a maniac ended Ray Durkin's life. The killer had no reason to pull the trigger. No reason to end any chance Ray Durkin might have had to beat the addiction. Any chance of redemption."

Unbearable. We cry. He looks at us in the front row, then over the congregation. The local reporter is wiping a page of her notebook with a tissue.

"Any chance of becoming the man Ray Durkin once was."

Katie is howling. I hold her tighter and hand her another tissue. She gives it back because my tears have already soaked it. I whisper an apology and give her a fresh one. She sniffles.

Jack is finished. He stands for a minute as if not sure what to do. Mr Mathers steps over and pats Jack's shoulder. Jack turns, nods and starts back to his seat. He stops and looks over the faces.

"Yesterday our Mum briefly regained consciousness." Murmurs ripple around the church. "She didn't say much to us. Didn't name the mongrel who nearly took her life. But she will. And then I will make him pay."

A mist of whispers rises around us.

Jack turns to the coffin. "And Dad, the only words she said were 'My Ray.'"

I vainly try to stop crying. Katie hugs me. She pulls away, leaving my ear damp.

Many other people, even one or two gossipers, are sobbing, sniffing, clearing throats. Katie slides away from me to let Jack sit between us. We grab each other's hands and squeeze. Mr Mathers speaks again. He's distracted by we three and I can't catch all his words. Auntie Meg says some tear-filled kindnesses about her brother. Another hymn. Shorter. The benediction.

Standing, we watch the coffin carried past by former teammates.

* * *

TUESDAY 12:15pm

They drove to the cemetery after a short time in the adjacent hall–tea and cakes and crustless sandwiches and stop-start, smiles-tears conversations. As if they were all talked out, there was little conversation in the car at first.

As they passed the town limits and drove into the countryside, however, breathing returned to normal, bodies relaxed, limbs moved and faces turned to each other.

Mary said: "All those people. Such a tribute to your Dad."

"I was shocked." Katie paused. "I mean stunned. I expected only a few… After all…" Her voice trailed off.

"Shocked is the word I'd use," Jack said. "When I saw all the faces looking at me, all the way to the back, right over to the sides… God, I wanted to hide. But there was nowhere. I looked at your faces. I had to go on. Thank you."

"You did so well," Mary said again. "We are so proud of you," she said also again. How could she not keep saying it after today? It would always be true.

Katie patted his shoulder and said: "You were just so amazing."

"One day I will tell your Mum and, through the sadness, she will be so proud of you too," Mary said.

They were near the cemetery now. They lapsed into silence. Jack slowed as they came up behind cars turning through the open gates.

A small group has gathered near the hole in the red earth, Facing the minister on the other side of the grave. Jack stands between his sister and Mary. The sight of the coffin is more confronting out here, beside the grave, near a pile of dirt. Stark reminders that Ray Durkin ends here.

Mary feared for Katie. And Jack. And herself. All beyond anything they have experienced in their young lives. So is murder, for that matter.

Grief sounds different out here: a cool breeze mixes sobs and sniffs with the rustle of leaves and chirping of birds. Quilted grey clouds loom ominously, like unwanted strangers peering over their shoulders.

More words by the Mr Mathers. Ray Durkin is lowered out of sight, into the darkness. Katie screams. Gone. They stand, family and friends, undertaker, two gravediggers, minister, and words blowing in the wind with handfuls of dust.

* * *

They left the cemetery. Nobody said anything, lost in their own thoughts. As they approached Manderville, Jack drove off the road at a rest area. He switched the engine off and sat with his hands clasped at the top of the wheel.

Mary turned to Katie. Both released their seatbelts and reached to hug Jack. He dropped his head on his hands and cried. It was a loud, long release of pent-up emotions. Katie cried, leaning forward to touch her brother. Mary cried, leaning her head against Jack's.

It was about ten minutes before the crying quietened to a few sobs, mostly from Katie. Each dried their eyes and cheeks. White bundles of wet tissues lay at their feet.

They smiled self-consciously at each other and Jack drove back to the road.

"I'll drop you at your parents," Jack said. It sounded like a question.

"Oh… yes," Mary said. "Thanks."

He turned into a street near Mary's parents' home. She reached across and touched Jack's left arm.

"I'd like to come home. Would you mind?"

The speed with which Jack spun the car around showed he definitely wouldn't mind. He looked across at Mary. Smiled.

"You think I might need emotional support tonight?" Jack said.

"Maybe. I'm sure I do."

Katie rolled her eyes, but her smile was wide.

HANDY GUIDE TO MANDERVILLE

Honestly, we're a law-abiding mob.

By Councillor Bruce Mercer, Manderville Mayor

Mandervillians are a decent lot, even though the last part of the name might indicate otherwise. However, crime statistics are always low for a bustling town of this size. Serious crimes rarely occur. Many visitors, particularly from the cities, comment on how relaxing it is to walk around our streets.

It may be that we have got better things to do with our time than breaking the law. Or it could be that our local Police Force is outstandingly efficient. It is probably a big chunk of each.

Officers are often on the beat around our CBD and are always available if you need to stop them with a query. The recently refurbished Police Station is 'open for business' 24/7. Officers of all ranks have been trained to deal compassionately with people in sad circumstances, such as motor vehicle accidents, domestic disturbances and family tragedies. So, if anything untoward happens during your visit, you can be assured of kind, professional attention.

One of our local families learnt this, after losing their little boy, drowned in a flooded creek. The police determined that there were no suspicious circumstances. They heard there might have been some big boys nearby, but they couldn't be identified. The boy's schoolbag was lying near the creek where his body was found. A big shiny pocketknife was also found nearby but did not belong to the boy and as there was no bloodshed, it was not considered a weapon.

The parents spoke in the highest terms of the kind and compassionate way that the officers came to them to break the news.

So, wherever you come from, you can be assured of a safe and happy holiday in our lovely town.

<h1 style="text-align:center">32</h1>

THE BOOK KEEPER

Just as I expected it was not all good. Funerals are like that. Usually no joy. I know that. Oh, yes.

It was fine to start with, of course, watching family and their sycophantic friends. More than a few crocodile tears there. Still, I saw enough sadness to justify my stressful week.

A jolly occasion. For some... me. The usher gave me a queer look when I let a chortle escape. Very careless of me. Luckily, that detective near the door did not hear me.

It was very enjoyable, until that pathetic Durkin boy said his mother might recover. Sloppy job. There is a tiny chance she could identify me. I cannot have that.

Difficult. There is always a police guard on the door.

The nurses are another problem, hanging around, everywhere. Doctors, too.

I should have done the job properly in that house. I should not have been scared off by noises in the yard. Nobody there. Probably not.

Ah well, we learn as we go.

I am sure I could look the part as a doctor. Suit, white coat. Stethoscope would cap it off. I have to get in there quickly and do it. We cannot pull back now.

After that, finish the job: sister and girlfriend. Then we shall see how he goes at those funerals.

I am determined to balance the books.

For a while the police will be kept busy by a body in a bedroom. Identification of it will not help them find us. The town's gendarmes will be puzzling for a while. Soon, the missing piece will be gone forever and they will never know about me.

* * *

WEDNESDAY 8.48am

It was later than they thought when Jack and Mary emerged, bleary-eyed and tousle-haired, from the bedroom. The time on the wall clock didn't faze them. This wasn't a morning for an early start.

With the electric jug burbling and bread in the toaster, they grinned at each other across the table until the jug clicked and the toast popped up. They crunched toast and Vegemite and sipped tea, lost in themselves, oblivious of the radio in the background: music, ads and insignificant chatter, from a DJ sounding as if he was putting himself to sleep.

They had tumbled off to sleep quickly last night, with barely a kiss. When they awoke this morning, or more precisely when Jack woke Mary, it was a different story. A story with a happy, prolonged, ending. And an emotionally satisfying climax. For both, Mary was sure. She knew she was looking forward to the sequel. She smiled over the top of her cup, at the memory.

But, as always, reality was creeping in.

"Will Mr Jacobs mind you being late?" Mary asked.

"Nah," Jack said, swallowing a piece of toast. "He's a good bloke. He told me to come in late."

"How thoughtful. Granting you hot sex leave."

He looked at her, saw her serious expression, and began to protest, stopped mid-sentence by Mary's lips opening into a cheeky grin. She pushed her chair back and went to his side. She bent to kiss his lips and was soon glad she had kept her grin wide.

Coming up for air, she said: "Just being silly, you do have a good boss, considerate. Me too. I'm also going in late. Soon, unfortunately. When do you have to be there?"

"Oh, in about…" He looked at the clock. "Twenty minutes ago."

He dropped the last half slice of toast so quickly it missed the plate and fell into his cup. He stood, pushing his chair back.

"We both better get going then," he said.

Mary laughed. She put a finger to her lips. "Shhh," she said, "Katie will hear us."

"If she didn't hear us half an hour ago, a bit of kitchen conversation won't stir her," Jack said.

She rinsed both cups at the sink, removing soggy bits of toast from Jack's.

He kissed her forehead and whispered: "Thanks, Mary, for all you are doing."

"It was just tea."

"You know what I mean. All through these shit days… weeks… you saw how I was coping and did your best to be there for me–"

"But I left you. Walked out on–"

He shrugged. "That was a bad night. I was distraught with the implications of Smithson's new stuff."

Mary started to speak, but Jack quietened her with a hand gesture.

"It got out of hand. You were struggling to make sense of it, but I… I lost it."

She smiled. "I learnt that lots of coffee doesn't always help."

He laughed, his head shaking. Mary enjoyed the sound she had missed and laughed also.

"I learnt no coffee doesn't help either." His tight smile flickered away. "Mary, I love you and that has steadied me at times when I was wobbling in the wrong direction. I know you love me. That's sustained me when all around is dark and threatening. Still is. But we still are, too. You and me, we, us, we still are. Still together."

"Yes," Mary said, hugging him. "As we were even though the world caved in around us."

Jack said even the brief separation was too long. "I know now how essential you are in my life."

Mary's tears ran down her face. She wiped her face on his shoulder and kissed his neck. She shivered, realising the danger in being precious to Jack Durkin.

She pulled away and rubbed his shoulder, hoping her hand would dry his shirt without leaving a stain.

He wiped his lips with a piece of paper towel and dropped it onto a plate alongside a small heap of once-was toast.

Mary, standing near the sink, waited until he turned from the table. Speaking quietly and calmly, she said: "Jack, what can we do to protect each other?"

"We'll keep close together–as much as possible," he said. "Today I'll drive Katie to the hospital. They'll be guarded by a cop." Except when he takes a toilet break, Mary thought. "If you come with us, I'll drop you at work first, then, lastly, I'll go to work."

"Good plan."

"And I'll pick you up after work and we can visit Mum and bring Katie home."

Mary frowned. "Yes, that'll work. But look at what this maniac is doing to us. Having to plan like a military mission. Just to get to work and visit Bev and come home."

Jack nodded but didn't comment. Instead, he brought up the Martins, who had disappeared according to Constable Smithson. "Apparently, nobody has seen Edie for a few days," Jack said. "Seems Colin has taken off too."

At the table, Mary picked up her cup and considered making coffee. She checked her watch, put the cup down on the saucer.

She said: "Col didn't come back from lunch on Thursday. More like brunch, he left about 10.30. I tried to talk with him, but he wouldn't open his office door to anyone. Then he almost ran out, brushing off questions.

"He said something about an early lunch and being back soon. But we didn't see him again."

Jack poured a glass of orange juice from the fridge and leant against the bench. Mary was glad they both had understanding workplaces.

"Sounds like he took off," Jack said. "Bloody guilty for sure." Pause. "Wonder if I could find him."

Mary gasped. "Jack, don't even think about it. You are too impetuous."

"We mustn't let them escape."

Mary gave in to her need for coffee. She filled the jug and switched it on. "I just can't see Col as a killer. He's such a gentle, kind man."

Jack drank the last of his juice and rinsed the glass. "Finding out your only child had been murdered after years of accepting it was accidental would shatter any parent," he said. "Sure to twist anyone."

Mary nodded and put her cup and saucer on her plate, along with a spoon and knife. She couldn't be bothered making coffee now. Better get Katie moving.

"But despite what you told me the other night," she said, "about revenge being the motive, I just can't reconcile the friendly colleague with a cold-blooded killer, or woman basher. Just not him."

Jack reckoned similar opinions could be expressed about whoever it turns out to be. Still be a Manderville citizen, someone they might mix with every day.

"Killers don't wear badges on their chests."

They heard the spare bedroom door open and the main bathroom door close.

"Katie's up," Mary said.

Jack said: "I better get ready, too."

He went to the bedroom.

"Enough of this," Mary said to herself. Time to get ready for the outside world. She went to turn the radio off. Her hand stopped, finger on the button. The local news was on. Sucker for punishment she thought, living within the bad news lately. Why wait to hear council's road maintenance plan, Rotary Club golf day report, debutante ball date, twins born overnight…

"Police have identified - "

Her finger jolted away from the button, as if it was electrified. Her heart missed a beat, then pounded.

" - the body found in the bedroom of a Hillview Estate house on Wednesday as that of Colin Martin." Mary clutched her mouth. "Mr Martin was an accountant with a local firm - "

Mary called out for Jack. He rushed into the room, to see Mary staring at the now-silent radio, hand in mouth.

"What is it?"

"It's Col. The radio. The body we saw was Colin Martin, they have identified it. Jack, he's dead."

He held her tight. She was shaking.

"Maybe he knew the cops were onto him. Killed himself. That'll tie it up nicely for Mr Detective Sergeant Brogan."

She looked up at him, brushing hair from her eyes. She said: "Will all these killings end now?"

He kissed tears on each cheek. "If Col was the killer, then they will."

She wondered about Edie's role, but didn't say anything.

"What's all over?" Katie walked into the kitchen, dressed ready for the hospital.

Mary kissed her 'Good morning' and said she looked 'smashing' before answering the question.

"Police say the body found… it's Col… Colin Martin."

"Oh My God, Mary. We thought it might … your friend … I'm sorry."

"My line manager—and, yes, my friend."

"Edie's husband." Katie hugged her. "So sad. I'm sorry that's who it was." She paused. "Was it suicide?"

"They didn't say on the radio."

Jack said: "I'll ring Brogan a bit later, from the shop. Now, I'm going to finish dressing, so we can leave soon."

"I'm ready," Katie said. "I'll get brekkie at the cafeteria."

Mary said: "I thought you might sleep in a bit longer after yesterday."

Katie rolled her eyes, grinned. "I wish. I didn't set my alarm last night, but, as it turned out, I got a … rude awakening earlier than I planned." She paused. "The walls here are rather thin, aren't they?"

Jack and Mary exchanged embarrassed glances.

"We didn't mean to wake you up," Mary said.

"Didn't sound like you were thinking of anyone else. And I'm glad about it." She smiled broadly.

Mary changed the subject. "You look great. Dressed very smartly for your Mum."

"Thanks. I want to spend more time with Mum today. I think they'll let me sit by her bedside, don't you?"

Jack took keys out of his trouser pocket.

"Sure, come with us, gorgeous. I'll take you there after I drop Mary at work."

33

SMITHSON

Don't know where to look next. He's vanished. In a place this size. Need to talk to him. Not home. Not at work. Behaved oddly at the funeral. Not like a mourner. So, why go to the funeral? Weird one. Smiled a lot, laughed, too. Looked edgy. Took off quickly at the end.

Need to have a yarn. Might shed some light on what's going on. Can't see a link, but you never know. I sure don't. Is this bloke after the Durkins or in fear of the killer for some reason? Martin was a prime suspect and look at what happened to him.

* * *

WEDNESDAY 3:15pm

Katie sat beside her mother's bed. There was no one else in the room. As usual, a constable stood outside the door. Katie wondered why anyone had to guard their mother if the man who had attacked her and killed their Dad was now dead himself.

Her mother hadn't stirred, hadn't opened her eyes, hadn't said a word. Depressingly, when a nurse came in to check everything, she said Bev had not regained consciousness to any noticeable degree. Whatever that meant. She either had or hadn't, Katie thought. As the minutes and then the hours passed, Katie was overwhelmed by hopelessness.

She had left the room twice. Once to get coffee and later to go to the toilet. Now, she needed to stretch her legs again and kissed Bev on the forehead before leaving the room. She walked along the corridor, passing the nurses' station. A short, dark-haired nurse was bent over an untidy pile of papers on the counter. A taller, younger blonde nurse was talking softly on the phone.

She looked up and nodded as Katie went past. Katie waved and continued on to turn the next corner. She strode quickly, anxiety building with each step. Before she reached the next corner, she swung on her heels and headed back to her Mum. Exercise could wait. Retracing her steps, she said "Nervous Nellie", loud enough to cause a male attendant to stop and shoot an offended glance at her back.

Silly, she told herself. There's always–almost always–a cop at the door. Now guarding her Mum against a dead killer.

She turned the corner. Her feet stopped mid-step, her heart mid-beat. The cop was gone. Bev's room was unguarded. Probably at the toilet. They should post cops with better bladder control to these jobs. Maybe getting coffee. Someone could bring him that, but he'd have to look after toilet essentials himself. Can't deny him that. She'd left her Mum for similar reasons. And even for lesser reasons, like treating herself to a stroll around the hospital. Be OK. But she couldn't reason away her anxiety. Her legs having recovered their movement, her heart its rhythm, she broke into a fast walk.

She was relieved to see a doctor at the nurses' station, talking to a nurse behind the counter. He was a big man in a white coat over brown trousers. Somehow, this reassured her that her mother would be safe until the cop returned.

Nevertheless, she maintained her pace, hurrying past the doctor and nurse, her eyes fixed on the ward 204 door.

The doctor raised his voice, speaking over the nurse. Katie didn't get the gist as she rushed on.

By the time she reached the doorway, the doctor was shouting. Glad he's not Mum's doctor, she thought.

"It's a simple request, nurse. Surely Mrs Durkin's ward number can't be a secret."

Katie froze. That voice. She had heard it shouting outside her prison room. He had dropped his voice as the nurse raised hers. But Katie had heard enough. It was him. He wasn't dead. It hadn't been Mr Martin.

Where was that cop? The man still had his back to Katie, arguing with the nurse. His voice was low now and Katie grabbed a chair from the corridor to prop the ward door closed. That won't work, the bloody door opens outwards.

"Are you looking for something, Miss?"

She jumped. What? Who?

She turned and, relieved, put the chair down. The tall figure of the police officer was walking towards her. His face was serious, but not unfriendly.

"Umm, needed a … a weapon…," she said, knowing how silly it sounded in a quiet hospital corridor. She looked over her shoulder. The fake doctor was looking at her. His face was twisted with anger – or was it hate?

The nurse, oblivious to the threatening danger, had gone back to her paperwork.

Convinced she was right, Katie turned back to the policeman. "Officer, that's him," Her voice trembled, making her cry for help sound wobbly and unconvincing. She said it again, louder this time, then louder still, said: "He kidnapped me."

"What do you mean? The doctor? Kidnapped? You're here now –"

"Days ago, locked me in a house. He's –"

"Hang on." The constable rubbed the side of his nose and looked from Katie to the man and back again. Katie glanced over her shoulder. The man was undeterred, walking towards them still.

She shouted: "He's a double killer. Probably."

"Excuse me, doctor," the constable said.

Doctor? Bloody hell.

"Could I have a word with you?"

Good god, the cop wants to chat with a killer. Ignored what I said. Maybe took it as a teenager's fantasy.

But the fake doctor indicated he wasn't in the mood for a discussion, by turning abruptly and running. Not bothering with the lift, he headed for the stairs. As if at last suspecting something was amiss, the policeman made chase. He was slow, lumbering rather than running. He hesitated at the top of the stairs, took a loud breath, exhaled with a sigh, before going down a step at a time.

Katie muttered: "The cop won't catch the crook." And if he does, what then? The cop was smaller, older. Be like a weekend angler hooking a marlin. Better stay here. Out of the way. Guarding Mum.

She hoped the constable would quickly realise he had lost his man, give up, and return to his post. She stood in the corridor for several minutes, continuously looking left and right. After a while, she went in and sat beside her mother.

The nurse who had scotched the fake doctor's plans came in and asked, "What was that all about?"

"Better ask the cop," Katie said, getting up and patting Bev's blanket-covered arm. The nurse paused, nodded and left the room. Katie sat again. She looked at her watch. Where was he? She looked at the wall clock. Frowned. Both clock and watch were in agreement: the constable was taking a long time.

She went to the corridor. No cop. She closed the ward door and went to the nurses' station.

"Excuse me," she said.

The nurse looked past Katie. "You can't leave the door closed."

"My Mum might be in danger. Please call Security."

The nurse began to protest. "I can't just –"

Katie snatched the pencil from the nurse's hand, snapped it in two, dropped the halves on the counter. She shouted: "Now. Bloody well do it now."

The nurse, open-mouthed, obviously thought Security was just what she needed right now. She picked up the phone and poked at the numbers, warily watching the angry teenager.

Katie watched her put the phone down. She looked at Katie with an expression that alarmed her.

"He's not answering. Ted always answers."

"Call another one," Katie said, hands gripping the edge of the counter.

"Tony's at lunch. He –"

"Bloody late lunch." Katie's voice shrilled. She hated that. She took a deep breath, paused, then said: "That man you were talking to, the fake doctor, he killed my Dad and put my Mum in the room up there."

"Oh my god." She looked at the phone, looked at Katie, back at the phone, poked at buttons, stopped, peered at the numbers, hesitated.

She looked at Katie as if hoping she could tell her what to press. Katie touched the nurse's hand, settling its wavering movements.

Katie scanned the corridor in both directions. Nobody. She had to get back to the ward. Protect her Mum. Somehow secure the door. At least it was still closed. As she had left it.

She turned back to the nurse, standing, phone in shaking hand, watching the teenager with wild eyes watching everything.

Katie forced herself to speak calmly. "Can you get your boss? Or a couple of attendants?"

The nurse looked down at the buttons again.

"Yes."

"Nurse," Katie said, "I'm sorry I shouted. You may have saved my mother's life by delaying the fake doctor. Thank you."

She turned and ran towards her mother's room. She was nearing the doorway when she heard footsteps behind her, thumping down more heavily than her light steps. She stifled a scream. She didn't look.

"Wait," a man shouted.

Wait? No way. She rushed into the ward and gripped the door to close it. Tried. A big hand grabbed the door edge. Katie couldn't budge it. The man outside was too strong and gradually pulled the door open, dragging Katie with it. She wouldn't scream near her mother.

"Jeez, miss, you make it hard." The constable stuck his face around the door. Katie felt like falling to the floor and lying flat out. She walked into the corridor.

The constable was holding his phone but not talking on it. Relieved, Katie nodded at him.

He smiled ruefully, said: "Sorry, Miss, he got away." Obviously. "He stabbed Ted, the security guard. Left him lying at the bottom of the stairs. Doctors got to him quickly, of course. Not a bad place to get stabbed. A hospital. I just rang the boss. Brought him up to par."

Katie nodded again and smiled encouragingly at him for doing what he should have done. His duty.

"He kidnapped me," she said. "Probably killed my Dad, bashed my Mum."

"I told Detective Sergeant Brogan I didn't know who he was."

Katie rolled her eyes but refrained from saying, "I told you what he did".

"I don't know his name, but it's not the poor sod left dead on the bedroom floor."

It could have been construed as a question. The constable looked uncomfortable.

"You'll have to speak to Detective Sergeant Brogan about that."

"Right." No point asking this cop.

"I'll be away for a minute or so," Katie said. "Make a phone call."

The officer nodded as if he cared what this teenage girl did.

Along the corridor, at the top of the stairs, Katie rang Jack's mobile phone. No answer. Probably switched off again. Don't know why he bothers carrying one. She tried Mary. She was always on the ball. Sure enough, she answered.

"Hello, Katie —" There was a clunk, bouncing thuds. A shout. Muffled voices. Silence.

Katie looked at her phone, hung up and called Mary again. No answer.

34

KATIE

Mum, what's wrong with your son? What's the point of sticking a phone in his pocket if he's not going to answer it? Must have it turned off. At a time like this, for god's sake. Sorry Mum hope my thoughts are not getting through to you. I know, I know. Jack turns the sound off while at work, has it on vibrate.

But Mary… why didn't… worried about her. She answered but sounded like she dropped it. Very hard. But why didn't she call back? Said my name when she... Oh. Try again. Maybe broke in the drop. Yes. That's it. Maybe she fell over. Sounded hard. Voices too. Seeing if she was all right?

Come on, Jack, turn the sound back on.

What should I do, Mum? You'd know. Call the cops? About people not answering their phones? Get cab to Jack and Mary's? They might be there. Yes. One or the other….Or that bastard…

Call Aunty Meg. And cops. Wait here. Jack's picking me up here. Any minute. Tell this cop? Please sir, they won't answer my calls. Mum, what is best? Try Jack again.

* * *

WEDNESDAY 5:15pm

Jack whistled as he drove to pick up Mary from the Hardwicke Accountancy Practice. He was fifteen minutes early, but Mary was sometimes allowed to go before five-thirty. Good boss. He parked close to the office and got out.

He waited on the footpath. He didn't mind standing around. He would never leave Mary standing alone in the street at this hour when there weren't many people about.

All shops in that part of town were either closed or closing. The sun was setting, gleaming redly on the shiny tops of parked cars and casting shadows of low buildings and tall poles on the road, undulating over occasional passing vehicles. He turned at the sounds of the office front door closing and two women talking. He knew them.

Heather, tall, slim, blonde, No Mary. And Charmaine, shorter, rounder, auburn hair. No Mary.

"Hey, Jack," Heather called out. "What you doing here?"

"Picking Mary up," he said, walking towards them.

"She's not here. Didn't she tell you?"

"We arranged it this morning. Not changed since then."

Charmaine said: "She's gone off with the boss, half an hour ago." She was chewing gum and the words came from her mouth stickily sloppy, as if agitated out of shape by her chewing. Jack got the gist: they had spoken before. He didn't know what she sounded like with a gum-free mouth. Despite distortion, the words struck fear into Jack.

"She can't have," he said. "We arranged to meet here —" he checked his watch — "now. We were—"

Heather broke in: "Very sad about your Dad. We've all been thinking of you." Jack turned when the office door opened again. Not Mary. He looked up and down the street. Back at Heather. "You did good yesterday. Great funeral speech."

"Are you sure Mary isn't still in there? Is there a back entrance?"

"Nahh," Charmaine said. "Youse getting back together, Mary told us."

"Look," Jack said, "do you know where they were going?" Both women shook their heads. Charmaine pushed gum from one side to the other.

"She's all right, Jack. Safe with Mr Hardwicke," Heather said.

"Only natural to be worried," Charmaine may have said. "After all your poor family is going through."

"Yes, how is your poor Mum?" Heather said, lifting her wrist to see the time.

Jack said, "Maybe someone inside can tell me where they are." He took a step towards the office door. "She's not answering her phone."

The women exchanged glances and shook their heads.

Heather half-turned to go. She said: "Not many in there now."

Charmaine said: "They might be back soon."

And, with that hesitant piece of gummy optimism, they walked away.

Finding the office door was not locked, Jack went in.

The five staff left were standing among the desks, preparing to leave for the day. They all knew Jack, so they responded politely to his questions as he went from one to another.

He walked out onto the footpath five minutes later still without any idea of where Mary was. Out on business with her boss, was the sum of knowledge in the Hardwicke Accountancy office.

At least she's safe if she's with him, Jack reasoned. His staff were quite adamant that Mary hadn't been driven away by a stranger. Thank god, for that. Hardwicke was a big bloke. Should be able to look after himself. And anyway, with Col Martin dead, the danger is over. But what to do? Wait? Go home.

Freddie thought he overheard Hardwicke say he would drive Mary home. OK, which home is home? Theirs or her parents'? Anyway, Freddie wasn't sure he had heard what his boss had said.

He tried Mary's number again with the same result: "Sorry, I can't talk to you at the moment. Please leave —"

Jack shut it off. That lovely, sweet voice. His mother's was silent. His father's gone forever.

35

THE BOOK KEEPER

They think they are putting the pieces together now. Pity. I thought they would have taken longer. It is not that our police are smarter than I had estimated. It was bad luck for me that the annoying teenager was there and heard my voice. I will talk softer next time. And that brat's luck will run out soon.

Edie is no help now. I did not realise how weak she would turn out to be, how squeamish.

She was close to collapse when Peter died. She said she would never get over it. So much worse to learn our precious little boy had been murdered.

It was me alone who never gave up. I found the truth. Me. Peter would thank me.

Edie agreed we could not close our eyes to that terrible crime. The enormity of the crime, with its multiple contributors, burns me up. Not like reading about murders in the paper or hearing about such horrors on the television or radio news. We heard it direct. Edie and Colin from the police; me, later.

When you find an accident was, in fact, a sadistic murder, it becomes a part of you. A pain deep inside like a diseased organ, aching day and night. No surgeon can remove it. None can perform a griefectomy. Useless profession.

The second time a son.

Jeremy and Lisa stolen by the woman who lied about loving me. Taken when my back was turned.

Edie should be happy that we are balancing the books. But she…

First things first.

Taking Mary will throw a spanner into their foolish works. They do not get it. Just think they do. Or did, until pathetic Colin Martin dropped into their realities.

Mary's boyfriend and his mate could have saved me all this stress. And the extra work. It is not as if I have a lot of time to spare.

She keeps looking at me. Perhaps she wonders why I have not said much. She will find out before the day is over. She may realise then that silence is golden.

* * *

WEDNESDAY 4:44pm

Mary was uneasy. Hardwicke was tight-lipped, gripping the wheel, eyes focused on the road. He wasn't a naturally jovial person, but he usually spoke about work matters when driving to see clients, like today. Her attempts at small talk elicited grunts. She was unnerved by his silence. She turned to look out the window again.

Mary usually enjoyed drives in the countryside around Manderville. She and Jack had spent many pleasant hours on walks and picnics and lovemaking in the Great Mander Forest, which was now to the left of the car. She smiled, remembering the last time they had lain together on the grassy floor, overseen only by trees and ferns and bushes. When they finished and rolled apart onto their backs, a kookaburra cracked the restored quietness of the forest with its loud laugh. Jack quickly dropped his trousers over his lower body. Mary laughed. "He's not laughing at that Jack."

The car rolled on, leaving the forest behind. Now, on both sides, with low, tree-dotted, brown hills sloping down to wide green pastures and flocks of merino sheep, Hardwicke seemed preoccupied and Mary kept her thoughts to herself, reasoning he was sometimes the same in the office. Nevertheless, after another five minutes, she tried again.

"Lovely country, isn't it, Mr Hardwicke?" No reply. Keep trying. "Nice day, too, for what… we're … for … this …"

Success.

"Indeed, yes, it is a perfectly lovely day," he said, turning to her with a broad, toothy grin. It wasn't the breakthrough she hoped for. He concentrated on the road for the next ten minutes.

She said: "Where did you say we're going? I didn't catch it when —"

"I did not tell you. You know that, Miss Bourke." No smile this time.

"Oh."

He slowed the car. "I see no harm in telling you now," he said. "I am calling on Mr Thomas Hud—"

Mary gasped. "Tucker. You mean Jack's mate, Tucker?"

"I believe that is what his friends call him. I never use such frivolous names for people."

Outside, the country was darkening into an idyllic scene under the last rays of the sun; inside, Mary felt the air chill and she wrapped both arms around her body and pressed back hard into the seat, trying to control a shiver. She almost succeeded, but Hardwicke glanced across with a slight smile.

She was determined not to let her Jekyll and Hyde boss see her apprehension.

She said: "What's this all about, Mr Hardwicke?"

He briefly looked at her. He turned back to the road without answering.

"Why him?" Mary said. "Tucker? He uses Maxwell's."

"Sam Maxwell. Amateur. Mr Durkin's friend has a record of making bad decisions."

"No point coming out here," Mary said. 'He's away.'

"No matter. It is probably all to the good. It is his wife and son I want to see."

Oh shit. Mary's mind struggled to form words into a coherent sentence; her tongue trembled, waiting for instructions.

"He is…He's … Tucker … His wife … He has … He's taken them with him. Nobody is… nobody's home."

Hardwicke banged a fist on the wheel.

"I don't blame them," Mary, more confidently said. "Not after some cowardly mongrel ran their boy down."

Hardwicke cursed. The car momentarily wobbled sideways.

Mary saw the Hudsons' two-storey red brick house, standing about thirty metres from the low matching brick fence. A wide drive led to a long, silver, corrugated iron shed and out of sight from the road, Mary knew, was a sprawling fenced area for Tucker's hundreds of chickens.

With some satisfaction, she said: "Gone to New Zealand." An outright lie, but she had no qualms about lying to a killer. She feared that was what he was.

Hardwicke jammed on the brakes so sharply that the car slid sideways before stopping off the road, several metres from the driveway. The gate was open, which surprised Mary. She hoped somebody had called in. Hardwicke might speed away if anyone appeared, but where to?

He was angry at what Mary had said. He bashed the wheel again. And again. He slumped back and stared at the house. At Mary. Back at the house.

Mary watched in silence, fearful of what her boss was thinking. She could almost hear his brain ticking and felt the fear rising and a sourness filling her mouth.

Hardwicke put the car into gear and drove slowly through the open gate and stopped on the drive alongside the house. Mary's stomach tightened, her breathing staccatoed into short in-and-out puffs. Get a grip.

He looked at her and smiled—more to himself than at her.

"I told you they aren't home," Mary said. "House is empty."

He turned the engine off. "I know."

"Why have you stopped here, then?"

He looked at the house and back at Mary. "We can go in there. We will not be disturbed. It will be that way for longer than I need and much longer than you will be aware of." He smiled just like he did in the office when he made a joke and waited for obedient staff to laugh. Mary didn't laugh. She stifled a scream and gripped her knees tightly, as if crushing pain would distract her from the chilling fear that froze her mind. Undisturbed for…

He was going to leave her lying on the floor, her body undiscovered for months, perhaps until Tucker returned. She blinked a tear away and released her knees from destruction. She might need two good legs before the night was over.

She concentrated and regained control of of her tongue again. "You can't break into their home." That'll dissuade him–not. Break-and-enter is way down the crime scale from murder and attempted murder. How did she ever win debating contests?

"I'm not going in there," she said. "It's … it's… trespassing." Good point, Mary.

"I am sure you will." He leant down to his right and came up with a long knife. He held the brown wood handle and aimed the tip at her throat. She saw stains on the blade, but instantly dismissed it as a trick of the fading light. She pulled back as far as she could and watched the man who had praised her work, promoted her, cried in his office telling her of the long-past day when his wife and children left him. Now he smiled down at the big knife in his hand like a father smiling at a new child.

Mary relaxed taut muscles in her shoulders, slumped slightly, when Hardwicke put the knife on his leg; his hand still around the handle.

"Yes, relax for a minute." Huh? Was he for real? Too real. Crazy real. And Mary was scared stiff real. Wanting Jack right now real.

Hardwicke said: "I will get a way in for us." He locked her in the car and walked through the shadows, across the lawn to the front door. He stood for a few seconds, testing the knob. Mary hoped someone, somewhere, would hear the rattling. As if aware of her thoughts, he left the knob to pull something silver from a coat pocket. He bent slightly over the lock. From the distance and in the darkness, it was hard for Mary to see what Hardwicke was doing. But it was now or never. Do something now, quickly. The car doors were locked and couldn't be opened from inside. Childproof. Prisoner proof. The windows were too small for her to unobtrusively squeeze through. Smash one. Stupid idea. Ring Jack. Anyone. Her phone was in her handbag, which Hardwicke, against her protest, had put on the back seat next to his briefcase. On the driver's side. Long stretch. She swivelled around, reaching across the back area. The bag was beyond the reach of her outstretched fingers.

She risked a quick look at the house. Hardwicke was pushing the door open. Shit. Desperately, she thrust her legs against her seat and lunged at her bag. Her fingers touched the leather and snapped sharply around the handle. She turned to the front with the bag on her lap. Time was running out. Her boss was coming back.

She scrabbled inside the bag, took out her phone and closed the bag. She pocketed the phone and flung the bag back where it had been.

Hardwicke was at her window. She turned away. He tapped on the glass. She ignored him and he gave up. Mary hoped he had locked himself out. No such luck. He went to the other side and opened the door.

Mary turned to the front and saw hope appear through the fog of night spreading thinly over the property. At the top of the drive, two men in overalls had walked from around the back of the house. One carried a bucket; the other a torch, lighting their path towards the shed.

Mary leaned across and pressed repeatedly on the horn, startling Hardwicke, who had apparently not seen the men.

"That won't help you –"

"They will," she said, pointing through the windscreen. The men now stood, looking at the car and the big man standing at its open door. The one with the bucket dropped it against the shed door and called out.

"Are you looking for Tucker?"

Hardwicke bent into the car. He glared, pale-faced, at Mary, but she saw he was stunned, like last year when a long-time client said he was moving to another accountancy firm.

He pulled back and stood facing the men who had magically appeared to wreck his plans.

"I… I wanted—"

"He's away, mate, on a break. We might be able to —"

Mary blasted the horn several times, causing the man with the torch to swear and wave the light around.

Hardwicke mumbled something about his mistake and apologised for his daughter's impatience on the horn. He jumped back into his seat.

Oh god. "Help." She shouted over the sound of the engine starting and the radio suddenly blaring. Hardwicke put the car into reverse.

Mary kept shouting and waved wildly, hoping her gestures would be seen as coming from a distressed woman calling for rescue. Hardwicke was smiling and waving jovially.

The men smiled and waved them off. Hardwicke reversed onto the road and turned right, heading further away from Manderville.

The headlights shone on the black road and lit tree by tree by tree as they ghosted past. Mary turned her head away from Hardwicke. She stared through her reflection into the night. No light. No hope. Her left hand sneaked up to wipe her left eye, then her right to the other eye.

Behind her, Hardwicke began humming. Shit. Deep shit. Tucker's workers were unlikely to report a crime, not after waving off a confused, but smiling, man and his looney 'daughter'.

They were now travelling along a narrow, bush-lined, road that Mary had seldom been on. She remained silent, glad the radio was, also. She clasped her hands on her lap and waited for Hardwicke to say something. What now? Whatever it might be, she feared she might never see the Welcome to Manderville sign again. Probably not sunrise either.

A loud melody made her jump, and Hardwicke glanced at her. She jerked her phone out with relief. Sure to be someone who would rescue her. At last, help was at hand. Literally. She slammed the phone to her ear so quickly she winced as it thumped into her ear.

"Hello," she said.

"Mary, I saw–"

"Katie–"

Mary got no further. Hardwicke swung his left hand from the wheel and whacked the phone out of her hand. It flew from her grip and thudded onto the back seat.

Mary swore and rubbed her stinging hand.

"You utter bastard. I was on a call. I've got friends."

"You have no need of that anymore, Mary," Hardwicke said. "I am sure you do not want false hopes raised. You have always been an honest, forthright woman. That is why I like you."

Mary wanted to vomit.

He had both hands back on the wheel.

Mary said: "You are the only person I have ever hated. And I despise you for causing me to have that emotion."

"Perhaps you will now know what drives me."

He had lapsed into silence. Her hand still tingled. She sucked her thumb and forefinger. The childhood comforting habit brought more tears. She wiped her hand on her blouse and turned back to the window. There wasn't much to see along this country road in daylight. Now, in the pitch-black of night, with even the moon and starlight blanked out by clouds, only an occasional light from a farmhouse scattered Mary's reflection. Once, a white hatchback overtook them and Mary watched helplessly as its red lights shrank into the enveloping darkness.

They came to a crossroad and Hardwicke turned to the left. Mary thought it was back to town but wasn't sure. But, so what? Safer there?

Her hand still stung.

She said: "Mr Hardwicke, what's going on? You wanted me with you to go over a new client's books. That was a lie. So, why am I here?" Silly question, she knew. Might draw something out of him. Actually, state the obvious. Anything's better than this damn silence. Or was this as good as it was going to get.

Hardwicke kept his grip on the wheel, his eyes on the road.

"No, Mary — do you mind me calling you Mary, Miss Bourke, now that we are out here alone?"

She didn't answer. He'd used her first name before without asking permission.

"What I said was that I wanted you to help me balance the books of a new client."

Mary shook her head. Mincing words. "What's the difference? Tucker was never going to become our —". Suddenly she shivered, as if someone had left a door open. She saw the difference.

"You did not pay proper attention, Mary." He chuckled. "Mr Hudson was already on my — not our — books, as is young Mr John Durkin. As are others."

"This is crazy. We aren't your clients —". She stopped. It was futile to argue against the man's twisted logic. Her mind was racing faster than she thought possible, ideas tumbling over the ones in front, falling under new ones coming behind. What to say? Do? Play dumb? Pray? Dumb.

"I confess I don't understand all about your business, Mr Hardwicke. I want to learn more, but … Oh, look at the time. I'd better get home. Can we turn around now, please?" Too dumb a play for her boss.

He shot her a quick glance. "Problem with that, Mary, is that we each have different priorities. I am sure you know what I mean." She didn't reply or nod. "Now how can we resolve that?"

She knew he had no intention of resolving anything in her favour.

"Should it be ladies first? Or age before beauty? Or— " He was toying with her. "— I know, I think a boss would take precedence over an employee."

Hardwicke had switched to silent mode again. The car turned to the left, then left again and in about ten minutes, Mary sat up at the sight of the Manderville welcome sign. They were soon passing houses lining streets, their window lights taunting her with unreachable hope.

But she was back in 'civilisation' and even though held by a barbarian, she was cheered by signs of life around her: a strolling couple, man putting a garbage bin out, cars coming and going, criss-crossing at intersections, woman standing at a tree waiting for a small dog to relieve itself. Oh, for boring normality.

"Have you changed your mind?" She waited for the obvious answer.

"Not a lot, Mary. I have changed from Plan A to Plan B and now to Plan C. To succeed in life, we must be flexible. And I did not want to go directly to our destination."

He spoke as if addressing a weekly staff meeting.

"Our destination? Somewhere I know?"

"Wait and see. Patience, Mary."

Wait to be killed. She stared out, hoping to attract someone's attention, wishing the interior light was on. If only someone she knew was on the street. Looking in her direction. Recognise her in the shadows in just one of the cars whizzing past. She slumped back in her seat. They passed the Memorial Gardens and sports ground. As they turned another corner, she saw the lights of the hospital in the distance. Would Bev ever learn what her assailant did to others?

Hardwicke again intruded into her thoughts. "Bit chilly, Mary? That probably explains why there are so few people on the streets at this time of day. Pity, you may well think." He chuckled. The dry sound in his throat chilled Mary more than the night air.

"Yes." Her mind was racing, agitated by the fear that couldn't be allayed. The car slowed to go around a corner. Mary took a chance. Maybe Hardwicke had inadvertently unlocked the door when he was knocking on the car window and shaking the door handle at the farm. Not likely, but desperation led her on. She grabbed the door handle and pulled with both hands. No go. The handle wobbled slightly but the lock didn't budge.

"I thought I would never have need of childproof locks again," Hardwicke said. "Sadly, until now. I have not needed them since — "

"Since your wife took your children away?" Mary said, not caring about Hardwicke's feelings now. He gave her a baleful glance.

"Yes. I have never seen them for all those years. So long." He paused, swallowed hard. "Yes," he said again. "And more recently."

Mary looked across, expecting him to say more, but he left it at that.

She realised they were going down familiar streets. What is this? A game? Is he going to let her out? Just say "See you tomorrow, Miss Bourke?" Hardwicke drove past their home without slowing. Jack's car wasn't there. Surely, he wasn't still waiting for her at her workplace.

"Your journey will soon be over," he said.

Literally or figuratively?

Both, she thought.

She shut out the negative thoughts and concentrated on the route he was taking. Could be important later, if — *when* she broke free. Wait, this is near…

"Familiar streets, Mary?"

He turned into the street leading to Ray and Bev's lane. She moved in her seat hoping to see neighbours who might recognise her. What on earth? Was he returning to the scene of…

Then, before Mary had processed this, Hardwicke had turned into the often-visited lane and in less than a minute, was slowing down on the Durkins' driveway. The last time she had been here was with Jack. Hardwicke switched the engine off.

She was confused, her mind slowed by a jumble of apprehension, even dread, and tinges of curiosity and hope. Could she run from Hardwicke when released from the car?

He got out and locked the door. She watched as he strode around and opened her door. He roughly hauled her out, banging her elbow on the door pillar.

"Do not try anything silly. Lives may depend on your silence, not the least being your own."

He held the long knife in his left hand. He touched the point to her cheek. She jerked her head away as far as his tight hold would allow. He paused to survey the area. Mary did, too, as far as her limited movement permitted. No cars or pedestrians in the lane. Bugger. Apparently satisfied there wasn't anyone watching, he turned his attention to the front door of the house, as if estimating the distance and the time the job would take, allowing for negotiating the paths through the gladioli beds.

"Get going," he whispered. Tightening his grasp on her left upper arm, he pushed her onto a short path, parallel with the lane, between big square beds of massed gladioli. Not pausing to admire the moonlit display, he roughly swung Mary around onto the path that ran from the front gate to the veranda and shoved her towards the house. All the while, his vice-like grip never loosened.

Ray's wondrous array of the tall flowers was stunning in a way that Mary thought rivalled the sunlit gardens. All around her were more colours than any rainbow ever assembled. Dark and light, plain and variegated, show-offs and mysterious, familiar and rare, a carnival of hues; each green-sheathed sword flower standing proudly in random array.

There, in the midst of Ray's legacy, with a killer's knife at her throat, Mary was overwhelmed by the beauty and the perfume and sense of peace. Tears welled in her eyes. She blinked. "Thank you, Ray," she murmured.

"Get going. No maudlin dawdling." Hardwicke gave her a push along and she almost overbalanced. He yanked her to her feet and chuckled.

"You don't have to squeeze so tightly," she said. He replied by pushing harder and flashed his knife in her face, as a reminder. As if she needed one.

Mary bit her lip. She wondered how long it would take to get normal feeling back in her arm. Thankfully, it wasn't her right arm.

Not that even two full-strength arms would prevail against this brute.

Under Hardwicke's 'guidance', Mary stumbled up the three steps to stand trembling on the veranda floorboards, facing the dark green door. Hardwicke pushed the door open. Mary knew then that he had been there recently. It may have been his hiding place.

He shut the door with his foot and push-marched Mary down the hall, dimly lit by the light from the kitchen.

There was at least one person in that room, someone sitting, quite still, on a chair, back turned, facing the closed back door.

36

KATIE

Oh god, Jack, answer your bloody phone. Mary, too. Where are you? Both can't have disappeared. No. Can't be that. And Aunty Meg, not picking up either phone. Nor Uncle Doug either. Probably asleep. How could he in the middle of all this? Asleep in front of TV cop shows while we're in a real life-and-death drama.

Mary… Mary… Has that bastard got her? No. I won't have that. Helpless.

Try Jack again… might know something by now… Ring. Ring. … at last…

* * *

WEDNESDAY 5.56pm

Mary wasn't in a hurry to get anywhere but Hardwicke pushed her along the hall. Her shuffling, stumbling and falling sideways into the walls didn't bring any reaction from the woman sitting in the kitchen.

She wasn't showing any interest in the new arrivals. Probably expecting us, Mary thought.

Hardwicke shoved Mary to the kitchen doorway. There was nobody else in the room. The woman didn't turn around; her shoulders shook and her head dropped to her chest. She didn't look at them.

As Mary was propelled further into the kitchen, she cried out. "Hardwicke. You — "

The apparently disinterested, unresponsive woman on the chair was Edie Martin. Although the woman was facing the other way, Mary could see enough to recognise her former colleague, despite the brown scarf covering her mouth. She was trussed like a moth in a spider's web, tied to the chair, with thin rope winding around and across and down and up. No wonder she hadn't turned around.

"Why is ..." Mary began, conscious she was within reach of the giant spider himself. "What's going on?" No answer. A grin. Does a spider grin when contemplating its trapped victim? Stupid question.

Mary took two steps sideways. Hardwicke moved in step. She was still within reach of his iron grip. Edie's face was almost white, her eyes red, frightened and flitting from side to side, as if never finding what they sought. Her gag twisted and jerked as the mouth struggled to summon what the eyes couldn't see.

"I believe you have met my lover, Edie Martin."

Stunned, Mary could only stammer broken sentences of denial. The smirk on Hardwicke's face made her sick.

"The office gossip didn't catch up with that one, did it Mary?"

"You and Edie? No."

"Strictly speaking, not now, sadly. Not since she said too much to her husband."

"Did you kill Col?" She regretted asking, talking like this with Edie tied and gagged metres away.

"He was pathetic. He thought spray painting a few walls was sufficient to cover the debt."

Mary looked around the room, for familiar objects, things that existed in the world she had been dragged out of. Table, chairs, fridge, pantry... but here a killer and waiting victims. She shook her head. Deal with it. This was the only reality she had.

"Is that why you shot him? Just that?"

"He was on to us. I could not let him go to the police."

"They will get you. I know that. Edie knows that."

Edie squirmed, trying to speak, but her words were smothered by the gag.

"She is a shy person at heart," he said. "So forgive her if she doesn't say much."

Mary turned angrily on him, cursing his cruel, lying mockery. He seemed amused by the wild look on Mary's face as much as by the words. She wanted to slap the frozen smirk off his face, but that would be a fatal mistake. She unclenched her fists by her side and tried to calm herself. Although her mind was screaming, she spoke quietly: "What are you doing to Edie? You killed her husband and now you call yourself her lover. How dare you– "

He pushed Mary against the wall and stared into her eyes. She winced at the pressure of his hand on her shoulder. She shuffled, considered bringing her knee up into his groin. But he had placed himself out of reach of attack from that direction. His eyes were watery. Spittle dripped onto his chin.

"Edie lost her son and this week you killed her husband, Peter's father," Mary said, tightly controlling her voice but unable to prevent an underlying tremor.

"His son!" he said so viciously that droplets splattered on her blouse. "Peter was MY son, not Colin Martin's."

Mary tried to laugh in his face but it came out as a gurgle. She feared any moment could be her last. She didn't know how to reason with a lunatic. A crazy killer.

Edie was squirming and had pushed her feet on the floor. The chair rocked. Mary tried to break away from Hardwicke to help Edie. She couldn't budge his arm. He tightened his hold, smirking into Mary's face.

"You utter bastard," Mary said, shouting now. "So twisted up you don't know right from wrong." Pathetic insult, she thought. Should do better…

"You should have learned, working in my practice, that everything must be balanced. I have always made sure of that. I have failed you as a mentor if you do not get that basic tenet of accountancy."

"You're talking murder, not bloody accountancy."

That brought a string of invective from Hardwicke, during which he turned to Edie, as if soliciting her support. Mary felt his grip loosen. She jerked free, swinging both arms. The knife clattered to the floor. She spun in a half circle, avoiding his flailing arms. Her right foot trod on the knife. She kicked wildly, sending it skidding past the stove to end against the fridge.

She thudded into the kitchen table.

She yelped and automatically bent to rub her thigh. Her eyes never left Hardwicke, who had pulled a drawer out from next to the sink. With his eyes fixed on Mary, he rummaged around in it. She heard the metallic clink of large utensils as his hand scrabbled for another weapon. They stood metres apart, eyes locked: two glistened with terror, two glowed with hatred. Neither spoke.

His hand rose from the drawer holding a long, wide, heavy, wooden-handled chef's knife. Oh my god, it's bigger than the first. He twisted it and shifted it to his right hand. The blade flashed silver and deadly.

Oh shit. Mary backed slowly along the table edge, pain in every slide of her leg. But that was nothing compared to…

She saw a more extreme pain a few steps away. Hardwicke took his time. Mary tried to calm her mind. Getting harder. She needed to think clearly. Ignore the threat inching towards her. Do prey do that? Can they assess the odds, decide clearly what action could save their life? Shit, wouldn't know they… it had a life. No, she does. Don't freeze. Don't panic, run hither and thither. Calm. How to do calm with a chef's knife waving a metre from her face?

She was familiar with the kitchen but couldn't see anything that could save her life. Her eyes flicked around the room, but she had to keep her focus on the madman with the big knife. Nothing. Nothing.

Desperately, she picked up a kitchen chair. Held it high. A flimsy, green, wood weapon. It might do.

Hardwicke laughed at her.

"That is a good idea, Mary," he said. She trembled, knowing he didn't think that at all.

He suddenly changed direction. He swung around quickly to stand beside Edie and waved the knife near her throat.

"Now, Mary, put that chair down and sit on it."

"You must be joking." As if. Dumb.

"I never joke." Except when trying to impress office juniors.

Mary hesitated. The chair waggled above her head. She was terrified for Edie's sake, but didn't want to put her only weapon down.

"It is a bit heavy for you is it not, Mary? Be a good girl and put it down. And then sit on it."

He put the knife closer to Edie's neck. She squirmed and a whimper came through the gag.

Mary put the chair on the floor, but didn't sit, standing behind it, holding the top back rail.

Hardwicke shouted: "If you do not sit on that chair, I will slit Edie's throat. That will be a pity because we had a lovely relationship when she was my secretary. And, of course, she is the mother of my son. But what must be done must be done."

He theatrically swiped the knife back and forwards under Edie's chin. The gagged woman rocked back just centimetres and gurgling sounds came through the brown cloth.

Mary gasped. She had to obey Hardwicke. She pushed the chair to the end of the table and sat on it. Hardwicke stepped away from Edie

"That is better".

"Why do you want to hurt Edie? Who you claim is the mother of your son?" Get him talking.

"She is not as committed as I am —"

He should be committed, Mary thought, but didn't say.

"— to setting things right."

"How can killing people set anything right? You must—"

He banged the knife handle down on the table. Mary jumped in her seat. Edie whimpered.

"You cannot feel what … we, what I went through. We mourned terribly when Peter… it happened. Tragic accident they said…"

Mary hoped his attention would stray, even a little. Might give her —

Suddenly he banged the table again and shouted into the air. "Lies. Lies all along. All those years of grief."

His voice dropped and he smiled at Mary. A conspiratorial smile that scared her more than his shouting and banging.

"I found out the truth. That Peter had been murdered. Did you know that?"

His voice cracked and he gave up. He paced back and forth to the outside door, which had the big key in the lock, then over to the hallway entrance. But, so far, he hadn't moved towards Mary, who watched his every movement, her fingers stiff, gripping the seat edges. Her legs were poised to leap away if she was approached. She doubted she could be quick enough. Her eyes stung from staring at him.

She said: "How did the police miss, from the start, that Peter's death wasn't an accident, was murder?"

Hardwicke had stopped pacing and was opening the kitchen cupboard. He looked at Mary for a minute or so, until she was about to repeat her time-gaining question. He blinked. A tear perhaps? Another blink. His left hand was still in the cupboard. Was he hungry?

"Incompetent. They said it was the way those now-dead bullies did it. Mullins told me—after a period of persuasion— they held Peter by the legs in the creek… until he …"

Edie rocked sideways, sobbing into her gag, wet from mouth and streaming tears.

Hardwicke, who had brought another rope from the cupboard, turned a tear-stained face to Mary. He said nothing. He went to Edie and his shoulders shook. He turned around to Mary quickly as if suddenly realising she might make a break.

"Can you imagine that, Mary? Peter calling for his Mummy, Daddy and not meaning me."

"But Edie," Mary began, "Mr Hardwicke, surely there were signs that someone caused his death?" She struggled to finish the sentence, her eyes were on the rope in Hardwicke's left hand and the knife in the other.

Edie vigorously shook her head. Hardwicke paused to wipe his eyes with the back of his knife-free hand.

"They said — the police — that there were no signs of trauma—" His voice trembled. "— on his body other than would be expected …" He trailed off, then became audible again— "flooded creek."

He put the knife down on the table. Thank goodness for that. He shifted the rope to his right hand and fished a handkerchief out of a pocket and wiped his eyes. He hesitated, went to Edie. She shrunk back as far as she could. He bent and wiped her eyes.

Mary's eyes needed drying, also: tears released by sadness, aloneness and fear for her life. She wiped them with her sleeve, one eye at a time. Then her fear increased. She pushed her feet to the floor, ready to jump up.

Hardwicke's grin was back, as was the threat in his now dry eyes. He had moved to Mary's side of the table. He took a step towards her, big knife in one hand, looped rope dangling from the other. His grin chilled her.

Ray was dead, Bev in hospital, nobody would come to this house looking for her. To rescue her. She estimated the distance — the time — to the back door. She wouldn't make it: The table and chairs in the way and she would have to fiddle with the key; it stuck sometimes. Needed oil. She considered the hall leading to the front door. No good. Hardwicke's in the way.

"Now, Mary, I have seen how clever you are. Your bright intelligence stood out in my practice. You were destined for bigger things. Did you know that? I knew you were trying to distract me from my work here tonight. Keep me talking. Playing for time. It did not work."

"Mr Hardwicke, I just didn't understand what changed you. We didn't know of your grief when Peter died. Nobody knew he was your son. Colin was grief-stricken."

The gag only distorted, not fully silenced, Edie's heart-rending shriek. She was shaking violently, and the chair rocked under her.

Hardwicke laughed harshly. "Of course he was, he thought he was Peter's father. But Edie and I knew differently. Peter was my son and he was taken. I grieved in secret — except when I was with Edie."

Hardwicke took another step. Mary shifted her grip on the chair seat, ready to move at any second.

He stopped. "I try my best. You understand? I will balance my personal books."

Bizarre. Mary moved her feet further back, tension in her legs.

"And the little brat who ran away. She is still on my books. Free now, but not forever. I'll get her back."

He paused, as if he had lost the thread of his rambling rant.

"So, Mary, we come to you. Your beloved partner, Jack Durkin. We can guess how he'll be overwhelmed with grief at losing you. Can you picture that, Mary?"

His face showed he could see it clearly and it excited him.

"You bastard, Hardwicke," Mary shouted, standing. "If Jack was here, you wouldn't be so cocky –"

"You mean the kid who was beaten up by a girl? You look shocked that I know that, Mary. I do my research."

"He was just a boy. And he –"

"And when he was older," Hardwicke said, "he could have saved my son's life. But he turned his back. Skulked away. Do not count on rescue from him, Mary."

He took another step towards her. She knew he would rush her at any moment. Tie her up like Edie. She lifted her hands off the seat and stood stiffly, her thigh still sore. She grasped the back of the chair and lifted it to waist level. He laughed.

"A bit desperate, then, Mary? Not many useful weapons in here. I noticed a big wooden rolling pin in the same drawer as this knife. What a pity you are so far from that drawer."

"Keep your fucking mock pity to yourself, Hardwicke."

"Oh, no more nice girl. Now I am scared." There was no fear in his laugh. Nor in his voice: "If you yell out again, I will kill Edie as I told you I would."

A crash spun both Mary and Hardwicke around to see Edie and chair on the floor. A chair leg was broken off in the fall. Hardwicke ran back towards her. Mary hobbled fast to the other side of the table. Maybe she could make the door now. She wasn't even close when Hardwicke looked up from Edie. He got to his feet and moved towards Mary again.

Desperately, she pulled the drawer open and grabbed the rolling pin that Hardwicke had mockingly suggested. She didn't think her strength with a rolling pin would overcome his with a knife. And rope.

"Quick thinking, Miss Mary." She knew he wasn't concerned by her weapon. "But you are only delaying the inevitable."

He took another step and swirled a loop of rope above his head like a lasso.

"Your darling Jack will be grieving you by morning."

Mary screamed.

"Like hell I will, Hardwicke," Jack said, bursting into the kitchen from the hallway.

Hardwicke turned so fast he staggered and had to brace himself against the table. The rope slipped from his hand and fell to the floor.

"How did —" Hardwicke said.

Jack hadn't called in for a chat. He charged into Hardwicke's back and grabbed his knife-wielding arm with both hands. Hardwicke tried to pull his arm free, but Jack was too strong.

"Give up, Jack, I've got the knife. You can't beat me." Hardwicke kept up his arrogant talk as they wrestled for control of the knife. "You've just arrived in time to see the end of your relationship with Mary. How romantic."

With the initial impetus of his charge into Hardwicke slowed by the impact, Jack was struggling to keep on his feet as the big man pushed and pulled.

Mary stood, back to the wall, fearful for Jack's safety.

Hardwicke, now recovered from the shock intrusion, had regained his smirk.

"Well, well, Mr Durkin. Or should I call you Mr Sissy? A girl beat you up, so you have no chance with a real man."

Holding Jack at arm's length, he half turned to Mary. "No hope of a rescue here, Mary. I am more afraid of you than Mr Sissy."

Jack swung and hit him on the jaw. "She wasn't a coward who sneaks up on a defenceless woman in her home and bashes her, who tries to kill a teenager and shoots a man in the dark."

The smirk had been knocked off Hardwicke's face and he swung his left fist at Jack.

"You bashed my Mum. You killed my Dad. Now it's your turn to suffer. It's over, Hardwicke."

Mary saw Edie was trying, unsuccessfully, to untangle herself on the floor. Satisfied that Edie wasn't badly injured, she trod carefully around her, to help Jack. A difficult task. The men were shifting and shoving and shuffling, stamping. Hardwicke's talk had stopped, replaced by grunts, growls and curses.

The big knife, slashed in all directions, controlled by three straining arms–two of them Hardwicke's. With his free left hand, Jack repeatedly punched Hardwicke's upper arm.

When Jack had miraculously appeared in the room, Mary's dread had lifted, but it soon settled over her again. Jack was unarmed. The odds were against him. Unless she could…

"Jack. Be careful." Stupid waste of breath. "I've got a rolling pin." Even dumber. Shut up. Action is needed, not inane comments.

She slid along the wall, only centimetres from the entangled fighters.

At the end of the table, Edie pushed herself to her feet, bringing the broken chair and rope with her. She stood unsteadily, leaning against the table.

Mary pressed hard into the wall as the men suddenly twisted towards her. She lifted the rolling pin high and stood, poised, waiting for a clear shot. A window of opportunity to whack her boss. There he was, his face distorted with rage. Mary struck with all the vicious force she could summon.

Hardwicke screamed as the heavy wooden implement slammed into the side of his face. Blood ran from his nose. "You bitch. You'll never work for me again. You'll never leave this place alive. Any of you."

A combination of shock, pain and Jack's unrelenting attack were too much for Hardwicke. The big knife clattered to the floor.

Jack kicked it across the tiles. It clinked against the bucket near the stove.

"Thanks," Jack said to Mary through gritted teeth, without turning from his battle for their survival.

Hardwicke pushed Jack sideways, causing him to slip. While he was off balance, Hardwicke punched him in the face. Jack slithered on the tiles, now wet with drizzled blood. Hardwicke changed his angle of attack. Jack was ready for it and, with his greater strength, wrenched Hardwicke's left hand down before it struck home, released it, punched back, hitting Hardwicke in the pit of his stomach. With a loud ooff, the killer doubled over, showering Jack's shirt with red droplets.

"You murderous bastard, you spilt my mother's blood on this floor, now yours is there."

Mary had retrieved the unused rope.

"Jack, I've got some rope," she said, adding unnecessarily, "to tie him up."

Jack was too preoccupied trying to subdue Hardwicke, to acknowledge this helpful information. Hardwicke wasn't about to accept his defeat. Jack tried to tighten his hold on the big man's arms, but he broke his right arm free and grabbed a chair. He swung it into Jack's knees.

Jack fell to the floor with a primal cry that tore at Mary's heart. She ran to him, skidding the last metre. With arms under his armpits, she tried to lift him to his feet.

Hardwicke looked around the wreckage and started for Edie who backed away, hands raised in front of her face. He didn't seem to know which way to go.

Jack was again on his feet and ready to continue the fray. Hardwicke ran for the back door. He turned the key and pushed at the door. Jack moved quickly but the door opened and the killer ran out into the darkness.

Jack's foot slipped on the floor and he grabbed the table for support. He groaned in frustration but recovered his balance and set off for the door again.

Edie snatched the opportunity and ran for the hall. Mary moved to chase her. Jack called "Cops will get her," as he flashed past her to the back door.

Mary followed him and stepped out onto the back step, fearing Hardwicke had escaped—or was attacking Jack again. She looked into the shadowed yard, turning at the sound of cursing. She burst out laughing more in relief than amusement. Hardwicke was sprawled on his back, legs tangled in the wire-mounted rabbit skins that spread across a patch of grass near the corner of the house. He had obviously tripped on them.

Jack had him pinned by a spare frame, which he had forced apart enough to fit around Hardwick's neck. He had pushed the ends of the stiff U-shaped wires against Hardwicke's throat into the ground pinning him until it pressed against his throat. Hardwicke was helpless, but still kicking.

Mary went into the yard to help Jack, constables Smithson and Higgins brushed past her, so she left it to them.

She heard Edie crying in the house and turned to see she was handcuffed next to another police officer.

Detective Sergeant Brogan walked into the yard, giving a slight nod to Mary, then to Jack, who had left the killer in the hands of the Force.

Jack and Mary hugged. She laughed and wished she hadn't. Jack kissed her strongly and she was glad her laughter had been silenced and glad that tears were running down her cheeks. They stood together for a while.

The quiet was broken by a tentative voice coming from the chook house. "Is it all right to come out, now?"

Jack slowly opened the gate, so no chooks escaped.

"Come on out, Aunty Meg." So she did, giving a shy smile to Mary, whose eyes were widely questioning.

"Been feeding the chooks," Meg said, as if that explained everything.

Mary suddenly remembered her phone and bag were in the locked car. She ran to catch up with someone who could open Hardwicke's car.

A constable she didn't know was holding Edie on the driveway near a police car with a back door open. Mary walked past them towards Constable Smithson and Higgins on either side of Hardwicke, also handcuffed.

"Mary." Surprised, she turned back to see Edie's tear-stained face.

"Mary," Edie repeated, her lips trembling.

Mary waited. The constable tried to push Edie into the back of the car, but she fought against him.

"What, Edie?" She said. The constable relaxed his efforts. Edie leaned forward, looking up at Mary, who was keeping an eye on Smithson, anxious to get her phone from the locked car before he left.

Edie said: "Tell Katie I saw her in the boat."

"What?" Mary was lost for a moment. "Boat?"

"She hid in a boat from us. I stopped to catch my breath. Leant on a big boat. Cat jumped up. I saw Katie's sneakers."

The constable resumed his job. "That's enough," he said, pushing her shoulder.

"Wait," Mary said. "You didn't call out to Hardwicke?"

"Tell Katie, please. Somebody might hate me less."

Her smile was so sad that Mary's next words caught in her throat. When they emerged, the door had slammed and the car had disappeared into the lane.

"I'll tell her," Mary said, her words snatched into the darkness by the billowing wind.

She turned around and asked Smithson – both Hardwicke and Higgins ignored her– if she could get her property from the car.

"I'll get your stuff, Miss Bourke," the constable said with a smile. "I have the keys." After Hardwicke was deposited in the back seat of the police car, Smithson got her bag and phone. "Detective Sergeant Brogan will want to talk with you and your Durkin mates sometime soon." She nodded.

"Good work there."

Mary took out her phone. Better return Katie's urgent call. Poor girl must be worried sick.

A short time later she found Jack and Meg in the lounge room. Meg was sitting in a single-seater chair, with unopened magazine on her lap. Jack was sprawled on the three-seater with his eyes closed. Mary sat in the small space left by Jack's legs. He opened his eyes and weakly waved a hand in her direction.

She spoke into her phone, then held it towards Jack.

"Katie wants to speak to you. It's about your Mum."

37

BEV

I can see sunlight sparkling through the filmy white curtains. I feel the warmth as it settles over my face, easing injuries; I smell the flowers, bravely trying to cheer me with gentle scents and many-coloured smiles; I taste the sweetness of the purple grapes left by the even sweeter Mary; I feel the rough landscape of my face and arms and rejoice that I survived such brutality.

They said I had been in a coma ten days.

Now, I again see and hear and feel and touch and smell and taste, but those returned senses fill my heart with grief and the terror of hopelessness.

My ears heard words that snatched joy from awakened happiness. My eyes will never open on the first and forever true love of my life. My Ray will never walk into my field of view again.

My mouth will never again taste those oh-so-sweet lips, the salty tears when he sorrowed his missteps. I will never again be enveloped in the scents of a hard-working man at the end of his day or a lover preparing his body for me. The sweaty grime, the freshness of newly showered skin, his teenager-like efforts to add scents before we went out, when we went to bed. I'll miss the marvellous mix of scents that identify this complex man of wonderful goodness and imprisoning faults.

What use are my senses in this world, dimmer without Ray?

Soppy thinking. Ray is still around. Here, when Jack, oh-so-strong-and-straight and our beautiful, brave Katie wrapped me in their exuberant love. So hard the bed creaked and the nurse tut-tutted through smiling lips. Both so much Ray, so obvious. No wonder I cry; cry even while laughing. Katie called it a sun cry, like a sun shower.

Inspector — I think he was — Grogan, maybe, said Jack, Katie and Mary were strong, brave and clever right through it all. They were "amazing", he said.

I know you're not surprised, Ray.

So tired. Sleep. But awake to my new future. Ray… I …

* * *

THURSDAY 10:55am

They sat in the hospital coffee shop around two small square tables that Jack had pushed together. For minutes at a time, they looked down in silence at the orange and brown cups on yellow saucers containing varying levels of tea or coffee. Plastic plates with remnants of biscuits and muffins were jumbled together in the middle. Jack's cup sat askew on a saucer, cushioned by two wet serviettes.

At first, the small group—Jack, Mary, Katie, Meg and Doug— had said little, as if thankful for the non-distraction. After a while, they looked up with glances, accepted and avoided, smiles hesitant and open. Gradually, small talk went back and forward, while bigger matters built up, like flood waters rising behind a dam wall.

Jack thought that, like him, nobody was quite sure how to express their mix of feelings. They looked at each other like people unexpectedly coming together in a maze, uncertain of the way out.

A smile from one breaking the sombre mood of another, a grim face of one freezing another's happier face, a mention of hope silencing a sob. Mum's back, but Dad's gone. They were free of the killer's threat but not from the scars he had left.

Sentences petered out.

Jack lifted his cup, dripping coffee on the table, he took a sip and looked at Mary. She raised her eyebrows and Jack nodded.

"You know, Meg," she said, "I nearly fainted when you called out from the chook house." Everyone laughed. "Funny, I know," Mary said, "but, seriously, without your initiative—"

"And sharp eyes and ears," added Jack.

"Margaret sees too much, sometimes," Doug said. "I can't get away with anything."

Meg gave him a gentle nudge.

"Doesn't stop you trying, though," she said, as she mopped up dribbled coffee from Jack's cup. He nodded thanks and put his cup on Meg's wet serviette rather than the more sodden ones on his saucer.

"Mary's phone cover stands out," Meg said, "you know, all those colours and photo of Jack on it." Mary brandished her phone in mock show-off.

Jack said: "Lucky for us you looked into the car."

"When I was passing it, I heard your distinctive ditty and shone my torch in. Your bag was on the back seat near your phone."

"Probably me," Katie said. "I called over and over."

"Me too," Jack said. "I also reported Mary as a missing person."

"I've never been a missing person before."

"They told me to go in and fill out a form and so on. I didn't have time for that nonsense."

"I could do it for you tomorrow," Mary said with a straight face. "They might give me a copy as a souvenir."

Her face broke into a smile, triggering laughter.

"Or a reward for finding yourself," Katie said.

Meg continued as the laughter died down. She told of her puzzlement at seeing Mary's phone ringing in the back of a strange car. She tried to get in, but it was locked.

Katie giggled. "Good on you, Aunty. You tried to break into somebody's car."

"Of course. Seemed odd. Then I reckoned it was none of my business. The ringing stopped, so I went on to feed the chooks."

"Something none of us thought to do," Jack said.

Mary said: "Among other things." She looked at Jack, who lowered his eyes to the table.

"We didn't come back to clean the room after—"

"A lot of… you know," Meg said. "And broken crockery, even a busted chair."

"Another one, now," Mary said.

"There was a tipped-over bucket, too," Meg said. "Near the stove. Looked like a burnt jumper."

Jack and Katie exchanged glances. Meg gazed at brother and sister in turn, as if expecting an explanation of the bucket's unusual content. They didn't provide one, so she continued.

"I was appalled that Ray might have done that. I thought my brother had gone off his head. The entire room made me cry to see the wreckage of an attack that put dear Bev in hospital. By my brother, I thought."

She was teary and Doug held her hand on the table, inadvertently pressing it onto Jack's saucer of wet serviettes. Meg tried to move her hand but Doug's attempted consolation pushed harder, tearing the paper. Small pieces stuck to her palm, but she didn't appear to notice.

Katie got up and leant down, hugging her aunt.

"I was so wrong—" Meg said.

"We all were, Aunty," Jack said. "No one more than me."

"Don't cry, love," Doug said. He kissed her forehead and she touched his cheek, leaving three serviette remnants there, looking as if he had cut himself when shaving.

Mary covered her smile with a hand. Jack frowned at her. She removed the hand revealing straight-set lips. Jack hastily pulled out a handkerchief to cover a smile. Despite Doug's suggestion to not cry, Meg did. Katie lifted her head from Meg's hair and looked at Mary, her eyes glistening.

Mary wiped her eyes, swallowed and said: "Last night, Meg, you saved lives. I was a goner. Sure I was going to be another of Hardwicke's victims, but you saved me and Edie with your phone calls."

Meg sniffed, wiped her nose with Doug's proffered handkerchief, and said: "Never thought I'd be calling the cops while squatting in the middle of chooks."

She looked at Mary. They smiled at each other. Mary reached over and squeezed Meg's hand.

"Good job you didn't come into the house," Jack said.

Meg laughed half-heartedly. "Gosh, no. I heard you shouting like a crazy man. Scared me off."

Jack looked at Mary. "I wasn't doing that was I?"

Mary said: "Someone was shouting. Hardwicke, or Edie."

"Or you." Jack said. "You were pretty scary wielding that massive rolling pin."

"Seriously, though," Meg said. "I thought I'd better ring the cops and Jack." She smiled. "Yes, Jack, I didn't hear you until much later."

Mary hugged Jack and he kissed her lips. Katie rolled her eyes and Doug studied all sides of a muffin he had picked up.

"Of course," Mary said, "you called Jack before the police."

"I was shaking in the chook house, in two minds. I could hear that man's mad talk and your quiet attempts to reason with him. Thought maybe cops would be too late. You know how it is in a small place. Often other stuff going on."

She looked around the table, as if seeking approval for her emergency thought processes. The smiles and nods seemed to encourage her.

"In the end, I called Jack. I knew from Katie that he was out driving around looking for Mary. He might be closer. As he was. He beat the cops there and he and Mary Rolling Pin Bourke were too much for one maniac.

"My brother to the rescue," Katie said, patting his arm. Jack hugged her. He and Mary had decided not to tell Katie what Edie had said. That was for another day.

"I peeked in the window," Meg said. "I was very scared. Then you got the better of him. When he headed for the door, I headed for the chooks."

"Good job done by all," Katie said. "Mum just glowed when we told her how you ended that bastard's terrible reign of vengeance."

Meg said: "We had a few tears together but at the end she was so relieved it was all over and nobody else was in danger. She will take a long time to get over losing Ray."

"Never will," Jack said.

"None of us will ever forget Dad," Katie said.

Jack stood, pushing his chair back and it squealed on the tiled floor. He clapped his hands. "Right, let's go. Who's first to see Mum this after…" He stopped, his eyes on something beyond their group.

Mary followed his gaze. The old lady they had seen in the cafeteria a few days ago was sitting alone at a table near the far door. To Mary's surprise, Jack walked to her. The lady looked up, seemingly surprised, perhaps alarmed. He squatted beside her and said something. She replied softly. Jack touched her shoulder. Mary joined them.

"Is something wrong, Mrs Palmer?" She knew there was.

"My sister Elsie passed away this morning." She picked up her half-finished cup of tea and took a sip. Put it down.

Mary pulled a chair alongside her and sat close, a hand on Mrs Palmer's arm. They talked for some minutes. Then Mary said: "Can we help you in any way? Drive you home?"

"Your young man has already offered to drive me home. My son said he can't leave work just yet. He asked me to wait, perhaps an hour." She looked at Jack and then Mary. "But I would like it if you could take me."

"I could ring your son," Mary said. "Tell him you're with us."

"No. Thank you dear. I'll ring him from home." She paused. "Sometime."

They stood and walked towards the exit, Mary's arm around the old lady's shoulders. As they passed the others, still standing near the table, Jack waved at them.

"We'll be back in an hour or so."

* * *

ONE WEEK LATER

Mary walked into the lounge room carrying a large, flat object wrapped in brown paper. Jack was sitting on the lounge, flipping through the Manderville Express. Without looking up he said: "Been disinherited then?"

"Ha, not quite," Mary said. "In the end, she was glad I called."

"Gladder than when I called in person, that night?"

"To be fair, you gave her a shock, out of the blue saying I had disappeared. That I might have been abducted."

"I know. I was pretty frantic by that stage. Thought they might know where you were."

She put the big package upright on the floor, leaning against the desk and went to him, ruffled his hair and kissed his forehead.

"You are wonderful, darling. I explained how heroic you were, bursting in and saving my life. She cried. Mum wants you to come to dinner one night soon. Dad wants to have a drink with you."

"Worth being punched about by Hardwicke, then." He smiled. "Now, what's that you brought in?"

Mary brought the big, flat package over and held it in front of Jack, arms stretched to grip the edges.

"This is intriguing," he said. "Not shoes or jewellery."

He reached out to touch it. She backed away, her face shining with excitement. Jack sat forward, hands on knees, and waited.

"I have something for you," Mary said.

"Let's have a look then."

She sat beside him, setting the rectangular object vertically before them. The top was higher than their knees. She peeled away the sticky tape that ran from one side to the other, holding overlapped paper edges together. She looked at Jack with a here-it-comes smile as she removed a large sheet of wrapping paper from the entire front in one long flourish. The torn paper fluttered to their feet.

"Ta-da," she said, revealing a giant, glass-fronted, framed colour photograph of Ray Durkin in all his glory, running with his signature lean as he swerved around would-be-tacklers, ball tucked under his right arm, his left hand palming off another player who wasn't going to stop him scoring that day.

Mary held it higher so he could see it better, but his face showed he was seeing it very well indeed.

"Wow!" Jack said. He went closer and squatted down studying it in detail. He looked up at Mary.

"Wow" again. He paused. "That's just so wonderful, Mary. Magnificent. Where did you get such a fantastic photo?"

"From the Express. They have lots of photos of Ray in his heyday."

He carefully took the photo from Mary and held it in front of them. Mary put an arm around his waist and hugged him. He kissed her and whispered, "Thanks".

He carried his precious picture to put it on the desk, leaning it against the graffiti-splattered wall. Threats of violence stood as a background to Ray Durkin, footy hero. Jack went back to Mary and embraced her with breath-taking passion. After several exhilarating minutes, Mary slowly unwound and leant back, still in his arms.

"Do I take this to mean you're pleased with my gift?" she said, when getting her breath back.

"No, this means I love you dearly. But I also love your gift. It's just so… so… magnificent."

He paused a moment. Things are looking up, Mary thought.

They stood, arms around each other, gazing at the action photograph. Mary was warmed by the emotion it had elicited in Jack. I love him so.

Jack broke the silence. "Mum will love that photo. We must take it around when she's home and stronger."

Mary beamed. "I'm glad you think so. I got her one, too."

Jack went back to the desk and stood looking down at his father in full flight.

"Despite all the bad things, things that nearly wrecked our family, I loved that man, Mary."

"I know you did, darling."

She wrapped her arms around him from behind, snuggled in tightly, and kissed the back of his neck.

"Jack," she said slowly, "are you feeling tired?"

"Not at all," he said.

"Sure? After having that big dinner?"

"Not so big," he said.

She knew it wasn't. He turned and kissed her.

She pulled away and tried a different tack in this game: "Not too tired to go to bed?"

Without waiting for his answer, she took his hand and they walked towards the bedroom. Jack grinned like a kid. Mary wanted to skip like a kid.

Then she stopped, letting his hand go. He looked at her with what Mary took to indicate disappointment.

"What is it?" he said.

"Just wondering how we're doing in the cricket." She struggled to keep a straight face.

He looked puzzled but answered her odd question.

"Since you ask, just won the first Ashes Test. Beat the Poms."

Mary smiled broadly and grabbed his hand again.

"So we've beaten the Poms, hey?" He nodded. "That sounds just fine, then."

She skipped to the bedroom.

<u>**THE END**</u>

HANDY GUIDE TO MANDERVILLE

Chamber of Commerce

By Simon Hardwicke, Chamber President.

There are many thriving businesses in Manderville. This is a wonderful place for successful commercial ventures. More than 250 commercial ventures are represented in the Chamber of Commerce. We exist not only to further the success of our businesses but also to serve the people of Manderville in the best way possible with service and quality goods.

It is always important to have a balance in any town's activities. Balance between life and work. There are times, of course, when one side impinges on the other. Times when the business people of Manderville can band together to help.

For example, the sadness of loss in a local family and the attempts of parents to get their lives together after this tragedy took a combined effort of townsfolk led by the Council and this Chamber of Commerce.

Accidents happen, of course. At times it is reassuring to our people to know fellow citizens are ready to step in.

As the head of Manderville's largest accountancy practice, I am very aware of the need for balance in our responses to unforeseen eventualities...

Acknowledgement

The book you are holding would not exist without the assistance of my family of talented people who stepped in when my sight stepped out, never to return.

When my sight all but disappeared in the latter stages of writing what would now be my last book, I was stuck — literally and literature-ly.

Despite steadily declining vision, I finished writing the book and revising the first draft. That is where further essential improvement became difficult. I could no longer see well enough to revise or proofread.

That you can now read my novel is testimony to the unstinting love and support I received from my family of talented professionals: teachers, librarian, novelist and journalist/author.

My heartfelt thanks go to Rebecca Davis, Emily Maguire, Ben Pobjie and Alice Pobjie for their encouragement and practical help.

I would have been lost before my sight was without my beloved wife Gaye Helen, who could write a *Handy Guide to Being Nice to All People in All Circumstances*. She supported me in this project before the first words were written and gave countless hours reading what I had written but could not see. Gaye Helen's sharp eyes and steadfast concentration have improved this book in many ways.

Thank you all. I will forever be prouder of you than of this book or any other achievement.